Praise for *Rabbit: Chasing Beth Rider*

"Maze's storytelling is fast and fun, overflowing with ideas and spiritual insight." ~ Eric Wilson, author of *Fireproof*, and *Valley of Bones (The Jerusalem Undead Trilogy)*

"Riveting and eye-opening…a powerful testament to the often overlooked spiritual strength that lies within us all." ~ *Apex reviews*

"What a great book! It kept me on the edge of my seat, waiting for what was going to happen next. With all the strange powers at work in this world, this book reveals the greatest Power of all." ~ Rabbi John Giddens, *www.ChavurahShalom.org*

"I've often wondered what makes vampires so intriguing to humans…The characters in this book are solid and each scene is more vivid than the next…The author opened my eyes to a unique and interesting new world leaving me thirsting for more as I read the last page." ~ Stacey Pierce, *www.diligentwriter.blogspot.com*

"I absolutely love it when an author can take a myth or legend…and weave them neatly and efficiently into a brilliant and original tale…This book is definitely not simplistic in nature. Ms. Maze gives us a fast-paced plot with many twists and turns, not just in the action, but also for the mind…*Rabbit: Chasing Beth Rider* will grab your attention from the first page and will not let go until the end, and maybe not even then. Enjoy the chase!" ~ Stephanie Nordkap, *Bestsellersworld.com*

Maze takes us on a vampire journey with a one-of-a-kind twist! Rabbit is a fast-paced, action-packed, exciting vampire thriller…As an avid reader of vampire fiction, this gem unexpectedly has become one of my very favorites. ~ Marcia Freespirit, CEO, *JimSam Inc. Publishing*

"*Rabbit: Chasing Beth Rider* delivers a fresh new twist to vampire lore. The strength of the plot carries it from page to page as all the pieces fall into place, painting an exciting tapestry. This book is a must have for those seeking a real, refreshing vampire novel." ~ SB Knight, *Premium Promotional Services*

BOOKS BY ELLEN C. MAZE

NOVELS

Rabbit: Chasing Beth Rider (Book One)
Rabbit Legacy (Book Two)
Rabbit Redemption (Book Three)

Anomaly: Beyond the Rabbit (Summer 2018)

The Judging: The Corescu Chronicles Book One
Damascus Road: The Corescu Chronicles Book Two
Tree of Life: The Corescu Chronicles Book Three
Anathema: The Corescu Chronicles Book Four

PARANORMAL SHORT STORY COLLECTIONS

22 Sideways: Twenty-Two Bloodthirsty Tales
Loose Rabbits of the Rabbit Trilogy
Feckless Tales of Supernatural, Paranormal, and Downright Presumptuous Ilk

ELLEN'S LINKS:

www.ellencmaze.com
Email the author at ellenmaze@aol.com
Ellen writes and illustrates children's books and nonfiction under the pen name Ellen Sallas.

ellen c. maze

Rabbit:
Chasing Beth Rider

Rabbit: Chasing Beth Rider
By Ellen C. Maze
Sixth Edition
©2018 by Ellen C. Maze

This Sixth Edition is released in tandem with the long-awaited Book Three in the Rabbit Trilogy –Rabbit Redemption—freshened for old and new readers.

ISBN-13: 978-0615678306
ISBN-10: 0615678300
Also available in eBook

Little Roni Publishers
Byhalia, MS
www.littleronipublishers.com

Cover Design: Hyliian Graphics, http://hyliian.deviantart.com

Mild Language, Sexual Situations, Vampire Violence

PUBLISHED IN THE UNITED STATES OF AMERICA

Book One of the Rabbit Trilogy

Rabbit:
Chasing Beth Rider

Choose your friends carefully
for the wicked will lead you astray.
Proverbs 12:26

Prologue

The monster had him boxed in, and it wasn't even close to sunup.

"GIVE IT UP, RABBIT! You don't have a chance!" he barked, his growling tenor reverberating the very walls.

Schaffer cringed at the sentiment and tiptoed faster along the corrugated tin wall. Up ahead and much too far away, the exit emptying into the dark night mercilessly teased. The warehouse sat on the river's edge—how far from the pier was he? Maybe fifty feet once he cleared the threshold. There was a good chance he could jump into the water and swim away. Hadn't he overheard one of them say their kind abhorred open water? Schaffer didn't have time to ponder. Taking a deep breath to gather his nerve, he burst forward only to slam into the outstretched arm of his enemy after four short strides.

"Oops," the monster giggled. "Down you go."

Schaffer struggled to find his feet, but the creature grabbed him by the collar and dragged him back the way they had come, his boot heels plowing the red clay.

"Silly wabbit," the monster snickered, "Come on, we have a *big night* ahead of us."

Schaffer uselessly wrestled against his attacker's grip. The thing that held him fast was not his master, but he was still one of *them*. A *Rakum*. A devilish miscreant with ancient roots whose strength was outdone only by his cruelty. They would be sure to punish Schaffer for the stunt he pulled against Elder Rufus.

Schaffer fought futilely until they reached the monster's rusty Dodge pickup parked in the unlit abandoned lot. He got a glimpse of the Rakum's face; it was not one he recognized, but that mattered little for he heard they were a hundred-thousand strong...

"In ya go!" The Rakum gruffly tossed him into the passenger seat, and in a matter of seconds, zip-tied his hands together. With a smirking peek into Schaffer's horrified face, he then yanked his bound wrists over his head to tie to the headrest. Schaffer cried out, but only

1

a few syllables escaped his lips before the monster shoved a greasy rag deep into his mouth.

"Where're your matches now, Rabbit? Hmm?"

Schaffer paled in terror. Yes, he had set Rufus on fire and it had been a glorious sight. Schaffer watched with round eyes as his attacker settled into the driver's seat and turned the ignition.

"Might be fun to burn you up. See what that smells like."

Schaffer moaned. An hour after he set Rufus aflame, he'd been captured by one of the other Elders, who forced him to drink his blood and then told him to "start running." Schaffer had no time to wonder why he'd been released. He had made it to the edge of town before being captured by the brute in the driver's seat. As his mind raced seeking escape, an Airstream trailer emerged nestled deep in the thick forest ahead.

The Rakum hit the brakes hard and didn't bother to come around to extricate his catch. Instead, he jumped down and reached in to yank Schaffer out the driver's side. The stiff plastic ties raked across his flesh and he yelped through the filthy towel as his skin gave way. His wrist bones fractured as his hands popped free of the bonds. Bleeding and crying, Schaffer was tossed over the Rakum's shoulder. He watched the weeds go by in the moonlight, his bloodied fingers dangling in his line of vision. They no longer stung, but he was too terrified to be thankful. They entered the trailer, the door closed and was locked, and he was dropped onto a tattered yellow couch. Schaffer grunted as he hit the sofa, but one glance at his wrists and he realized that skin was not ripped after all.

"Let the party begin," the Rakum said, rubbing his palms together as he stood over Schaffer's position. "Do you know what happens to Rakum Rabbits?"

His heart pounding, Schaffer shook his head. His tongue pushed at the rag in his mouth and he pleaded with his eyes.

"We *eat* Rabbits around here. Yep. But we take our time."

Schaffer cringed as the monster approached and stopped inches from his sweating face.

"And Rufus wants to be sure you suffer."

Rufus? Present tense? Are they fireproof? Schaffer choked back a scream as the monster withdrew a knife and brought to his chin.

"We ain't in no hurry, Rabbit. We can go all night…" The sharp blade pressed into Schaffer's throat until it pierced the skin with stinging pain. Blood coursed from the wound and spilled out before ellen c. maze

him onto the monster's chest. But as his assailant hovered over him, an evil grin on his dark face, Schaffer felt something else entirely. The fiery pain in his neck subsided and was replaced with a peculiar tightness. The blood that spurted forcefully from his body ebbed and then ceased.

His knife wound had healed—as if he was one of them.

The marking procedure did this!

Horrified as the gravity of his situation sunk in, Schaffer violently leapt aside. The Rakum backhanded him into place and straddled him on the couch, holding him down with his body weight.

"See, Rabbit? Now you get it."

Schaffer straightened up in his bonds as the monster raised the knife and slashed again, this time across the chest. Dark oxygenated blood oozed down his shirtfront and again, the pain subsided and the flow eased. Schaffer's face twisted into a mask of horror.

"Yep. That's right. We'll go on all night. And tomorrow night. And the night after that..."

Schaffer watched as his attacker brought the bloody knife tip to his mouth and cleaned it with his red tongue.

"Oh, shit, that... is... so..." he whispered, closed his eyes and smiled. After a moment, he sought Schaffer's terrified eye. "And Rabbit," he said pausing drunkenly, "when I get tired of you, we'll have my brothers over and let them see what fun you are."

The knife rose again and plunged into Schaffer's middle. He grunted, his gag preventing him from screaming no matter how his lungs fought to expel his terror.

"We'll never get tired of you," he whispered as his gory tongue circled his lips, seemingly intoxicated by the ingestion of Schaffer's blood. The knife was thrust in again, this time into his ribs. "And you'll never die. *Never.*"

As Schaffer felt the skin tighten and knit itself together in his middle, he had no doubt that the monster was right. His punishment would go on. Schaffer was in hell and his hell would last forever.

Watch Your Back

"Well, if it ain't Beth Rider," a deep voice rumbled above her head and Beth raised her eyes.

"That's me! How are you?" she said disguising her startle response. She had been signing books for two hours and this didn't look like a fan.

The corners of the man's mouth turned down as his fierce gaze sought hers. He was a giant; even hunched above the author's table, he would be nearly seven feet standing. His skin was as black as ebony and his teeth too white and too large behind full lips. A long, deep scar furrowed his hairline, down his temple, past his cheekbone and faded out beneath his chin. Dark blue lenses shielded his eyes and he wore a scuffed black leather jacket with no insignia. A myriad of tattoos covered what she could see of his neck, the ink three shades darker than his impossibly dark flesh. Beth had to remind herself to breathe as her keen observation skills took in every disturbing detail.

"I got a message for you," the man said as he leaned heavily on the table with both hands, looking hard at her through his Ray-Bans.

Beth straightened her back and cleared her throat as an unnamed fear welled inside. "A message from whom?"

"From me." The huge man swished off his sunglasses and fixed his gaze on hers. His eyes were dark and hidden behind an immense brow. The small amount of sclera that surrounded his black irises was yellowed and streaked with blood vessels. His giant hand snaked forward and covered her left on the tabletop.

"Watch your back!" Words she heard even though the man's lips did not move. Beth squealed and jumped up, sending her folding chair crashing dramatically behind her. Wrapping her arms around her chest, she backed again, stumbling over her fallen chair. All around

4

her, people came to her aid, but she couldn't respond, frozen, her eyes locked in the hateful gaze of the man across the table.

Beth put her hands to her ears in case she heard his voice in her head again, but he said, or *thought*, nothing else. He simply held her with his gaze and waited for her to react. Beth remained as she was, standing in the supportive arms of two young store employees. They fanned her with their hands and asked her repeatedly what happened. They did not fear the hellish Goliath only a few feet away. Had she overreacted?

"Jesus, help me!" she whispered, looking into the face of the giant.

At her words, the man stood off the table. He tossed Beth a malicious grin, then turned on his heel and disappeared in the throng of customers. Beth exhaled and broke free of those who held her.

"I'm okay," she began as a doctor came forward to check her pulse at her wrist. Beth made an excuse to the worried faces. Smiling, she scooted past the crowd and entered the ladies room at a trot. Inside a private stall, she leaned against the door and collected her thoughts. Her novels attracted a plethora of diverse characters, but the dark maniac truly frightened her.

Why had he focused his hate on *her?*

Beth took a deep breath, asked God to help her, and sincerely hoped that would be enough.

2

The Book

Javier didn't ask Simon for his blood tonight. Instead, he spent the entire evening discussing a book the kid was reading, enjoying the passion in Simon's voice and the sincerity in his eyes as he gave his dramatic narration.[a] Somewhere in the house, a clock chimed the hour. Javier glanced at his watch and Simon looked at the digital read-out on his bedside alarm clock.

"It's only three. You're not leaving, are you? You haven't heard the best part."

Simon's expression was hopeful. Javier's stomach grumbled uncomfortably, but he didn't want to interrupt the telling to fill the void. His young friend was sharing the strangest tale he had ever heard. So far, they'd only covered two-thirds of the story. He put both hands into his wavy black hair and massaged his scalp, then gave Simon a winning smile.

"Go on. What happened next?"

A huge grin consumed Simon's face and Javier leaned back in his chair beside the youth's bed. With no human experience, the religious-themed plot made little sense, but Javier enjoyed the bloodthirsty nature of the main character. The storyline featured a priest who had been transformed into a vampire by the devil. The priest murdered a hapless mortal every night until the novel's protagonist, an aspiring preacher, convinces him to stop. The spiritual struggle of the protagonist intrigued Javier more than it should. Did such faith exist in the real world? Most bewildering of all, did their God *pop in* to save them as He did in this novel? Javier didn't know. In fact, he didn't know any gods. He'd never been to a church, synagogue, or temple, nor had he ever uttered a prayer in a time of need. Yet, as his favorite donor sat on his lumpy bachelor's bed, reading to him from this mortal woman's novel, something deep inside fluttered. For the first time in his long life, Javier experienced a desire to know this God. The sensation was peculiar and he didn't resist. Instead, he watched Simon's lips move and concentrated on the words, the syllables, and sentences that built the suspense the author intended. When Simon reached the last page, it was five-thirty in the morning and Javier was stunned into silence.

Falling quiet, Simon closed the book, set it aside, and fell back onto his bed lengthwise. Javier chewed his thoughts, absently watching Simon watch the ceiling. Only when the kitchen clock rang in the quarter-hour did either of them speak.

"Sun-up in forty-five minutes." Simon rolled his head to the side to meet his pal's gaze, but Javier's face was red and his mouth a straight line. Simon sat up and threw his legs over the side of the bed. "What? Is something wrong?"

Javier clenched his jaw, losing the battle with the words that wanted so badly to exit. Rakum were not permitted to speak of mortal abstracts. There was no religion among the Brethren, yet something deep inside of him was proving stronger than the ancient tenets of his people. He looked into Simon's bright blue eyes and took a deep breath, ready to relinquish the fight. Leaning forward, he took his longtime donor by the forearm that he normally drew blood from and asked him point blank. "Will you tell me about God?"

There. It was out and Javier was mortified. His people did not hold such frivolous and foolish notions. To do so would contradict the Ten Fathers, as well as the Elders assigned to educate them to adulthood. To do so would nullify his own deity, of which he had always been certain.

Until now.

Simon rubbed his eyes. "Sure. I mean, I never said anything before because I thought you weren't interested in that stuff. Do you want me to start from the beginning?"

"No," Javier sighed, sensing the unpleasant nudge of the sun nearing the horizon. He was disappointed that he would have to leave without finishing what he had started, but his time was up. "I'll come back tomorrow. Same time."

"I'll be here," Simon replied softly.

Javier nodded, stood, and turned for the closed bedroom door.

"Um, you didn't want..." Shyly, Simon lifted his forearm as well as his eyebrows.

Javier held up his hand. "Forget about it. I'll see you tomorrow." Simon's face fell and Javier turned to leave. The kid's blood would ease his discomfort, but he had made his choices and tonight's preoccupation with the novel had erased any interest in a buzz.

Javier jogged the two blocks to his own residence. Once home and preparing to bed down, he thought about the characters from the novel and about the question he had asked Simon at the last. Mostly, he thought about the answer and what it might mean for him, his future, and that of his entire race. It meant *something*, but what? Had any of his brethren read the story? Did it move anyone else and wake something hidden deep inside of them? Was it ultimately going to be a bad thing that he peeked the human concept of a Creator-God?

Javier slept fitfully and longed for the evening. To finish what he had started. Perhaps to learn about a God he had never known existed, one that would care for him and give him purpose. Ironically, he never knew he desired those things until he sat and listened to that silly woman's book.

Beth Rider's book.

3

Beth left the room dark and collapsed face down on the hotel bed. She had no energy to even turn on a lamp. She'd spent the last two days and most of both evenings in various bookstores signing novels for her readers. Her left hand was numb from the effort, but for the most part, each book signing had been a joy. Only the dark maniac at the Buckhead BooksAMillion left a sour taste in her mouth. She had put him out of her mind, but now, she shivered as she recalled the hellish encounter. Beth flipped onto her back, still lying long-ways across the king-sized bed. A furtive movement to her right, beyond the glow of the tiny nightlight caught her attention and she sat up.

She was not alone.

"Is this the way you watch your back?" a husky whisper rasped.

Beth jumped to her feet and lunged for the door. Before she could take three steps, the dark form across the room grabbed her from behind.

"Don't bother to scream…"

As one steel-like arm wrapped uncomfortably about her chest holding her immobile, the other hand covered her mouth. Beth could not see her attacker, but it was definitely the tattooed monster from the night before. Beth prayed in her heart for help and went limp in her attacker's grasp.

"You're quite the nuisance. Have you any idea the trouble you're causing my people?" The voice paused and then continued in a guttural chortle that chilled Beth's soul. "I could handle this so many ways, Miss Rider. So many ways…"

Beth squeezed her eyes closed, unable to fathom the meaning of his accusation.

"Bel suggested I snuff you out, right here, right now." The

stranger waited briefly for a response, but then continued his one-way conversation in a gleeful tone. "But Tomás, on the other hand... his idea intrigues me. Want to know what Elder Tomás suggested?"

Beth did not respond, still praying for divine rescue.

"He said you'd make a delightful Rabbit." The giant smacked his lips. "Hah! I haven't marked a Rabbit since... *damn*... it's been a long time. Would you rather die now or become a Rabbit for my pups to play with?"

Beth didn't attempt to answer, even though the thought was moot with her mouth covered. She opened her eyes and trained them on the outline of the curtained window across the dark room.

"I'll tell you," the man continued in a teaching tone, as if she had asked a question. "A Rabbit is a toy for my pups. You know, a papa wolf finds a rabbit, marks it with his scent, turns it over to his pups, and they play with it. They practice their technique on it. They attack it again and again until it's worn out, or insane, or both."

The man paused and Beth worked to ignore the rising panic in her gut. Somehow, she knew he was not going to end her life, but whatever he had in mind was going to be horrible.

"Most of the time, Rabbits give up *long* before we're done with 'em. I wonder how long you'll last? I wonder how many of my pups you can entertain before you kill yourself?" The man's tone turned wistful as he finished his thought. Still with his left arm around her from behind and that hand pressed firmly over her mouth, his right arm disappeared and she felt his fingers against her throat.

"Now, hush, this might sting a bit..." His fingernail pressed into the curve of Beth's neck and continue inward until the skin split and blood trickled out of the small wound. "Are you the quiet type, little Rabbit?" He encircled the wound with his lips, his tongue pressing against her skin.

Not even aware that she was going to do so, Beth leapt into action. With mighty effort, she pushed off with all of the strength she could muster. Although she didn't break free, the man's lips slipped away and she grunted victoriously. As she struggled to free herself from the death grip on her face, the man secured her once more with his strong right arm. His left hand shifted slightly and now covered her mouth *and* her nose.

"Can you wriggle free from this, you brat?"

Beth increased her attempts to break loose; she couldn't breathe and as panic crept in, all of her internal prayers ceased.

"I'm gonna mark you now. It'll only take a minute if you're still."

Beth continued to strain, all of her senses on alert. She was no longer a rational being, but rather a wild animal fighting for her life. Just as she thought she might lose consciousness, the man's hand slipped off her nose and she took in a painful breath. The man shuffled her to the bed and forced her into a lying position, his looming shape taking a straddling stance over her. Beth's eyes grew wide in the dim room and she thrashed wildly.

"Be still, you shit," the monster hissed and again, closed her airway with a slight movement of his hand. His weight over her abdomen caused enormous pressure to her diaphragm and Beth grew still.

"Move again, I beg you," the man rasped. "I don't like you enough to explore what else you might be good for."

Horrified at his vaguely sexual threat., Beth quieted every muscle.

"That's right, heheh," he chuckled, his putrid breath falling on her cheeks. "You're too school-teacher for me, but I have *lotsa* brothers." The monster leaned down to sniff her hairline. "*Yeahhhh,* I can think of three or four who like them clean and innocent..."

"Mmmm!" Beth mumbled into his hand, her eyes vainly seeking his in the dim light.

"My mark will change you, make you smell like me, and then *all* of my pups will like you—*a lot.*" He stressed the last two words and held her gaze. "I am about to uncover your mouth. Hush, submit, and this will be over quickly. Understand?"

Beth nodded, her eyes bulging with terror. She didn't know what he intended to do, but he said it would be quick. Beth held on to that assurance and closed her eyes. The man's clammy hand slipped from her mouth and a warm liquid touched her lips, her tongue, and rapidly filled her mouth.

"I hope you're a swallower, Miss Rider," her gruff attacker jibed and pinched closed her nostrils. "All of it. *Swallow.*"

Beth's mind flashed to her novels. Her characters were forced to drink blood. Did this lunatic think he was a vampire? Is that what the entire ordeal was about? A psychotic and deluded fan of her novels acting out his fantasies? Even as her mind raced with comparisons, Beth swallowed to keep from choking. Immediately, the man removed his hands from her face and placed them down on the pillow to either side of her head. He looked upon her and now his fetid breath fell on her forehead.

"Wait for it..." the dark giant whispered.

He was waiting for something to happen and Beth opened her eyes to meet his glittering gaze. In the darkness, she saw only the reflection of the nightlight in her attacker's reddened eyes. Focusing on the general area of the man's scar, Beth worked to regain her composure. *What now?* Her mind was clearing, her morbid fear passing... What was he waiting for? Precisely five seconds later, Beth's stomach turned inside out.

"*Ugghhhhh!*" she groaned, writhing in pain beneath her monstrous enemy. The man did not cover her mouth as she twisted and strained beneath him, every nerve afire.

"*Shiiiiit...*" he chuckled, "that looks painful."

Beth made an attempt to conceal her discomfort, and soon, the acid burn in her middle subsided. As she settled her frightened but angry gaze into that of her attacker, her pain melted into nausea and then was gone altogether.

"You're hilarious," he said, spittle falling on her face. Beth didn't respond and the dark brute sat up, still holding his bulk up just enough to prevent crushing her. His right hand lifted and dropped to her shirt, dragging heavily across her breasts. "*Ehhhh*, so tender; my pups are going to be thanking me forever," he muttered. With one last lewd pass, he put both palms to his thighs and looked upon her. "Do you have any idea what just happened?"

Beth only glared, unsure of what she should say and unsure of whether or not she could control her tongue if she spoke.

"Mad little bunny," the man chuckled and patted the top of her head. "My mark is on you and that makes you a Rabbit. Now, I am releasing you into the world so my pups can hunt you down. No matter where you go, they'll seek you out. Did you know that a wolf can sniff out a rabbit from as far away as a mile? My pups' senses are far greater than that and you will smell like steak roasting on an outdoor grill. You know how wonderful that smells? *Mmmmm.*"

He paused for Beth to respond, but again she refused.

"All of my brethren will want a shot at you. A juicy new Rabbit is a rarity they will exploit to the max and in every way imaginable."

As numbness seeped up her spinal cord, Beth realized was losing consciousness. She watched the silhouette of the big man as he crawled away and then stood.

"Let's see...where is it?"

He reached for her purse on the nightstand. Through heavy

eyelids, she watched him locate her wallet and pluck out a plastic card that glinted in the low light. Beth whimpered as he dropped the purse beside her, her driver's license in his possession. Beth's head swam. She was done fighting, but the monster spoke again and she made an attempt to comprehend.

"I like to know where my Rabbits are headed. Montgomery, Alabama? I have some pups *'round them parts*." He spoke the last few words in a put-on Southern accent. "They haven't seen a Rabbit in a *long* time," he laughed to himself with a shake of the head. "My favorite lieutenant's in Montgomery; he'll find you first. You won't like him; he's horny and hungry *all the time.*"

Chuckling, the man backed toward the door and wiggled his fingers in Beth's direction.

"Sleep now, Rabbit. But tomorrow..." He opened the door and bright light spilled in from the hallway. "You better start running." And he was gone.

Beth tried to thank God she was alive, but numbness overtook her brain and she slipped away, falling into a deep sleep. In her dreams, she was running and staying out of reach of the wolves.

Just barely.

No Donation Tonight

Javier's bunkmate opened a vein for him before he left. As a result, when he arrived at Simon's, he was comfortable and ready to listen. Dietrich was an amicable fellow that Javier had been saddled with ten years ago. Elder Roman expected him to teach the rabid Rakum a little couth, but so far, Dietrich showed little sign of amending his wild-child ways.

Simon answered the door dressed for bed, a surprised but pleased look on his movie-star face.

"Hey, I was afraid you got busy with something else." Simon led him into the house, apologizing. "I'd already gone to bed. We got the place to ourselves. Bart's out of town for the week."

Bart was the reason they usually met in Simon's bedroom, but Javier stopped in the den without heading for the back of the house.

"We can sit in here. There'll be no donation tonight."

"Oh..." Simon padded barefoot back into the living area and watched his guest settle into the sofa. "How about some water?"

"No, sit down. Tell me more about the God in that novel."

Simon sighed and collapsed into the recliner to Javier's left and kicked open the footrest. "Okay, but I'm no expert." Simon nodded when Javier urged him again. "The *whole universe* was created by one God, *the* God. All of the other gods and goddesses are fairy tales that man created because he couldn't control the real God. Get it? Over time, Man worked it out so he could be the *creator of god*. Make sense?"

"Is this what you believe?"

"Sure."

Javier was surprised at Simon's noncommittal answer. "What else? What's He like?"

"Oh, that's easy. God is all about judgment and rules, limits and

14

parameters. He is *holy*—whatever the flip that means—and He thinks humans need to be holy, too. In the old days, the humans He made turned out to be all wicked and despicable, so God decided to make a nation of people who would worship only Him. That was when Israel was born..."

"The country? Or the race—the Jews?" Javier tried to follow, but so far, Simon's story was more far-fetched than the fiction novel that started their conversation.

"The Jewish people."

"Aren't you Jewish?"

Simon shrugged. "God created *my* people. And *we* were given all these laws and promises and stuff. And one day, He's supposed to come and take His earthly kingdom back into His control. Then there will be peace on earth forevermore." Seemingly done, Simon rubbed his chin.

Javier responded with a tiny shake of his head. "Wait. He'll come *back?* Where is He now?"

"Oh, sorry," Simon said and cleared his throat. "You really don't know any of this." Javier held his face static and waited for the youngster to continue. Simon grinned. "God is everywhere, He's a spirit. The rabbis say that eventually, God will send us a mighty King to establish His throne in Jerusalem and the whole world will know the God of Israel is the one true God." Simon chuckled, but Javier was dead serious.

"And the preacher in your novel followed this God?"

"Uh, well..." Simon cleared his throat. "That character was a Christian. And Christians think Jesus is God. I don't know much about that stuff."

"But the novel is filled with characters that follow this Jesus..."

Simon lifted both hands, palms out. "What? Like I could tell you anything more? I was raised by an irascible aunt whose entire contribution to teaching me of my heritage was to show me how to get a good deal at the market. I'm telling you what I remember from shul, and that's like a lifetime ago. Religion is a drag."

Puzzled, Javier asked, "You don't care about this God that you say created you especially for Him? If you believe all this stuff, how can you dismiss it so easily?"

Simon scratched his head and offered a half-hearted grin. "I never think about it. I mean, I don't hang out with religious Jews and I've never met a Christian I could tolerate." Simon shrugged apologetically and his smile faded.

"How would one go about learning more? What would happen if we talked directly to God, like the preacher in the story? Do you think He'd listen, I mean, if He's up there?" Javier realized as he spoke that he *knew* there was a God. Somehow, he'd come to the realization without consciously doing so. He dropped the disclaimers. "Can I speak to Him without Him calling me first?"

Simon shrugged. "Sure. You can pray to Him, ask Him anything you want." Simon reached for a large hardbound book on the side table on his right. Flipping it open, he shuffled through the pages looking for a specific passage. "I dug this out for you. It's my bar mitzvah Tanakh.[1] Let's see…"

Javier watched him, his mind pondering what questions he might ask the Creator, and of course, if he'd receive a reply. The Rakum Elders spoke telepathically with the Ten Fathers, but for the rest of them, if they had larger questions, they turned to the Elders. Javier cleared his mind; sometimes Elder Roman read his thoughts and it would be better to keep the God-search to himself.

"Here it is," Simon said, bringing Javier out of his thoughts. "I always liked this one. It says, 'Call to Me and I will answer you and tell you great and mighty things that you do not know.'[2] How about that? Call to Him. I think it's that easy."

"What's He called? Just God?" Javier sat up from his position on the couch.

"Ummm," Simon stuttered and leafed through his book. "He has dozens of names. I guess if I was you, I'd just call Him God. I think if He's the real God, He's the only one that'll answer."

Javier chuckled. "Got it. Can I borrow that?"

Simon handed the Tanakh over and yawned. "Keep it as long as you like. They say those are His actual words."

"I'll see what happens." Javier stood, the heavy book under his arm. "How about the Rider novel. Are you done with that one? I'd like to read it myself."

Simon reached to the counter and grabbed the novel. "Sure. Keep it."

"Thanks." Javier caught the tossed book. "I'm shoving off. Thanks for everything."

"Oh, okay." Simon stood up. "When will I see you again?"

---

[1] Collection of Old Testament Scriptures given when he came of age at thirteen.
[2] Jeremiah

Javier sighed and shook his head, distracted by his plans for the evening discovering more about Simon's God.

"Come on, Javier," the youngster whined. "This is twice in a row."

"Let me work on this and I'll call you. This is going to sound crazy, but…" Javier was about to stop himself, but didn't. "I think God is calling me. Does that sound crazy?"

Simon shook his head, his eyes to the side. "No. That's what He does. He's pokin' me, too, since we've been talking." Simon looked up then and stepped closer. "Just call me later, okay? Promise?"

Javier nodded and squeezed the youth's shoulder briefly before making a hasty exit. He reached the house in record time and headed down to the basement, prepared to begin reading about—and hopefully *listening* to—God.

5

A Pleasing Aroma

Michael inserted his time card, satisfied with the loud click. His shift had been uneventful, as they all were, and he was ready for a quick dinner before sunup. Because of his need to stay in during the day, he put in six five-hour nighttime shifts a week as Airport Security Personnel, working 7:30 to 1:30, nightly. His salary plus the interest on his investment holdings kept him in his cozy two-bedroom house in the city. What else did he need? When his Elder sent him to manage the area, Michael found that police work suited him best; Rakum grunts either worked or siphoned a living off their Cows— Michael had never been a slacker. Plus, law enforcement allowed him a measure of brutality now and again, and aided in keeping an eye on the ever-evolving mortal world.

I've earned a little peace and quiet, Michael thought with a satisfied nod. He'd policed city streets and when he took the job at the airport, the excitement ceased.

Dannelly Field was equipped to welcome only regional jets, so between arrivals, the various gates emptied often. Tonight's Delta CRJ from Atlanta arrived forty-five minutes late due to weather delays in Georgia. Michael locked away his sidearm and followed the noise of the disembarked passengers milling about seeking their luggage. He re-entered the terminal from the restricted area and immediately noticed a pleasing aroma. His stomach responded and he licked his lips. Then he stopped walking to lean against the wall. The glorious and fulfilling odor tickled his head and Michael's eyes darted over the heads of passengers. With one last deep inhale, he stood off the wall to follow the unmistakable scent of the Rabbit.

18

Oh! It's headed this way... Michael smiled with confidence. He was the only one of his brethren in the area so he would have this one to himself. Jesse, who always came in on Tuesdays, was expected within the hour, but he wouldn't be averse to allowing Michael a little privacy to start. Michael further scrutinized the travelers as they filed past his position. Rabbits were easy to spot. They were contemptible creatures, the dregs of humanity, marked by the Elders for slow and deliberate execution by the brethren.

Judas Priest! We haven't had a Rabbit around here since...

It had been nearly a year since the last Rabbit came through the region, and Michael wasn't the first on the scene that time. Boris caught the scoundrel at the train yards, sneaking in and out of the abandoned warehouses like the rat he was. That particular Rabbit had been marked for treason. He was a pretty useful Cow before he turned on his master, Rufus, and tried to kill him. Michael heard through the grapevine that he had nearly succeeded by dousing his master with gasoline and setting him on fire. However, Rufus was no mere grunt, but an Elder, and an extremely powerful one at that. He had not been consumed beyond redemption, and in his anger, he had the Cow marked as a Rabbit for the others. Michael grinned as he remembered how they tormented the fat little man when Boris let them in on the game.

Me and Jesse, and that loose cannon, Tyson. We were merciless. That was a good time...

Michael allowed the memories to flow as he waited for the new Rabbit to cross his path. They had gone at that guy again and again, even moving him to Tyson's rented cottage for a few days to work him over even more. By the time the other brothers had their shot, the Rabbit was ready for the loony bin. The man threw himself in front of a train the first chance he had to slip away. Broke his sorry back, severing his spine, one of the few ways to kill a Rabbit. It had been a shame to lose such an entertaining food source, but despite the longevity and healing power the marking procedure provided, Rabbits had pretty short life spans.

At that moment, Michael noticed a young woman across the wide hallway, a distraught look on her face. She was lovely and delicate, with wavy, dark blonde hair; the kind of woman Michael enjoyed the company of when he had time. Dressed in a modest yet alluring pastel blue business suit, she carried a laptop case in one hand and a soft leather briefcase in the other. Michael crossed the foot traffic to assist her and remained on the lookout for the Rabbit. He was nearly at her side when the realization hit him full force: this beautiful woman was his goal. Someone had marked her as a Rabbit. As she turned to ask for help, Michael recognized the scent of the Elder who marked her.

Jack Dawn. His Elder. *His* Master.

It didn't get any worse than that.

"Hi, can you help me?" the young woman asked with a smile. Preparing to shake hands, she switched her briefcase to her right hand alongside her laptop. "My name is Beth Rider and I left my purse on the plane. Will they let me back on to fetch it?"

Michael looked at her hand, hesitating only a millisecond, and then shook it briefly, knowing all the while that her scent would be on him and as far as his brethren were concerned, that meant he had claimed her. *But ...no way.* Michael's mind rambled on its own track. *There's been a mistake. Why would Jack mark a young woman? What crime against the brethren could she be guilty of?*

Covering his bewilderment, Michael matched the woman's friendly expression. "What flight was it?"

"ASA 5128. Is it too late to go back and get my purse, Officer?" Beth asked looking back the way she had come.

Michael held out his right elbow. "It's Michael, Miss Rider. I'll take you down there. They'll be sweeping out the cabin about now."

He waited until she placed her small hand on his arm and then walked the two of them back to her gate. Nearly sixty seconds since he met the Rabbit and her scent was beginning to sink into his subconscious to no longer distract him mercilessly. He steered her through the foot traffic and made way for her more than once with an authoritative swish of his hand. At the jet-way, Michael pulled open the air-sealed door.

"Hey, Jim," he called down the hall to his ornery coworker. A second later, Old Jim's head appeared at the curve of the hallway, clipboard and pen in hand.

"What's up, Stone?"

"This young lady left her purse on that flight. Grab it for her." Michael opened the door wider so Jim could see the woman on his arm.

"Highly irregular, Stone." The man narrowed his gaze and eyed Beth up and down. Michael didn't reply, but waited for Jim to comply. The old man cursed under his breath. "What seat was she in?"

"Eleven B. My purse is brown leather with a shoulder strap..."

"Eleven B, Jim. We'll wait." Michael winked at Beth as the codger turned and ambled back down the jet bridge. Then the scent of the Rabbit hit Michael afresh. He forced a smile and consciously repressed all memories regarding the Rabbits of his past. Just one look at the woman, and every delightful moment spent torturing them came to mind as clear as crystal.

But...

This one would not be like the others. At least for the time being. Until he discovered her crime, Michael would look upon her as a normal human woman. Noting the arrival board posted by the door, Michael engaged her in some harmless small talk.

"Did you fly in from Atlanta?"

She nodded. "I'm happy to be home, I'll tell you that." The woman paused and looked away; Michael thought she might have shuddered. He picked up the slack.

"I lived in Atlanta a few years back," Michael offered. Even as he stood so close to her, the heavy scent of Jack Dawn draping her like a cloak, he couldn't imagine her under the fearsome Elder's attentions. Jack Dawn attacked her. Marked her. Maybe even *raped* her—that was his style. But Beth Rider didn't look like a woman traumatized. Presently, the woman checked her watch and sighed.

What did she do to enrage Jack? Michael couldn't figure it out.

Jim's heavy work-boots cleared the jet's door. He would be in view in moments and Michael opened the door wider to receive him.

"Wow, that was fast." The woman craned her neck to see the man shuffling down the gangway, her purse in his free hand.

"Here ya go, Miss. Sign this, Stone." Gruff and business-like, Jim held out a clipboard. When Michael had jotted his initials, the grumpy Gus disappeared down the hall without another word.

"Problem solved." Allowing the air-tight door to close with a swoosh, Michael turned to face Beth and her hand slipped off his arm.

"I can't thank you enough, Michael. If I hadn't run into you, I don't know what I'd do. Everything in a woman's purse is so hard to replace."

"Yes, I imagine so," Michael replied already wondering if she was missing her ID. He'd been discipled by Jack Dawn and retaining the victim's driver's license was one of his signatures. Instead of asking her about it, he pointed loosely to the purse in her hand. "Maybe you should have a look. Make sure everything's in there."

Her lips parted to respond and she shook her head. "I'm sure it's fine." She had a faraway look in her eye and then the corners of her mouth turned up.

"What? There's a smile. What are you thinking about?" Michael put his hands into his pants pockets and watched her features glow, her creamy skin smooth and blemish-free, her bright green eyes large and doe-like. She didn't seem to have an evil bone in her body. How did she end up a Rabbit?

"Oh, was I smiling? Hmmm. It's nothing. I'm so exhausted. I didn't sleep well last night..." Beth's grin faltered, but she regained her composure and turned as if walking away. "It is *way* past my bedtime. I shouldn't hold you up. I'm sure your boss doesn't want me to monopolize all of your attention."

"I'm off duty. Let me help you with your luggage," Michael said and they matched pace toward the baggage claim. He didn't know how many Rakum were in the Tri-County Area at any given time, but the knowledge of her presence would be making the rounds. She would not be safe alone from this point forward.

"Thanks. I think the Lord sent you to watch over me tonight. Did you know that Michael is the name of an archangel?"

"No," he replied.

"Yeah," she said with a child-like grin. "It means *who is like God.* Neat, huh?"

"Mm-mm," Michael responded hoping a non-word response would end the line of discussion.

She said no more and Michael made way for the two of them through the crowd. They were almost to the baggage claim when he sensed one of his brothers disembarking.

Jesse's plane had come in.

Here we go, he thought to himself.

Michael hastened his step, dragging Beth along with him, and rounded the corner. They were standing at the entrance of an airport novelty store and as Beth peered curiously into the window, Michael stole a glance back at the arrival gate to see if they'd been noticed.

He didn't have to search long, he noted, for his brother was seeking *him.* And, of course, the Rabbit on his arm.

6

"Are you *reading?*"

Javier closed Simon's Tanakh with a fluttery thump and set it down, embarrassed to be seen with such a book. Roman, his Elder, had stopped by unexpectedly and he had been so engrossed that he hadn't heard him enter the basement. But then, Roman had always been the king of stealth.

"Yes." Javier thought to rise off his cot, but Roman gestured for him to remain as he was.

"It has truly captivated you." Roman stepped to the makeshift bed of plywood and a homemade mattress to peer at the two books. "Is that what I think it is?"

There was no need to respond; Roman could read, both the Tanakh and Beth Rider novel leaning now upon his pillow. His Elder was a fair man, not given to hysterics or drama, but Javier watched his eyes, hoping to guess his opinion of the books before he made his excuses.

Roman's mouth remained in the same tight line as when he first spoke. His gray eyes were calm behind the round-lens spectacles he donned as an affectation as all Rakum had extraordinary vision. Finally, he stooped down and lifted the novel, taking a seat on the cot next to Javier.

"Since when did you become a reader?"

Javier had no reply and Roman scanned the novel's back cover. When done, he raised his eyes, Javier still unable to read anything of his Elder's opinion on the matter.

"Speak up," he instructed, narrowing his eyes a fraction as impatience crept in. "You read this book?"

Javier considered what he should reply. Reading wasn't

23

forbidden, but his brethren didn't read anything of substance. A book with the word "God" on the back, or inside, for that matter, was usually taboo. And Javier understood why; religion was for the mortals and Rakum avoided all such human abstracts as idiocy.

Weary of Javier's avoidance, Roman posed another question. "Was it an entertaining read?" Javier shrugged and Roman added, "Who gave this to you?"

"Simon." Javier's heart sank as he spoke his young friend's name. Roman had not yet overtly reacted, but Javier expected repercussions against the youth to be harsh.

"He's on Meriwether Court, correct?" Roman asked as he thumbed through the novel. Javier nodded with a noise of agreement. Roman closed the novel and set it back on the lumpy mattress. He repositioned to sit against Javier and then leaned over his knees, resting on his folded arms.

Curious at the movement, Javier looked at him sideways and imitated his posture.

"I read it some time ago," Roman whispered, his eyes trained to the rough cement floor.

Javier's lips parted in surprise and he studied his Elder's profile, awaiting an appropriate remark. Roman was a relatively new Elder and was only 372 years old; although to a human, he looked no more than forty. He was tall, over six feet, with shoulder-length reddish-brown hair that curled curiously at the ends. He tugged at his costume eye-glasses and held them in his hand. After a few more seconds passed, he considered Javier and offered him a weary smile, his storm gray eyes sparkling with a secret shared.

"I'm bunking-in with you today."

Dietrich clambered into the room just then at full speed. He slammed the door at the top of the stairs and jumped to the floor. He made popping noises with his mouth, as he usually did when he was feeling particularly fine, and had not noticed their VIP guest. Javier watched him throw his body onto his bed with abandon and only then did he look over to the room's occupants.

"Master! Elder Roman!" Dietrich gasped and rolled out of bed to his knees. He was being overly dramatic, for Roman never required that they be prostrate, but Dietrich often behaved oddly.

Roman shooed him with one hand. "Make yourself scarce."

Dietrich met Javier's eye before casting his gaze to his cot and the basement door seven steps up. "Master," he whispered with respect, "sun-up is upon us."

"Your master has eyes, pup. Sleep in the closet."

"Your will is my will," Dietrich replied, as if not at all distressed at the prospect of spending the long daylight hours folded up on the closet floor. He scrambled to his feet and disappeared into the tiny space.

Roman turned to Javier with a wry shake of the head. "As I was saying, I will bunk with you today and at nightfall, we will leave."

"We're leaving?" Javier was still unsure if he'd committed a crime.

The Elder stood and crossed to Dietrich's cot. "Our brethren who read this book are on the run and their Cows are winding up dead or missing. At sundown, we will start running, too."

Javier was shocked to hear such words leave his Elder's mouth. "Where would we go?"

Roman lay back on the yellowed mattress and his heels hung off the end. "Your master has this well in hand." Roman closed his eyes and sent his last thought telepathically, perhaps guarding it from Javier's roommate a few feet away in the closet. *We will find Beth Rider. Sleep now.*

Javier shoved the books aside to lie back on his bed and ponder Roman's words. *Find Beth Rider.* And then what? What could she do?

"Sleep, Javier," his master reiterated aloud.

Javier looked at his Elder, but Roman's eyes were closed. *Sleep?* Javier was more confused than ever. Maybe he could be strong and fearless like the preacher in Miss Rider's story. After all, her character was physically small and weak, where Javier was tall, broad, and muscular. Her preacher-man was mortal, where Javier was an earth-bound divine entity.

However, Miss Rider's preacher had God...

Javier closed his eyes and one hand caressed the leather cover of the old Jewish Book. Maybe by evening, he would have God, too.

7

It Must be a Mistake

"**W**ill you wait for me right here?" Trying not to sound desperate, Michael placed his hand on Beth's shoulder. "I'll be right back." He absorbed more of her scent every time he touched her, but he couldn't worry about that; the damage was done.

The woman nodded and pointed into the shop with her brief-cased hand. "Sure. I'll see if they have my books for sale…" Her voice trailed off and she stepped inside.

Thankful she asked no questions, Michael walked briskly through the crowd back to the place he last saw one of his brethren. Jesse smiled ear-to-ear as he approached and nodded a greeting.

"Is that what I think it is? *Please* tell me you will share with your favorite brother." Jesse did not amiably pound his shoulder and Michael understood why: he didn't want the Rabbit scent transferred to him too soon. "So? Give. Details, man!" Jesse said quietly and with passion. "What's the problem? I've never known you to be selfish."[b]

Michael found his tongue. "Listen to me; there is *no way* this woman should be a Rabbit. Something's wrong…" Michael turned and Jesse followed. "See for yourself and tell me the honest truth."

"Okay, I'll play. But a female…" Jesse sucked his teeth. "Let's not look a gift Rabbit in the mouth," he said with a chuckle. Maintaining his grin, Jesse accompanied Michael to the store.

Michael stopped at the doorless entry and met his friend's eye. *"You know me better than that,"* he whispered. *"I'm serious—nothing about this fits!"*

Michael held his gaze a second longer and turned to call Beth over. He and Jesse had been partnered up by their Elder decades ago and of all of the Brethren, he was the only one Michael considered a friend. Jesse would be truthful, no matter how distasteful. In addition, Jesse had a questionable romantic history with at least one mortal. Keeping this in mind, Michael hoped for Jesse's wisdom regarding Beth Rider.

†

Beth peeked around the shelving and spied her handsome new friend at the door. Tall with wide shoulders, Michael had dark brown hair cropped close and a square jaw. Although intimidating at first glance, Beth had seen kindness in his hazel eyes. She smiled as he looked at her and started over. Beth also walked forward and met him and another man halfway.

"Beth," Michael said, his voice less animated than before. "Allow me to introduce my friend Jesse Cherrie."

"Hi, Jesse, I'm Beth Rider," she responded and nodded to the stranger. Jesse's look was refined and elegant with an olive complexion, carefully-styled thick black hair, and flashing hazel-green eyes that met hers without shyness. Beth stuck out her hand, but Jesse only sent her a small mysterious smile.

"It is nice to meet you, Miss Rider. Did you just get off a plane from Atlanta?"

"How did you know?" Beth asked and dropped her hand.

"How did I know?" The man gave Michael a knowing smile and continued. "Let's just say, part of Atlanta is still hanging on you like a blanket. Mike, I have a date." He waved at Beth without touching her hand. "Be nice to my man, Michael," he said with a bow and turned.

"I will," Beth replied haltingly as the man had already stepped away. Michael asked Beth to excuse him and he chased after his friend.

Watching the men walk out of earshot, Beth tried not to yawn. If she allowed her mind to wander, she might start thinking about the monster with the tattoos and his ferocious—

"*No!*" Beth shut down her brain and hoped Michael would hurry.

†

Michael jogged a few steps to come up beside his friend. "Well?"

Jesse slowed, but did not stop. "I'm not hanging around for this one. I can see that you have no intention of obeying our master's orders."

"Jesse—"

27

"No, I get it. This woman is marked, but she doesn't fit the profile..." Jesse finally stopped to look Michael in the eye. "We don't make the rules. We follow them. We submit. It's good. We have a chain of command that is irrevocable."

Jesse paused and glanced back toward the store. Michael watched the old pain return to his friend's eyes before he shook it off.

"We don't ask *why* our Elders do what they do," he continued. "They don't owe us an explanation."

"What if he made a mistake?"

"So, what if he did? She's still the Rabbit. She has to go. Surely you don't think..." Jesse shook his head incredulous.

"What?"

"No way." Jesse chuckled and touched his temple. "You're thinking that since Jack favors you, he'll lend you an ear. Hah!" Shifting his briefcase to his left hand, Jesse placed his right on Michael's shoulder, ignoring the fact that he would now absorb the Rabbit's scent. "Have you lost your mind? Jack Dawn would eat you for dinner if you asked him to admit a mistake. Elders are never wrong—you are well aware of this."

Michael grit his teeth. All Rakum were taught the infallibility of their leaders, and even if one made a mistake, they would never own up to it. Thus was the beauty of being in charge of thousands of brethren; no one disputed an Elder's word.

"Mike, I like you—too much, maybe. Don't go to our master with this preposterous rebellion. What are you thinking?"

"If Jack made a mistake he can..." Michael knew how asinine he sounded, but he couldn't stop now. "He can let her go."

Eyes filled with concern, Jesse shook his head. "There's no going back for her. She'll always be the Rabbit. Buddy—you're starting to scare me. Did you hit your head?"

"Well..."

Jesse read his eyes—and as a decent telepath—his mind, and scoffed. "The Lost Rabbit? *Judas Priest!* Let me get out of here..."

"*Why not?*" Michael whispered knowing how absurd he sounded. Jesse answered as he expected.

"Rumors, Mike. Legends. It has never happened."

"It must have happened at least once for there to be a law against it—" Michael stopped himself. He had some far-out theories regarding the origin of the Lost Rabbit legend, but the Rakum weren't permitted to think on such things. The High Father doled out the history and questioning his version meant certain punishment. Jesse had heard enough anyway.

"Stop. You're on your own." Jesse exhaled slowly and lowered his voice. "Mike, it does *no good* to get attached to these mortals. You're setting yourself up for disappointment." Jesse's voice choked. "Walk away if you don't want to be the one to catch her. Go home. Someone else will be along. You don't have to get involved. You don't have to get hurt."

Without waiting for a reply, Jesse turned and walked briskly toward the cabstands. Michael didn't follow. His friend had his reasons for his emotional outburst, but Michael had to watch over Beth Rider no matter how crazy the notion. With every fiber of his being, he knew Jack had made a mistake.

Michael sighed and headed back to the bookstore, Jesse's private pain and the story of the Lost Rabbit circling his mind.

Love is Weakness

Jesse caught a taxi and headed for the Hotel Renaissance, the lushest such establishment in the city. If he had to leave the comfort of his New York apartment, at least he'd have a concierge. As the hired car meandered toward the interstate, Jesse alternately stared at the cabbie's head, the lights outside, and the torn carpet at his feet, Michael's lunatic attachment to the Rabbit erasing his peace.

Dealing with the mortals he worked with night after night wasn't difficult; he met most of them online or on conference calls, and when he dealt with them face-to-face he kept the meetings short. As far as he knew, Michael also avoided anything more than casual contact with the humans in his world. So what was it about this one woman that turned his head?

Jesse sighed and narrowed his eyes at a passing truck's headlights. *We've had female Rabbits before,* he thought and huffed. His favorite brother was setting himself up for tremendous trouble and unfortunately, was blind to reason. Yet, Jesse had been blind once. He got her out of his system, but the memory of Dae Lee was bleak, and he worked hard to erase it.

"Mind if I put on the ballgame?"

The taxi driver put his fingers on the radio knob, his eyes on Jesse's in the rearview mirror. Jesse shrugged and looked out the window. In his mind, he touched ever so slightly the recollection of Dae Lee's small, heart-shaped face. Her big eyes were brown like her Chinese mother's, but round like those of her father, Johann, a Rakum Father of Swedish descent. She had a way of batting her eyelashes that never failed to make him grin, and she would swish her long black bangs out of her eyes as she spoke.

Jesse's chest hitched. Tonight was a good time to revisit the pain. It could help him keep Mike's preoccupation with the Rabbit in perspective. Pain was good medicine when a pal faced a similar threat.

Jesse began by recalling the girl's mother.

Dae Ping had been grabbed off the street in New York's China Town by Father Johann's scouts. It was 1945 and the population of Rakum fell off by one the year before. As the rotation among the Father's lay, Johann was the next in line to choose the new Breeder. As the rumor went, he sought a Chinese woman with the notion to meld her ethnic features into his strictly blond Nordic traits. His scouts collected Dae Ping one evening as she bought groceries for her parents. From a strict household, Dae Ping was eighteen and still a virgin, which although not a requirement for Breeders, appealed to Johann when she was presented. He indoctrinated her into the program and nine months later, Dae Ping delivered two healthy babies to the Rakum physicians.

The boy, Dae Kim, born a Rakum, was sent to the nursery to be raised among his people. But the girl, Dae Lee, was sent home with her mother and put in an apartment in New Jersey. It was the normal practice among Rakum to make use of the Breeders as Cows after a live birth, so Johann assigned Senior Elder Jack Dawn to make sure the mother and child were properly attended. Being newly planted in Atlanta, Jack called on his only proselyte in the New York area to govern her care until her death. Thus, the lot fell to Jesse. He went to her home when the baby was four months old, put Dae Ping on a twelve-week rotation, and in a sideways fashion, watched the youngster grow.

Dae Lee grew quickly, especially since Jesse saw her infrequently. The child was naturally inquisitive and by age eleven, she actively sought his presence. His method was to meet Dae Ping in her bedroom privately and evade the child, but as she matured, Dae Lee was not easily distracted. She took to knocking on the door as Jesse drew her mother's blood, asking to come in, and prodding for information. Dae Ping did what she could to schedule her daughter's away-time to coincide with Jesse's visits, but one night when the girl was fifteen, she caught Jesse leaving her mother's room and grabbed him in a tight hug. She cooed into his coat, *"I love you, Jesse Cherrie."*

At a loss on how to respond, Jesse asked her a few questions and before long, they were sitting on her bed in her small bedroom discussing the things of the universe. To Dae Lee, the world was

31

gigantic and she had ideas covering a myriad of subjects. She held opinions on important things Jesse didn't give thought to anymore, and she had solutions—how to address the country's social issues, what to do about immigration, health care, racism. The youngster enchanted Jesse to the extent that he soon consciously timed his visits around *her* calendar. By the time Dae Lee was eighteen, Jesse had placed her in his heart in such a way that it pained him to be apart from her. That was where the real trouble lay. Not only did his affection push the boundaries of Rakum allowance, she had matured into an adult. She saw Jesse as a man and decisions would need to be made regarding the nature of their relationship.

On her eighteenth birthday, Jesse made an unscheduled visit and took Dae Lee out to her favorite Italian restaurant. He sat quietly as she filled him in on everything that had transpired since she last saw him. At the end of the meal, he asked her plans for the future. A Rakum Father provided half of her DNA, which had imbued her with unmatched intelligence. She graduated high school with honors and was now being courted by several Ivy League colleges. All of that notwithstanding, Dae Lee informed him that she did not want a career—she wanted to move in with Jesse.

"No, you don't want that," he had told her. He lived well, owned an apartment on Central Park West, and traveled plenty. His associations with females were strictly sexual ones, more than often, prostitutes and high-end escorts—he had no need for a mate. Yet, Dae Lee...

The mouth-watering offer to add her to his life *was* tempting, but no—the girl should seek out the American Dream. With her looks and intelligence, she could have it all. When Jesse pictured Dae Lee's defeated mother who considered him her god, letting her blood with religious fervor, his heart sank. Jesse wanted the girl as far away from the Rakum as possible, the sooner, the better.

That night as she ate spumoni ice cream and sipped her black coffee, Jesse told Dae Lee to forget about him. To move on, go to college, get married, and have some kids. Dae Lee didn't take the advice well and the night ended in hysterics. Angry and rejected, she avoided him the next two times he visited her mother.

When Jesse saw her again shortly after her nineteenth birthday, she'd forgiven him. With passionate kisses that erased the past, she convinced Jesse that all was well. Jesse arranged to take her into New York to catch *Funny Girl* on Broadway. At Times Square, they ran into two Rakum Jesse knew by reputation only. These two worked out of the Cave as errand boys for the Fathers and they told Jesse they were in the city on holiday. Jesse had his suspicions that they were on the hunt, but for what, he couldn't read. He reluctantly introduced them to Dae Lee who blushed and dazzled them with her charm. When both of his brothers were thoroughly enamored, he left them in the street and took her to the show. Afterwards, he made his goodbyes and scheduled his next visit for three months as usual. When he returned at the allotted time, Dae Lee was gone.

When asked, her mother joyously announced that she had been recruited for the Breeder program and Jesse's heart broke at the news. His innocent one, more valuable than any treasure, was submitting herself to the cruelest of creatures only to receive disdain and humiliation as a reward. Jesse made plans to visit her, but because of obligations with the brethren, he wasn't able to get to the Cave for several months. When he arrived and found her in the underground Breeders apartments, she was six months pregnant.

Dae Lee jumped for joy when she saw him and held him a long time about the neck, but Jesse was saddened by her appearance. Besides the round protrusion in her middle, she had shrunk to a shadow of her former self. Her once bright eyes were dull and cheerless, and her luminescent complexion now yellowed and wan. She had been "bred, bled, and hardly fed," as the Rakum were fond of saying, but for the first time the phrase made Jesse angry. Helpless and unable to do anything about her condition, he left. A few months later, he discovered she died in childbirth and the baby, a girl named Dae Jae, lived only a few hours. Decades later, Jesse still lamented the entire misadventure.

"Here you are, Sir. Have a good evening."

The cabbie had pulled into the hotel reception area and Jesse grabbed his briefcase, shoving a few bills in the driver's proffered hand. Walking through the impressive lobby to the desk, he set about shelving every memory that had cascaded home during his ride in.

The girl's mother, Dae Ping, passed away a decade ago so he no longer had her as a constant reminder, but her Rakum son, Dae Kim, was well-established in the New York area and Jesse ran into him frequently. Each time their eyes met, he thought of the beautiful and tragic Dae Lee who held his heart in her hand for several years, only to unintentionally fracture it forever.

Jesse tromped up to his room avoiding eye contact with those he passed. He would seal up the wounds in his heart tonight, but remember the pain so he could be the most help to Michael. If his friend continued on his current path, he too, would be nursing a broken heart soon enough.

Jesse pushed open his door and locked it behind him. Dae Lee was dead and gone, but even when the bleeding stopped, there was nothing to be done about the scars. He picked up the phone and dialed the familiar number. She went by Miss Kitty, and the comfort she brought would have to do. At least for now.

9

Nip It in the Bud

Jack Dawn shoved Kite to the ground and beat his chest like a gorilla. He'd never been bested, not in twelve hundred years; no way this feeble pup was going to get the better of him tonight. Jack feigned toward him and the kid winced. It was good to be the king.

He'd begun his evening at a local brothel with a few of his brothers and now they were winding down, enjoying their nightly ritual of pounding each other until they collapsed or cried uncle. Kite endured a special beat-down for something he'd said over a month ago. There was no need to remind him of his error; it was more fun to slap the snot out of him and watch his eyes grow wide with fear. It would make the kid stronger. Jack was slapped around plenty when he was young and he recalled every excruciating millisecond.

"So, what about that Rabbit you marked, Jack?" Elder Tomás spoke with a thick Spanish accent, watching from a few feet away.

"What's to say?" Jack booted Kite in the shoulder just to hear him yelp. When the kid fell silent, he turned to Tomás. "Well?"

"There's a whisper going around that Stone isn't playing fair."

"Don't you know better than to listen to gossip?" Jack approached his friend and swatted his shoulder hard. Not quite as tall as Jack, but nearly as muscular, Tomás braced himself, effectively nullifying the jab.

"It's not gossip, Brother. Tyson said—"

"Tyson? That miserable waste of space? Come on, Tomás. Shut up about Tyson!" Jack growled his words and threatened the Elder with a raised fist.

Tomás stepped forward and bared his teeth, wrapping a strong hand around Jack's closed hand. Jack pushed against him and soon added his upper body strength, leaning in to press through, but

Tomás matched his great physical might perfectly. As they tested each other's strength, Tomás spat his next words into Jack's sweating face.

"Stone's gone soft," Tomás grunted with effort. "Let's go down to Montgomery and check it out." Tomás brought his free hand up and clocked Jack under the chin. "If Stone's behaving, no problem. But if he's—"

Jack returned Tomás' uppercut with a powerful double blow to his kidney. Tomás crumpled to the ground, but didn't cry out. He remained on the carpet, drew up his knees, and caught his breath.

"Behaving? That's my *lieutenant*, you asshole." Jack kicked the other Elder's nearest shin hard.

Tomás made no notice of the blow. "If he's gone soft," he said in a forced whisper, "you're gonna want to nip that in the bud."

Jack frowned. "Seriously? What does Tyson know?"

"It's not Tyson alone." Tomás put out his hand and Jack pulled him to his feet. "Others sense the same thing. Don't you? He's *your* favored one—surely you've read his intentions," Tomás said and raised his fists, pugilist style.

Jack ignored his offer and turned away. He left the large, empty room modified especially for roughhousing, and entered the kitchen. Tomás was right behind him, followed by a very bloody Kite, and Beryl, one of a set of twins Jack was discipling.

"What about it?" Tomás pressed as he pulled a beer from the fridge. He tossed the can to Jack who caught it without looking up.

"I got this, Tomás. Shit. End of discussion." Jack popped open the can and drank the entire contents without pause. He tossed the empty to Beryl who tossed it into the trash. "I should have killed that woman and been done with it. Why do I always listen to you?"

"Blame yourself for lovin' me so much." Tomás smiled and then his eyes narrowed. "Did you hear? Bel had two of his pups disappear tonight. That makes at least twenty."

Jack cursed and hit the wall with a closed fist. Powdered plaster filtered down from the ceiling onto his bald head. "This is *ridiculous*. Stone's a real monster. That woman has unleashed some sort of disease on him. *On us.*"

"That makes no sense," Tomás countered, his fists to his hips. "*How?* And why *now*? Thousands of years and nothing like this has ever happened…"

Beryl cleared his throat and Jack glared at him out of habit. Beryl was part of Jack's inner circle and had been for the last few years.

When he sent Michael Stone to Montgomery to manage that area, he moved Beryl and his identical twin brother, Meryl, right under him. The boys performed as two bodies with one magnificent brain, and it was no use to separate them for long. Tonight though, Meryl was taking care of a mission for Jack across town and Beryl stayed behind. He liked to have one of them around at all times. He liked to watch them work. And he liked to watch them, period. Identical in every way, the boys had soft, curly brown hair, and their fawn-hazel eyes often left speechless any mortal careless enough to be caught in either boy's gaze. The kids had the looks they all wanted—perfect facial symmetry, skin the color of creamy coffee, a killer smile—but both with the disposition of their true father, Umbarto. Father Umbarto was also Jack's natural father, and he was a nightmare when perturbed. Beryl and Meryl could be great; they were natural leaders. And Jack was just the man to disciple them up.

"You got something to add, B?" Jack asked, knowing his normally terse tone inevitably lifted when he addressed the twins.

Beryl carefully chose his words and in a voice as smooth as silk, he said, "Father Abroghia once told a story." He paused and met the eyes of each man. "Two thousand years ago, many Rakum fell away, grabbing onto a new religion circling the planet at that time. Abroghia was there."

Jack considered the tale. Abroghia was the only Father that went back that far. The other nine were old, no doubt, but Abroghia had seen at least two millennia and was widely respected as the ultimate leader of their Race. He nodded at the boy who returned a tight smile. It was the closest thing to affection that they had between them and it suited them both.

"Well, it's coming around again," Tomás interjected. "Twenty of the brethren gone underground. Hiding from us. Hiding from *you.*" Tomás headed out of the kitchen. "You need to go to Montgomery and eliminate that Rabbit. Hell, I'll go with you. It'll be fun."

Jack watched him go and then glared at Kite who stepped back, as if awaking from a trance, his marbles scrambled.

"We'll leave at sundown," Jack called to Tomás and then reached for Kite's upper arm. The boy knew better than to evade him and he stood under Jack's hard gaze suppressing a shudder. Jack eyed Beryl and he stepped behind the younger Rakum to wrap his arms firmly around his chest. Kite closed his eyes and pressed his lips together. It stunk being least in the kingdom.

10

Old Cow, Good Cow

Michael avoided the elderly man's gaze as he drew his tired blood into a disposable cup. After making his good-byes with Beth Rider at the airport, he surreptitiously tailed her home and made sure she got inside safely. He had a small window of time before she was in any real danger; Jesse would deflect anything mentioned to him and none of the brethren were nearby. Michael returned his attention to the work at hand.

This particular Cow entered Michael's life five years ago and was one of the first added to his current rotation. Of course, five years ago, the man had been virile and productive, working full-time at his family-owned hardware store. But during the last eighteen months, he developed pneumonia and was beginning to show the first signs of Alzheimer's. None of this mattered to Michael. The old gentleman remained a ready food source and Michael never turned down a free blood meal.

It was the acceptable method of feeding; to select a few human donors who were willing and able to give blood regularly on a schedule, and Michael had nine such Cows in the area. Many of his brethren lived off less than half that, but Montgomery had been good to Michael and he was envied for it.

As a rule, Michael maintained an amicable relationship with those inclined to let blood to him, but not all Rakum treated their donors with such respect. Some Cows faced constant terror at the whimsy of their Rakum masters; but, *hey, they volunteered for the duty. You lay down in the bed you make.* Michael had a hard time feeling sorry for any mortal who consciously submitted to such practice and Jack Dawn was infamous for his cruelty. Michael smiled despite the gruesome recollection of the last time he accompanied his Elder on a visitation.

Jack was fond of ripping the Cow's skin with his teeth where most of the brethren used a knife. Michael's mind poked him with a new quandary: what compelled Jack to sick the brethren onto Beth Rider? A mortal would have to threaten a Rakum's life or his possessions to be marked as a Rabbit. What did Beth Rider do to raise their oldest Elder's ire?

Michael cleared his mind as the errant thoughts threatened to ruin his mood as the aroma of Norman's blood tickled his nose. This Cow liked Michael to draw his blood into a cup and drink it holding eye contact. Michael didn't care—all Cows were mentally unstable, so he expected each to have his or her own perverse fantasies. Michael finished off the quickly-cooling liquid and licked his lips.

"What'cha gonna do when you come by here one day..." The old man paused to take a ragged breath. "When you come by here one day and I'm gone?"

Michael didn't respond, his brain alive and his every nerve tingling from the hastily-downed ambrosia. Norman knew better than to interrupt; Michael allowed a small smile, but didn't reply until the orgasmic effects of the buzz filtered away. Norman waited, his lungs rattling, and when his tongue was no longer numb with pleasure, Michael feigned surprise.

"Where're ya going?" he teased. "You can't even get out of bed."

"When I'm dead, you idiot!" Norman spat the last, his flying spittle a happy accident.

"Hah! If you even die, I will be very surprised," Michael said with a laugh and finished wrapping gauze around the man's withered arm as he had done every eight weeks for the last five years. "Hard old coots like you never die. You'll be here another hundred years lying in bed, waiting for me to come through that door and brighten your miserable life."

Norman struggled to respond and fell silent.

The man watched Michael as he rose from his kneeling position to toss the cup into the trashcan. This particular Cow had always been belligerent, but it was a farce. Norman was in awe of him—as were all his donors. And why not? He was a living, breathing god. He strode back to the man's side and knelt to his eye level.

"Norman, if you're going to die, be sure to leave me the name of someone I can carry on with. *I'm* not dying any time soon, and I'm still going to need my supper on time with or without you."

Michael knew his careless words would get a rise out of the tired

Cow, and for some reason, the cruel banter pleased the man more than anything.

Norman took a careful breath into his ravaged lungs and let out a string of profanities, cursing Michael profusely as he rose and headed toward the door. He was still cussing like a sailor when the door was locked automatically behind him.

Michael reached the elevator and pressed the down button as an unwanted aroma hit the air. It was a Rakum and not one he liked.

"Hey, Brother. Where's the Rabbit?" Tyson exited the stairwell and walked up to Michael pressing into his personal space.

Wondering how the creep got past him, Michael ignored the elevator and returned to the hallway. Although they had shared adventures in the past, Tyson was nobody's favorite. Short, greasy, and repulsive, he had come to live with the Southern Packs only a few years ago. He had zero social skills and his only positive attribute was his generosity—he had a lot of dough and he shared it with anyone who treated him with any measure of civility.

Michael was not going to earn any money tonight.

"Come, now, Stoney-boy. I know you nabbed a Rabbit. I smell him all over you. Where'd you leave him? Is he in there?"

"You've got a nose, idiot. I'm keeping this one to myself, so stay away." Michael leaned into him and even though the smaller Rakum shrank back, in no way did he fear him. All Rakum enjoyed violence and Tyson had always been tough as nails.

"You gotta share. The Rabbit was made for all of us. You can't keep him to yourself." Tyson thoroughly sniffed the air, his eyes half-closed.

"I'm about to squash you," Michael hissed and meant it, his fists clinching. He could not leave Tyson with notions of hunting down Beth Rider. Michael pushed further into him, menacing with his bulk.

Tyson opened his eyes and put his palm to Michael's pectoral region. "If you want to dance, take a number. I have all the lovers I need," he jibed with a wink. Then his jaw dropped and he stepped back to look Michael up and down. "It's a *Bunny! Yesssssss!* Is she pretty? Is she soft?" Tyson's beady eyes glittered. "Same rules apply. You get first dibs, but then, she's ours. *Judas Priest!* I can't wait to get my hands on her soft fur..."

Michael grit his teeth, working to hide his unRakum-like behavior. He couldn't allow his brethren to take turns at her, assault her until their horrible lusts were satiated, just as he had done himself his entire life. Tyson's second palm pressed into Michael's chest and he looked down upon the brother's oily face.

"Look, handsome, we all know Elder Dawn favors you. How about you put in a good word for me with your master and in return, I'll preoccupy myself a while..." Tyson nodded smugly. "But next weekend, the Bunny is mine and you know I have just the place to enjoy her."

Having entertained Rabbits with Tyson on more than one occasion, the man was correct—he had a private killing field of his own not too far away. Michael said nothing and watched the ridiculous snot turn and head back to the stairwell.

There was no time to fume over his interaction with the disgusting inferior; it was less than an hour to sunup and he wanted to be in Beth's house before then. Michael pressed the elevator button and planned his route. Tyson saw it—Michael was acting fishy, and all of his brethren would know it soon, if they didn't already. And of course, his master would be furious.

Riding the elevator down, Michael shook his head. It was going to be an interesting week.

Don't Open the Curtains

Situated on Beth Rider's couch, Michael listened as she rose from bed and proceeded through her morning rituals. He had made entry before dawn and having silently scoped the townhouse's layout, he mapped two bedrooms and a bath upstairs, with the kitchen, dining nook, and living room on the first floor. His ears and nose informed him that the woman lived alone with no pets, she did not often entertain guests, and Michael did not detect any masculine aromas.

The Rabbit is single and a loner... he pondered and rose to stand.

Still wondering how she earned Jack's mark, Michael imagined her brushing her hair and preparing to come downstairs. The clock read 10 a.m. and on the other side of the woman's light-blocking curtains, the sun threatened him mercilessly. Michael positioned himself so he blocked the drape cords and prepared to surprise her as gently as possible.

Presently, Beth Rider clomped down and as predicted headed for the curtains. Michael closed his eyes behind his Raybans and cleared his throat, the woman seeing his shape and gasping at the same time.

"Beth, it's Michael Stone," he said with his free palm facing out. "Don't be afraid, and *please,* whatever you do, don't open the curtains."

"Oh, my god!" she hissed and grabbed her own arms. To his amazement, she calmed almost immediately and scrutinized him from the bottom stair. "Michael?" she muttered, darting her eyes behind her to the upper floor and then back to her uninvited guest. "What are you doing here? And why are you covering your eyes?"

"I'm allergic to the sun—and I'm sorry about sneaking in. Please, don't open the curtains," he repeated. "I can explain everything."

Beth's shoulders relaxed and she moved backward one step up. "Okay, I believe you. Why did you break into my house?"

Michael mumbled sincere thanks and added, "You were attacked in Atlanta. I know about it and I'm here to help you." Michael lowered his hand and she took one more step up, still facing him.

"Are you a police detective?"

Michael smiled and her face softened. She liked him, and for some reason, the thought made him glad. "If you can trust me a tiny bit, I promise to tell you whatever you need to know."

Beth nodded with round eyes and her hands touched the sides of her thigh-length sleep shirt. A blush blossomed across her cheeks and she spun around. "I'll be right back," she said and Michael listened as she moved about her room.

Minutes later, she was back wearing blue jeans and a soft green sweater that perfectly complimented her eyes. She met him at the first floor landing, her musculature tight with stress, but her flight response erased.

So this is how she dealt with Jack Dawn—she simply compartmentalized. Impressed, he offered her a friendly grin. "You're the bravest woman I've ever met. I'm sorry I scared you."

She nodded absently. "We'll deal with that later. How did you know about that monster in Atlanta? I didn't tell you…"

"Let's sit down. Is this enough light?" Michael asked referring to the single lamp on his right as he sank into the sofa. Beth did, too, a cushion between them.

"Take off your sunglasses," she said, her head to the side.

Michael sighed. Jack Dawn wore the same kind, which she might find troubling. Forcing a calming breath, Michael pulled them down and held them in one hand.

"You have kind eyes," she said softly. "Tell me about that man. Are you working a case?"

He shook his head. "I know the man who attacked you, but I don't know *why*. Maybe if you tell me about it, I can figure it out. Had you met him before that night?"

Beth shook her head. "I was hoping it was all a dream. I mean, I'm fine. I don't have any physical proof that I was even attacked."

"Is your driver's license missing?"

Beth nibbled her bottom lip.

"Tell me exactly what happened."

"It was weird. I was signing books in the bookstore…"

43

Michael was about to ask her to clarify and she caught on.

"I'm a novelist and my publicist sets me up with book signings."

"Okay, I'm listening…"

"I signed books all afternoon and into the night, but one of the guys in the line threatened me." Beth tittered nervously and Michael arched his eyebrows.

"And?"

"Don't laugh, but I thought I heard him threaten me in my mind, as in, *telepathically*. I know that's impossible, but I freaked out. I heard him say clearly, 'watch your back.'"

"And then he left for a more opportune time," Michael mumbled, his eyes to the side. He knew the drill: frighten and intimidate the intended victim and mark them later in private.

"Huh, I think that's a Bible verse," she said when he grew quiet.

Michael grunted a reply, noting his new acquaintance seemed overly preoccupied with religious notions. He refocused his questions and continued. "When did you see him again? In your hotel room?"

"As a matter of fact, yes. The next night, he was already in my room when I went in. Do you think he stole a key? Does he have a confederate at the hotel?" Beth turned to glance at her front door. "Come to think of it, how did you get in here last night?"

"I promise to explain everything, but this first," Michael said gently. "What happened next?"

Beth furrowed her brow, but acquiesced and retold the entire event. When she was finished, Michael leaned into the couch and trained his eyes to the ceiling.

"Well?" she asked, probably anxious to hear the explanations he promised. "You're taking this so seriously, but if it happened as I remember, I should have a scab on my neck." She put her fingers to her throat.

Michael did not look over; she still smelled delicious and he endeavored to keep blood out of the conversation as long as possible. "You never saw that man before that night in line?"

"No. I'm certain of it. I'd remember that brute."

"I'm sure," Michael agreed, allowing a quiet chuckle. "Why did he target you? That's what I need to figure out."

Beth had an answer. "Michael, he thinks he's a vampire. He's crazy." She wanted him to agree, but he shook his head in thought. She added with more fervor, "Crazy people don't need a reason to do what they do."

"No, I know this man very well and he's not crazy. He's rational and his decisions are based on a millennia of experience..." Michael pondered and his hostess shook her head.

"You're not making sense," she said quietly trying to get him to turn her way.

Michael finally met her gaze and again, her eyes softened in his. She should be terrified—what was holding her together?

"How do you know him? He's not like you," she said then, perhaps protesting too much. Michael was more like Jack Dawn than any of his pack, but since he met the Rabbit, his behavior had skewed *way* off center.

"His name is Jack Dawn and he marked you for a reason, only I can't imagine how you incited his ire."

"*Marked*—that's what he called it." Beth flipped her hair off both shoulders and leaned over her knees. "Okay—tell me what all of this means to you. I'm ready."

With a deep inhale, Michael leveled his gaze. He'd tell her everything. Why not? She was up to her neck in his world and not likely to escape. "Beth, listen closely," he began, his voice even, "Jack Dawn isn't a man, he's a Rakum, one of our oldest. If you would hold your questions, I'll explain about my kind. You may as well know it all at this point."

"Your *kind?*"

Michael held up his hand. "I'll talk. You listen." Beth's lips parted, but then she nodded and sat back into the couch cushion. With a grave nod, he continued. "My race lives below mortal radar. We are 100,000-strong and we live across the globe. In English, we're sometimes referred to as *Wraiths,* but we prefer our ancient name, the Rakum."

"It sounds like you're saying you're not human," Beth interrupted.

"Correct," Michael grunted. "I was born in 1859, the product of a human woman and a Rakum Father. I was raised in a group-lair—like a group home—for Rakum. My people age normally until puberty when our aging slows to a crawl."

"1859?" Beth whispered, but Michael continued without a pause.

"At age thirteen, I was taken in and proselytized by an Elder named Jack Dawn. He is the one who attacked you."

"You're over a hundred years old?"

"That's right."

"And the monster that attacked me is your... boss?"

"*Master* is a better term," Michael corrected. "He oversees a thousand brethren and I'm his top lieutenant."

"*The lieutenant in Montgomery,*" she whispered her gaze going blank.

Michael recognized her meaning; Jack must have threatened her with his lieutenant's famous reputation.

"This is unbelievable. I have a million questions," she said with cautious wonder.

She closed her eyes, slowed her breathing, and when she opened them again, Michael recognized the emotion in her gaze— *determination.*

Beth took a deep breath. "Your master told me that I better start running. He thought you'd hurt me. Why are you helping me instead? Are you going to get into trouble? He seemed sociopathic—aren't you taking a huge risk?"

"Whoa, hang on," Michael chuckled softly even though she brought up a few terrifying points that he had not had time to ponder. "I can't explain my behavior—and I hope I'm not wrong. But until I figure out why you were marked, I can't concentrate on anything else."

Beth rolled in her lips, her expression thanking him without words. "Do you think they're after me?"

"Without a doubt." Michael clasped his hands in his lap and watched for her reaction.

"Are you sure? How do you know?"

"It's complicated and I have to get away from that window." Michael flicked his chin to the curtain. "Here's the condensed version. In the airport, you met Jesse Cherrie. He's no danger to you, he's a friend and trusts my judgment. He'll tell everyone that I'm keeping you to myself. My reputation will keep them away for a little while." Michael shrugged off the rest of that topic, but Beth pressed him.

"What reputation is that?"

Michael sighed. "Jack Dawn is my Elder—that means before this shit—pardon," he said with a stumble, unsure why he suddenly didn't want to curse in her presence. "Before I saw you, I idolized and mimicked my Master as best I could." Beth paled and he regretted that there was still much more to tell. "If Jesse tells the brethren I'm keeping you to myself, they'll give me a week. A week is standard."

Beth frowned. "You've seen a lot of people like me?"

"Rabbits? Yes. Like you? No."

"You don't usually help them?"

"First time," Michael answered flatly. "I want you to be aware of the danger you're in—last night, another brother approached me across town. I diverted him, but he won't stop searching. Any Rakum that comes within nose-shot will try to get to you, even during my solitary week."

"This is horrible," she mumbled.

"It's going to get worse. We haven't discovered why you were marked and we'll run out of time. Eventually, Jack will send someone to correct me." Michael got to his feet. "I can see that you like me and I'm glad you trust me, but my behavior is not normal—none of my brethren will care if you suffer." Michael took in the room in a furtive scan. "Beth, I have to get out of the light." When he took a step backward, she got to her feet, her eyes worrying on his behalf.

"In there—it's a laundry closet," she said softly and Michael nodded, having already scoped it out earlier.

He stepped to the door and put his hand to the knob. "I'm winging it, I admit it. And I have no idea how to keep you safe. We don't do this—" Michael waved his hand in a small circle. "We don't care about your kind. My behavior will be considered a weakness and I'll come under reproach, or punishment for disobeying my master. Nonetheless, I'll need to stay by your side during the night hours."

"What about the daytime? That's when I do most of my running around."

Michael replaced his sunglasses. "Rakum cannot go out in the day. You see that light seeping around the edges of your curtains?"

"Is that bothering your eyes?"

"Yes. You'll be safe until twilight." Michael opened the small room's door and stepped inside. Beth followed and he must have registered surprise at their sudden close proximity for she grinned when their eyes met.

"Sorry—I got in your bubble there," she said and leaned against the now-closed door to give them both room.

A nightlight in the single outlet provided light for human eyes and Michael decided to further increase the distance between them by hopping onto the lid of the washing machine behind him.

"Your story fits, but there's a big question you haven't answered." Beth bit her lower lip and then set her jaw, as if about to ask something horrible. "You assured me that I didn't imagine him cutting my neck. Why don't I have a mark of that? Does he have the power to heal?" Beth's hand ran along the surface of her throat as she spoke and Michael imagined that was where Jack did the deed.

"No, Jack's not a healer. My guess, he was trying to scare you. You probably seemed a little too calm—he enjoys a victim's fear." Michael smiled and lowered his head. "Come to think of it, you are extremely calm. Aren't you afraid?"

Beth sighed. "Yeah, but I don't control what happens. God does, and I trust Him more than anything."

Michael's thoughts clouded as he realized she spoke of the mortals' infatuation with religion.

She waved her hand once. "I'll explain my peace later. Please finish." Beth rubbed her invisible throat wound as she spoke and Michael chuckled wryly. Had any of his brethren ever exposed himself to a Rabbit in such a way?

Michael's slipped off the dryer. "It goes like this. When you swallowed Jack's blood, your body chemistry was altered. If you were to have tissue samples drawn right now, they wouldn't match those of the previous Beth Rider. By now, every single body system is producing and reproducing cells tainted by Jack Dawn's personal physiological identity. You've been changed into a new being. A Rakum Rabbit."

"I don't feel any different," Beth said and shook her head. "Are you saying that the reason I don't have a cut on my neck is because Jack's blood in me caused it to heal up and disappear?"

"Yes," he said watching her expression.

"So, he doesn't think he's a vampire... Why blood? He could have done all sorts of things to scare me..." Beth's voice trailed off and Michael realized she missed a huge point.

"Rakum drink human blood. Did you not figure that out already?" he asked in a kind tone.

Beth slowly shook her head and looked at the floor. "It feels like I'm living in one of my novels. I wrote this. I know it."

Michael lifted his brow. "You wrote about Rakum?"

She met his eye, offered a shy smile and shook her head. "You first. Why do you drink blood if you're not vampires?"

Michael acquiesced with a shrug and hopped back onto the machine behind him. "Vampires are fiction—a creation of a man's active imagination. Rakum are a flesh and blood race, and there is nothing fiction about us." He lowered his gaze until she accepted his seriousness. "We eat anything we want, but human blood scratches an itch deep inside. We can live without it, but none of us ever would."

"That's horrible," she whispered, looking to the side. "Why not just substitute animal blood?"

Michael shook his head. "Bad food—it devolves us."

"Then, drink each other's blood and leave us alone," she suggested and met his eye.

Michael offered a kind wink. She did not like discussing blood-drinking and the more he spoke of it, the hungrier he grew. He cleared his mind and attempted to answer gently. "We do sometimes, but it's not good food for the long run. Rakum blood is like Coke without caffeine—it doesn't satisfy."

"Geez," Beth whispered. "Poor humans. It doesn't seem fair."

"Oh, it's not like that." Michael shook his head. "We drink from human *Cows*, not just anyone off the street."

Beth's eyebrows went up and Michael quickly explained.

"We call them *Cows,*" he said with a nod. "Like a Cow gives milk? There are mortals that are drawn to us and they live to let their blood. We don't have to steal it. We don't have to kill. There are plenty of freaks who offer it up freely. It doesn't take that much and it can be relatively painless."

"That sounds really wrong." Michael shrugged noncommittally.

Beth tilted her head. "I swear, I could have written this. It's very close." She put her hand to the knob to leave. "This is incredible."

"Wait." Michael replaced his sunglasses as a precaution. "Will you bring me your books? If this seems familiar to you, maybe it seemed *too* familiar to my Elder."

Beth nodded with a sad smile, exited, and then returned with copies of her novels. Michael thanked her and she left him alone, probably wondering what lay ahead.

It's gotta be strange, but damn, she's taking it well, he thought and settled onto the cushions to read. He hoped the clues jumped out— he'd never been much of a detective.

12

It Opens Your Eyes

Javier woke thirty minutes before sundown and stared at the dark ceiling. Roman's breathing was steady a few feet away on Dietrich's bed, and a throaty snore trickled from the closet. In a little while, he and Roman were hitting the road. Could things be as bad as Roman indicated? Why were the Elders so upset about the Rider book? Javier rolled his head to the right to see Roman looking at him. All of the Elders were telepathic and he was no doubt reading his thoughts.

"You know why, Javie."

Javie—his childhood nickname. Javier stared back. He had a long history with Roman. Most Rakum were housed in group-lairs to be assigned Elders in their teens, but Javier had been raised by this man, and from the beginning, whenever a stressful situation arose in his training, or life in general, his Elder called him by this endearment. Javier smiled, but the line never curved up.

"Jack Dawn is leading the crusade against this book and every Rakum who reads it. His actions are not sanctioned by the Fathers, but..." Roman sat up and leaned over his knees. "...it is likely once involved, they will take his side."

"Because of God?"

Roman's head tipped a fraction and he stood to his feet. "Store those books in your satchel before Dietrich awakes."

"He knows I read the Rider novel. I told him yesterday. He was cool with it. In fact, last night he buzzed me so I could get to Simon's faster." Javier came to his feet and stuffed the books in his backpack anyway.

"That is unfortunate. He is dead inside."

"Dietrich?" Javier raised his brow. His roommate was a bit of a doofus, but dead?

50

"The Rider novel opens your eyes. I can *see* things now and I can see *hate*. Dietrich *hates*, Javie. He hates you, he hates your congeniality, and he hates my authority." Roman strode over to the closet and put his hand to the rusty knob. "He can buzz me tonight and we'll get underway."

Javier nodded, still amazed at Roman's impassioned words. He watched his Elder pull open the closet and tug Dietrich's long hair.

"Ouch! Master, I—" Dietrich stood, his knees popping, and then he grabbed Roman's hand buried in his dirty yellow curls. "Good evening, Elder Roman!"

Roman said not a word, but held Javier's housemate by the back of the head with one hand, and with the other, he produced a six-inch switchblade that popped open with a click. Dietrich's eyes widened momentarily, but then fell on Javier in an accusing glare.

Javier shrugged and held his gaze, even as Roman plunged the sharp tip into Dietrich's throat and slurped up the blood that coursed from the wound. Dietrich clenched his jaw, but remained silent. Rakum experienced pain like anyone else and Roman was being particularly brutal.

Javier unexpectedly thought of Simon. A painful image of the boy dead in the street behind his condo popped into his mind. Javier looked away from Dietrich and toward the basement door. He'd never been especially telepathic, but that thought was not his own. Another Rakum sent it and he didn't need to know who to be alarmed. He took a step toward the stairs and was stopped by Roman's voice in his head.

"It is day a few more minutes. We will go together to be sure your friend is safe. Be patient…"

Javier stayed put and slung the backpack over his shoulder. He stole a glance at the couple across the room and Roman was showing no mercy. Dietrich was a hardy specimen, but he was going to be sick tonight, nauseated and perhaps too dehydrated to go out.

Javier shifted his weight and after what seemed too long, Roman released Dietrich and dropped him to the floor. The Rakum with the dead spirit did not move as their Elder stepped away. To Javier, he gestured for the steps.

"He'll do us no harm tonight. Come." Roman took the lead and yanked open the sturdy door to lead Javier through the littered and abandoned kitchen. Roman owned the run-down house and allowed Javier and Dietrich to reside there. Javier wouldn't miss it. He fell into

Roman's dusty black Camaro and didn't look back.

"Simon will come with us." Roman shifted gears smoothly and reached the boy's nearby house in minutes. When the car came to a halt, Javier jumped out and sprinted to Simon's front door. The boy answered at the second knock.

"Javier? The sun just barely went down." Simon backed to make way, his face filled with concern. "What's wrong?"

Javier walked past him with Roman a few strides behind. He took Simon's arm and pulled him away from the door.

"This is Elder Roman. You met him once before. Now listen and don't speak." Javier waited for his Elder to close the door and both men watched as he threw the deadbolt.

"Javier—" Simon started, but Roman held up his hand.

"Javie, we need food. Fill your satchel with whatever you can find and I'll fill in your Cow."

"*Hah-vie?*" Simon wrapped his mouth around Javier's nickname. "What's going on? Doesn't this guy know we're friends?"

Javier ignored the boy's questions and tore into the kitchen to grab whatever edibles might keep a week and could be stuffed into his backpack. When the bag was filled to capacity, the food plus his two books, he zipped it and returned to the doorway. With a small bag over his shoulder, Simon looked ready to step out the door.

"We will take young Simon's truck." Roman led the way to Simon's silver extended-cab pickup. The Camaro would have been tight and Javier nodded with approval. Roman went to the passenger-side front and after only a moments' hesitation, Simon dropped his keys into Javier's open hand and climbed behind the wheel.

"Dig out that Rider novel," Roman said to Simon and motioned to Javier's pack. Simon rummaged around until it popped free and handed it over quickly, as if unsure of Javier's companion. Roman gave the boy an exaggerated smile and then held the back of the paperback up to Javier. "Montgomery, Alabama. Head west."

Javier nodded and started up the truck. From Athens, Georgia, to Montgomery, Alabama, they would be there before midnight. Roman looked out his window, Javier stared hard out the windshield, and Simon looked alternately to the backs of their heads, probably wondering what had he gotten himself into. Javier only hoped whatever lay ahead would leave them all alive.

13

More Answers at Michael's House

Despite everything, at seven o'clock, Beth bounded down the stairs humming a tune, hoping God would give her the courage to face the night ahead. She reached the bottom of the stairs and peeked around the living room searching for her new bodyguard. The laundry room door was closed.

"Michael? Wakey, wakey." Calling through the door and then as she entered the kitchen in the next room, Beth allowed her voice to maintain the sing-song quality she had coming down the stairs. She was dressed for the authors' party in a soft black pantsuit and a pair of comfortable loafers. The house remained quiet and as she drew a glass of water from the refrigerator door, she called again.

"I have to go to a party at eight so anyone interested in protecting me from night crawlers might need to be waking up soon…" Had she told Michael about the party? She couldn't recall. Should she cancel? Beth stepped out of the kitchen and approached the small room's door, tapping lightly. "Are you awake?" Her voice lower now, Beth wondered if she should open the door. She put her hand on the knob. "Mike?" Still no response.

Beth turned the knob slowly; the room was empty. She whirled around and her eyes landed on the front door.

"Did you go outside?" Speaking to herself, Beth strode over, unbolted the deadbolt, and swung it wide. The sun had gone down and Beth stepped onto her stoop and looked around the complex parking lot. In the bright sodium streetlamps, he was nowhere to be seen. Bewildered, Beth shrugged and reentered the house, pulling the door behind her. A movement out of the corner of her eye grabbed her attention and she focused toward the back window over the dinette table. The outline of a huge man filled the glass, hands on hips, head to the side. It was probably Michael, but suddenly cautious, she stared at the shape as it turned to meet her eyes. Beth sighed with relief, placed her hand over her heart, and then waved, grinning. Michael must have taken his call outside either to avoid disturbing her or to keep his conversation private. Either way, he was heading in through the back door as she waited. Beth crossed the room and met him at the kitchen threshold.

†

"I made a few calls to some guys who owe me favors," Michael said in lieu of a greeting, wiping his feet on the rug. He glanced up to continue his remarks when he noticed Beth's dressy attire. Her suit fit perfectly and her thick hair was piled high off her neck effecting an elegant, timeless look. Michael nodded with appreciation. "You look nice," he managed and she grinned.

"You like?" Beth swirled around, posing, and then resumed a more serious tone. "So, what did they say? Those guys you called?"

Michael arranged his thoughts, still distracted by his attraction to the Rabbit. He searched for Jack's mark on her and thankfully only detected her citrus shampoo. Finally, he clapped his hands together.

"Yes. My favors." Michael maneuvered past Beth in the narrow doorway. "I called a friend in Atlanta who was able to locate Jack. It wasn't easy. He likes to remain mysterious and inexplicable." Michael moved his hands around as if casting spells as he spoke and Beth smiled.

"Why? Are you going to see him?"

Michael shook his head. "Anyway, there's no need. He's heard about my apparent rebellion and is making plans to come see me." Michael began replacing the couch cushions that he had borrowed for sleep and Beth helped him with the pillow.

"That doesn't sound good. What do we do? Will he know to come here? How long do we have?"

She had asked her barrage of queries in a calm tone and again, Michael found her composure impressive. "I'm still gathering intel," he answered and gestured to her outfit. "Where are we going?"

Beth grinned and her cheeks tinted pink. "You said you will stay with me during the night, and tonight I'm supposed to go to a gathering at my publisher's loft." She looked at her watch when he nodded. "I'm due there at eight. I don't have to stay long, but I *do* have to make an appearance if you think it's safe. So..." Beth motioned to her watch while keeping her guest's eye. "What do you think?"

"Let's do it," Michael stood. "Jack's not here and I can best any of my brethren we might run into." He tucked his uniform shirt into his pants. "Where is the party?"

"Downtown," Beth said gathering a small handbag.

"Good. My place is on the way. I'll get cleaned up and we'll make it by eight."

"Great." Beth followed him to the door and turned when he hadn't yet moved.

Michael chuckled and shook his head, an odd sensation tugging his chest. "You must hear it all the time, but you're very pretty. I'm a bit of a caveman, so I'm sorry if I'm staring." He laughed again and passed her to open the door.

Beth blushed. "I honestly don't ever hear that," she said looking aside. "Thank you, though."

Michael led her to the car and let her in. Once settled behind the wheel, he said, "I read all of *The Judging* and it didn't offend me in the least. Maybe it's not the book that triggered him."

"If it matters, the book signing was for my second novel, *Damascus Road*. It's been on the shelf four months."

"I'll read that one next if I have time. For now, let's get going." Michael listened as Beth filled the drive with polite conversation but inside, he pondered all that he wouldn't say, and how odd the woman made him feel.

†

Beth followed Mike up his front porch steps. He put his key in the lock and turned to catch her eye.

"Try not to laugh when you get inside. I don't spend much time here so it is sparse in there." That said, Michael opened the door and switched on the light.

Beth didn't laugh, but grinned at him, eyebrows up. He wasn't joking about having little furniture. She took a few steps and peered down the hallway to her immediate right.

"Make yourself at home. The kitchen..." He pointed in the general direction in front of her. "The guest room and extra bath." He pointed loosely to the hallway to her right and then disappeared down the left.

Beth stepped to the hall threshold and stopped. Her guardian's house was a newer brick home with polished wooden floors and neutral-painted walls. He had no rugs or wall hangings and every window was completely shuttered by thick, velvety curtains.

Taking a step into the hall, Beth peeked into the guest bedroom. No furniture in sight, aside from a computer desk and matching chair. A dark computer screen topped the surface and the power strip was off. Out of morbid curiosity, Beth peered into the guest bath where there was no shower curtain and no towels. She returned to the great room at the front and chuckled softly at the brown two-seater loveseat and a gigantic four-foot-square pillow cushion on the floor. She wandered into the kitchen and found no dining room table, but one barstool tucked neatly beneath the counter/bar inside. The glass-doored cupboards sat empty and one plate and fork lay on the counter near the sink.

Beth marveled. Her new friend had no use of furniture. Beth's mind went unwillingly to one of her novel characters. She had placed her evil vampire character in a sparsely-furnished apartment where he mercilessly tortured the hapless protagonist.

And what about Rakha's place? Beth pulled the stool out and sat down, pondering. Her vampire character, Rakha, lived in such a place. But that novel would not publish until late December. How would Jack Dawn know about a book that wasn't yet available?

"Rakha..." Beth said the word aloud, her wheels turning. The name of her Book Three character sounded a lot like the name of Michael's race—the *Rakum*. Was there a connection? She named her evil character after a Hebrew word meaning 'vain thing'. Did the Rakum have ancient Hebrew roots? Before she could ponder further, Michael waltzed in, showered and changed into crisp blue jeans and a red button-up shirt. He was a looker and heat rushed to her face at the sight of him.

"What do you think? I keep it simple, eh?" Michael stepped over to the refrigerator and rummaged around. "I bought this house five years ago and you're the first human guest I've had. Congratulations."

Beth laughed and looked around once more from her perch on the stool. "I like it. Very Spartan. Very clean."

"I don't do well in filth," Michael replied.

"I was wondering, what does *Rakum* mean?" His eyebrows lifted and she asked another way. "Does the word have a meaning to you other than the name of your people?"

"I don't think it means anything. Why?"

"It sounds like a word in the Bible. *Rakhah*, a curse word."

"Hah," he laughed. "A curse word. Thanks," he teased. She offered a tight grin and he looked at her sideways. "You're serious? I think it's a coincidence, that's all."

Beth sighed. "I guess so."

"Keep at it. You'll think of something." Michael grabbed an apple out of the crisper. "Are you hungry? Can I get you something to eat or drink?"

"No, thanks. If you want, we can go out for dinner afterward. I'm looking forward to learning more about this mess I'm in."

"Sounds good. I am *starving.*" Michael bit into the apple, squirting juice. He laughed and turned away to wipe his chin.

Beth watched Michael's wide back and when he faced her again, his gaze caused her to smile anew. She slid off the stool and held out her hand. "Come and sit in the living room with me. I think I thought of something useful."

Michael wiped his hands on his jeans and allowed her to pull him into the next room.

†

Michael sat beside Beth on the small sofa and concentrated on detecting the Rabbit mark. Somehow, he had become desensitized and that had never happened before. He let the notion slide as he gave Beth his full attention.

"Okay, let's hear it."

Beth nodded. "Besides the fact that the word *rakhah* sounds like Rakum to me, I created an evil vampire character named Rakha. Could that have made Jack Dawn angry?"

Michael shrugged and waited for more.

Beth huffed softly. "Think about it a moment. You don't think the word Rakum sounds like *Rakim*? That could be a Hebrew plural form of the name of your people."

"I'm fluent in Hebrew, but I don't hear it that way," Michael said honestly.

"Okay, drop that for now," Beth sighed. "Your house, the inside, looks a lot like my character, Rakha's. He lives in a cottage by himself with no furniture. He sleeps on the floor and he can't go into the sunlight. Do you think that means anything?"

"I sleep on the floor," Michael said with a small grin.

Beth blushed and shook her head. "That notwithstanding, do you think that would make your guy mad?"

"No." Michael left his answer short. Her novel was fiction and a Rakum Elder would never be offended at an unreality.

Beth sighed wistfully. "This is a mystery, isn't it? Why does this Dawn guy want me dead." Making a statement instead of a question, Beth leaned into the couch cushion and closed her eyes to think.

Michael watched her eyes move beneath closed lids and wondered what it would be like to wake up next to her every evening. Rakum did not marry in the mortal sense, but they were permitted to take a mate. Only the Fathers were fertile, so birth control among the Brethren was unnecessary. Beth wore little make-up and glowed with health. She wore no flashy jewelry, only a simple watch and a thin silver chain about her neck that sported an odd combination of unfamiliar figures. He was staring at her necklace when he realized that her eyes were open and she was watching him watch her.

She smiled demurely and sat up. "What about female Rakum? Are they pretty much the same?"

Michael shook his head. "Females cannot carry the Rakum gene."

"Then how...?"

"When our Fathers mate with a mortal woman and she conceives a male child, he will be Rakum. But if she has a girl, she is always mortal."

"Oh. I don't want to know anything else about that." Beth put her hand to her stomach.

Michael inclined his head. "The Breeders lives are a little stressful."

Beth grimaced and forced a convincing smile. "Let's head downtown. Bob and Carol have a loft on Perry Street."

"29 Perry Street?"

Beth nodded. "You've been there?"

"A friend of mine lives there, on the third floor."

"Oh, what kind of friend?" she asked, her head tilted to the side.

Michael chuckled and stood, unwilling to reveal the nature of his relationship to the man on Perry Street. Instead, he played it off. "He's not my brother, if that's what you mean. I'm the only of my brethren who keep residence in Montgomery. This guy on Perry Street is an artist. I'm his... *muse*. Maybe I'll stop in and check on him while we're there."

Michael walked Beth to the door. He was actually quite fond of Jeremy, the brooding starving artist he had set up downtown. The kid was bright and interesting, and head over heels in awe of Michael. Also, he was not starving. Since Michael began to visit him, Jeremy's work had become quite valuable. Michael knew of at least seven galleries around the country that badgered him constantly for new work and three of those were in New York City. Still, it was three weeks until his scheduled visit. Michael tried to convince himself that seeing Jeremy too soon was a bad idea. He would most assuredly want him to come in, have some brandy, look over the new work he'd completed since last time...

And I know he's going to want me to milk him...

With that internal admission, Michael's stomach grumbled and he glanced to Beth. If she noticed, she didn't show it. She slipped into the passenger side of his coupe and Michael fell in beside her feeling more or less normal. He could almost forget that he had a price on his head. Almost, but not quite.

14

Simon and the Nephilim

In their Montgomery hotel room, Simon slept as late as possible in the enormous king size bed. Roman and Javier slept the day away in the spacious bathroom, the door locked against the sunlight that trickled in beneath the thick curtains. Out of respect, Simon kept them drawn, but he so wanted to fling them wide and face the day. Hanging with Javier had been fun in the past, but running and hiding was the pits.

Simon watched TV, daydreamed, and explored the huge facility until the sun neared the western horizon at five forty-five. He was proud of himself for the way he was handling the current inconvenience. He was two hundred miles from home in the company of two amazing beings who unintentionally led him into terrible trouble. Javier's domineering Elder warned him of the danger he was in, but it was hard to fathom. All he did was read a book and then share it with the one person who he thought might appreciate it. So now he was on the run for his life?

A sound from the bathroom reached his ears, like the shuffle of feet on tile. Maybe they were rousing. It was weird—sleeping in there together with only pillows for comfort. Of course, he long realized Javier's people were unusual; that's what attracted him from the beginning. Simon thought at first he was an angel, which wasn't too much of a stretch since when they met, Javier healed his broken bones with his touch. But when his friend explained over time who and what he was, Simon thought that was even cooler than being an angel. For who knows what an angel is anyway? It certainly wasn't a flying baby or a gorgeous winged woman in flowing robes. No. Even the Bible wasn't too clear on it.

Simon remembered the Hebrew word for angel was the same as

messenger. That could be anything. Because the messengers brought tidings from God, they were considered supernatural, winged and fairy-like. But what if they were like Javier? Traipsing through time, part man part something else, outliving the mortals around them by centuries, helping now and then and destroying now and then. It was supposedly God's prerogative to love who He would love and hate who He would hate.

Simon heard a clunk and glanced at the bathroom door. Would they be sore from sleeping on ceramic tile? Did Rakum get sore? Simon humphed and shook his head. What did he know about angels' sleeping habits? Or Rakum's?

Simon rose and grabbed the Tanakh off the nightstand where they'd left it. He would have to rethink his pathetically limited theology if he was truly being pursued by a posse of angry Rakum. If they were offended that their brothers got religion, maybe Javier wasn't a messenger of God after all. Maybe Javier was just another creature swimming through life, waiting to ultimately meet the same Judge as the rest of them.

And what if—

Another noise in the bathroom, then the sound of the shower.

Simon snickered, shook his head with wonder, and looked back at the book in his hand. *Half man, half something else.* The idea had merit. What if Javier and his people were descended from angels?

As a kid, only the supernatural elements of the Bible interested him and he definitely recalled the tale of the Sons of God. Simon flipped a few pages to Genesis 6 and read aloud to himself.

"The Nephilim were in the earth in those days, and also after that, when the sons of G-d came in unto the daughters of men, and they bore children to them; the same were the mighty men that were of old, the men of renown…"

The Sons of God had babies with mortal women. Simon looked at the bathroom door; sounded pretty close. The commentary running along the bottom said that the Hebrew word *Nephilim* may mean "causing others to fall or stumble." But that didn't fit Javier. If the Rakum were descended from angels, that was one thing. But Javier never did anything to cause him to fall. *Simon* hadn't fallen. He was still a great guy. He was the coolest guy he knew.

Simon smiled.

Maybe you're not good just because you think you are.

Simon's brow furrowed and the corners of his mouth turned down. That thought didn't sound like one of his. He read a little further down the page and stopped when another errant, un-Simon-like thought popped into his head.

Maybe you are supposed to be holy because God is holy.

Simon closed the Book with a thud and placed it down heavily on the bed stand. The Bible was speaking to him, nudging him. He remembered now why he had tucked it out of sight all those years ago. The thing was alive and had a mind of its own. In his youth, and even in his teens, when he got confused and sought answers in the Book, he was always brought around to the same understanding: *Simon is bad and he needs to submit his life to God.*

Every time, *every single time,* he opened the Tanakh and read from it, God called to him through it. Simon scowled and stared at its puckered leather cover. So what about Javier and Roman? They read the Rider woman's novel. It definitely was *not* the Bible.

But it has lots of Bible verses in it...

"Oh, my god!" Simon said aloud and slapped his forehead. If God reached for people from his Word, then maybe even a small part of it could grab you, too.

Simon rolled forward to the nightstand and grabbed the Rider novel. Flipping hastily through the book, he noted the Bible verses stuck at the beginning of each chapter.

"Dang. That's sneaky," he whispered.

"What's sneaky?"

Simon startled with his hand to his chest. Javier was standing inches away towel-drying his hair and Simon hadn't heard him leave the bathroom. He was redressed in the same clothing, wrinkled Dockers and a pale blue Polo, but had obviously showered.

"How did you get out of there so quiet? Can you walk through walls?" Simon's voice was higher than he liked and he made an attempt to man-up as his heart rate returned to normal.

Javier laughed. "No, of course not. But I'm very quiet, remember?" Javier finished with the towel and tossed it to the far corner. His hair stuck out everywhere and he did not pat it down. "What're you doing? You said 'dang that's sneaky.'"

"This book—the author put Bible verses in it. I think I know what happened to your people." Simon held it out as if it were evidence in a criminal case. Javier's eyebrows went up. "It's the same thing that happens to regular people."

"What's that?"

"God's word is alive." Simon shrugged matter-of-factly, unsure if

62

he would come across as stupid or brilliant. Javier rolled his hands to get him to continue and he cleared his throat. "This novel is packed with Bible verses—and when we read it, God is able to speak to us. It's weird, but it's the truth. I swear."

Javier looked thoughtful and then re-entered the bathroom. Simon heard the two Rakum sharing words out of his hearing and then Javier returned with a different book in his hand.

"I read the back part of this while we were waiting for sundown. Have you read it?" He held it out for Simon to see. It was a Gideon Bible. A *Christian* Bible.

"That's the one the Jesus-freaks read." At the advice of every Jew he knew, Simon avoided the Gentile Bible. Too many Jews fell away after reading it.

Simon's stomach knotted uncomfortably. What if they were not falling away—*but falling in?* What if they were falling into the arms of God? He was busy preaching to Javier that God's Word could change a man and give him ideas, and the Christian Bible had been swaying Jews from the Old Way for two millennia.

"This book explains a lot." Javier set the Gideon Bible down and straightened his damp hair with his fingers. "I know now where Tony Agricola's faith lies."

Simon narrowed his eyes. Agricola was the novel's preacher character; the most irritating and intriguing character of the bunch, and his faith was the reason why.

"Roman and I are going to ask Jesus to help us."

Simon's skin prickled at Javier's proclamation. Every fiber of his being resisted the idea of speaking to Jesus, and the reason why blared in his mind like a clarion. He didn't want to because He might be real. Because He might actually *be God.* Just as the Gentiles said He was.

Simon cursed under his breath. He reached for the Gideon Bible and opened it to the New Testament. It fell open to the Gospel of John and he read the first words under his breath.

"In the beginning…"

Great. It began exactly like *Beresheet*—Genesis 1:1—in the Hebrew Bible. Simon rolled his eyes and kept reading.

"…and the Word was with God, and the Word was God. The same was in the beginning with God. All things were made by him; and without him was not any thing made that was made."

The Christian Bible was not saying anything new so far as he could tell. God was always there in the beginning. God was always the

Creator. Why did his people hate to read the words of those who followed Jesus of Nazareth?

Simon sat heavily onto the elevated king-size bed and cursed again. Was he falling in? Was God waiting to catch him on the other side? And what if he didn't want to go? What if he liked his life the way it was? And more importantly…what if God was mad at him?

Simon shook his head. The Jesus fellow promised *shalom*. Simon didn't know much about true peace. He read a little more and hoped God would make it plain.

15

Young Cow, Good Cow

Michael and Beth stepped into the old-fashioned elevator on the ground floor of the refurbished building. The metal grating that served for a gate pulled closed soundlessly and they headed up to the fourth floor party.

"These lofts were opened to the public five years ago," Beth remarked. "Bob and Carol use their loft for parties and to put up celebrity authors when needed. What about your friend? How long has he lived here?"

Michael smiled. "I set my friend up here when they opened. He needed a place to stay and I know the developer." Michael fell silent, lost in his own thoughts. An Elder named Tomás owned the property and resided in Florida. Michael kept an eye on the place and was happy to rent the space for his favorite Cow until he got on his feet.

"I've been here at least a dozen times. I'm amazed I never ran into you when you were here visiting your friend," Beth said, interrupting his train of thought and Michael nodded absently. The elevator stopped on the top floor and Michael pulled open the gate.

"What a noise!" Beth exclaimed as they exited the elevator. It opened to a small twelve-by-twelve foyer, but the door to the residence sat ajar. The noise from the party inside spilled out with substance and the air was heavy with cigarette smoke.

Beth covered her nose. "In and out, fifteen minutes tops."

Michael grinned and then walked directly behind her as they wove their way through the initial cluster of people near the door. He glanced around, quietly taking in the occupants and finding himself 100% certain that he was the only of his kind in attendance.

"Let's find Bob and Carol," she shouted over the din and Michael motioned that he would follow.

They picked their way across the living room and into a wide hallway with tapestry-covered benches along both walls. Party-goers filled both of the long seats and Beth waved at a bony older woman on their right with a martini in one hand and a cigarette in the other.

"There's Carol. Let me introduce you."

Michael allowed himself to be tugged through the throng, but heard his name being called as they reached the bench.

"Michael! Michael! Michael Stone! Over here!"

Michael turned and far across the room near the door to the great room stood Jeremy, gesticulating wildly. Michael shot him a finger gun and Jeremy stopped calling out and stood still.

"Good," Michael mumbled and turned his attention to Beth who was busy introducing him to her publisher.

"Carol! I want you to meet my friend Michael. Michael Stone, meet Carol Stein." Beth stood aside so the two could shake. Carol came to her feet and gawked, her eyes reddened by too much vodka.

"O my *gawd!* He's *adorable!* Where did you find him? Hunks R Us? Gawd!" Carol leaned into Michael drunkenly and squeezed him in a half-hug with her free arm, her hand falling low on his back. "Nice to meet you, *dahling!"*

Michael answered appropriately and caught Beth's eye. She understood the meaning behind his look and patted Carol's hand before moving them off. Then she took Michael's arm and stepped through the couples toward the way they had come in.

"You okay?" she asked when he looked over her head and nodded to Jeremy.

"My third floor friend is over there." Michael hooked his thumb toward the door and Beth followed his line of sight. Slight and mousy with watered-down Hispanic features, Jeremy wrung his hands, his eyes riveted to Michael's face. Michael sent him a wink and he visibly shuddered. Noticing, Beth made a short laugh.

"He looks happy," she said watching Jeremy bobble in his impatience.

Michael agreed, ready to move away and see what Jeremy had to offer. The promise of an impromptu meal had cemented in his mind and he wouldn't go without. He said to Beth, "I checked the room, it's safe. What do you think about me heading over to his place for a minute?"

Beth waved her fingers to the artist who frowned and looked away. "Sure. That's fine with me. I'm making one round and then I'll pop down there and knock on his door. Fifteen minutes, tops."

"'Kay," Michael said and just as he initiated his turn, Beth tip-toed up and pecked his cheek. Without a pause, he continued and showed her his back. Maybe she blushed, maybe he read a fraction of embarrassment on her part to be so forward, but Michael wouldn't ponder any of it. Clearing his mind of possible female motivations, he carefully moved through the crowd until he met up with Jeremy. The youngster leapt at his approach and grasped his arm.

"Michael, Michael, Michael!" Jeremy said once in the hall, still holding Michael's elbow. "*I can't believe it!*" he whispered and jumped up and down in the elevator. "What are you doing here? How wonderful! I've been trying to reach you. Why haven't you answered my calls? My emails? Where have you been?"

"Slow down, Jay-Jay," Michael said entering big-brother mode; sometimes it calmed him. "Breathe in, breathe out. In... Out..."

"Okay, okay, okay, okay," he said, nodding his head.

Jeremy always spoke rapidly and in a staccato accent. He had Latino roots, but never discussed his family. Michael had long assumed he was an orphan. Why else would he have put his trust in a stranger who periodically drank his blood?

"Come see my new babies. They're shipping off tomorrow. Do you see now why I needed you to call me back? You almost missed them. You have to see them off. *You* made all of it possible and the shippers are taking them to their new home in L.A. *tomorrow!*"

Jeremy violently yanked open the gate when the elevator stopped at his foyer. He pulled Michael to his front door and unlocked it. Once inside, Jeremy flipped on the overhead and warm golden light filled the room.

"Nice," Michael remarked, realizing his Cow changed the bulbs to suit Rakum eyes.

"I'd do anything for you. I'm always wondering how to make your life better. I never stop thinking of ways to make you happy."

Jeremy motioned ahead of him where his entryway had become a spontaneous art gallery. Michael stepped around the space and studied the dozen twenty-by-thirty canvasses encircling him. He'd never had an eye for art and Jeremy's newest endeavors confounded him more than ever. Nevertheless, he smiled and pointed to the nearest one.

"This is your favorite, isn't it?"

Jeremy nodded his head wildly and touched the wooden frame with tender affection. "How did you guess? How do you always guess?"

Michael shrugged and pretended to study the others a bit longer. He knew that it made Jeremy happy to think his art meant something to his mysterious benefactor so Michael feigned interest. The abstract lines and shapes made no sense to him, but he easily fooled the young artist with flattering comments.

"This is all I have. There it is. Poured out. It all poured out after your last visit. Look." Jeremy gestured to the one to Michael's right. "That was the last one. I am all out. You have to help me again. I can't do it without you…"

"Jay-Jay, it's too soon. I'm not due here for three more weeks." Michael did not try to be convincing. "It's not smart to jump the calendar."

"You have to!" Jeremy insisted, his pitch rising. "Michael!"

"Shhh. Show me your arm." Michael received Jeremy's right arm and examined the wound. The tiny laceration was nearly healed, but Michael shook his head. "I can still see it, Jay…"

"But I can't paint without you! I'll die!"

Michael shrugged. "I can't help that."

"But the gallery consigned a new series for *Paris,* Michael. *Paris.* I can't even think about Paris with no vision. I have no vision! I'm going to lose everything! You are *the art* in my artwork. I can't do it alone. I won't!"

Jeremy's complaints were coming faster and faster and fat tears leaked from the corners of his eyes. Michael softened his gaze and nodded his head.

"Jay-Jay, don't get yourself so worked up." Michael sighed dramatically. "This will count as your regular visit, you know. I'm not coming for another eight weeks, understand?"

"Oh! Oh! Oh! I knew you would. I knew it! Because we're best friends! Oh!"

Michael followed an animated Jeremy to the next room and mumbled for the young man's benefit, "Damn it, Jay. Now, my schedule is all screwed up. The things I do for you, I don't do for anyone else…"

"I know, I know, I know. I'm your favorite. I know. Here, here, here…" Jeremy led Michael into the room. "I made this for you. I found the headpiece in Boston and one of my pals at the gallery made it into a necklace. Look, look, look."

Michael received the item from Jeremy's shaking hand and

studied it closely. The eighteen-inch leather thong had a metal puncturing tool affixed to the center. It resembled the incisor of a lion, but it was polished steel and sharpened to a wicked point. Jeremy gamely took the trinket back and whisked off his windbreaker.

"Look how easy..." Jeremy sat on the edge of his messy bed and held his muscular bare arm open to Michael. Then, quick as a flash, Jeremy stabbed his inner elbow with the tooth and withdrew it. With a grin, Michael yanked the wound to his lips.

"You can wear it around your neck," the youngster said, his voice finally growing softer. "Or on your key ring... There are a thousand places you could keep it handy..."

Jeremy's phrasing slowed significantly and he rambled as the seconds stretched into minutes.

"And you'll think of me...every time you use it... because I'm your favorite... I know it... because we're *amigos*... friends... best friends."

Michael closed his eyes. The kid was a keeper.[3]

---

[3] Read the delicious account of how Michael met the excitable Jeremy at the end of this book, BONUS: *Loose Rabbits*, #3, p.252

16

Inspired by Demons

The unmistakable sound of the elevator reached Michael's ears and he sat up, tightly covering Jeremy's puncture wound with his finger. Swallowing, he opened the drawer nearest him in the nightstand and pulled out a cotton ball that he knew from experience would be there.

"Hold this, buddy." Michael pressed the cotton into Jeremy's arm, his mind buzzing. He made an effort to resist a drunken grin and rose to his feet.

"Wait, wait, wait." Slower, but with the same sincerity, Jeremy reached for Michael's arm. "I see the new ones. I see them."

Michael stood by the door as his dearest Cow received the visions that he treasured more than life. "What do you see, Jay-Jay?"

"Yellow and white," Jeremy mumbled, smiling, but his brow furrowed just the same. "Not even yellow ochre, but I see bright yellow and Chinese white. Odd…"

"Okay, then," Michael said and shook his head. The significance of the artist's piqued interest after a milking had never been Michael's concern. "I gotta get the door. Stay here and rest up." Michael chuckled and left the bedroom.

As he reached the front, Beth knocked twice. Michael opened the door and this time, her smile struck him more than the Rabbit mark. He backed to one side and she stepped in at the invitation.

"Let me show you something," he remarked and led her to the circle of canvasses. "This is Jeremy's artwork. What do you make of it? I usually just *pretend* to look at them, but tonight…" Michael said, his voice low in deference to the artist in the next room, "I wonder what you see."

"Sure…" Beth squinted in the low light and looked to the overhead fixture. "Is this all the light we have?"

70

"I'm afraid so," Michael said and watched her face as she stepped to the closest canvas.

"Ugh," Beth grimaced.

"What?" Michael asked, truly interested.

"Well… it's grotesque. Not my taste, for sure." As she glanced around, she repeated her first response absently. "Ugh."

"You don't like them, either?" he whispered. Michael pointed to the one on his left. "This is his favorite. What do you think?" Beth shivered and Michael furrowed his brow. "What?"

"You don't want to know what I see."

Beth wasn't kidding and Michael tried to catch her eye. When he did, she was visibly upset. "They're that bad?"

"Michael…" Beth lowered her voice to a whisper. "This man is severely *disturbed*. This art is *psychotic*. But what disturbs me the most is that he has fixated all of his talent on *you.*"

"What do you mean?" Michael turned to look again at the artwork and studied them as they spoke. "They're just blobs. Abstracts. What are *you* seeing?"

"I know I haven't had a chance to explain myself to you yet, but suffice it to say I can see beyond the obvious. I can see the intention…the spirit and soul. These are all paintings of you. Look." Beth gestured to Jeremy's favorite. "This is you hanging on a cross, crucified."

"What? No, it's not…" Michael tilted his head, but saw only swaths of black and red.

"This is your head and your shoulder. Look how the arm is stretched out and fastened to this dark area. It's a detail of a man on a cross and it's not Jesus."

Michael concentrated and slowly, her perspective began to make itself known. What he had only perceived as formless blobs of color began to take shape. Although the man's head and right shoulder were all that fit on the canvas, he could now see that it was a loose rendition of a crucifixion.

"You think that's me?"

"I know it is. Look at this one." Beth stepped back to point to the one on her left. "Surely you see this. See the hunched over, blackened figure…the red and purple landscape splattered with blood—this is the likeness of a Rakum drinking someone's blood." Beth shook her head in unabashed disgust. "This one has your profile."

71

Michael watched as the painting Beth referred to moved and shifted in his perception until he could also discern shoulders, a head, then teeth and claws. "Why didn't I see this before? This is crazy. Are you doing this? Making me see this for the first time?"

"No, but maybe you're *looking* for the first time."

"What about this one?" Michael pointed to a dark red and purple monstrosity to Beth's right. The black, amorphous shape was more erect in this scene, but beyond that, he saw nothing.

"Look at this area. This is the head and here's the mouth. It is gaping open and look." Beth placed her finger close enough to touch the oil painted surface. "What is that?"

"Well…" Michael paused and then laughed nervously. Once she pointed out the head of the creature on the canvas, the details fell into place as before. Hanging from the roof of the gaping maw were long, sharp teeth erupting, curving cruelly back toward the tongue like those of a poisonous snake. Slinging in all directions from the horrific mouth were dozens of painted strings representing highly oxygenated blood. Michael was too embarrassed to say what he saw so he remained silent.

"Exactly," Beth replied to his non-response. She turned from the gallery with an audible sigh. "Sadly, these are the most hideous paintings I have ever seen. Like something from the depths of—"

"They bring ten thousand dollars a pop, Missy!"

Jeremy entered the room and Michael watched as Beth scrutinized him. He scowled at them both; she'd insulted his work and Michael had invited her in.

"Looks like your friend has no taste for art. Doesn't she know that this stuff is gold?" The artist sneered and walked toward them, clutching his right arm to his chest.

He was probably light-headed and Michael wondered if Beth would notice. Instead of replying to the kid, Michael looked back to the remaining works and tried to see what else he might find. Concentrating, he readily saw the form Beth described, over and over, hovering, menacing, attacking and otherwise brutalizing any number of faceless, helpless victims on every reddened, tortured canvas. He faced Jeremy and placed his hand heavily upon his shoulder.

"That's not supposed to be *me*, is it?" Michael physically pulled the kid closer to the third canvas and put his finger to the painted ghoul's face. "I don't have teeth like that. I'm not a monster, am I? This isn't me, right?"

Jeremy stole a glance at Beth then faced Michael once again. He made a small noise in his throat and shook his head.

"Jeremy, do these images come to you in visions?" Beth asked flatly. "If so, they're coming from demons."

Jeremy ignored her and trained his eyes on Michael.

"Michael, your friend needs to leave. Now!" He pointed for the door with a jerk and his blood-stained cotton ball fell to the floor. By the hitch in Beth's breathing, Michael knew he was busted.

"Yes… I'd better go."

Speaking softly, Beth would not meet his eye and Michael read the disdain on her face. Jeremy stooped down and tucked the cotton back into his elbow, then looked to Beth with wet and angry eyes.

"What do you know anyway? I get these visions from *him*. He visits and paintings are *born in my soul*. There's nothing wrong with that!"

Jeremy's voice took on a desperate quality that Michael recognized as his normal tone, but Beth would think he was becoming hysterical.

"They're *killing* your soul, Jeremy. You know they are," she responded from the door, and Michael thought she hadn't meant to sound unkind.

"You don't know me! You don't know what I can do! Michael, she's trying to hurt me! She wants to ruin me and make me poor again. She wants me to go live in a box on the street. Michael, you have to make her leave! Leave! Leave! Leave!"

"Shhh…" Michael inclined his head to Beth to encourage her to proceed out. Then he lowered his voice to Jeremy. "You never lived in a box, kid. You're exaggerating. Aren't you? A little?"

Jeremy shook his head like a spoiled child and then grabbed Michael tightly about the waist. "You can't leave me. I need you. I'll kill myself if you wait two months to come back. I will, I will, I will." Jeremy held on, his words muffled into Michael's chest.

"Oh, hush, you big baby." Michael held his arms out. "You couldn't kill a fly. Look, you have your new vision, right? With new colors, too." Jeremy nodded hesitantly. "It'll take weeks to complete the new set. You'll be fine."

"No, no, no." Jeremy shook his head, wiping tears and sweat on Michael's clean red shirt. "I have another deadline. Not only Paris, but Hamburg. They just called me yesterday. It's too much. Too much. Too…"

"I'll call one of my brothers." Running out of patience, Michael cut him off and pushed him away. "How would that be? You could see me one month, and him the next." Michael had been contemplating this plan for weeks because of Jeremy's special needs. It was uncommon for Rakum to share Cows, but sometimes the circumstances warranted such measures. Loyalty out the window, Jeremy didn't protest. To the contrary, his eyes grew wide and a faint smile came to his pale lips.

"Your brother?"

"You might remember him. He was with me the day you moved in. His name is Jesse. You liked him, didn't you?" Michael nodded his head in time with Jeremy. "I could call him for you. I'll call him next week."

"Oh, no, no, no. You gotta call him right now or I can't sleep. I will worry myself sick. Please, Michael. Call him right now. Gotta be now."

Jeremy stole a paranoid glance toward the doorway where Beth stood dumbfounded, but Michael expertly drew his attention back.

"I'll call him." Michael pulled his cell from his pocket. "But if he doesn't pick up, you'll have to let me call him later. I have plans tonight and I'm already running late."

"That's cool. Yeah. Yeah. Yeah. That's cool."

As he waited for Michael's call to go through, Jeremy narrowed his eyes at Beth again and childishly stuck out his tongue. Michael waited three rings before he heard Jesse's voice on the other end.

"Bunny problems already?"

"I'm calling about Jeremy." Michael covered the mouthpiece with his hand for added privacy, *The Cow I keep on Perry Street. You helped him move in about five years ago.*

"Oh, yeah, cute kid. How's he doing?"

"Lonely. Could you put him on your schedule? Just say yes and give him a date. I'll fill you in the details later."

"Yummy," Jesse chuckled. "When?"

"About a month from now. No longer than that."

"Let's see…tell him I'll come on the fourth of next month. Will that work?"

"Yeah, okay. On an eight week rotation, okay?"

"Fine. What about your bunny friend? What've you found out?"

"Jack's coming to see me… and I guess her, too."

"Uh, oh. Good luck, pal. Been nice knowing you."

"Thanks a lot, brother."

Jesse laughed. "You're welcome."

Michael ended the call and gave Jeremy the thumbs up. "Jesse will be here on the fourth so write it down. I have to leave."

"Okay. Okay. Okay," Jeremy said and followed him to the door. "Come alone next time. *Alone.*"

Michael opened the door for Beth, irritated by Jeremy's rude remark, but she did not seem affected. She stepped to the elevator and waited.

"She's only worried about you, Jeremy."

"No. No. No. She wants to kill my muse. My vision. My art. My *babies.* I hope you dump her soon."

Michael clucked his tongue, but smiled at his diminutive friend. By the time he got the two of them to the ground floor, Beth was ready to speak.

"I don't feel very well. Please take me home."

Michael held his tongue. Her face was red and her eye hard. What did she have to be so angry about?

On the Run

Javier glanced at Simon. The kid was reading to himself from the Christian Bible. He then turned his attention to Roman whose eyes were trained on a door fifty yards away. They sat in the truck awaiting, a small man-made pond between them and the Rider woman's townhouse. It was his Elder's superior telepathy that led them directly to her front door. Roman skipped along the thoughts of men like a stone on a pond, and tonight his talents saved them time and effort. When they departed the hotel, Roman took over driving in order to follow his instincts on the fly. A miniscule movement in Roman's brow informed Javier he was using his telepathy even then. All Rakum were telepathic, but to what extent varied from man to man.

Roman tightened his grip on the steering wheel and looked hard at Javier. "Beth Rider has been marked by Jack Dawn."

Javier looked out the window. "I don't smell anything." He usually sensed Rabbits three counties away, but detected nothing on Beth Rider. Roman lowered his gaze. He hadn't noticed the Rabbit's scent either.

"What? What does that mean?" Simon asked from the back, setting the adopted Gideon Bible aside.

"It means she's now being pursued by our entire race," Javier offered in an exaggerated reply.

"There's a Rakum with her," Roman said to Javier, excluding Simon by lowering his volume. "Michael Stone—Jack's lieutenant. Do you know him?"

Javier considered the name and shook his head. Roman's gaze gradually softened as he received additional telepathic messages.

"Stone is keeping her to himself. He picked her up at the airport and has kept her to himself since then."

"Can you reach him?"

Roman considered the question and then shook his head. "No, Stone's telepathy is not as good as it should be." Roman's gaze admonished Javier in a sideways fashion since he never developed his as well as expected either. Javier had no response and Roman sent him a wink. "You have other talents, eh?"

Javier offered a small grin. "Yes, many."

Roman reached across the truck and clapped his shoulder. "Indeed. Don't worry about Stone. I've been in contact with Jesse Cherrie—also Dawn's pack. He answered my questions, but hesitantly. I got the impression that Stone is *protecting* the Rabbit, not chasing her. And if I'm right, Cherrie has a right to be consternated."

"Do you think he read the novel?" Javier asked, wishing the evening could get underway.

"I don't know." Roman looked back to the house. "Be patient. Also, we have company. Did you sense your brother nearby? Watching the house, as we are?"

Javier looked into the dark night. He was not as adept at sniffing out the brethren as some, but should have sensed at least a vestige. He apologized for his shortcomings with his eyes. "Friend or foe?"

Roman grinned. "You don't practice anything I taught you," he said with a wink. "I'll move you back in with me and start over if you're not careful."

Javier chuckled at Roman's levity. First Ritual ended for him more than a century ago and no Rakum would enjoy repeating any of the vicious trials.

"Okay, lazy bones. Be quiet, listen, and wait." Roman's instructions were final.

"Who is Jack Dawn? Is he the guy out to get us?" Simon had scooted fully forward between the two front seats during Javier's conversation with Roman.

Javier answered. "He's one of our Elders, like Roman."

Roman sneered. "Jack Dawn is old and crotchety," he said offering his opinion, his voice neutral. "He's been doing things his way for a thousand years. Not one a mortal would want to cross."

"Huh, okay," Simon mumbled, then asked brightly, "How many Elders do you have?"

Roman didn't answer so Javier turned in his seat to see the young man's face. Simon's bright eyes sought his. It had been days since Javier's last blood meal, and as if waking an elderly lion, his stomach growled. Roman gave him a reproving glance as Javier offered Simon an answer.

"There are one hundred Elders. Each Elder has one thousand Rakum under him. Those are broken down into lieutenants and captains." Javier stole a quick glance toward the Rider woman's front door and continued. "The rest of us answer to the Elders and the Elders answer to the Ten Fathers."

"What are the Ten Fathers like?"

Javier smiled wistfully, looked at Roman and then chuckled. "There's nothing to compare them to. They pass judgment when needed, they set policy and law."

"That's enough education," Roman sent telepathically and Javier nodded. Roman did not care for mortals and dealt with them as little as possible, but that information wouldn't give Simon any confidence.

"I heard you say she has a Rakum with her. Is he on our side?"

Javier looked at Roman's profile, but he didn't turn. Javier took the hint and shrugged to Simon. "It's time to be quiet and wait." Javier faced front and Simon scooted backward, lifting the Bible into his lap.

"The book of the generation of Jesus Christ," Simon read quietly to himself. *"...the son of David, the son of Abraham..."*

When his young friend choked and cleared his throat, Javier turned to check on him.

"Jesus was a Jew," Simon said to no one, his gaze far off and his mind far away.

With a wry grin, Javier relaxed back in his seat and quieted his mind. Patience didn't come easy.

On the Hunt

Night Charter Jets was a private corporation owned entirely by Rakum and run by humans clueless of the supernatural nature of their employers. The mortal pilots were briefed on special safety measures, but nothing else. The regulations regarding the use of NCJ were loose so any Rakum at any time could order up a free flight to their destination and get there before sunup. As an added precaution, every Night Charter had blacked-out windows in the cabin, in the event the pilot had to make an emergency landing during the day. Tonight, Jack loaded his crew plus Tomás into the waiting jet an hour after sunset, now taxiing down the runway headed for Montgomery.

Jack brought more muscle than he needed; aside from Beryl, Meryl, and Kite, he brought two pups that he'd rarely worked with since they graduated First Ritual under his tutelage fifty years ago. They were strong, mean and hungry—attributes he favored in any Rakum chosen to work with him. The jet seated ten and the five underlings sat in the rear section, mumbling to each other about the coming evening. Jack and Tomás sat in the first row where two luxurious leather captain's chairs kept them comfortable.

An odd tingle vibrated behind Jack's eyes and he turned from his position to catch Beryl's eye. The kid was thinking about Father Abroghia and the old wives' tale they'd discussed earlier. Tiny nonsensical bits filtered to him telepathically and he waited to see if there was more. Unfortunately, even after several seconds of concerted effort, he received nothing else.

Jack frowned at his limitations. His telepathic ability was average, but his real propensity was as a Seer. Jack called Beryl over with two fingers. The kid hopped up and covered the distance quickly. Since

Jack's Seer method was tactile, he held out his hand and Beryl obediently lifted his arm. Jack grasped his wrist and held it firmly, looking deep into the youth's bright, fawn-colored eyes. To the kid, he gave one short telepathic command. *"Show me."*

Jack waited until the first image hit before he rolled his eyes closed to concentrate on Beryl's memory of the event. As a Seer, Jack could see others' memories, and he practiced this often over the centuries; secrets were impossible to keep with a Seer for a Master. Slowly the image cleared behind his closed lids and he saw what Beryl had seen half a century ago.

The twins were in the last year of First Ritual and the class's guest-Father was Johann. This Father was an intriguing and aloof character who kept to himself at Assembly and Jack knew little about him. In this memory, which may have been embellished over the years by Beryl's imagination, Johann was gesticulating wildly as he shared with the group the legend of the Lost Rabbit. His manner was like that of a human Scout Leader telling ghost stories over a campfire, and his voice fluctuated dramatically with the telling. At the part of the story where the mortal-turned-Rabbit escapes his captors for the third time, Beryl flinched and the image disappeared. Jack opened his eyes.

"What happened?" he growled in a low voice. The others would hear him, but they would know by his tone that the conversation was intended to be private. Only Meryl in the back row followed their exchange and he wasn't at fault—he was as attached to his brother mentally as if by physical bonds.

Beryl gave a tiny shrug. "Master, my memory ends there. But—"

Jack cut him off and pointed to his temple. Of all the up-and-coming Rakum in his pack, Beryl and Meryl were the most telepathic.

"My memory ends there, Master, but there is something crazy about the last thing I saw."

"What?"

"When Father Johann spoke about the Lost Rabbit, he envisioned Father Abroghia."

"What is so strange about that? He probably heard the tale from Abroghia first."

"No, Master. No. In Johann's mind, Abroghia was the Rabbit. I think I saw something in his mind that no one was supposed to see."

Jack was silent a moment and he looked back at Meryl. The boy's bright eyes met his in agreement with his brother. But how could that be? Abroghia as a Rabbit? High Father Abroghia was ancient, older than anyone really knew, and he definitely predated the Lost Rabbit stories. It didn't make sense. Jack considered the possibility for a second longer, but then shook his head.

"There are a dozen explanations for what you think you saw..." Jack glanced at the twin so he'd know he was consciously being addressed. Even though Beryl was the one with the original memory, the boys' thoughts were indistinguishable. *"You were a kid and you had not fully developed your telepathy. Your memory could be faulty—who knows what condition your body was in at that point of the Ritual. Or maybe, Johann was looking for a sneaky, mind-reading Rakum to catch in the act so he could punish him. Either is more reasonable than taking this memory at face value."*

"I'm sure you're right. I was kept in seclusion for a week after that meeting." Beryl blinked and looked back at his twin; he abruptly remembered something else. *"Michael Stone was punished along with me. He was proctoring our group that season so he was present during Father Johann's foible. If we were being punished simultaneously, perhaps he saw the same thing. Is he telepathic?"*

Jack scowled. Stone was not dependably telepathic—his gift came and went with his whim. His lieutenant's strengths were heightened natural senses and physical might. And of course, he was slated for Elder training in another century if he continued to mature. But telepathy? He didn't yet have the discipline to develop the mystical ways of their people on his own. If Stone saw what Beryl saw, it would have been a fluke.

Satisfied with his conclusions, Jack winked and sent the boy a compliment. *"If Stone is wigging out, you two will step into his place."*

Beryl almost smiled, but suppressed it; Jack caught the tiniest flicker of approval in the kid's eyes. This one had a ton of self-control. Cross that with his unmatched mental acuity, he could be a greater proselyte than Stone ever was. The twins could outperform Stone, if necessary.

Jack chuckled and then added aloud, no longer guarding their conversation. "Don't think on this anymore, Beryl. Wipe it from your memory, and never speak of it." Jack dropped his arm and clapped him on the back.

Beryl nodded and came to his feet. As he turned, he stiffened and Meryl stood up from his seat in the back. Both men looked at Jack with real panic in their eyes.

"What is it?"

"High Father Abroghia—he overheard us just now," Beryl

whispered, and Meryl's lips mouthed the exact phrase a dozen feet away.

Jack's eyes grew wide, but he recovered instantly. *Never show weakness to an inferior—even if you're truly unnerved.* Jack *lived* on Abroghia's hit list and it was Father Umbarto who got him off time and time again.

Jack grabbed Beryl's arm once more and replied in his mind only. *"What did he say?"*

"Nothing, but he heard. I felt him slithering away... spying..."

Jack nodded and motioned for the kid to return to his seat. It was okay. Abroghia was paying close attention to Jack's pack since he marked the Rider woman. Many thought he violated procedure by making the woman a Rabbit. Only Jack understood the woman's crime and as soon as he caught up with her, he would take her before the Fathers and show them. They would take his side. How could they not? The Rider woman was responsible for contaminating dozens of Rakum. How could they allow her to go on?

Jack swiveled his chair to face front and caught Tomás looking at him with a smug grin.

"What?" he snapped, but his old friend only looked back to the Playboy magazine in his hand. "Just what I thought," Jack mumbled, and leaned back in his chair.

One thought circled his mind as he dozed off. *Catch the Rabbit. Catch the Rabbit. Catch the Rabbit.* And then... *Abroghia as the first Rabbit?* Jack laughed at the ridiculous notion and fell off to sleep

19

The High Father's Secret

In his private antechamber, Abroghia, Rakum High Father, studied the top of his staff where his named had been carved three millennia ago, his original name, his *true* name. But the Rakum knew nothing of his origins, or their own, for that matter. They believed what he told them, and that was enough. He was meticulous in revealing only what he wanted them to see.

As for the few Rakum who peeked into Johann's feeble mind all those years ago, so what? Johann was an idiot. Of the nine understudies he appointed as Fathers over two thousand years ago, the useless ne'er-do-well from what eventually became Sweden was the only one he shared the smallest amount of truth with. And that was *because* he was the weakest link. Reality would blend well with fiction in the old Rakum's addled mind. Over time, Abroghia slipped him just enough false information to lead astray anyone clever enough to pry open a Father's private thoughts.

So, let them wonder and guess blindly about their past, so long as they never approach the truth...

Abroghia put his fingertips to the deep indentations that spelled out his name in the ancient cedar staff. The Temple of Solomon had just been destroyed and its gold and cedar looted when he acquired this treasure from a passing merchant. Most likely carved for the merchant's king, Abroghia paid a high price and then painstakingly dug out the words. For the next thousand years, the Staff of Abroghia would serve as a source of power in the minds of those he conquered. A source of fear for those who opposed him. And a source of security for all who joined forces with him voluntarily.

Johann alone knew that Abroghia himself birthed their race. But Abroghia never divulged to the dolt how the deed was accomplished;

how difficult and time-consuming the undertaking. Or what powers he possessed to make his own will come to pass.

Abroghia stood and prepared to return to the Chamber of Fathers where his cohorts awaited his presence for dinner. If Jack Dawn and his pups behaved, he would leave them be. But he would keep a close eye on them. As well as on his blood son, Michael Stone. Stone was a star among the Rakum, bred to lead, and if he was truly being affected by the Rabbit as suggested, there could be real trouble afoot. Yes, he would watch them all closely, but for now, leave the situation to Stone's Elder. Jack Dawn was a despicable animal, always had been, but he knew how to take care of business.

Abroghia headed to join the others, only slightly put out by the night's events. What had he to worry about? After all, he was god to 100,000 Rakum and six times that many human Cows. What could possibly happen?

Abroghia smiled, perfectly satisfied.

20

No Time to Freak Out

"**Y**ou aren't hungry? I'll take you to dinner," Michael said as they drove away from Jeremy's building.

"No, thank you."

Michael glanced over at her short reply and returned his eyes to the dark road. Her mood had shifted and Michael was reminded why he didn't spend time with a woman he hadn't hired.

"Just run me home, thanks," she added quietly, looking out her window.

"Did Jeremy's art bother you that much?"

"No."

Perhaps, she was trying to avoid an argument, but Michael had no such reservations. Remembering to be gentle, he prodded for more. "If it wasn't the art, was it me?"

Beth sighed and peeked at him for only a moment and then trained her eyes to her lap. "Maybe it's all just now hitting me. ...When I saw that kid..." Beth paused and Michael noted her increased respiration. Finally, her dispassionate manner had developed a crack.

"So it *was* the artwork," Michael offered.

"*No*. The way he stumbled into the room... his face... his arm..."

"I don't follow," Michael replied softly, trying to guess what had pushed her buttons. What he knew about dealing with women he gleaned from Hollywood, and he'd soon figure out why she seemed so upset. She hadn't spoken and her fingers went to her cheeks. *Is she crying?* "Are you okay?"

"How am I supposed to accept all this?" she asked angrily, looking out the windshield. "You're not human, I'm a victim, and right before I came in tonight...*you were drinking that man's blood!*"

85

"Oh," Michael murmured with a nod. "But I told you about that..."

Beth wiped her face hard. "It's not your fault. I just have to be strong. I have to remember where my true strength lies..."

Michael turned into her apartment complex wondering at her verbiage. It sounded vaguely Catholic and he didn't want to discuss religion. He made a noise of agreement and she leaned back and closed her eyes.

"There's not any time to freak out, is there?"

"Are you asking me?"

Beth shook her head with a sad chuckle. "Okay, this is really happening." She looked over as he parked and met her eye. "I'm in. You said we have a week before your brethren start coming and less than that before your master hunts us down, right?"

"That sounds right."

She shrugged with a sideways grin. "Guess what happens next."

Michael shook his head a fraction, wondering at her sudden mysterious air.

"We go inside. You've told me about your people. It's time I told you about mine..."

"Yes, ma'am." Michael nodded. He put his hand to the door handle and gave her a smile. "I'm sorry about Jeremy."

She opened her door as he did and spoke as they stood out of the car. "Did you know from the moment we were headed to his apartment building what you were going to do?"

"Yeah, I mean, whatever happens, happens."

"Believe it or not, I think I understand," she said looking at him over the car-top. A cool wind swept past as Michael came around to meet her.

"I don't keep mortals as companions, so I apologize in advance if you find my behavior unpleasant," Michael continued with an apologetic wink.

"Okay..." Beth nodded slowly, absorbing his meaning.

Michael took her elbow and started them for the curb. "My brothers and I live in harmony. One-hundred-thousand Rakum obeying laws that are mutually agreed upon, because they're conducive to everyone's well-being. You know," he added with a wry chuckle, "I prided myself on living in a secret society that runs better than any here out in the world. But now..."

"Yeah, what changed?" Beth turned to Michael's profile. "All I did was ask you to help me get my purse."

"Now... I think there's been a mistake." He met her eye and looked away, suppressing another unfamiliar internal twinge when their eyes met. "For the first time in my life, I have questions. It's like those awful paintings. I've never seen anything right or wrong about them in all the years I've been approving them for Jay-Jay. But tonight... I saw *myself* through someone else's eyes and I didn't like what he saw."

"I understand," Beth said quietly. "I think you should always ask questions and seek the truth, but also know that there's redemption. As long as you have breath, there is redemption."

"Not for Rakum. That's a human word, a *weak* word. No matter how you look at it, I am what I am." Beth laughed and Michael's eyebrows went up, the principle well used among his people.

"I'm sorry. I used that line in my book. I am seeing more and more similarities between this whole situation and that of my book characters. The answer to your master's rage might be inside the novels after all."

Michael inserted her key in the lock and froze stock still. He'd been so distracted that he hadn't sensed his brethren close by. He cursed softly and looked around the quiet lot.

This woman's presence isn't enough to distract me—something else is happening.

Beth began asking him what was wrong and he pushed her front door open, still scanning the expanse.

"It's the brethren," he whispered. "More than one. Also... one of them is an Elder." Michael shook his head.

"God, help us," Beth said just as quietly.

Michael stared into the darkness, his mind racing. "Elders don't chase Rabbits. He must be here for me."

"Where are they?"

Michael didn't answer, but continued to look into the night. Beth might follow his line of sight, but she'd see only the moon and streetlights reflecting off the surface of the pond.

Michael motioned for her to enter the apartment. "There's nothing I can do about it. If I go speak to them, you'll be alone. It's too risky. We will let them come to us." He waited for Beth to enter and locked the door once inside. A deadbolt wouldn't prevent Rakum entry, but it sent a message when tossed by a brother enjoying his solitary Rabbit allowance.

Beth headed for the kitchen. "I'll heat up some soup."

There she goes again, not a care in the world...

Michael peeked out the blinds. "I can't predict their behavior," he said, his voice barely carrying.

"What?" She poked her head around the wall between them.

"I don't know what they will do. I'm not much of a telepath. Plus, we've always worked in unison..."

"Do they know what's going on?"

"It's hard to say. We communicate telepathically, but only the advanced brethren will know I've gone off script. It's safe to assume that some of them, at least, know something hinky's going on..."

"Hinky?" Beth smiled at his choice of words.

Michael matched her grin with a shake of his head. "This is serious. Don't forget, they're drawn to you as the Rabbit. They don't have to know that I've lost my mind."

Beth wrinkled her nose in fun and Michael pushed back an unpleasant thought: *What if she's insane?* He wasn't a healer and could not diagnose any such condition. Jesse could. Any *Elder* could...

"Why are they hiding?"

His humor dissolving, Michael resumed looking out the window, his back to Beth.

"What do you think it means?" she pressed standing a few feet behind him.

"Maybe Jack sent them, or maybe they're simply following their noses." He turned his head to meet her eye. "I don't want you to take this so lightly. I haven't threatened you, but my brethren will want to drink you. Or worse."

Beth's face fell and she inclined her head. "Worse?"

Michael nodded morosely. "We're not priests."

"Oh," she said under her breath. Then she exhaled and clapped her hands together. "I say, until they make themselves known, let's get on with our evening." She sat in a cushioned chair and crossed her legs at the ankle.

Michael turned. "Just like that, eh?"

"Yeah," Beth replied and caught on why he asked. "I'm scared, but it's out of my hands. What can I do about it? I don't control the world. Either I trust God or I don't. That's my peace."

Michael frowned. "God? Your book is entertaining, but it's as fiction as the religions of the world."

"Really? How can I endure that horrific violation in Atlanta and go about my day as if nothing happened? How can I listen to you share about this race of Rakum—of *vampires*—as if they are real?"

"Beth..." Michael began, but she forged ahead.

"Did you understand the spiritual element in *The Judging?*"

"What do you mean?"

"How did my Tony-Agricola-character feel about everything that was happening? How did he deal with it? He *prayed.*"

Michael sighed; there were no resolutions to be found in man's dream-world of religion. "That's not *real*, Beth."

"It is. Tony's peace came from God. His predicament was fictitious, but his way of trusting in God is real. Michael," she said and didn't continue until he looked over. "I know who God is and that He watches over me."

Michael looked back out the window. "No offense, but we're going to need a better plan than '*trust God*'."

Behind him, Beth stood up and huffed. "I listened to your outrageous story. How can you dismiss mine from my opening statement?"

"It's a fairy tale," he replied, elevating his voice without intention. "It's a global human conspiracy. A money-making scheme that dates back thousands of years. It's pointless."

"No, *life* is pointless without *Him*," she said, her eyes flashing, but her tone soft. "God is not a fairy tale. Man has made Him into all sorts of things, but God has never changed. He is the same as He was in the beginning. He loves His children and He will protect His own." Beth huffed. "At least *listen*. I listened to you quite attentively, and your story is more a fairy tale than mine."

"Fine. Go ahead," Michael whispered from the window.

"If you can wipe from your memory everything man has told you about God, you could begin to know the truth. Man has always wanted to control God. Can you see that?"

"We have company," Michael muttered an instant before a knock sounded at the door, two short raps. "This is the time to start praying, Beth. Here comes obstacle number one."

"Open the door. God has my back," Beth whispered.

Michael's eyes darted behind him to check Beth's position and he unlocked the door.

"I hope he has mine, too." And with that mumbled sentiment, Michael opened the door and set his face.

21

Motorcycle Cow

From the front seat of the truck, Javier watched Simon sleep, folded like an infant in the back, the Gideon Bible in his right hand. Roman stopped watching the Rider woman's door long enough to follow his eye and frown.

"That kid is getting darker, Javie. I'm worried about him."

"Why?"

"He's unstable. Unpredictable. Do you not see it?" Roman faced front again and absently cleaned his useless glasses.

Javier attempted to see the same danger, but only saw Simon, the kid with the friendly smile and delicious blood.

Roman chuckled, getting wind of Javier's thoughts. "Taste notwithstanding, watch him. I'll kill him if he crosses me," Roman said flatly. "An Elder protects his own."

Despite the harsh statement, Javier was pleased, happy to be considered worthy. Javier's mouth went to the side and he returned his attention to the sleeping youth.

Simon was nineteen when they met, and the circumstances were peculiar to say the least. But hadn't Javier favored the kid at first sight? Javier closed his eyes and wandered back to that time in his mind.

It was two years earlier, a few months after they'd moved to Georgia from the Carolinas. Javier piloted Roman's new Camaro like a professional racecar driver down a deserted street ribboned with delicious curves. Roman rarely smiled, but when Javier glanced at his Elder briefly after the last sharp turn, the man didn't hide his amusement. Javier accelerated as the road straightened out and leaned into the steering wheel, blowing raspberries for added comic effect. Roman shook his head and chuckled. It was a good time. Not so different from their time together in Montreal where Javier grew up.

A brake light ahead caught his eye and he slowed the car to the speed limit. As he reached the curve, the red glow was off the pavement and in the grass, under a low-branched tree. Curious, Javier pulled to the curb and looked to his superior.

"A motorcyclist has crashed." Roman indicated toward the scene, but made no suggestions.

Javier discerned the shape of a man thrown several feet from the bike. A rush of emotion hit him deep inside causing him to inhale sharply; he recognized it well. It was the way he chose all of his Cows—superb intuition that bordered on premonition.

Roman discerned his reaction and came back with a retort packed with mock consternation. "Go have a look. Your curiosity will be your ruin one day."

Javier grinned and hopped out of the car. He reached the biker in seconds and stooped down. It was a boy—a teenager—and he lay on his side, the face shield of his helmet only partially down. Javier carefully unlatched the chinstrap and freed his head. Roman stood behind him and took the helmet from his hand.

"He's breathing normally," Roman offered when Javier gently rolled the boy onto his back. As the kid's shoulders rested flat he winced, but his eyes remained closed.

"What a mess," Javier mumbled and checked the boy's pulse at his throat.

"His clavicle is broken."

An expert in human anatomy and medicine, Roman made diagnoses as the seconds ticked on. "He has a compound fracture of the right tibia."

"Hey, you okay?" Javier spoke to the boy and brushed bright blond hair from his forehead. The kid was a looker and Javier rubbed open one lid and checked the pupillary response in his blue-green eyes. "You're going to be all right."

Well-trained as a healer, Javier tucked his fingers beneath the collar of the kid's T-Shirt, directly atop the fractured bone. With very little concentration, he convinced the bone to knit back together, the boy not stirring even a trifle. Satisfied with the result, he pulled back and sat on his knees beside his patient.

"The leg will need resetting," Roman offered from his spectating stance a few feet away.

Javier nodded and moved to the boy's legs where blood seeped into his jeans. Should he set it himself? He was capable, but out of respect, Javier looked to his Elder.

Roman shook his head and dialed his cell phone. "Leave it to the humans. I'll call an ambulance."

Javier moved back to the kid's head and now, the young man was looking right at him with eyes filled with wonder—an emotion Javier intuited he'd elicit from the handsome boy.

"You're going to be all right." Javier smiled encouragingly, automatically infatuated. He'd always had a soft heart, and since Roman rarely chastised him for it, he felt no need to disguise it. "You had a motorcycle accident. Broke your leg. I fixed your shoulder. How do you feel?"

"Like I fell off a cliff," the boy responded. His voice held a touch of humor despite his predicament. He offered a half-grin and lifted his hand to his hero. "Simon Miller."

Javier took his hand and shook it, the sirens of the ambulance a few miles away just reaching his ears. "I'm Javier. Nice to meet you, Simon."

"*Hah-vee-air?* Weird name," the boy chuckled and then sputtered with a frown. "Hurts."

Javier glanced back at Roman who raised an eyebrow.

"He busted up his leg. Other than that, he's fine."

Having come to the same prognosis, Javier smirked. The kid's pain threshold was lower than normal. He leaned over the boy, took his face into both hands, and smiled.

"Look at me, Simon. I'll take that pain away."

Simon did not question him, but did as he said. Cupping his face, Javier concentrated on the pain. It was only moments before Simon gasped with surprise.

"How did you do that? Wow..." Simon's eyes grew wide and he smiled anew. Javier released him, but stayed bent over, looking into his face.

"*Magic,*" Javier whispered and Roman snickered over his shoulder. After another moment, the sirens getting closer, Roman touched his shoulder and he reluctantly got to his feet.

"The medics are here, Simon. You're in good hands." Javier backed away from the kid, their eyes still locked. Roman would not want to be interviewed by the authorities and seconds later, he was in the Camaro turning over the engine.

Simon lifted his hand toward them and Javier stopped.

"Javier—come see me at the hospital. Please." Simon's plea was pitiful and Javier nodded. *"Hah-vee-Airrr..."* Simon played with his name as pain returned to his eyes.

It was unusual that Javier connected with a Cow so readily, and hadn't the boy attached himself unnaturally fast? *Easier is always better...* Javier smiled jubilantly as he slid into the car.

Roman steered them away from the accident scene as the ambulance rounded the corner. When they were a mile down the road, heading home at normal speeds, Roman held the wheel with his left hand and grabbed Javier's shoulder with his right.

"You go see him, Javie. It's a good match."

Javier nodded. He couldn't agree more.

Later that same evening, Simon was fast asleep in the hospital bed when Javier slipped into his room unnoticed by the staff. It was after two in the morning and he had no trouble circumnavigating the security guard or the errant nurse roaming the hallways. Javier took notice small circular monitoring pads taped to his upper chest. Simon was shirtless with the body of an athlete. There was no bandage across his shoulder leading Javier to assume his healing touch had been successful. The crisp white hospital sheet was pulled to Simon's waist and he snored little puffs of air that made Javier smile. Before another minute passed, Simon awoke and serenely stared into Javier's face.

"Javier.. Hey."

Javier sat down gingerly on the edge of the bed and Simon put out his hand. When the handshake was over, the boy held on, his fingers wrapped around Javier's.

"You're an angel, aren't you."

It was not posed as a question and Javier raised his eyebrows. "I guess it depends on your definition."

"You are. I can feel it—your hand..." Simon lifted Javier's fingers and then ran his other hand along the skin of his forearm. "Your arm. Too smooth. Too perfect."

Javier grinned and he watched Simon caress his arm. He could think of no reply, so he turned his attention to the boy's injuries. "How's the pain?"

"No pain... good drugs." Simon gestured to the crook of his arm and the plastic tubing attached to it. "Out of all the people who had wrecks tonight—why me? Am I special? Are you my guardian angel?"

Javier smiled. "I'm not an angel."

"Aw, now, I can see you are. Your secret's safe. Hey—where's your friend? The tall guy?"

Javier offered a half-shrug. "He goes where he pleases."

"He was really cool." Simon nodded his head as he spoke, his words slurring from the painkillers in his IV.

"Here," Javier wriggled his hand from the kid's grip and stood. He guessed the location of Simon's injured leg under the sheet and laid his palm on the temporary splint. Javier concentrated with both hands now on the sheet. The bones had been set and needed to grow together. "I'll accelerate the healing so you won't need a cast."

"I knew you were an angel."

Javier chuckled at the boy's imaginative deductions as he sensed the bones knitting together. After another fifteen seconds, it was done. He lifted his palms and sat on the edge of the bed.

Simon reached for his hand again. "Thanks, man. I can feel it working." Simon was growing sleepy, but valiantly resisting.

"Where do you live?" Javier asked thinking ahead.

"Meriwether. The blue house. You can't miss it." Simon closed his eyes still holding Javier's hand. "You'll come see me, won't you?"

"Oh, yes." Javier stood and waited for the boy to release his hand. He did but only after several long seconds. "Bye, Simon."

"Bye, *Hah-Vee-Airrrr...*" Simon exaggerated his name and smiled, falling off to sleep. Javier slipped out of the room and as usual, not a soul witnessed his departure.

Two weeks later, Javier stood in Simon's bedroom and waited for the boy to enter. He'd been watching the kid's house a week, learning his schedule. Tonight, Simon stayed home watching TV and his housemate left carrying a backpack. Javier slipped into the house unnoticed. The toilet flushed in the hall bathroom and the bedroom door swung open right after. Completely healed from his broken leg, Simon strolled in strong and balanced. He yanked off his T-shirt and only noticed Javier when he raised his arms to stretch.

"Hey!" He ran across the room and threw his arms around his visitor as if greeting a long lost friend.

Javier stiffened and held his arms away from his body, but Simon didn't notice. After another five seconds, Simon was still hanging on, his face against the collar of Javier's leather jacket, and he laughed.

"I guess angels don't hug, huh?"

"I'm not an angel," Javier replied matter-of-factly, his arms still sticking awkwardly outward.

"Then what are you?"

"I'm a Rakum," Javier answered softly.

"*Rah-kum...*" Simon sounded out the word slowly, still hugging. "Yes."

"Rakums don't hug?"

"No," Javier said quietly.

"Is it awful?"

"No." Javier relaxed a fraction, but still held his arms away from Simon's bare skin.

Simon released him and stepped back. "Enough of that. Sorry," he apologized with a sheepish grin. "Didn't mean to act so stupid."

"It's okay." Without forethought, Javier touched Simon's chest with his fingers and the kid blushed. He made a grab for a T-shirt on the floor and Javier turned his attention to a shelf of trophies. "You play baseball?"

"I'm on a scholarship at the college. How 'bout you? You play?"

"No." Javier shook his head. "But I'd be good at it if I did."

"I'll bet. I'll bet there's nothing you can't do," Simon said, wonder in his voice.

"You'd win that bet," Javier said, and looked about the rest of the room. Trophies and plaques denied any space for books, and three photographs of the same teenaged girl sat framed on his dresser.

Simon stepped closer to Javier then and lifted his hands toward his face, stopping just short of touching him. Simon waited for the surprised look in Javier's eyes to soften into consent before he touched the skin of his cheek. "Smooth. Just like I thought. Your skin is different."

The young man then ran the fingers of both hands into Javier's slick black hair. He withdrew them with a humph and stepped to his bed to sit.

"Unreal," he said and motioned for Javier to sit, too.

His entire life, his Cows became infatuated with him, so Simon's behavior fit right in. "You like?" Javier joked.

Simon shook his head in unbelief. "My girlfriend is a senior at the High School, she's a cheerleader—" Simon made a kissing noise and pointed to the nearest picture frame. "She has it all, and then some, but her skin's not half as smooth as yours."

Javier settled into the chair on top of several pairs of discarded clothing. "Interesting."

"Rakums don't get pimples, huh?" Javier laughed and shook his head. "So what do Rakums do besides rescue kids on the side of the road in the middle of the night?"

Javier chuckled. "That was the first time I ever found a kid on the side of the road."

"Nice." He nodded. "It was the first time I ever crashed my motorcycle. My aunt bought me a truck yesterday. Much safer." Simon laughed and pointed to his leg. "And you were right about the cast. In the morning, after you left, the doctor couldn't understand why I could walk. He's recalibrating his machines. My leg healed overnight, thanks to you."

"I've always been a proficient healer."

"What else do you do?" Simon leaned forward, his tone more serious. "Why do you care about me? You could be anywhere tonight, couldn't you? You just popped in here like a ghost—poof!"

Javier shook his head at all the questions. "I didn't *pop* in. I walked. I'm just really, really sneaky."

"Cool." Simon meant the word sincerely. "So, what else do you guys do?"

"We accept *donations,*" Javier said holding the boy's gaze.

Simon's head went to the side. "You're not talking about money, are you." Again, not a question and Javier grinned.

"Donations of blood." He expected the kid to be blasé about letting his blood—all Cows were—and this boy had it bad.

Simon cackled and slapped his knee. "I knew it! So a Rakum is like a vampire, then? A friendly vampire?"

Javier smiled. "Whatever helps you understand."

"Unreal," he mused then looked hopeful. "So…do you want my blood?"

"Oh, yes." Javier nodded, pleased that he had chosen well.

"I'm guessing I don't have to die."

Javier smiled again. The kid was smart; if he intended to kill him, he'd never have rescued him from the crash. "No. You'll be fine."

"Okay." Simon got to his feet and awaited instructions.

Javier stood and reached into his pants pockets, retrieving a three-inch pocketknife.

"After I leave, drink a glass of water. Eat plenty of iron-rich foods, especially after my visits."

"You'll be coming back?" Simon's countenance brightened.

Javier chuckled. "I will visit every month on this day, okay?"

"*Nice.*" Simon beamed another smile. "So how do we do it?"

Javier stepped forward and grasped his new friend's wrist. It was so easy. *Simon* was easy. Life was good.

22

Toothless Snake

"Hey, Brother," Michael offered in an even tone at Beth's front door. The Rakum on the stoop was young, slender, and clueless, with a gentle face and a guileless expression. Usually generous to his more humble brethren, Michael regretted the gruff role he had to play for Beth's sake.

The visitor returned the nod and stood respectfully at the door, hands behind his back, expecting to be allowed entry.

"I'm not ready for family." Michael lowered his voice. "What's your name?"

"They call me Snake." The visitor shrugged at the unfitting name. "And you're Michael Stone?"

Michael maintained his static expression, but everything about the kid was ridiculous. "What have you heard about this party?" he asked and hooked his thumb behind him without allowing Snake to see into the room.

"Only that Elder Dawn sent a Rabbit to Montgomery. I got here as fast as I could." Still exuding a shyness that did not match his name, Snake shuffled his feet and did meet Michael's eye.

"It's like this, *Snake,* I'm having a private party. You do know that I have that option, right?"

"Of course. But…"

"Then go away. If you run into any of the brethren, tell them as well. They'll know when the party goes public. Got it?" The brethren Michael sensed earlier still waited in the dark and he had no way of knowing if Snake was with them or on his own.

"I came a long way…"

"Not my problem. Do you have a place to stay?" The boy shrugged and Michael gave him a stern look. He would need a place

97

to escape the sun. "Are you an imbecile? Did you come here without a back-up plan?"

"I don't know. I guess so." Snake's eyes filled with water and Michael tapped his shoulder to force him to look up. It was highly uncharacteristic for a Rakum to weep—in general, they were incapable of manufacturing tears. But this Rakum was doing it and Michael hurried to halt a display.

"Look. I have a house nearby. I'll call you a cab. Stay at my place until tomorrow night and then leave town." He noted the kid's eyebrows go up in defiance. "You heard me. I'm not allowing you to stay in my place longer than one night. Got it?"

"But what about the party? You said…"

"Better luck next time. Make a plan, have a place to stay. You act like you've never left the Lair, *shit!*" Michael whispered the curse and had to work hard to keep the kid's eye. "And look at me when I'm speaking to you!"

"I…I don't have anything." Snake's pitiful voice rose an octave. "I've been exiled. I don't know anyone here. Truth is, I was just following my nose…"

Michael sighed. He actually was the kind of Rakum an orphan like Snake could count on in the past. But now? He could no more help himself than he could the Rabbit and this foundling. Michael shook his head again, "Brother, what's your real name?"

"David," the kid replied, lowering his eyes.

"Okay, *David,* go to my house and stay there a few days. You still can't join this party."

"Oh, let him come in. He's harmless." Beth stepped up to the door and peeked over Michael's arm. "If he gets out of line, you can take him. Look at him. He's just a kid."

Michael looked over his shoulder to glare at Beth. She had let down her hair and he wished she hadn't; none of his brethren needed the added distraction. "Beth, I'm handling this."

"Yeah, Michael, I won't be any trouble. Can I come in and have something to eat? Are you guys burning something in there?"

"My soup!" Beth whirled from the door and raced to the kitchen.

"David, go to my house. I have food there. Help yourself."

"But I'll be alone. Please, let me come in. Like the Bunny said, I'm not a threat. You could tackle me in no time."

"The *Bunny* has a name. Her name is Beth."

"Beth said I could come in."

Unafraid, Beth called to the men in the door. "Bring him to the table. I already set three places."

Michael sighed and gave the kid a hard look. "She wants you to come in, but I'm warning you. She's not your Rabbit. You can have soup—not blood. Do you understand?"

"Yeah, okay. Hands off." He held up both palms.

After one more unhappy exhale, Michael lifted his arm and David stepped tentatively under to walk inside.

"Smells good. I haven't had anything to eat in three days. Ooh! Bread!"

Michael watched as the youngster took a seat and grabbed the Italian bread Beth offered.

"Just when I thought things couldn't get any worse," he mumbled.

"Oh, come on, it's not that bad." Beth sat across from David and watched him devour his bread. "Come sit with us."

Michael secured the door and walked slowly to the table. "Why don't you trust my judgment? This is not a kid from down the street."

Beth regarded Michael only a millisecond and then smiled at David across from her. He grinned with bread in his teeth. Michael slapped the table top and sat down beside him.

"David, look at Beth. What do you see?"

Obediently, David stopped chewing. "She looks like a nice lady," he said through a wad of dough.

"And how does she *smell.*"

David swallowed his food and then took a dramatic breath. "Like heaven..."

Michael nodded and swiveled his face to Beth's. "See? He's not seeing what I see. He's thinking about food. *Rabbit,* to be exact."

"Is that wrong?" David looked between them innocently. "She is a Rabbit, right?"

Michael sighed, his face turning red. "David, shut up. Beth," Michael said and sucked his teeth to buy a moment, "you think he's a lost child searching for his mommy, but this Rakum is a killer, like all of his brethren. Like I am."

"You're a killer?" Beth asked Michael sideways as if she doubted his words. Michael huffed.

"Yes. Your puffy pink dream world is over." Michael took a deep breath and attempted to soften his tone. "We take what we want, we do what we want, and sometimes humans die when they get in our way. We're above you on the food chain." Michael further gentled his tone, but wanted her to be sure to get his meaning. "Beth, this sweet-looking little guy is a killer."

"But I'm not." David looked to Michael, probably surprising himself with his impertinence.

"Yes, you are," Michael disagreed and stood up to put his hands to his hips next to David's chair.

"I'm sorry, Mr. Michael, but I have only killed in self-defense."

"Self-defense?" Beth asked and David nodded sincerely.

"Yes, Ma'am. A few years back when some thugs tried to kill my friends…"

Michael huffed, not interested in hearing anything of David's history other than what he could use right now. "Focus, little brother. How old are you?"

"I was born in '35. I've never killed anyone for sport or food."

It was difficult to believe. Even though he didn't actively seek opportunities to destroy human life, Michael had done so, especially in the beginning when running with Jack Dawn. Human life was cheap; always had been. Finally, he leveled his gaze at the youngster. "How can that be?"

"I just haven't. Never wanted to." David slurped his soup, ignoring Michael's confounded state.

"Who is your Elder?"

"Tomás. Do you know him?"

"Yes. Very well." Annoyed, Michael pulled out his chair and sat down again. He put his spoon in his soup, but didn't eat. The kid was not making sense. Tomás was a thug; he would've forced the kid to exercise brutality.

"You said you had been exiled," Beth said in her soft voice, the sound of it, in an odd way, calmed Michael's mind. "Did you break some kind of law?"

"Naw, but Master Tomás got disgusted with me and sent me away." Tears threatened again and David sniffled.

"No—shut that sh—, *crap* right now," Michael barked, editing his profanity for Beth.

David turned away from him to Beth. "I did the best I could, but he didn't like me. I didn't measure up," he whined.

Michael's skin crawled at the sound. Tomás very likely hated it even more.

"Why were you exiled? Because you didn't fit in?" Michael asked trying to make sense of Tomás' behavior.

"I think that's mostly it," David replied, his voice stronger. "I guess I'm not tough enough. His pups are pretty brutal."

Michael humphed. "You don't look like Tomás' type." He then nodded to Beth. "They're a vicious crowd, that Miami Pack. Elder Tomás is tight with Jack Dawn, if that gives you any idea."

Beth stopped chewing.

After taking a deep breath, David slurped his soup and continued evenly. "Master Tomás sent me to live in Gainesville pretty early on. I was only twenty, but he wanted me to be alone, said it would make me tough. I've lived in Gainesville since '55, but a week ago, he sent some of the brethren to tell me I was officially kicked out of his family."

"What are your skills? Your strengths? Didn't you have anything to offer your pack?" Michael asked thinking of his own talents that his Elder exploited regularly in his youth.

"Nothing Elder Tomás appreciated," David said with a shrug. "I don't register pain. I'm an empath. I'm a so-so telepath. None of those are anything my brethren consider worthy. Oh, and my tongue…" David put out his tongue and touched it with his pointer. "Closes wounds." He looked at Beth, tongue still sticking out, obvious pride in his gaze.

"Your tongue?" Beth asked and gave Michael a suspicious look.

"Yeah. It's handy when drawing blood. I only know of one other Rakum who can do it. Aside from the Fathers, of course…"

"Being weaker than your brethren isn't a reason to be excommunicated and Elders do *nothing* on a whim…" Michael rolled his eyes to the door working the problem.

"If that's not normal, maybe this correlates to your Elder marking me for no reason and David's Elder kicking him out." Michael read her gaze and them looked to the kid who nodded with round eyes.

"David," Beth said softly, "do you believe in God?"

"Uh, yeah. I think so."

"What?" Michael interrupted, unable to rein in his disgust. "No, you don't. What are you talking about?"

"I don't want to make you mad, but I've recently learned about God." David pulled his eyes from Michael's and turned to Beth. "Terrence—one of my Cows—shared his faith with me. It made sense. I don't know what to do about it, but I believed him."

"There's your connection," Beth said with a grim expression and Michael had to agree.

"Did you read a novel called *The Judging*?" Michael asked him and he nodded, grinning as if relieved to speak of it.

"I loved it. Terrence loaned me a copy. He said it would explain God to someone like me. I also read the sequel. Why?"

"I'm the author, David. I'm Beth Rider."

The youngster's green eyes grew wide and his smile increased. "What? Oh, wow..."

Michael tapped the table. "Focus. David, did Beth's book lead you into religion?"

"Um, I'd say it made me want to know who God is. In fact..." David turned to look at Beth. "Maybe He led me here so you can teach me more. If anyone could explain it to me, it'd be you..."

"SHUT IT!" Out of patience with the topic, Michael stood and leaned on the table with his palms, effectively hulking over the wiry youth. "We are in grave danger and this God-talk won't help us find a solution." Michael sensed Beth about to interrupt him and he cut her off. "No, I'm serious. Jack Dawn is on his way here. He'll want to finish the work he began with you and he'll want to punish me *and* this kid from Florida. If Jack has taken exception to your writing style, I think I now know why."

"Because my book led this kid to God?"

"It may have led this *Rakum* to God. Because it probably is leading more of us down a road we can't take. There is no room in your theology for Rakum, Beth. We are incompatible with your concept of God. We don't lead human lives and we don't keep human values. Why can't you see that?"

"Because it's not true."

"It's not?" David stopped chewing.

"Of course not. Any of you who hear the Good News and choose to believe it can be saved. And *redeemed*, Michael."

"THIS IS LUDICROUS. What have I gotten myself in to?" Michael left the table and disappeared into the living room, not caring in the least that Beth and David heard him cursing all the way.[d]

23

The Delight of the Dying Buzz

Beth reached across the table and placed her hand atop David's. Even though his slippery-smooth skin felt alien to her touch, it was hard for her to believe that he was anything more than a regular human kid. He could have stepped right out of her youth group at church. He had friendly green eyes with eyebrows set in a constant state of apology. His reddish brown hair was short and spiked on top, giving him if anything, the look of a kid who liked skateboarding and loud music. Beth chuckled with wonder at the expanse of differences between the four Rakum she'd met thus far. Because they varied so much in disposition and motivation, she was more convinced than ever that they were more human than they were aware.

"I'm sorry I made Michael mad. He seems like a good guy."

"Don't mind him, David. He's wrestling with the truth, just like you must have at first."

"Oh, yes, ma'am. I was awfully confused. Terrence was being as plain as possible, but it was like I had cotton in my ears or something. But by the end of the week, I understood, and I needed him to explain it to me further."

"Did he?"

"He disappeared, Miss Rider. He vanished about the same time they came to kick me out."

"Oh, I'm sorry," Beth sighed and patted David's hand before pulling back. "Tell me about him. He was a good friend?"

David's expression changed immediately and his gaze softened. "He was one of my Cows, but he was a friend, too."

"He sounds really nice," Beth offered, trying to forget that no matter how great Terrence was, he still voluntarily let his blood.

"Terrence O'Henry," David whispered, and his gaze fell to the table. "Like the candy bar, only not as rich..."

It sounded like he was imitating someone's voice and Beth smiled. "But he was just as sweet, right?" she added making a joke. David glanced at her and then away quickly, smiling, and Beth recognized the double entendre and she blushed.

"Yeah," David continued, a faint blush also touching his cheeks. "He rescued me one time, Miss Beth. If it weren't for him, I'd be on the run again. He took good care of me."

"What happened?" Beth asked happy to move away from her embarrassing remark.

"Remember I mentioned that I once killed in self-defense? That night, I killed two dangerous intruders. But that wasn't the problem. My problem arose when I took a Dying Buzz and became paralyzed. I couldn't move. Terrence was the one who got me upstairs before the authorities arrived. If it weren't for him, I would have been arrested and then I would have had to go on the run and I hate running more than anything." David gobbled the last bite of his bread and looked at the empty plate.

"What's a Dying Buzz?" Beth asked innocently and picked up the plate to add more bread from the kitchen. David waited to answer until she returned and his face was red again. "What? Is it embarrassing?"

"No... I haven't ever explained it before. We don't talk about it..." David grinned and wiped his mouth with his palm. "We learned about the three buzzes at First Ritual."

Beth waited for more, now increasingly curious.

David smiled and cleared his throat. "As recently as five centuries ago, Rakum consumed blood from any human source. Alive, dying, and even recently dead." Beth grimaced, but David nodded and smiled. "No, it's not bad. I mean, before the rules were changed, Rakum had access to all blood. It was easy to evade human authority." David took a fresh slice of bread in his fingers, but held it on his plate. "A Dying Buzz is from a dying person, or someone who will die because you're drawing their blood."

"Oh. So, a Dead Buzz is drawn from a dead person?"

"Yeah, and a Live Buzz, which is all we do now, is from a live and relatively healthy person."

"But the Dying Buzz is bad for you? You said you were paralyzed..."

David looked down sheepishly and chuckled. "I'm pretty young and it hit me hard. See, the Dying Buzz can paralyze an immature Rakum with pleasure." He glanced up briefly then looked down, still smiling. "It's bad because it feels really, really good..." David blushed again and shrugged. "You might find this interesting since you're human, but when a Rakum drinks dead blood, he develops characteristics not too unlike those of a zombie. For real. Flesh-eating, walking-dead type. Just like in the movies."

Beth was interested indeed. "And what did the dying buzz do?"

"Dying buzz makes us have long teeth and nails, our eyes dilate and change colors. I guess it is like a lot of vampire movies when we get like that." David poked his bread into his mouth, proud of the way he instructed his hostess.

Beth nodded, her wheels turning. "So, now, you only take live blood, you look almost human. You can pass for human, and take jobs to work and live right alongside us undetected. That's brilliant." Beth mused, unhappy at the wiles of the enemy.

"Pretty much."

"And now you've learned about God."

"Yeah..." David's grin fell and he looked at the bread in his hand. "I don't understand how it happened. When I read your books, it was like I could hear God for the first time. It scared me." David gulped and looked at her sideways. "It still scares me."

"I'll bet," Beth said, now piecing together a new puzzle. Three years ago, she didn't begin to write *The Judging* on a whim. She had received the story in a dream, but she never would've thought that her work would move the hearts of so many half-devils.

"Do you think God made you write those novels? To get through to us?"

"I guess He did." Beth shrugged, still working it out in her mind. "I got *The Judging* in a dream. And God can use our dreams to communicate with us."

"Did you dream about Rakum?"

"No, I dreamed about *The Judging*. That I was at Panera Bread studying the Bible and eating a bagel when someone came up behind me." Beth put her own hand on her right shoulder as she told her tale. "He said, 'Hello, Elizabeth.' I knew the voice, but I couldn't place it. Then he came and sat in the booth across from me."

"What did he look like?"

"Like a Pastor. Thirty-something with short, dark-blond hair parted on the side, his eyes were blue and his clothes outdated—" Beth smiled at the recollection, tickled that it was so vivid after so much time had passed.

"Did you know him?"

Beth shook her head. "No. ...Yes. I kept thinking that I *should* know him. He looked familiar and he *felt* familiar..."

"What did he want?"

"He put a book on the table and pushed it over to me. It was old and the title was engraved in gold. It read 'The Judging.'"

"Oh...cool..."

"Yeah, I thought so, too," Beth agreed. "Then he said, 'it is time.' I flipped through the book and it was blank. Then he said 'it is time' again and was gone."

"He disappeared?"

"I guess. But then I opened the book again and on the first page, in *my* handwriting, it said, 'go and do.'" Beth laughed softly. "The next morning, I had the whole story in my mind and I started writing immediately. That was three years ago, and all four in the series have been sold."

"It could've been God who gave you the story, huh?"

"I think it was. And I think I know who that guy was who gave me the book."

"Really?"

"Yeah. I think he was my guardian angel."

David laughed and held his hand up in an apology. "I'm sorry. I've seen angels in the movies—they're usually big winged fairies."

"No, angels can be anything. Whatever they need to be to perform their task. What are angels but ministering spirits sent to serve those who love God."

"What?"

"That's what an angel is. A ministering spirit. And the Bible says that God's children have guardian angels that keep watch over us."

"So your angel came to you in a dream?"

Beth shrugged. "Why not? He's probably here right now, watching and protecting me. It would explain why I've been so safe up to now."

David looked warily around the room and into the dark kitchen nook. "What does he look like?"

"I don't know, but I have an inkling that we'd take him seriously. In the Bible, they always say, 'be not afraid' when they show up, so I guess they look pretty scary." Beth watched David's expression turn sour and she put her hand on his. "But they only do the will of God and His will is that we succeed in our purpose. Be happy he's here."

"Do I have a guardian angel?"

"I think you might." Beth sat up again and rested her head on her folded hands. "You heard God call you. You must be His child."

As she spoke, Michael left noisily through the front door. David hung his head.

"I'm messing everything up."

"No, Michael's angry at God, not us. Now ask me a question."

"For starters, how can I be God's child when I'm not even human?"

"That's lie number one. Your people have fed you this lie to perpetuate their lifestyle, but they *are* human. Mutated and altered by unclean spiritual forces sure, but human just the same."

"How can you know that? We live off human blood. We outlive our human counterparts by centuries."

"Yes, I know. But I also know this. You have a soul. You were born to a woman, right?" David nodded. "Then you have a soul. That means you have a *choice*. If you put your trust in God, He will deliver you. You'll become a new creature in Him—a *human* creature. And you'll serve Him for the rest of your days. When your time is up here, you'll go to be with Him in paradise forever."

"Really? How do I put my trust in Him? What do I do?"

Before Beth could reply, across the open floor, the front door opened. Michael's tall form filled the doorway, his gaze hard as glass and his mouth a grim line. Beth counted at least one other head behind him and her chest tightened. In her imagination, her guardian angel puffed out his chest.

24

A Rabbit, a Cow, and Four Rakum

Michael Stone blocked the way as Javier peeked over Roman's shoulder at the Rider woman standing across the space with a young Rakum he didn't recognize. The tension in the air was high, but who was the most apprehensive? What was Stone thinking? And the Rabbit—what would she make of them? A posse of Rakum and a feckless Cow gathered in her tidy, all-American home?

After an awkward moment, Stone allowed them access. They lined up in the living area facing the table where Miss Rider stood, a delicate hand to her chest and her lips parted with surprise. She was pretty in a small-town way, with large eyes and flawless pink skin. Her best feature was a full mane of honey-blonde hair that trickled over one shoulder. It was no wonder Stone wanted her for himself. Most puzzling, Javier still caught no scent of Elder Dawn's mark. Presently, Simon positioned himself between Roman and Javier; it was a good idea—Stone was an unknown variable and anything could happen. Javier didn't expect what did.

"Hi. I'm Beth Rider. The Rabbit," she said with a wry grin, "the accidental author of this chaos." The woman stepped forward, her hand outstretched in the normal human greeting.

Javier was the first to reach out and Stone tensed with a low growl; he had his answer—the guy was protecting the Rabbit. Now to figure out for what purpose.

Roman stepped forward to take her fingers and he brought them to his lips. Stone made another warning noise in his throat, but restrained himself. Was Stone prepared to physically take on an Elder? If he was, he was crazier than them all. Stone had size on Roman, but that mattered little when going against a superior Rakum with training only Elders receive. But Jack Dawn's lieutenant stayed put and only his nostrils flared as the introductions continued.

Simon didn't shake the woman's hand, but lifted his fingers in a wave, his smile tight. He was clearly unhappy and Javier pitied him. Twenty-four hours ago, he had the world at his feet; a Rakum for a best friend, a baseball scholarship taking him to the good life, and a brand new truck to tote his girlfriend around in. And what did he have today? A contract out on his life.

"So? Where do you stand on all this?"

The woman was speaking to Roman, instinctively discerning him as their leader. Javier watched his Elder's expression, anticipating his response. The woman was incredibly calm for a Rabbit and it made him think of the preacher from her novels. She was probably leaning on that same faith and the realization left Javier empty.

"Miss Rider," Roman began in his most genteel voice, "will you pray for us?"

A smile as bright as the sun and bookended by dimples spread across her face. "Of course! Come in, let's sit down." She gestured for the couch and then turned to the youngster behind her. "David, bring some of those chairs in here. We'll have a little prayer time."

Stone huffed and looked at the faces surrounding him. It looked like he might speak; his mouth opened then closed again, and he dropped his shoulders. "I have some calls to make," he grumbled and turned to the open door, closing it resignedly behind him.

Javier sought the woman's reaction, but if she had one, she didn't show it. She arranged the chairs, assigned seating and then brought in a tray of sliced Italian bread, toasted with butter and garlic. Everyone reached for a piece, and Javier and Roman grabbed three. When everyone was munching the flavorful bread, she returned with a tray of bottled water and passed one to each man. Lastly, she took a seat and with a contented sigh, started with the first person on her left.

"Who are you?"

Javier was first. He checked Roman's expression before he began. It was unheard of—sitting next to a Rabbit and opening up so willingly. Even after what he had seen so far, Javier could hardly imagine Roman doing the same. A few moments ticked by and Javier didn't see anything in Roman's face that indicated he was unnerved. He looked back to the woman, held her gaze, and gave her a brief testimony of the last few days. When he was done, he was emotionally drained, and even that sensation impressed him; he was changing rapidly and he didn't loathe any of it.

After a long reassuring look, the Rabbit looked to the next in line and went around the room. When each person had his shot, she began to explain God. Javier listened intently and watched Roman across from him also soaking up every word. The kid, David, grinned like a loon, and Simon nodded in all the right places. At one point, Miss Rider was going over what God expects of His people when Roman leaned forward.

"Am I to understand that God will forgive the murders I have committed?" Roman removed his glasses and didn't return Javier's concerned gaze. "Miss Rider, before now, I have had no regard for human life. I have considered mortals an entertaining diversion." He looked sideways at Simon seated next to him, and apologized. "But I no longer feel that way. I feel that up to now, I've been deceived."

"Exactly."

Miss Rider put her hand on his forearm as she replied. Javier's eyebrows went up, but Roman did not react, where in the past he would never allow such casual and uninvited contact.

"Things are getting weird," he mused to himself, but the thought traveled to his Elder who shot him a disapproving glare as Miss Rider continued.

"You *have* been deceived. Let me explain…"

As she launched into a description of what happened in "The Beginning," Javier listened out for Stone. He was indeed on the front stoop talking on his cell. Now if only he could concentrate and overhear the conversation. He focused hard, was able to filter out Miss Rider's words, but he couldn't hear Stone at all. Javier stopped trying and looked down at his hands.

I don't smell the Rabbit, I don't smell my brothers, I can't hear Stone and he's only a few feet away… Javier was losing something. And although he knew what was causing it, he hoped that what he gained in return would be well worth it.

†

Michael shut off his call and took a deep breath. Jack Dawn was in Montgomery and was seeking them with ferocious intent. He looked up at the full moon and frowned. Half of him wanted badly to get in his car and drive away, leave the zealous Beth Rider to her God. But the other half was stronger and it wanted him to stay, to protect her to the end. There was nothing else he could see himself doing, even if it meant dying for her.

Would I do that? Would I give my life for that mortal woman?

Even though it went against everything he knew, Michael was certain that he would, and this change of heart frightened him more than Jack Dawn's punishment. Her novel may have led the other Rakum to her God, but if it did anything to him, it made him crazier than she was.

Michael leaned against the threshold and decided where to hide her for the remainder of the night. His phone call to Jesse had been helpful—Jack had already been to his house. He had Beth's driver's license so he would be here next. The last thing Jesse told him was that an Assembly had been called. Michael would have to break up the prayer meeting and divide the group.

He would send Elder Roman and his two shadows to his house now that Jack had already been there. And he would take Beth and David to Jeremy's loft. Jesse agreed that since Michael had nine such Cows scattered throughout the tri-city area, it might take Jack until sunup to investigate them all. They would have to risk it.

He checked his watch and it was nearing midnight. Michael pushed open the door and the group turned to face him. He wanted to say something that would send fear into every heart and get them moving without any ado, so he put his hands on his hips and lowered his gaze.

"Jack Dawn is coming. He has been to my house and is headed here. We have less than ten minutes to clear out."

It worked. All parties came to their feet and awaited instructions, recognizing Michael's affinity for leadership. Michael was glad for the cooperation. Things were about to get ugly.

25

A Broken Stone

"**W**hat's happening? Everything okay?"

Dressed in silk pajama bottoms, Jeremy watched with sleepy eyes as Michael checked the locks on the door and pulled the blinds all around the living room. Michael had entered without a key, as he had at Beth's earlier. Opening locks by will was something every Rakum learned during First Ritual, but there was no time to reminisce as he turned his friend toward the bedroom.

"No, everything is *not* okay. I'm on the run, little dude. Get dressed. I'm sending you to a hotel tonight. The best in town, your pick. Now go on, get dressed." But Jeremy was too curious about the impromptu visit, and now about the young man stepping out of the kitchen.

"Who's that? What's going? Is that guy with you?" Of course, Jeremy was asking if David was a Rakum.

"Yes, Jay-Jay, this is one of my brothers. We're in a hurry and I need you to throw on some clothes and get outta here."

"But I don't wanna go anywhere. What's going on? Who's after you? Is it the police?"

"*Michael...*" Beth urged him in a whisper now poking her head out of the kitchen, too.

With growing frustration, Michael grasped Jeremy by his upper arm and dragged him into the bedroom. He shut the door with a bang and looked him square in the eye, not allowing him to look away.

"Listen to me! You're in danger. If you stay here tonight, if you don't leave like ten minutes ago, you're going to die. I don't have time to explain and I can't protect you from what's coming. Do you understand?"

"But, who'd be chasing *you?*"

Michael released the smaller man and spun for the door.

"I'll bet it's that woman's fault. I told you—" Jeremy stopped at Michael's sudden angry glare.

"*Fine.* Fine, Jeremy. You had a good run. A lucrative career. Your art is going to be worth ten times more tomorrow when they find your dead body down in the basement." Completely out of time and patience, Michael left the room, Jeremy apparently stunned into silence. *And it's about time,* he thought as he joined the other two in Jeremy's kitchen.

†

"So, there's nothing we can do but sit here and wait?" Beth asked, not believing for an instant that there were no options. "Why don't we make a run for it? Get in the car and drive away?"

David shrugged and turned to Michael, who answered brusquely.

"Because it's less than three hours until daybreak. Because only one of us can handle the sun."

Michael's facial expression and body language revealed his exasperation and Beth looked aside. But he wasn't done.

"Jack has us in a corner. By now, he's been to your apartment, and has killed two of my Cows in his rampage. He's following his nose and he will come here." Michael slumped into a kitchen chair.

Beth lowered her gaze. "That means we can only rely on the Lord, now."

"*Please,*" Michael groaned and put his head in his hands.

"No, really. I belong to Him, He wants all of you for Himself so let's see what He does next." Beth met Michael's eye when he looked up again. "He's with us. He'll do something to help us."

Michael made a louder groan and stood up.

"Really?" David leaned closer, his eyes shining. "If we trust God will save us, He will?"

Beth lowered her voice to a whisper even though she was certain Michael's Rakum hearing allowed him to hear every word. "It's like this. Once you know God, you can trust him to take care of your *soul.* That means we will spend eternity with Him in paradise. It *doesn't* mean we won't be murdered tonight by that monster who hates us. I know it sounds nuts, but believers are sometimes martyred for God."

"*Judas Priest!*" Michael said as a curse. "It doesn't *sound* nuts. It *is* nuts. I don't believe my ears!" Michael's anger welled and he was shouting by the time he finished. "What have I done?"

"But," Beth continued and cut her eyes at Michael's histrionics. "I believe there is a HUGE purpose to all of this," she said and waved her arm across her body. "*Somehow,* what we are involved in tonight will affect hundreds, maybe thousands, of your people. I trust God to do His thing." Beth ignored Michael's continued noises and focused on her young proselyte. "Whatever happens next is ordained by God. I'm going to pray about it and ask for help."

David glanced at Michael with a serious nod. He then placed his hand on top of hers. "I'll pray with you, Miss Beth. Go ahead."

"Oh, this is too much!" Michael spat, disgusted. "I'm going to do my dying in the living room where I can have some peace and quiet!"

Michael stormed out the swinging door and Beth turned to David, who still held her hand.

"Okay, let's pray. Maybe God isn't finished with us. Whatever He wills, we'll accept."

Beth prayed and David nodded his head in agreement. Neither of them heard Jeremy's muffled scream two rooms away, and neither did Michael until it was too late.

†

A faint gasp and the whispery sound of cloth on cloth was enough to draw Michael to Jeremy's room.

"You okay, Jay-Jay?" Even as he spoke to the closed door and prepared to shove it open, he didn't have to see his Elder to know that he would be there. And he was.

Michael pushed the door in time to see Jack Dawn dropping Jeremy's lifeless body to the floor. No mess, no blood, he'd broken the artist's neck. A pang of regret hit Michael deep inside, but there was no time to reflect. Jack stepped over the Cow's inert form and reached out for Michael's lapel with his huge right hand.

"Michael, how naughty you've been! And to think I had once favored you above all others!" Jack's eyes were red with madness and his lips curled into an animalistic snarl.

"Wait… Master, I can explain…" Michael stumbled backwards into the living room and Jack followed holding tightly to his jacket.

"No, you shit, you can't." Jack struck Michael across the jaw with his free hand. His body recoiled from the blow, but didn't escape Jack's grip. Michael's Elder pulled him upright and looked him in the eye.

"Master…let me…"

"Shut-it. You're dead to me, Stone," Jack said and lifted Michael over his head wrestler-style as Beth and David pushed open the swinging kitchen door. He waited for them to comprehend their friend's condition before he dropped Michael over his upraised knee.

†

Michael's back broke with a bone-crunching crack and Jack enjoyed the scream that emitted from the Rabbit's pretty mouth. He dropped Michael's body to the floor and shook his finger at the woman.

"Ahhh, you again," he cooed as the Rabbit ran to Michael's side and reached for his head. Jack pulled her to a standing position by her long hair. "You've cast quite a spell on my pups. A witch, eh? And who do you have with you? Little brother, what's your name?" Jack tossed the woman aside and she slammed into the carpet near the windows.

"David! Be careful!" she cried out, sobbing near Stone's broken body. Jack savored her tears as much as her terror.

"David... what a sweet name. What are you doing with these traitors? Who's your Master?" Jack crossed the room and stood before the young Rakum, looking down on him and feigning affection. "Where did you come from?" The kid was scared stiff and Jack laughed derisively. "Are you a fwightened, baby-doll?"

He touched David's cheek and laughed again when the boy jumped at the contact. Jack dispensed with the forced levity and roughly grasped the kid's shoulder.

"Stand still," he commanded and inhaled deeply, prepared to divine answers from the youth's addled mind.

The kid wouldn't open his eyes, but it didn't worry him. He liked that the boy was terrified. He had every right to be.

"Oh, you're Tomás' pup, eh? But you've been naughty. You've been excommunicated. It's because of this female..." Jack turned his head and fixed his gaze on Beth. *This disgusting Rabbit.*"

The woman on the floor wept quietly and quiet prayers fell from her lips. Jack shook his head grinning.

"Babble all you want, *Rabbit,*" Jack said, spittle flying. "I want you to see this. Watch what your magic spell gets this boy..."

†

Beth watched Jack lift a large wooden sculpture of a rearing horse off the end table by his hand. He was preparing to swing it at David's temple and Beth cried out, leaping to her feet to grab the monster by his free arm. But it was too late and David never even opened his eyes. The sharp carved edge of the horse's mane struck him squarely on the temple, the cracking noise alerting that his skull had fractured. Almost-black blood bubbled from the wound and the young man stumbled and then dropped to the floor with a lifeless thud.

"David! I'm so sorry!"

"You should be," Jack snarled and grabbed her by her arm. "You bad Rabbit!" Yanking her into his full embrace, Jack bit down on the soft flesh of her throat. His blunt teeth could not make a clean incision, but his objective was no doubt pain and terror. Beth froze in the monster's grip and gasped. The pain was terrible, but there was nothing she could do but hang helpless, enduring a nightmare she never could have imagined.

When he tired of the futile bite, he pulled away, and she was flung to the floor unceremoniously, holding her hand to the raw but swiftly-healing wound. Two strangers emerged from the swinging door and looked at her with matching hungry grins.

"Beryl, Gage, take the traitor to the car," Jack barked motioning to David's body. Then he called two other men from the kitchen. When the first two Rakum heaved David's body in their arms and pushed the swinging door, Beth noted the large picture window near the kitchen table was wide open. "And you..."

Beth returned to her own predicament at the sound of Jack's voice close by. The two summoned goons were approaching with a mixture of lust and duty in their eyes. She shuffled backward as they neared, until she was stopped by the wall. She listened as Jack gave parting instructions to his cohorts.

"...take this Rabbit to the car."

The Rakum grunts nodded and grasped Beth by her arms, pulling her roughly to her feet.

"And Kite..." Jack wiped his mouth as if removing Beth's germs from his lips, "this Rabbit has been in hiding. I want you and the boys to initiate her properly *all the way to the airport.* Got it?"

Beth glanced back and forth between the three monsters that loomed above her and loathed the looks they exchanged. Whatever horror Michael prevented by keeping her away from his brothers when she was first marked was about to be visited upon her in force.

She remembered her faith as the two men tugged and dragged her to the kitchen door, praying it would sustain her no matter how badly she was treated.

The two Rakum rudely pushed her to the open window until they got her legs over the sill. Beth looked down three stories and a long black car waited below in the dark, white plumes coming from the tail pipe. As her feet dangled over nothingness, she thought of Michael in the next room, half-dead and paralyzed, alone with a true demon. She held on to the window frame and squeezed her eyes closed, praying for Michael in a forced whisper and ignoring the cruel hands that pried her fingers off the wood to shove her out the window.

Down below, one of the earlier goons waited as if to catch her. At least, she hoped that was the plan, because as she prayed, the two behind her shoved her free of the building. Before she even realized she was airborne, Beth landed heavily into the arms of her catcher and was tossed into the back of the waiting car.

"Go!" she heard one call to the other as all four of them piled into the limo. Peeking around the dim interior, she saw David across from her against the window, head lolling, black blood above his right eyebrow. Next to him was a bronze-skinned Rakum, his face in a perpetual sneer. This one looked her up and down and shook his head.

"This tiny thing is causing all this trouble? *Mierda!*[4] he spat in a thick Spanish accent. "To the airport. We leave in an hour."

Beth looked right as one of the goons pressed against her to bark the same directions to the driver. Done with his orders, the Rakum named Beryl looked down on her and she shivered. He had the countenance of an angel, but death filled his shining eyes.

"Beryl, use my knife."

The big guy across from her tossed a shining switchblade. He then turned to David beside him in the spacious interior of the limo and buried his left hand in the boy's hair. He slammed David's head against the glass and Beth squealed. She attempted to help, but was pressed into the seat by the one Jack had called Kite. Beryl readied the knife and awaited permission to proceed.

"*¡Cállate, Conejo asqueroso!* He can't feel anything!" Slamming his head a second time, the Rakum continued, directing his venom at David. "Didn't I teach you to stay away from religious nuts?" He

---

[4] (Spanish) A curse word.
[5] (Spanish) "Shut up, disgusting Rabbit!"

slammed the boy's head against the glass a third time, reopening his healing wounds and smearing the window with blood.

This was Elder Tomás and Beth strained against Kite's arm as David's words regarding his Elder returned to her mind. However, her waiting for the attack was over. Beth looked around the car, catching the eyes of all four monsters circling her in the back seat. She was caged and there was to be no escape. Beth inhaled sharply as Beryl took her by the wrist, sliced it deep in one quick motion, and brought the wound to his lips. She peeked out from teary eyes as the knife changed hands to Kite who scooted from his seat and fell onto his knees before her. Somehow, all four of the Rakum were going to drink from her simultaneously, just as Michael described in the beginning. How long ago was that? It seemed a lifetime.

Sweet Michael. Gave his life to save a little lost Rabbit.

Tomás laughed when Beth's skin was sliced open a third time and she gasped with pain, sitting under the combined weight of the creatures that drank from her. She could feel the first two on her right hand and upper arm and the third had made a burning incision on her left shoulder. One of the Rakum had his cool hand on her midriff, under her silky top and his explorations of her body caused her to moan with fear. Tomás egged them on with rude comments, but Beth was too much in shock to pay him any mind. She mumbled audibly, asking Jesus for help, until one of the men placed their palm over her mouth. Nevertheless, they couldn't stop her heart from calling out to her God.

And call she did until she fell unconscious.

26

Black Reasons

Stone's house might have been ransacked by Dawn and his minions, but it was so bare, Simon wouldn't be able to tell if it had been. Maybe he'd been robbed or maybe he just didn't care about material things. Considering the odd nature of his supernatural friends, he figured it was most likely the latter.

Once inside, Simon heard the sound of locks thrown and he turned to see Roman hanging the chain. Was he frightened? Simon shuddered at the possibility. If Javier's master was afraid, a helpless mortal should be terrified. He mulled his sad position, standing in the middle of the empty room, and noticed Roman staring at him, his expression grim.

"I am not *afraid*, little one." Roman watched him over the top of his round glasses. "I'm locking out human dangers—nothing more."

Javier stepped forward, damage control, Simon mused. *Try to keep the Cow safe from the unpredictable Elder.*

"Who's hungry?" Javier slung the pack off his shoulder and rummaged around as he spoke.

Simon shook his head. "I'm not. Ya'll go ahead."

He peeked sideways at the Elder who was still regarding him with serious gray eyes. Did the guy have a problem? Was he going to stop ogling? Just then, Roman smiled and Simon broke out in goose flesh; the guy was reading his mind and it was grossly invasive.

Out of his line of sight, Javier exited for the kitchen and left him alone with Roman. He tried to think of something totally disgusting to see if the Elder would catch it. It wasn't easy, but he finally formulated a coherent thought that might get some reaction other than that retarded grin.

I'd rather lick the dirtiest toilet than to look at you one more time...

Roman stepped into his face at speed and wrapped his spidery fingers around Simon's throat, pulling him close. They were nose-to-nose with Simon a good three inches shorter. He didn't know how he should react and in a split-second decision, he called out Javier's name.

"Javier is not going to be able to save you. And neither am I. You'll have to turn to God, young one. Stop resisting." Roman lowered his chin and rest his forehead against Simon's. "Or I will *make* you stop."

Simon stared blankly into the Rakum's face, too close to focus on his sharp features. Could he *force* him to submit to God? Simon had no response. Thankfully, Javier appeared and tugged on Roman's arm.

"I don't think you can *make* someone believe," Javier said with respect to his superior. "Once someone hears the Truth, the Bible says the rest is up to God."

Roman lifted his head and regarded Javier. "It says that?"

Javier nodded and said as if quoting, "One plants, one sows, but God gives the increase."

Roman swallowed, looked at Simon in his grasp, and frowned. He opened his hand and moved it to Simon's shoulder.

"Okay, kid. You work it out, but if you get in the way, I will protect Javier over you in a heartbeat. I don't know this God well enough to sacrifice one that I cherish for one who is a fool."

Simon smarted at the insult, but Javier pulled him away from Roman and toward the kitchen. The Elder followed and took a seat on the only barstool. Javier positioned Simon on the opposite side of the bar and pulled the single pan off a wall hook.

Simon looked between them and sighed. "Sorry," he whispered to his friend. He was angry at the Elder, but for Javier's sake, he wanted to smooth things over. Javier was a good friend and he still loved him, even if it looked like he may never let blood for him again.

"Why do you let blood, Simon?"

Roman grabbed the thought uninvited and Simon huffed.

"Stop that!" Simon looked hard at the Elder, but the guy's mouth turned up in a smile, as if happy to have irked him.

"I am truly asking," he continued with mock concern. "Why would a mortal do this? Part of accepting that I am *not* God is accepting that I no longer have all the answers." Roman wove his fingers together and rested his head on his hands, elbows on the countertop. "Please, indulge me."

Simon looked to Javier, but he turned to his soup; he was on his own. So why did he do it? Simon sighed and leaned on the counter. "Well... he saved my life."

Roman shook his head. "Javier healed your shoulder, took away your pain, but you would've lived if we never arrived on the scene."

"Maybe. And... well... I thought he needed me. I guess I enjoyed being needed. Appreciated." Simon paused. There were other reasons. *Black* reasons that he never fully faced and he certainly wasn't going to drag them into the light now.

"I would like to hear these black reasons." Roman leaned in and Javier stopped stirring and came to the bar.

"Yeah—what are you saying?"

Simon scowled. "I didn't *say* anything!"

"Okay, kid, just think it," Roman offered in a near whisper.

Simon hated the guy intensely. He was manipulating his memories now. Inviting him to think about them caused them to float to the surface.

Why did I voluntarily offer my blood to Javier?

Because it was cool. It was sexy. Because the lust for blood was *in.* And because maybe, just maybe, if he played his cards right, one day Javier might make him a vampire, too.

Or a Rakum.

Whatever they called it.

Simon's eyes narrowed as Roman read every last iota of his private run-on thoughts.

"You have to let that go or you'll never get close to your Maker," Roman said in a fatherly tone. Simon wasn't buying it.

"Stuff it, Roman." When Simon threw in a few expletives describing Roman's mother, Javier was immediately at his side.

"Simon," Javier grasped his forearm and waited for him to meet his eyes. "Take your time. Roman's only trying to help."

Javier's eyes were as deep and as sincere as ever. Why did Roman have to be here? He was ruining everything. To Javier, he offered another apology.

"I'm sorry." Simon took Javier into his arms in an awkward embrace. After a few seconds, Javier carefully rested his arms around Simon's back. Still in the clumsy hug, Simon glared at Roman in hard-won triumph, but Roman responded with a derisive chuckle.

"This is a first. Well done, Javier. You're becoming more and more human every second."

Roman laughed again and Simon wondered what he meant. He released Javier to catch his expression, but his friend was looking off in the distance considering the Elder's words.

Is that what's happening to him? If he became a Believer in Rider's God, was he going to become human? It didn't sound like a fair trade.

When Javier stepped back, Simon grabbed his hand and stared at his profile. Was his angelic hero giving up his deity? And for what? Some assurance that when he died he would go to heaven with Beth Rider? Simon's pulse increased, an odd panic rising in his gut. If he lost Javier, he'd lose his hope. If Javier became mortal… who would make him *immortal*?

In his peripheral vision, Roman was smiling, his face the picture of mirth, and oh, how Simon hated him.

27

Left to Die

"Stupid, short-sighted, ignorant... I had plans for you, Stone. *Big* plans..." Grumbling as he spoke in the now-quiet loft, Jack Dawn pulled Michael across the room by one arm. "You were bred to lead. The High Father is your frikkin' blood Father! How did you screw this up? *Shit!*" Jack dropped his body on the hardwood under the large living room windows.

"Uhhhh..." Michael moaned, not fully conscious.

"It lives." Jack booted the man's shoulder. "I hope you wake up in time to see the sunrise. It's gonna be a sight."

Michael did not or could not respond and Jack growled, still angry that one of his best pups would turn on him. He pulled the cord on the blinds to open them all the way and then tied back the thick red curtains assuring that when the sun came up, it would fall directly across his paralyzed disciple. As a general principal, death was not part of the Rakum penal code, but the unforgivable trespass had always been grossly subverting one's master.

"You were next in line, idiot. Did you know that? My pride and joy." Jack nudged Michael again with his toe. "I want to cleave your head from your body!" Jack swore loudly and then quieted. He needed to depart as soon as possible and the sun would finish the already-weakened Rakum quickly enough. "I wish I could be here to see it. You're a big disappointment. *Big.*"

"Master..."

Jack whirled around at the soft sound of Michael's tortured voice and placed the heel of his work boot on the side of his head. "If you say one more word to me, I'm going to crush your skull."

Michael did not speak again.

Jack turned back toward the kitchen and the open window. In the morning, Stone would be toasted to death and whoever eventually came to check on the artist would find quite a surprise. Jack jumped to the ground, not happy in the least. A night of murder was always invigorating, but a night of uncovering deceits stole the fun out of it. In addition, there was still the problem of the Rabbit, the source of the spiritual virus that had affected over one hundred of his kind. She had to be stopped. Her influence, whatever it was, needed to be reversed on the affected as well as eradicated forever.

Jack nodded to no one; he'd turn her over to the Fathers after they heard him out. The oldest of their kind would drill the truth out of her and he'd wipe her from his hands.

†

Michael viewed the sky through the open blinds, his gut warning him the night wouldn't last much longer. The pain in his back had subsided to a dull throb and he tilted his head to glimpse his lower half. He was lying on his back and his legs looked normal. If left in a light-tight environment a few days, his spine would knit together on its own, but rejuvenation powers were useless in the sunshine. Michael propped himself onto his elbows, happy his arms still functioned. When he told his legs to move, they didn't respond. Michael tried until the exertion showed on his face and he collapsed with a gasp.

Gazing blindly out the window, he sought a solution. He had to get away from the window, but he wasn't strong enough to pull his broken body out of harm's way.

"I should have listened to Jesse..." Michael's voice was too loud in the quiet house and he whispered the follow-up. *"It's Tuesday. Jesse flies in on Tuesdays..."*

Resolute, Michael reached into his jacket pocket and pulled out his cell. He punched a few keys and closed his eyes as he waited. Thankfully, Jesse picked right up.

"Speak, brother."

"Jesse," Michael gasped, making an effort to sound normal, a vanity because of Jesse's telepathic superiority. "I'm in a jam. Can you come to Jeremy's? Right now?"

"Oh, Michael," he *tsked* and sighed into the phone. "I'm just leaving the airport. Perry Street, right?" Jesse calculated the distance. "I can be there in twenty minutes. I'm going to regret this, aren't I?"

"I hope not," Michael said softly, still trying to disguise the desperation in his voice. "But if you don't come soon, you'll have one less brother."

Jesse barked to the taxi driver and then snickered good-naturedly. "I can see you, Mike. You're a mess, *shit...*" he chuckled.

"I know, brother. I know. Just hurry. And come in from the alley, Jack disabled the lift. There's a window. You'll see the light."

"See you in twenty."

The call disconnected and Michael was alone. He peered around the room, his face upside down. Jeremy's body would still be in the bedroom, but what of Beth and the kid? He hoped they were okay, but he knew better. Jack would kill Beth and turn David over to the Fathers for reeducation.

Michael shuddered with a new wave of pain muddled with despair. He said to the air, "Let them be okay."

The loft was so quiet, Michael half-expected a reply. But from whom? Who did he just speak to? Was he praying now? Like the preacher in Beth's book? Michael scoffed without venom.

Rolling his head to face the kitchen, he spoke to the air once more: "And make Jesse hurry."

What if her God *was* listening? Just in case Michael added, "Amen."

28

Chartered Jet to Hell

Beth returned to consciousness groggy and bleary-eyed, her bra unclasped beneath disheveled clothing. She remembered nothing of the nightmarish trip in the limousine and now she was aboard a medium-sized jet, the kind movie stars and politicians used to avoid the public. The second string players were present, all except their boss, Jack Dawn. The bloodthirsty bunch was seated toward the front near the cockpit doors, facing inward and conversing outside of her hearing. Alone in her corner, Beth thanked God and took stock of her body. Even though she had no visible wounds, she was paralyzed from blood loss without even the strength to look for David.

Outside, a car screeched to a halt and Jack Dawn climbed into the plane, bending his enormous frame to fit, and faced her right away.

"What's the status of the Rabbit?" he barked to no one in particular and not guarding his words.

"She's on empty, Master," the one called Beryl answered, holding her gaze as he spoke. He rolled in his lips and then moistened them with his tongue. "Want me to continue?" he asked his master without turning from Beth.

"Wait until we get in the air and then have at it," Jack said with a laugh. "I think your brother might get jealous." Jack looked behind him just as another young Rakum boarded, identical to Beryl in every way. Every detail of the man matched his twin, from his lustrous curls to his flat black pants and shirt. Jack whispered in his ear, the kid looked at her and grinned.

"She couldn't handle me, Master," he said with a sneer and left the plane. Jack chuckled and patted Beryl's back. "Go sit with her, killer."

Beryl had a few words with the other grunts on his way to her seat. Beth's stomach lurched in trepidation but could not lift her arms, much less fend off the advances of a devil.

"It looks scared," Jack joked to the other Elder and dropped into the nearest captain's chair. "Try to make it cry, B," he called while facing front. Beth watched every Rakum on the plane laugh and then fall into their independent conversations.

The cockpit door opened a crack and a middle-aged pilot poked his face through the opening. "Destination, sir?"

"The Cave," Jack said and the door closed. To the Rakum sitting around him, he spoke again. "Call your people. We're gathering for Assembly. Thirty-six hours. Go ahead, start callin'."

The Cave? Assembly? It didn't sound good and Beth whispered a prayer. Beryl had filled the seat beside hers and lifted the arm-rest. When she stopped praying, he pinched her chin between two fingers and forced her to look into his face.

"Say a prayer to me, Rabbit," he said, his voice silky smooth. "I'll be your god."

Beth inhaled and averted her eyes. The grip on her face grew firmer and his right hand tangled into her hair.

"Pray to Beryl the Beautiful and you might even enjoy his attentions," he cooed and pressed his mouth hard against hers. She held her mouth closed and whimpered. The fingers bruising her chin fell away and in her peripheral vision, the Rakum tugged at his leather belt. Beth gasped and commanded her muscles to resist, but she was as weak as a baby.

Beryl pressed her into the seat and climbed onto her lap, straddling her. His brothers cheered and he shouted to the cabin ceiling, "And the congregation said, AMEN!"

Beth prayed for help and trained her eyes to the black window on her right. All around her, the Rakum applauded their brother who pawed at Beth's body and whispered vulgar come-ons in her face. Somewhere between her final plea for help and a desperate reciting of the Lord's Prayer, the Rakum's weight disappeared and the monster left to sit with his brethren. Beth remained as she was and thanked God in her heart.

29

A New (hu) Man

Javier had had few sleepovers with Roman since he moved out a century ago, but he remembered the protocol. Serving one's Elder came naturally as he'd spent his early years under Roman's wise tutelage as well as under his roof. Earlier that evening, after they'd split some soup, Javier shuffled through Stone's bedroom closet for a change of clothing Roman could wear while his were laundered. He found a pair of work-out pants to fit Roman's slender frame and by borrowing Stone's washer and dryer, he washed his Elder's clothing and had them ready to don hours before sun up. As for himself, he'd wear Stone's leftovers; they were roughly the same build and he mostly had Roman's comfort on his mind. Now, it was forty-five minutes until sunup and Simon was asleep in the living room on a two-seater love seat.

Once in Stone's light-tight bedroom, Roman locked the door, most likely because he didn't trust the kid. Redressed in his own clothing, Roman sat on the floor against the door and Javier, dressed in Stone's faded blue jeans and a Doors T-Shirt sat adjacent to him on the perpendicular wall, his legs crossed Indian-style. The only thing in the bare room now was the two of them, the Tanakh, and the Rider novel. They left the other Bible with Simon hoping he would read more during the daylight hours and hear from God.

The room had been silent a long time and Roman periodically drilled Javier with his gaze. Before his spiritual awakening, Javier could sit for hours in total silence and lose himself in his own thoughts, but now his mind raced and his thoughts much more difficult to corral.

He read disdain in his Elder's countenance and Javier sighed, exasperated. "What is it? What did I do?"

Roman lowered his chin, but maintained eye contact. "Where did your Cow—" Roman corrected himself with a grunt. "Where did young Simon get the idea that one day he could become a Rakum?"

Javier lifted his eyebrows. "Say again?"

"Your Cow—your friend Simon—he wants to be like you. And it's not a fantasy. He believes it's possible. He's waiting for it. What have you told him?"

Javier creased his forehead in thought. He never told the kid he could be a Rakum. He thought back to their conversations, and he spent a lot of time with Simon between donation periods. He'd been to the movies with the kid. They'd been camping. They'd even taken a week-long trip to Montreal. They had hundreds of conversations under their belts. Where did Simon get such a crazy notion? Then Javier remembered.

"It might be the Lost Rabbit legend."

Roman inclined his head, "And?"

"We were talking about the Rakum and the legend of the Lost Rabbit came up." Javier shrugged apologetically now as it dawned on him that such a story might lead a human to hope for things out of his reach. The *Lost Rabbit* was one who did not suicide from his mistreatment. This mythical creature escaped his captors and while fending for himself away from the brethren, he morphed into a full-blooded Rakum.

Roman scoffed at Javier's internal monologue. "Simon's heart is wrapped around this vulgar fantasy—and he cannot reach out to God when his heart is imprisoned by this lust."

Javier's countenance fell. The last thing he wanted to do was to hurt Simon and now that he had read the New Testament, he realized he had inadvertently caused the boy to stumble. Simon couldn't hear the Truth because the delicious power that Javier spoke of as a Rakum was more appealing to the boy than a holy life spent with God.

Roman said no more. Javier closed his eyes and wondered if he should pray. And if he did, would it make a difference.

†

An hour later, they were wide awake and the sun had fully risen in the Alabama sky. Stone's bedroom windows were expertly blacked over and only severely diffused sunlight filtered through the thin crack of the doorframe. Roman imagined Javier's difficult man-boy in the other room with the curtains thrown wide, no regard whatsoever for the sun-sensitive Rakum in the back of the house. The kid was more trouble than he was worth—and he was getting worse, not better.

Roman shuffled through the pages of the Rider novel, periodically shaking his head. He had no trouble reading in the dark and he peeked over to Javier deep in thought only a few feet away. He had lain down flat, his head supported in his hands, his knees bent. He could be eight years old again if Roman thought back. He had raised a hundred youngsters since the Fathers promoted him to Elder, but Javier held his black heart. Why, Roman could never pinpoint. There had been smarter Rakum, smoother ones, more attractive ones—although Javier had a distinctive look that Roman favored. So what made this one stand out all those years ago?

Was it the way he was delivered over?

The traditional method of proselytizing adolescent Rakum involved waiting until year thirteen before taking them from the Group. But Javier's group-lair was situated on the outskirts of the infant city of Montreal where an influx of immigrants kept the population on the rise. The Rakum considered moving the facility when local community disputes between the Scots and Irish turned violent. They delayed their decision too long and Javier's home was burned to the ground in an incident unrelated to the nature of its inhabitants. The youths were hastily divided among available Elders.

It was 1885 and Javier was only eight years old, still more human than Rakum. He was too old to be added to a new lair and too young to begin First Ritual, so he was plunked into Roman's life.

Roman chuckled at the memory. When the boy reached thirteen, and initiated the invariably painful transition of First Ritual, Javier was the only Rakum proselyte he'd ever known who needed assistance with the easiest assignments. Providing help was frowned upon, but not forbidden. Roman practically carried the boy through the worst of the trials, and in the end, Javier quietly graduated a full four years after his peers. But none of that mattered. Roman had kept Javier to himself in that formative decade. Only the Fathers were aware that the youngster had been so slow to adapt. The kid was a deep thinker and a skilled healer, but that scored him few points with the Fathers who measured worth in one's ruthlessness. Roman chuckled again and shook his head. Javier had never been very dangerous to anyone.

"What're you laughing about?" Javier asked with eyes closed and a half-grin on his face.

"You don't know?"

"I wish."

Roman grunted with understanding. Javier was a poor telepath and showed almost no propensity for any other extrasensory gift. Although bloodthirsty and keenly introspective, the kid was mostly only good for companionship. He gazed at Javier again, this time not hiding the affection in his expression, but Javier's eyes were still closed. Roman shut the Rider woman's book with a loud paper noise. Javier looked his way.

"I received this book a month ago from Elder Emil."

"Emil? He read it?"

Roman and Emil spent time together in Javier's presence so he knew him well enough. Roman shook his head, but his pup was losing his night vision so he spoke aloud. "No, he didn't read it because he was *afraid* of it."

"An Elder? Afraid?" Curiosity piqued, Javier sat up.

"Three of his lieutenants and fifteen of his pups had already been transformed."

"Transformed?" Javier sounded fearful.

"Two of the younger brethren—about your age, Javie—had become entranced with the God of Miss Rider's book. These two walked into a church one night with their Cows and when they left the building, were fully human, their Rakum identity erased." Roman paused for effect and Javier understood the unspoken meaning for the two of them. "This God can literally change you into a new man."

"A new man," Javier repeated, his voice soft.

"Think about it. You worry over your loss of power, your senses are weakening. I don't know how much longer we will be as we are." Javier agreed without speaking and Roman sighed. "And there's the blood. My bloodlust is gone. Is yours? Your Cow has been with us several hours and you haven't tapped him once."

Javier's lips parted, but again, he remained silent.

"Why would I have no desire for the food that has kept our people superior for thousands of years?" Roman had never uttered such an emotional treatise, Elders never displayed weakness, and he sounded like a child to the man he supposedly governed with an iron fist. *Govern? Did I ever see myself as his master?* Roman sucked his teeth. Rakum had no sentimental familial attachments, but as his heart changed along with his understanding of the Maker, he realized he had favored Javier as a son—as if they were *human*. And now that they were aware, he worried for Javier's safety. This was *definitely* not a

Rakum attribute and Roman clasped his hands together.

"I know why Stone is protecting the Rabbit," he said quietly to Javier who listened with empathy in his gaze. "His heart has changed." Roman lowered his voice to a whisper. "He can't help himself. I know, because Javie—I am desperate to protect *you*."

"I know you are," Javier replied, his voice subdued.

"This is our trade, as you have rightly discerned," Roman continued. "If we choose to follow this God, *the* God, we will no longer belong to the race into which we were born. If we choose to follow this Maker, we will join His people. We will be mortal." Roman set the paperback beside him and slid down the door until he was lying on the smooth hardwood.

"It's already happening," Javier whispered in the dark room and held his hand up in front of his face. "I can no longer see in the dark."

"I know. Come here," Roman whispered. His vision remained sharp and he grabbed the hem of Javier's untucked T-Shirt, pulling him until he scooted over. Javier laid his head on Roman's chest.

"What will you choose when the time comes?" he asked.

Roman's heart pained for him then; he must have always had the predisposition to love, because now that the Rider woman's God had touched him, his heart ached at the drop of a hat.

"I will choose God," Roman replied and smoothed Javier's unruly hair.

"So will I."

Javier spoke his answer loudly, as if convincing himself, as well as his Elder. Perhaps, he was trying to convince someone else. Someone who may have been calling him since he was brought into the world. His biological father was a Rakum, but his mother was human. Roman frowned. The God of the humans is tenacious, and according to His Word, He always gets His way.[6]

---

[6] Read about Javier's first Cow, discovered on a passenger train to NYC, in the back of this book, BONUS: *Loose Rabbits*, #1, p.241

30

Be a Pal

Jesse stared at the light in the open window of the artist's loft three floors up. Through a shadowy haze, he saw what Michael saw when he stared at his broken body, but that was all the telepathic information he could glean from his friend.

Studying the brick wall, the metal piping that ran up it, and the fire escape attached to the wrong window, he opted for the climb. It had been years, maybe decades, since he scaled a wall and he was perturbed that he was being forced to now. He was above adventure and excitement. He had moved on. His life was now peaceful, calm, and serene. He held a lucrative job as a freelance trader and his success on the Stock Market allowed him freedom to travel, see the sights, entertain his lusts, and live well in all things. Climbing crumbling brick walls in the wee hours of the morning to rescue a soon-to-be dead brother was not his idea of fun.

Jesse cleared his mind to concentrate. Scaling the wall should be easy, but he didn't want the embarrassment of losing his footing. Just because a Rakum leaves the jungle, the jungle is never supposed to leave the Rakum. As he secured a firm hold for his manicured but strong fingers, his cell phone rang. He fished it out, knowing who it was.

"Patience, Mike! I'm right below you. Hang on!" Jesse dropped the phone into his trouser pocket and returned his attention to the wall. Taking a deep breath and hoping for the best, he climbed for the light. Hopefully, Michael had a good excuse for putting him through all of the drama.

†

Michael watched the swinging door intently, sweat popping out on his brow, hoping to see Jesse's face soon. When the door swung wide and his eyes met Michael's, he swore loudly into his raised fist.

"Jack do this?" Jesse asked, rushing to Michael's side.

"Yeah. Wouldn't even let me explain. You were right." Michael spoke with effort and pointed to his legs. "Broke me in half. You gotta help me."

A decent Healer, Jesse took stock of Michael's lower half and then glanced out the floor-to-ceiling window, unshuttered to the encroaching sun.

"The sun was supposed to finish you off, eh?" Jesse looked down at his friend's face. "What do you want me to do? This is pretty bad and we're both stuck here until nightfall. Do you have a plan or would you like me to be a pal and die with you?"

Michael made a tiny chuckle and was glad to see a return smile on his friend's face. "Get me into Jeremy's bedroom. He keeps it light-tight. We'll be safe there. You'll need to shut down the house, lock it up good. Jeremy has very few friends so maybe no one will call while we're here."

Jesse nodded, but didn't move. "And then? What about your back? I'll bet you have a plan for that?"

"Your magic fingers."

"At least," Jesse chuckled uneasily, measuring the extent of the damage to his friend's body. "Okay, here we go."

Jesse lifted Michael gently underneath his armpits and pulled him into the bedroom. Lifting his six-foot-three frame without obvious exertion, he eased him onto Jeremy's bed and did not comment on the corpse at his feet.

"Sit tight while I shut everything down." Jesse made for the door and then turned with a sad smile. "You owe me big time, buddy. You'll never be able to pay this one back."

In slow motion, Michael nodded in agreement. He purposefully averted his eyes from seeing Jeremy's body below him on the floor. *What a waste.* He had been such a nice kid.

31

A Second Dose

The Rakum jet's windows were blacked over, but the motion and sounds of the plane alerted Beth they had entered a hangar. They'd been in the air for at least two hours so she could only guess where "the Cave" was located. Still weak from her previous abuse, Beth barely reacted when the dark-skinned brute called Kite rose from his chair and hurriedly approached, hiding something in his palm. Beth managed to bring her arms to her sides as he reached her and knelt down.

"I'm all tapped out," she whispered, wishing she sounded stronger. It sapped her strength to concentrate and speaking was more of a chore than she imagined.

Kite said nothing. He grabbed her wrist and forcefully pulled it out, exposing the underside of her arm. Unable to resist, she watched with wide eyes as the Rakum jabbed a syringe into her flesh and compressed the plunger. The blackish fluid hit her bloodstream and within seconds, a surge of pure energy flowed up her arm and into her heart. She inhaled with surprise and sat upright in her chair. The fire and power that had begun in her left arm had spread to her chest, all of her extremities, and was now making its way into her brain.

Beth hopped to her feet and whirled around, seeking David. The young man slouched in the seat behind her unconscious, his head wound matted with dried blood.

"David!" she whispered, although her normal voice had returned along with her vigor. Beth knelt beside him. One of her overseers would be yanking her away soon enough, so she laid her hands on his knees and prayed aloud in the small cabin. As predicted, a steel-like hand yanked her violently to her feet. She whirled into the face of Jack Dawn, and he was seething.

135

"It makes me sick to stick more of my blood in you, but I want you standing when the Fathers take you apart." Jack smirked and waved to the closest goon. "Kite," he growled, still staring into Beth's face, "I want you to put her and her little boyfriend in the Population."

"The Population, Master?"

"Yes," Jack snarled again, inches from Beth's face. Then with a last huff of disgust he thrust her bodily into Kite's waiting hands.

When Kite had a good hold on Beth's upper arms, Jack turned and approached David. He prodded the kid's shoulder before slapping his cheek hard enough to draw blood. When David flinched and opened his eyes, Beth released a short cry of joy at the sight. Jack ignored her and pulled David to his feet.

"Gage, you escort this waste of space. Beryl, Ray, you're with me."

Her eyes smiling despite the horror of the moment, Beth stood quietly and waited for the Rakum called Gage to take possession of her friend. She couldn't believe he was alive, and even more of a miracle, that he was conscious and able to stand. Gage flopped David's right arm around his own shoulders and supported him with his left, then nodded to Kite that he was ready to exit the plane.

Beth walked as well as she could while being rudely shoved, pushed and pulled alongside Kite, and looked around the edge of the door to see where they were headed. The plane had stopped inside a windowless underground hangar that housed at least two other similarly-sized aircraft. The high ceiling was unfinished and arched with bedrock. Steel beams crisscrossed the space supporting wiring and ventilation shafts. The lighting was sufficient and there were only a few people milling about in and around the floor space.

As soon as her feet hit the hangar floor, the movement of the wandering figures came to a stop, and every eye turned to her and her keeper. Kite ignored the attention and heaved her towards a doorway at the far end of the huge room. At one point, Beth heard David mumble something that sounded like the name Terrence and her heart broke for him anew. She prayed for them both as they reached a black door marked "Private".

Kite pushed open the door with his toe and shoved Beth into the next room. Gage followed closely with David, half-pulling him as he stumbled weakly along. Beth was free from the Rakum's grasp, but she didn't know which way he wanted her to walk. The room was dark and she had no sense of an escape route.

"Hang on," one of them barked. "Let's see how this jerk's doin'."

Beth strained her eyes and could just make out the outline of Gage supporting David with his shoulder and arm. He shook the youngster roughly and then slapped his cheek nearly as hard as Jack had earlier. David didn't respond as favorably this time and her heart blossomed with concern.

"David, you can do it. Wake up," Beth whispered in the darkness. Without thinking, she reached out and touched the sides of his face with her palms. The two Rakum didn't object, so she rubbed David's cheeks softly and prayed under her breath, *"Please, Father, please…"*

David took a deep breath as she prayed and his eyes fluttered open. "Oh! Miss Beth, I'm so sorry."

"No, shhh. You have nothing to be sorry about…"

Beth was cut off as Kite again secured her painfully by the upper arm and pulled her across the room, apparently satisfied that David was well enough to walk on his own.

"What do you think will happen to them in the Pop?" Kite questioned Gage as they walked through the dark room.

"I have no idea, but they won't like it," Gage answered, and neither Rakum acknowledged their hostages in any form for the rest of their walk. Beth, for one, was happy for it.

32

What if it was Dae Lee?

"**M**ike, you up?" Jesse whispered across the room. "Sundown in fifteen minutes."

Michael lounged in a recliner by the tightly-shuttered window. He slightly shifted his weight and then twisted his now-healed back until the joint cracked. "Yeee-owch! Damn-it!"

"You're healed so quit whining, you big baby," Jesse jibed as Michael rose from the chair and stretched his fingertips to the ceiling. "Dr. Jesse at your service."

"Best Rakum doc I know," Michael grunted. Jesse's gift of healing came in handy and the blood he donated didn't hurt either.

Jesse shrugged and rubbed the stubble on his chin. "I hate not shaving."

"Now who's a baby?" Michael stepped to the bedroom door and pressed his ear against the wood. Jesse's lack of shaving supplies was the least of his worries. So the man would grow a beard. Would it kill him?

"I can't pull off a beard, Mike. My face is too pretty. You know that." Jesse fluttered his eyelashes.

"Private thoughts are private, Jess," Michael mumbled, his ear still to the door. Surely no one had entered the loft since he and Jesse holed up in there the morning before, but it didn't pay to take anything for granted. He didn't put it past Jack to post a guard, even if it meant someone endangering his life just to be certain that Michael Stone met his end. Nevertheless, there was no evidence of anyone outside the door. Michael exhaled and sent Jesse a nod. "So, what was the plan?"

"Hah! Fine question, brother! I'd like to disappear and pretend I don't know you," Jesse said with a resigned grin. "But we're called to

138

Assembly. That's where I'm going. Should be fun," Jesse said in a laugh, no distress evident. "I've likely signed my death warrant helping you. You see how they treat their beloved; I'm not even anyone's favorite." Jesse didn't rise from the tousled bed, but instead, propped his head up on his arms and watched Michael think.

"It'll do me no good to hide. I'm going, too. At least I now understand why Jack hates Beth Rider with such passion." Michael sighed and leaned his back against the door. "She's guilty. Jack was right to do what he did. How was I to know she was crazy? She looks so sweet."

"She's not crazy, Michael. She's *convinced*."

"Convinced?"

Jesse shrugged. "I've had to deal with my share of believers like Beth Rider. They're irritating, but they're not insane."

"You think so?"

"I have no interest in whatever they're smoking, but generally, they're okay, not completely unpleasant." He grinned and looked aside. "They have a strange calm about them. They're even-keeled."

"Beth is calm, that's for sure."

"I say, so what? I'm calm," Jesse replied. "And I don't have to answer to a big boss in the sky to be that way."

"Oh, you answer to a boss, we all do. One hundred and ten of them," Michael said sarcastically, lumping together the One Hundred Elders and the Ten Fathers. "Let's focus on Michael Stone, now. Do I apologize to Jack and take my punishment? Do I humble myself before the Council of Elders? Before the Fathers?" Michael closed his eyes and pictured Beth's friendly smile and gentle eyes in his mind.

"Or do you bust into the Chamber of Fathers and testify on her behalf?" Jesse added, joking.

Michael didn't laugh. He came back with another option all together. "*Or* ...do I sneak in, rescue Beth and that poor kid David, and take them into hiding? Then, for the rest of my life, hide and run and fight continually, living a hell on earth because of a woman?"

Jesse smiled. "Human wars have been fought for less."

"They say wars have been fought and *won* for the love of a woman," Michael added wistfully.

"Love?" Jesse sat up. "Rakum don't love. What did you mean?"

Michael held Jesse's gaze a few moments. How could he explain a completely illogical feeling? Plus... Jesse was being disingenuous; he had loved before. By his own admission, the dead Chinese girl still haunted him. Michael wasn't sure what love was, but he was certain that whenever he thought about any harm coming to Beth Rider, intense pain entered his soul. A sensation he had never experienced before he met her. It was unpleasant, but it made him feel more alive than any amount of blood consumed. Such a sensation of being alive—*really alive*—gave him a sense of purpose. A sense that what he did today could make a real difference in the lives of hundreds of his people. And, of course, in his own.

His eyes captured Jesse's. "Dae Lee," Michael said and Jesse flinched. "What if it was *Dae Lee* Jack turned over to the Fathers? What would you do? Answer wisely, because I'm going to follow your advice."

Jesse looked away.

"Brother, answer me," Michael pressed. "What if it was Dae Lee?" He needed guidance and more than that—he needed Jesse's support.

Jesse put his feet to the floor. Jeremy's corpse had been moved to the closet, so only the bedsheets remained on the carpet.

"If it was Dae Lee," Jesse gulped and met Michael's eyes. "I'd get her back. I would get her so far away from my kind that she'd never be in danger again."

Michael nodded, resolute.

"It looks like you've made your decision," Jesse mumbled.

Michael turned and unlocked the bedroom door. "Yeah, I have." He entered the living room and Jesse followed close behind.

"I can't go down with you. I don't feel anything for that woman. She's just a Rabbit to me." Jesse waited for his friend to meet his eye before he continued. "I care about you, though. I hate to lose you."

"Would you die for me? How deep does friendship go between Rakum? Have any of our kind ever given their lives for another?" Michael saw that his pal had no answer and he continued, mostly trying to answer the questions himself. "Beth talked a lot about sacrifices her God made for mankind, and sacrifices that man is expected to make for one another. She is absolutely positive that there is one God who watches over all of us and is constantly calling us to be His children. What do you make of that?"

Jesse shrugged, sorry that he didn't have a more profound response.

"Yeah, me, too," Michael replied. "I couldn't care less about these issues a week ago, but now my wheels are turning and my insides are all twisted. I'm different since I met Beth Rider. Is it possible reading her book cast a spell on me?"

Jesse shrugged again.

"Yeah, me, too." Michael smiled this time, a sad, faraway look in his eyes.

"Then let's go to it," Jesse sighed dramatically. "I don't know about all that sacrificing business, but I'll travel with you to the Cave. Why not? Hiding from the Fathers is impossible." Jesse walked toward the kitchen and went to the window that he had crawled into the night before. "I feel kind of weird now, too. Maybe we're both under a spell. I guess our humdrum days are over."

Michael joined his pal at the window and flipped the latch. "Let's go down the rabbit hole together, Alice. You first."

Jesse smirked at Michael's Wonderland reference and climbed out the window to jump soundlessly to the ground. Once down, he darted to the brick wall and awaited Michael's descent. When Michael was safely on the ground, they both headed quickly out of the alley and onto Perry Street. They could catch a cab fairly easily there and hurry to the airstrip.

"You could call ahead for us and…" Michael began, but Jesse was already on his cell, arranging a flight as they flagged down a taxi.

"Done," Jesse mumbled and closed his phone. The private jet would be waiting for them by the time they reached the airfield.

"Good," Michael replied, satisfied to have Jesse's help. It was going to be a nightmarish evening, but at least he didn't have to go alone.

33

Three Hundred Crazy Cows

The Population was a huge open warehouse deep inside the underground facility. Beth counted at least five floors as their elevator descended its shaft. In keeping with what she'd seen so far, the Rakum spared no expense when constructing their underground headquarters. Purposely keeping the hallways in their natural state, rock moist from interaction with the Water Table, but improving the dwelling areas with man-made reinforcement and steel, the place was truly a home for an inhuman race.

Gage and Kite shoved them through a set of double doors that revealed a brightly-lit room full of people. At the doors, an older man with graying hair and a shaggy beard approached them hobbling side-to-side.

"Yes, Masters? Have you instructions on these two?" He spoke with reverence and another emotion that sickened Beth to the core; holy fear.

"They go before the Assembly in a few hours. That's all," Kite barked and exited without another word.

Beth took a hold of David's hand. He was getting stronger as the minutes ticked by and she had no reason to believe that he might not be completely restored within the hour. He intuited her concerns and squeezed her hand.

The old man who had come to meet them eyeballed David and smiled, revealing only four brown teeth. "I'm Mathers. I run the Dungeon. There ain't nothing to say except that all of us down here are in the same boat so try not to make trouble. Are you the sort that makes trouble?"

Beth shook her head no, but at the same time realized that Mathers wasn't paying her any attention. He was looking intently into

David's face. It then occurred to Beth that the people in the population might not automatically know David was a Rakum and that she was something else entirely.

"Thank you," she said hurriedly and moved David aside to angle him out of view. "Where should we go? My friend has been injured and we need to sit down."

Mr. Mathers blinked and looked between the two new guests, then turned and pointed to a row of bleachers against the nearest wall.

"We got those bleachers and there's a row of cots across the way. Toilets are near these doors. Ain't got male and female johns, sorry, miss. We're all co-ed here. The masters prefer it if we keep movin,' so don't sleep too much. You gotta be ready to jump when they call." Mr. Mathers stepped aside to allow them to pass. "Don't talk too much to the others, either. The masters don't want you socializin'."

"Yessir," Beth replied and tugged David gently along.

Mr. Mathers wandered off the other direction. As he ambled away Beth felt sorry for him. How had he come into this predicament and what exactly was his situation? And who were all these people? The room was filled with at least three hundred souls, walking aimlessly about, and for the most part, ignoring one another. Why did the Rakum keep them and what did they do with them? Were they all volunteer blood donors? Beth pondered all these things as she led David to the bleachers and sat him down.

"Miss Beth," he said finally, his voice quivering, "Mr. Mathers recognized me and any of these Cows that look close will know it, too."

"*All* these people are Cows? All of them?" Beth scanned the group again. None of them looked their way, but she was paranoid at David's confession.

"I believe so, ma'am. I recognize a few of them."

"Why are they here? I don't understand." Beth leaned a little over her knees, hopefully blocking David from the crowd with her body. The sound of shuffling feet was all she heard, and every once in a while she'd hear someone hum a tune. "They came voluntarily?"

David nodded. "Cows love us," he said with his shoulders pulled to his ears. "They're Cows..."

"*This is nuts!*" Beth lowered her voice even more and stole a glance behind her. It was hard to believe that any human being would knowingly give up their freedom, not to mention their lifeblood, to a Rakum. Were they all crazy?

143

Beth asked a new question. "What is this Assembly? Where are we? How much trouble am I in?"

"This is pretty much the end of the line." David briefly caught her eye and lowered his gaze. "We're in Nevada, near Area 51. The Fathers bought this facility from the government in the '50s and we have a few contracts producing artillery and the like. The Cave is top secret and only select humans know where it is."

"Area 51? Does this have anything to do with the alien folklore in the region?" Beth was skeptical. Sure, she could believe in Rakum who drink human blood and defy the aging process, but extraterrestrials?

David scoffed along with her. "Maybe the alien business helps us stay covered, you know? One crazy story masks the truth."

"I can see that," Beth agreed. "How do you feel? Your head looks horrible."

David shrugged. "I don't feel pain, remember? And my skull fracture has healed..." David trailed off and Beth cleared her throat.

"Praise the Lord. Tell me more about these Assemblies."

"Not much to tell. They call them about every ten years, unless there's an emergency. I think this must be one of those." David paused and touched his temple.

Beth watched him scratch at the dried blood, thinking it must itch something fierce. And he'd be hungry, wouldn't he? She shivered as just then, his stomach growled. David snapped to attention, smiling sheepishly.

"I'm sorry. I'm tired." He yawned and caught her eye only for a second. "I'll try to focus. Where were we?"

"That's okay, David. I'm exhausted. Let's rest. Follow me."

Beth turned and climbed to the top of the empty set of metal bleachers and lay down longwise against the wall on the top step. She patted the footrest area of the first tier for David to slip his body into.

"I need you to lay in here, okay? If they can't see you, maybe they'll leave us alone to catch a few winks."

David did as she suggested and stretched out directly beneath her step. He closed his eyes and murmured softly, "There's a good chance my brethren won't come get us until nightfall. We're waiting for everyone to arrive and it takes at least two days to gather us all."

"That's a blessing. I don't think I can stay awake one more minute," Beth said honestly and turned her head to see David's eyes already closed.

"I'm a light sleeper so don't worry. If there's trouble, I'll know it."

"I know you will." Beth checked her watch. "It's 3 a.m. I'll pray for a good long nap."

†

"Hmmm," David agreed, already half-asleep. His mind wandered down the path of his past and he frowned. He'd been sent away. And what would they do to him now? How would they deal with his treason? Would he get away with reeducation—when they force a fully mature Rakum to repeat First Ritual as an adult? Or had be committed an unforgiveable trespass—would they burn him to ash or hack him to pieces and scatter his remains? Either way, he was going to meet his end.

Beth put her hand on his arm and her touch comforted him. She was so patient and kind, maybe he could be strong a little longer for her sake. She still had hope. He heard it in her voice and saw it in her eyes when she spoke. Maybe her faith could save him, too.

David dozed off and dreamed of heaven.

34

Beryl's New Game

Tucked into Barracks F, Jack rolled over and hung his right arm off the bed. He bunked with his crew and was the only one awake. Beryl and Kite were on either side of him with Gage and Ray on the far end. They snored like old dogs and Jack considered kicking them all awake to shut them up, yet he held off. His Master used to knock him out of sleep for fun. Sure, keeping the kids sharp was his job, but Jack drew the line at disrupting nocturnal bliss. Of all the abuse he endured under Father Umbarto's tutelage, sleep deprivation was the worst.

A thousand years ago, before the Fathers isolated themselves in the Chamber, Umbarto still discipled young Rakum. Jack closed his eyes and instantly saw the old Father's black, grim face; his full lips sneering, his bushy eyebrows white and invariably flaked with dry skin, and his eyes burning holes in Jack's skull with loathing only he could muster. Why Umbarto would father him and then hate him was beyond Jack's understanding, but what could he do?

Jack heard a small noise and opened his eyes to see Beryl staring back at him, his expression unreadable. Jack held his gaze to a count of five to see what he might say, but instead of speak, the kid reached out his arm. The beds were a mere four feet apart and Jack easily grasped the boy about the wrist.

"Tell me about Umbarto, Master."

Beryl sent his request silently and Jack narrowed his eyes. Never had the kid been so bold to interrupt his private mental processes, but also never had his gaze ever been so altruistic. Was the kid trying to help him? Jack snarled a response, but didn't drop his wrist. Maybe Beryl was offering his services as consoler. Maybe he overheard his mental ramblings against Umbarto and thought he needed comforting. Jack nixed the idea as soon as it arose. If Beryl thought he

146

needed comforting, that would be a sign of weakness. Now Jack was angry.

"What the shit do you think you can do for me?" His mental tone was harsh, but the boy's child-like gaze didn't flicker.

"Umbarto used to beat you."

Beryl's mental voice whispered and Jack hated the fact that it calmed him to hear it. And the kid's eyes—he could run the world with such a gaze.

"What else did he do, Master? Did he humiliate you?"

The beautiful twin must have concocted a new game to combat his boredom. If he got too cheeky, Jack would shut him down, but for now, Jack allowed a small grin and answered back.

"He used to break my legs every sunup. He would keep me awake for weeks on end. He forced me to endure the sunlight up to an hour every day even after I completed the Ritual. He'd watch my tissues melt and laugh... This scar," Jack touched the deep valley of healed-over flesh that ran down his cheek, *"he carved my face when I was five years old, knowing full well a wound like this, received before puberty, would disfigure me forever."*

The horrendous details of Jack's past did not register in Beryl's expression, so Jack continued, curious to know where the game would end.

"He starved me. Tortured me. Sent other Rakum to berate me when I was at my weakest. He..." Jack stopped, disgusted with the telling, but Beryl read the rest, pulling it right out of his mind like so much ticker tape.

What Jack refused to acknowledge in their current diversion was that Umbarto also delighted in degradation, parading the young Jack Dawn through Assembly, naked and chained. And when the laughing died down, Umbarto would compel the senior Rakum proselytes to urinate on him.

"But you survived, Master." Beryl's mental voice again, as soothing as cold water on a burned tongue. *"You are the strongest Elder. Out of one hundred, no one—not a single one—can beat you. You will be a Father one day, Master Dawn. You will replace Umbarto. You will have your revenge."*

Jack remained quiet, still locked in the gaze of the fairest of them all. The kid was right. He never met his equal, he never would among Rakum. Only the Fathers had more power, and their powers could be learned. He was intelligent and willing. He *could* replace Umbarto when the time came.

Jack smiled, showing teeth now, more of a genuine grin than he'd allowed in a long time. The kid was devious. Ingratiating himself to

Jack would profit him in many ways and Jack would not refuse him. The Beryl was lieutenant material, more than Stone ever was. And what was so special about Michael Stone? The Rakum was big and dumb, not nearly as smooth and definitely not as interesting to observe. Jack squeezed Beryl's wrist and tugged his arm until he rolled out his bed and knelt on the tiled floor beside him.

"Do you honor me?" Still using their contact to send his telepathic messages, Jack pulled the kid closer until they were inches apart.

Beryl nodded his head a fraction and without hesitation brought his free wrist to his mouth. Biting down hard on the underside and twisting his head violently to the right, he broke the skin with his strong teeth and thrust the wound at his Master. Jack received the offer and watched the kid's eyes as he drank. Beryl's gaze never faltered, his poker face never changed. He was tough. A lot tougher than Stone. Maybe as tough as Jack himself.

Jack drank what was offered and planned an inauguration. As soon as Assembly concluded, Beryl and his twin would step into Stone's shoes. When the final bell sounded on the last day of the meetings, the twins would graduate to lieutenant, supervising a thousand Rakum. Jack supped away, happy with his choice and Beryl's eyes twinkled.

So it has emotions after all. Jack smiled and dropped the pup's arm. "Go to sleep," he whispered as the boy crawled onto his own cot. He watched as Beryl closed his eyes and turned over. If Umbarto was a Rakum devil, Beryl was a Rakum angel. It balanced out.

35

David is Hungry

Beth considered the shadowy ceiling and forgot for a moment where she was. Then David mumbled and everything returned in a rush. They were in the Population and soon, they were to be taken before the Fathers. Beth shivered at the thought and checked her watch. Thankfully, the day had passed and it was nearing nightfall, although underground, only a timepiece could prove it. No matter; the ten-hour respite was a true God-send and she was fully rested. Beth said a tiny prayer and sat up.

"You awake?" she asked David softly.

"Yes, ma'am. I've been watching you sleep. You look like a princess."

Beth smiled. "Did you get any sleep?"

"A little. I hear a rustle among the Cows. They're curious about me. They might be getting up the courage to come over here and check us out."

Beth looked at the crowd and they did seem to be watching them, even though they still walked to and fro like zombies.

"Then let's resume our chat right away." Beth took a breath and smoothed down her long hair. She was still dressed in her silk pantsuit from the party and as she straightened the wrinkles subconsciously, she couldn't believe only one day had passed since she took Michael to the Stein's loft. *Poor Michael...* She barreled on and prayed for him in her heart.

"Tell me more about Assembly," she asked but David's gaze had gone soft, his face to the side. She cleared her throat and his stomach growled as a response.

"I'm sorry, I just can't concentrate. I'm getting really hungry and all these Cows..." His voice trailed off and he wouldn't meet her eye.

149

"It's okay, just try again," she said with patience in her voice. "I'm hungry, too." Beth also hadn't eaten in hours and she took his fingers lightly to ask God to stave off their hunger. Of course, David was craving blood and she did her best to put that information away.

David rubbed his stomach. "Assembly is a mandatory gathering so 99% of the brethren will come."

"Michael said there are 100,000." Now it was Beth's turn pause as without warning, her heart grieved again for her broken hero.

"Yeah, but there are supposed to be more like me. When they're gathered, they'll probably be dumped in here with us. I don't know how many there are and I don't know what they'll do in the Pop." David scanned the milling crowd. "Also, I don't know what they'll think of you. You're still the Rabbit." As if he had wounded her, David looked down embarrassed and covered his face with his hands.

Beth squeezed his arm. "Don't apologize. God has my back." Then she took a deep breath and asked a hard one—something she feared, but didn't want David to know how much. "Jack Dawn indicated that I was to be taken before the Fathers," she said with finger quotes. "Is that bad?" David rolled in his lips with a sad nod.

"*Never* has a mortal been brought to the Chamber of Fathers," he said quietly. "I'm glad you can't hear like a Rakum—dozens of these Cows are talking about it. Everyone expects you to die there..."

David trailed off and Beth worried he might tear up as he did at her house. She squeezed his forearm until he gave her a small smile. Beth was ready to encourage him further when the room's atmosphere shifted. The quiet shuffling of soft-soled shoes had ceased, and a low chatter rose up beneath them. Beth pulled David's arm.

"Let's get you to the bathroom. Maybe you can shut yourself up in there." Beth stepped carefully down the bleacher steps, David behind her. At the bottom, he put his hands in his trouser pockets and ignored the inquisitive glances they received.

Beth opened her mouth to address the crowd, but no words came. What should she say? She had no idea what they wanted or what they were thinking. As far as she was concerned, they were all stone crazy to volunteer for such duty. Beth stood mute, clinging tightly to David's right arm and waited to see what would happen.

One person in the shifting crowd broke loose and stepped tentatively forward. It was a bearded young man, mid-twenties, wearing tattered blue jeans and a soiled Nickelback T-shirt. He had dirty shoulder length brown hair, a gentle face, and huge green eyes. He stepped slowly at first, then mustered a semblance of courage and walked up to meet David face-to-face.

"Master, I'm Larry. Can I clean that up for you?" the kid asked in a Brooklyn accent gesturing to David's brow.

"No, thank you, Larry, we—" Beth began, but David cut her off with an upraised hand.

"Yes." David unhooked his arm from Beth's and held out his hand to the kid who took it. The two moved away from the bleachers, hand-in-hand like school children.

Beth reached out and grabbed hold of David's sweater. "David... don't..."

David turned to her, smiling compassionately, and pointed to one of the crowd nearby who bounded over excitedly.

"Yes? Yes? What can I do?"

It was a woman this time. Nearly seventy years old, with a tired gray expression, but her voice was full of vigor to please the young Rakum.

"This is my friend Beth. Keep her company while I am getting cleaned up. Sit with her and answer her questions. Anything she wants to know. It's all right." David winked at the woman and she giggled like a teenager.

"David? Wha...?" Beth protested, but the woman took her hand and walked her back to the bleachers.

The painfully shy and grossly introverted David was in his element, king of his domain, and for the first time since she'd met him, he looked comfortable in his own skin.

He was raised in this incredible social structure. It's all he's ever known. Beth marveled to herself and tried to make sense of the moment. She would have to let David go for now and entertain the woman who stood by eagerly to answer her questions.

Beth sighed and turned to the woman with a suspicious eye. The lady in the plaid overalls pulled her to the first bench, not releasing Beth's forearm until she was seated.

"So ask your questions, dearie," she said, hands now clasped in her lap, awaiting whatever words might spill from Beth's lips.

Beth sighed and put on a strained smile.

It was the best she could do.

36

The K'Vorkah

Many Cows were deathly afraid of their Rakum masters and for good reason. Some Rakum were extraordinarily cruel in their approach to taking the blood voluntarily given. The combination of healthy respect, reverential awe, and morbid fear was kept in balance by the particular Rakum in charge. In David's experience, every Cow he met and kept liked him, even *loved* him. He called it "the *k'vorkah*" after a popular sitcom, and it meant the same thing: he had only to pass by a human with the propensity to be a blood donor for them to come on to him wantonly.

Could he remain a mystery to this young man? Would that help them to escape when their chance came? Wondering if his hopes were in vain, David determined to let the Cow do the talking and he would try not to develop a rapport. When they reached the bathroom, Larry grabbed the handle to open the door.

"Have a seat, Master, and I'll fix you up." Larry motioned to a metal bench across from the sink and waited for David to sit before continuing. "I'm sorry I didn't see you earlier. I spent the day up top and just got back."

Larry chatted on and David worked to appear indifferent, although he liked the kid a lot.

"Old Mathers didn't seem convinced you were a Rakum; but I knew at first glance," Larry bragged with a shy grin and then pointed to David's wound. "Your blood is different, plus..." he put his hand over his stomach. "I feel it inside." He shook his head. "These Cows should've known, they should've helped you." Larry gathered a few paper towels and washed his hands.

David nodded and tried to maintain a straight face. He was so accustomed to being friendly that it was a chore to come off somber.

"Of course, it doesn't matter why you're here. You're still one of our masters." Larry offered an apologetic grin and sighed. "At any rate, don't worry. I have everything we need."

The youngster removed a small white box from the shelf and opened it, pouring the contents onto the counter at their right. He selected what he needed and gently lifted the dried blood out of the matted hair at David's temple. David smiled sadly to himself and the kid noticed right away.

"Oops, did I hurt you? I don't have to use alcohol, I could use water." Larry pulled back his hands, a bloody gauze pad in his left and a clean one in his right. He watched David's face and politely awaited his answer.

David shook his head and indicated the boy should continue and he did, expertly and with great care. When he was finished, he washed his hands, dried them on his dirty jeans, and stood before David, a wide grin on his face.

"What do ya think? Pretty good?"

David stood and stepped to the cracked mirror and examined Larry's work. His temple was free of any evidence of the violent blow he'd endured at the artist's loft. He frowned at the blood on his collar, but there was nothing to be done about that. He met Larry's eyes and nodded his approval.

"Great. This is great." Larry grinned wide and leaned back against the sink facing David. "I'd get you a change of clothes if I could, but we all came with the clothes on our backs. I'd give you my shirt, but I've been here four days and it's pretty ripe."

At that selfless and sincere offer, David broke his silence, moved by Larry's kindness. "No, that's all right. Thanks."

Encouraged by David's gentle tone, Larry replied enthusiastically. "What else can I do for you, Master?" Larry stayed in position against the wall, but raised his eyebrows. "Look." He pushed up his sleeves and held out his strong arms. "No marks. I gave a little earlier, but they healed me right up." Larry tipped his head. "One of the Elders gave me a huge jolt—said I earned it," Larry added with pride.

David feigned disinterest, while inside he was very interested indeed. The Cave was a full-time institution and some two hundred Rakum lived there year-round to keep the place running. Thus, at least a hundred humans were kept in the basement Pop on a rotating schedule throughout the year, to provide sustenance for the brethren on the job. Larry was called in for the current Assembly, and was now offering himself willingly. Add to that, an Elder rejuvenated the man after his last blood-letting; if David took his blood, some of that power would cascade to him and should feel amazing.

David rolled in his bottom lip trying not to grin, but the young man was no novice. He strode to the door and turned the bolt.

"Do you have a knife?" Larry went to the sink and splashed water all the way to his biceps as he spoke.

Out of habit, David reached into his pockets and felt his way around his keys and a few loose coins. Then he grasped a tiny wooden cylinder that housed his blood punch. It had been a gift from Terrence: a sharpened piece of oak, two inches long and narrowing to a sharp point. It sat concealed inside a wooden sheath that he could carry with him. David brought it out and Larry's eyes lit up. He took the trinket from David and pulled the sharp weapon free of its holster.

"Very cool!" he said with youthful vigor.

David thought about Miss Beth outside and what she might think if he took blood from the youngster. But even as he pondered, Larry was taking care of business. He plunged the sliver of wood into the crook of his arm, showing no sign of the sting it must have caused. Then he laughed and held his arm out. The decision made for him, David grasped the youth's arm.

"Great," Larry laughed with glee, a look of awe and satisfaction in his bleary eyes. "Just great."

David thought it was pretty great, too.

37

Rebellious Cow

Preparing to leave Stone's house, Javier sat next to Simon a long time after he broke the news. Simon leaned on his shoulder, trying not to cry. But Roman was right—it would mean certain death for the kid at the Cave. When his breathing had returned to normal, at least enough to argue, Simon sat up and frowned.

"I don't understand why you're going. Why don't you stay here? It doesn't make any sense to walk into a trap like that." Simon glared in Roman's direction, but he was looking out the window ignoring them both. Simon returned his watery gaze to Javier, his lip quivering with an expression more likely on a child than a man of twenty-one. "Stay, Javier. Please don't leave me."

Javier smiled tightly and executed a human gesture he'd seen many times; he put his arm across Simon's shoulders and squeezed, even feeling some of the emotion appropriate for such a move. He was indeed changing. How much longer would he belong to the Rakum? He shushed Simon's weeping and rocked him side-to-side.

"You'll be fine. You'll stay here three days and then return home. Whatever is going to happen will happen within the next seventy-two hours. Just sit tight and—"

"I don't care about me! I want you to stay! Let Roman go by himself!" Simon shouted, his angry words aimed at Roman. "I thought we were friends!"

Javier's gaze fell on Roman's back and he wished for some words of wisdom. When none came, he shushed Simon again, released him and stood up, frustrated that Roman didn't help more.

"Your Cow, your responsibility," his Elder sent silently.

Javier turned to Simon, happy he could at least receive telepathic transmissions even if he could no longer send them. "We'll always be friends."

"Always? How long is that?" Simon retorted still sniffling.

"No one knows how many days they have on earth."

"You can't be seriously considering giving up your power. I thought you were stronger than that. I thought—"

"Shut him up, or I will," Roman sent over without turning.

"Simon, stop it," Javier responded, rebuking with his tone. "Roman and I have to go to Nevada and you have to stay here. You have no choice. I'm sorry."

"You could choose," Simon said then stopped. He lowered his voice to a whisper and cut his eyes to Roman's tall figure. *"You can stay the way you are. Why would you want to throw away such an awesome life? You're awesome, Javier, awesome. Why would you want to be like me?"*

Javier's lips formed a sad smile and he shook his head. He could never go back. He couldn't pretend he'd never heard from God. Roman turned, as if interested in what he might respond. Javier avoided his Elder's gaze and looked at Simon.

"I *have* changed. My heart is human already. Soon my body will be as well. I hope you choose God. He's calling you, too." Javier put out his hand as if to help the boy to his feet, but Simon looked away and crossed his arms. Roman walked to Javier's side and bumped his elbow. It was time to go. Javier's hand hung in the air a few more seconds, then he let it drop.

"Simon," Javier said. The young man was still pouting and he refused to look up when called. "Simon," Javier called again gently.

Simon rolled his eyes upward, but did not turn his head. "What?"

"Listen out for God. He's trying to get through to you." Javier spoke softly knowing the kid would likely hate his advice. Simon sniffed once and nodded his head.

"Come." Roman bumped his arm again and the two headed for the door. The timing was perfect as the taxi pulled up out front, honking once. Roman was through the door immediately, but Javier hung back, his mind on the first time he saw Simon—how much he loved him. Now his love had changed into something selfless, something godly. Something holy.

Javier sighed, saddened that the boy wouldn't hear him.

"I'll try," Simon said finally and looked up to meet Javier's eye.

Satisfied, Javier nodded, waved his fingers and left the house.

On to the next adventure—to face the Fathers of their race. To face judgment. He hoped the punishment wasn't too painful.

38

Meryl Wrangles a Lonely Cow

Outside Stone's house, hidden inside a rented Tahoe, Meryl spied on his brethren as they entered the taxi and pulled away. Elder Dawn's instructions were specific: bring the traitor's Cow to Assembly by any means necessary and Meryl was supremely gifted in handling the mortals they all toyed with. Anyway, his superior telepathy picked up everything that transpired with the trio inside and they were none the wiser. One of the perks of the mental acuity he shared with his twin was advanced mental blocking; if he didn't want his target to notice his intrusion, they would never be aware of him.

Now Meryl focused his attention on the sad little Cow left behind in the dark house. He would be easy to manipulate, easy prey. He switched on the truck and pulled up the driveway. It was time to collect the prize and join his brethren at The Cave.

†

Simon exited the shower in his boxers and towel-dried his short hair. Clean again and in the master bedroom, droplets of water rolled off his head and stained Stone's hardwood floor. Simon snickered and purposefully shook his head again. Javier was gone. What did it matter to him if some bossy Rakum's floor was ruined? Simon snorted and threw the wet towel to the floor with a snap.

"That's some temper you have, little Simon."

Simon yelped into his fist. Standing in the doorway dressed in black slacks and a black pullover was a Rakum, a stranger. During his time with Javier, he met several of the brethren, but the Rakum held their personal Cows jealously. Now for the first time, he was alone with a Rakum he didn't know and Javier was nowhere in sight. The man in the doorway watched him and chuckled, humor in his gaze.

"Who...?" Simon mumbled, standing square, feeling exposed and wondering where he'd left his blue jeans. His mind was blank. It took a few seconds to realize that looking into the Rakum's gaze was making him lightheaded.

The stranger stepped toward him and stopped a few feet away.

"I'm Meryl. I heard you might be a little lonely."

Simon opened his mouth to reply, but didn't. The Rakum before him was Javier's total opposite. Javier's look was rugged, tall, broad and square-shouldered, not to mention he looked to be at least thirty. But this one, this Meryl, could pass for eighteen. He was Simon's height and weight with nearly luminescent oak-colored eyes and coffee-colored skin. The Rakum named Meryl was beautiful, and Simon had never attached that adjective to a man before. Doing it now caused him to blush and Meryl smiled wide revealing perfect white teeth.

"I like the way you look, too," Meryl said, his eyes roaming Simon's form. "So, you've been abandoned? That stinks."

Simon sighed and nodded his head. "It's not fair, either."

"No, it's not," Meryl agreed and stepped closer. Now he was an arm's length away and he reached out to put his palm on Simon's bare chest. "How 'bout you come with me? I'm not likely to let a guy like you out of my sight for long. What do you say?"

Simon looked at the Rakum's hand and swallowed. Meryl was more eccentric than Javier as well—Javier never touched him except to receive blood from his arm. Simon gulped, but enjoyed the adoration in the Rakum's gaze. He nodded his head and gestured for the bathroom behind him. "My clothes."

Meryl tilted his head to the side still smiling. "Simon, Javier's gone. You know that, don't you?"

Simon nodded his head reading everything in the Rakum's expression. Not only was Javier out of his life, Javier would be human soon. It was a revolting turn of events, but this new Rakum was regarding him with affection in his enormous eyes.

"Would you be my Cow, Simon? All mine? I want to take you places." Meryl ran his hand up until it rested on Simon's left shoulder, his other hand now touching his waist.

Simon shivered at the contact and wished he'd step back. Conflicted, he watched the Rakum's lips as he spoke. Wasn't there a musical quality to his voice that he never heard in Javier's?

"And the first place I want to take you is Assembly. Tonight. Right now. I will show you off to my brethren. Oh, how jealous they'll be when they lay eyes on you. My beautiful new companion." Meryl lowered his voice to a conspiratorial whisper to finish with, "Isn't it a joy to show off? I will *show you off*, Simon. Will you come?"

Simon furrowed his brow. Didn't Roman say he'd be dead meat at the Cave? He started to voice his concerns, but Meryl shook his head, his cool right palm now cupping the side of his face.

"*T'ffffft.* How could anyone hurt you when I am there to protect you?" Meryl stepped toe-to-toe with him now, his breath falling on Simon's cheek. "I'm an extremely covetous master and no one will come near you unless I condone it."

Simon's head spun. He blinked his eyes, knowing he was being hypnotized, but at the same time, he didn't object. He leaned forward and rested his hand on the Rakum's arm to keep his balance. "I will go with you."

"I thought you might."

Simon fought to keep his eyes open. He saw a flash of movement between blinks, Meryl was holding a knife and bringing it up, out of his sight. When the Rakum pressed the blade into the soft flesh of his neck, Simon barely felt it, his mind buzzing along, the memory of Meryl's gentle promises refracting in his mind.

As Meryl pulled him close by strong fingers in his short hair, Simon thought about the bright future ahead. He was still needed, greatly desired by the earth-bound gods he loved.

"You're a good boy." Meryl's last words before he pressed his mouth over the incision he had made in the valley between Simon's throat and shoulder.

Simon released a small sound and fell silent, leaning into the strong arms of a Rakum he'd only just met. But this one loved him already. How could they be devils when they were filled with such love? Standing in his BVDs in a stranger's bedroom, in the arms of an even stranger Rakum, Simon felt peace. All the pain he thought he would feel at Javier's departure faded away then and there.

As the seconds ticked by, Simon rested his head on Meryl's shoulder, knowing he was finishing up his impromptu meal. He had to hurry because they were headed to the Cave where everyone would see he belonged to the most beautiful Rakum in the world.

Plainly overhearing his thoughts, Meryl chortled quietly and pulled away, pressing his thumb against the dime-sized puncture wound. Simon regarded him with sleepy eyes. It was okay if this one read his mind. He didn't want to run. He was home.

39

Snake Bitten

His tiny cut healed, Larry covered the short distance to the exit and unbolted it, only to then lean upon the closed door. When David said nothing, he cleared his throat. "Master, is there anything else you need?"

David sat on the bench, leaning back with his long legs stuck out in front of him. He felt sublime and he wondered if his grin looked as stupid as it felt. Now Larry was trying to offer him something else.

"What do you have left?" David asked softly, still trying to be mysterious. The amiable Cow had made him as a softy, but he could still play it tough.

"Grant. He's one of my buds. He could join us if you think he'd be any help. You were pretty weak when you came in."

David's lips parted, taken off guard. Two Cows at once? He'd never done such a thing before, but the kid had a point. He *had* been almost destroyed only hours ago. Perhaps the extra boost would give him an edge in the confrontations to come. David nodded his head and Larry left the lavatory.

David got to his feet and stretched, his joints popping with renewed vitality. Briefly, he wondered how Beth Rider was faring. She was strong spiritually and he drew most of his strength from her, but in here, alone with Larry and soon a Cow named Grant, he was king. Was it so bad to enjoy his superiority a little longer?

Why do I feel guilty? I've never taken from anyone who didn't want to give it. David sought an answer within. When he couldn't find one, he sighed. It had something to do with Miss Rider and her Gospel, but what, he hadn't yet determined. As he stepped over to the cracked mirror, the door opened and Larry entered with his friend.

"Master, this is Grant. He came with me from Vegas. We've been

160

serving the brethren together for almost eight years." Larry hung back as Grant took one step forward and stopped, his eyes averted.

David leaned back on the sink and crossed his arms. Grant appeared to be Larry's age with bright orange hair cropped into a crew cut. His pale skin was dotted with freckles and his lips thin and drawn. In stark contrast of his pal, Grant did not look happy.

David tipped his head and frowned. "What's wrong with you? You look miserable." Larry punched Grant's shoulder and swore, but the man remained silent. "You got a problem?" David asked, his mood turning black.

"Grant! Your master is asking you a question!" Larry looked at David, his eyes pleading for forgiveness, but Grant didn't budge or speak. He stood stock-still, eyes straight ahead, looking at nothing. David waited another moment, but then sighed when the kid refused to reply. He had decided to set aside his indignation, as was his practice in general, and rejoin Miss Rider. As he passed Grant, the young man grabbed a fistful of David's loose sweater.

"I know who you are and I don't want my blood in you when they come to burn you up. Kiss my ass, you… you… *TRAITOR!*"

"Grant!" Larry cried out, but David raised his hand to quiet him.

"So, that's how it is?" David leaned into the young man. Now only inches apart, the kid flinched and stepped back. *"Nuh-uh…"* David grabbed his neck with one strong hand. "You would shout at your master?" David applied pressure with his fingers and narrowed his eyes. "Don't you know that I could twist your head off before Larry could cross the room?" Taking a cue from watching his Elder deal with those he disdained, David brought his second hand to Grant's throat and squeezed. "I'm your master, you shit!"

Grant gasped, a respectful terror finally reaching his eyes. David's heart pounded inside his chest—he had never been so incensed and the sensations alarmed him. *This is what Tomás wanted me to learn! This is the brutality my master said I was missing!* The realizations hit David invisibly as he watched the fear blossom in the redhead's gaze.

Larry came up behind his friend and pleaded with David. "Please, Master, he's not himself. Please, don't hurt him…"

"Leave the room and watch the door," David grumbled to Larry, never releasing Grant from his gaze.

"Master," Larry began, but David growled—again imitating Tomás—and the kid hung his shoulders and left. When the door closed on its pressure-sensitive bar, David turned the deadbolt with telekinesis and fixed his attention on his captive.

"Okay, little Cow, tell me again why you hate me, your Master." David watched his eyes dart back and forth, no longer interested in taking the man's blood, but as yet unwilling to forgive him for his insolence. "My brethren have a punishment for Cows who rebel."

Completely repentant, Grant whined, "Master, I'm sorry… I'm stupid!" he squeezed closed his eyes and David's chest constricted— he'd never frightened a Cow and he didn't like it. He was within his rights to punish the youth; even in his present dilemma, he was still required to discipline any Cow who lost perspective on who was in charge.

Grant pushed up the sleeves of his dirty shirt. "Let me make it up to you, Master," he replied shakily and lifted one arm to peel free a white bandage. David reflexively glanced at the wound; the Cow had given blood recently, the laceration deep and ruthlessly inflicted. Still, he didn't want to let the boy off, no matter how delightfully his stomach reacted to the scent of his blood.

"I will do anything—anything to make it up to you." Grant allowed his arm to drop as if David had lost interest in his offer. He grabbed David's gaze and furrowed his brow. "If you need something else, then? What? I will show you I love my masters."

The Cow had become pitiful, offering sexual favors that David read clearly. Not interested, he grasped his wrist and licked his lips.

"My brothers would be very disgusted to learn how you just spoke to me," he said, his voice calmer and his eyes on the scabbed wound.

"I'm not very bright…"

David dropped the contact with the man's throat and forcefully stretched out his arm. The scab ripped causing a small rivulet of blood to ooze free of the wound.

"Well, I'll take your blood, but I still might have to kill you later," David mumbled. And he was serious. At least he hoped the kid thought so, anyway.

40

Smells Like a Traitor

Within the hour, they were in the air. Roman sat in one of the swivel chairs in the first row and Javier was relegated to the rear of the plane. They weren't the only Rakum headed for Assembly and the jet was carrying four already when it was routed to Montgomery to pick them up. One was a reclusive Elder named Kilmeade and the three Rakum with him were his pups.

Javier reached for a magazine stuffed in the pocket of the seat in front of him and flipped through it, seeing nothing. He was too busy intuiting an array of mixed emotions from the brethren around him. Javier's telepathy had always been nearly non-existent, but since he'd read the Rider woman's novel, his gifts of intuition and empathy doubled. He sensed that Elder Kilmeade knew he and Roman were traitors, but what he thought about it, he couldn't read. The three Rakum sitting directly in front of him knew something strange was afoot, but they weren't sure yet what their super-keen senses were telling them. Javier decided to play it safe and remain mum. If Roman wanted their secret out, he would have to do the exposing.

After a few minutes, Javier turned another page and felt someone watching him. He looked up to meet the eyes of one of the brethren. He had turned in his seat and his gaze was none too friendly. Javier gave the normal greeting, but the Brother sneered in response.

"I thought I smelled something fishy." He jabbed the guy next to him who also turned in his seat to look at Javier. "There's something wrong with you, my man. You don't smell right. You're one of those traitors, aren't you?"

Javier opened his mouth to respond, but Roman beat him to it.

"Face front, pups." Roman spoke his command without turning.

Javier watched the two Rakum exchange a glance, deciding their next move. Roman didn't want them to think about it too long. He barked his command again and this time stood and faced them in the confines of the small jet. He stooped his 6'3" frame, one hand on the back of his seat and one at his chest. When the Rakum still didn't respond to his liking, Roman lowered his voice and put his free hand on the Elder next to him. Without turning and in solidarity, Kilmeade covered the hand on his shoulder with his own.

"Face front or I will *make* you face front."

The two Rakum settled back into their seats and Roman glared at them another moment before sitting. He had a quiet word with Kilmeade and then everyone fell silent.

Javier shook his head in wonder. Even if Roman was slowly morphing into a human, he still commanded the brethren with frightening authority. And why was Kilmeade so willing to back him? Javier hoped he'd have a moment to ask him when they reached their destination. What would their reception be like? He'd been to many Assemblies, but this time, things would be different. This time, the Elders would likely grab them as soon as they landed and take them into custody. And what would the Fathers order for them? Reeducation? Torture? Death? No one had ever been punished to that extent in Javier's lifetime, but there were rumors, legends that it had been done before, two thousand years ago when many Rakum fell away and were never seen again. Javier's heartbeat quickened and with a palm against his chest, he marveled at the sensation.

"We will be released into the Population where we will find Beth Rider." Roman's telepathic voice soothed Javier's frazzled nerves. Then he added, *"And she will pray for us."*

Javier nodded his head. *"And everything will be all right?"* Roman did not reply. Javier tried again. *"The God of the humans will take care of us, right?"*

"The God of the universe will save us. His Book says so. Rest easy, Javie. We'll be there in an hour."

Javier nodded his head again and leaned his seat back. If he closed his eyes and fell asleep, would he dream about God? Or would he dream about the life he was throwing away, his life as a Rakum? To clear his mind, Javier pictured a blank wall and stared at it. Before long, a phrase appeared on it in big bold letters. The wall read, *God is my Salvation.* Javier smiled and dozed off.

Gotta Bite the Bunny

The swinging double doors were forced open from the outside and Beth watched four men stumble in as if they had been pushed from behind. Beth stood from her seat on the bleachers and pondered what to do. The four men appeared to be no more than mid-twenties. Were they Cows, Rabbits, or traitor-Rakum? She had no way to discern the difference, at least not from fifty feet away.

The youngsters stood in a huddle, eyes darting about, not moving away from the door. As she watched, Mathers shuffled up to meet the quartet, spoke with them, and then bowed low and stayed there. Beth grimaced, recognizing the reverence and hating it as before. They were traitors like David, and there was no telling how many more would be coming before she was called out of the Population to go before the Fathers.

Beth took a deep breath and paced a few steps toward them. Two of them looked up and met her eyes and her courage evaporated. David said they would sense her condition and she looked toward the bathroom. He was still in there, doing what, she could only guess. When she retrained her eyes to the small group of men, they had started over. Beth hugged herself and called out David's name. Ignoring her plight, the Cows Wanda and Larry looked away. Beth sighed and waited.

"Are you Beth Rider?" A slender youth reached her first, rubbed his nose violently, and then shoved his hands into his pockets. He met Beth's eyes, but wouldn't hold her gaze. His dark brown hair was long, shoulder length, and his complexion ashen. But most of all, he looked starved. She nodded her head and the youth exhaled with apparent relief. The other three with him came to his side and stood in a semi-circle around her.

"I'm Peter, and this is Nally, Geoffrey, and Spinner." He pointed to each man in turn and spoke in low tones, aware of the crowd

165

milling around them. "We heard you were down here. Where's Snake from Miami?"

Beth looked toward the restroom and managed a half-smile. She still didn't know their intentions; they knew about she and David and that could mean different things.

"I read your books. I believe in God. Do you think you can pray for me?" the one called Nally said and took a step toward her.

Beth smiled warily. "Of course, Nally. How about the rest of you? Would you like to pray?" She glanced to the other men in turn, and only Peter nodded. "Okay, Peter and Nally, let's go over here to the bleachers."

Feeling braver, she caught the hungry gaze of the one named Geoffrey and gestured toward the restroom. "Why don't you two go check on David? He should be cleaned up by now. He's in the bathroom over there through that door."

The one named Spinner turned as if to obey her suggestion, but Geoffrey drew close and stuck out his hand, his jet-black hair and thin mustache in perfect contrast to his ethnically bronzed skin. "Miss Rider…"

Beth didn't trust the dark look in his eye, but what could she do? To these young wayward Rakum she represented her entire religion. If she wasn't brave, she was lost. Beth put out her hand, aware that the other three men were holding their breath. Was this one their leader or had they all met in the elevator? The Rakum took her hand and brought it to his face.

"You smell…" Geoffrey inhaled deeply as her fingers reached his chin and he kissed the back of her hand. "…very nice."

"It's is none of my doing, you can bet," she whispered and tugged at her hand. "Let go, please." Beth spoke firmly, but still in a whisper. If he didn't want to let go, there was nothing she could do about it. The Rakum mulled it over, his cool fingers grasping hers firmly. Finally, he opened his hand.

"My pleasure."

She turned for the bleachers and thanked God in her heart. It was so easy for her to forget that she smelled like dinner to the Rakum, and when Geoffrey reminded her, it made her blood run cold. Beth led the two willing Rakum in prayer and hoped for deliverance.

†

"Oh, sorry, dudes. Excuse me." A young red-headed Cow pushed into them as they entered the restroom. When he met their eyes, he gasped and sputtered, "Oh, I'm so sorry, please excuse me..."

"Don't worry about it. Just beat it," Geoffrey mumbled and entered the bathroom followed by Spinner. The Cow disappeared in the crowd and once inside, Spinner re-locked the deadbolt.

"Snake from Miami? David? You in here? I'm Geoffrey and this is Spinner. We're from Oklahoma."

David flushed the toilet and came out of the stall.

"So, you're starting to arrive? My fellow traitors?" he asked with a single nod.

"We're the first. I overheard my master saying that there are probably about a thousand of us." Geoffrey leaned against the wall and eyed the Miami Rakum up and down. He didn't look as if he'd been almost destroyed a few hours ago. He started to ask about it when Spinner interrupted him with a thought of his own.

"I heard that at least ten of the Elders are affected. That's pretty amazing." Spinner was shorter than his partner with hair more brown than black and features more akin to an Eskimo than a native Oklahoman.

"Really? Cool," David replied, washing his hands in the sink.

"Say, Miami, did you bite that Rabbit? She looks pretty yummy. How long have you been with her?" Geoffrey's eyes glittered.

"First, my name is David, and second..." David paused and then his voice hardened. "Miss Rider is our friend and spiritual leader, so leave her alone."

"Don't get sore. Geoffrey and I haven't eaten in almost a week. We've been incarcerated since Wednesday and they didn't feed us at all. Nuthin'." Spinner came to David's side, begging for sympathy. "Not even water."

David nodded his head and offered a tight smile. "I'll get you hooked up." He went to the door and turned the deadbolt. "There is a free ranger in here named Larry who will know who's available for donation. Wait here."

Spinner and Geoffrey nodded and watched him leave.

Geoffrey sighed audibly once they were alone and leaned against the tiled wall behind him. "Spin, I'm not gonna go down with the rest of you guys. You know that, don't ya? I'm obviously not as convinced as I was before."

"Me neither. I was so sure a week ago, but now?" Spinner sat on the bench across from his friend. "I rather like my stomach full."

Geoffrey laughed in agreement and walked over to the mirror. He turned the faucet and removed his sweat-stained shirt. "Maybe I can at least get cleaned up. I must smell horrendous. I don't think I've ever been this filthy."

Spinner mumbled his agreement and watched absently as Geoffrey splashed the cold water on his face, neck, and arms. His own stomach felt so shriveled that it might as well be dead and he felt like joining it in hell. Sure, the Rabbit's novels had somehow caused him to believe, but the hunger inside now was strictly the fleshly kind. Maybe living a life of pleasure and self-gratification would be worth spending eternity in hell. Spinner sighed and rubbed his face.

"What's on your mind?" Geoffrey asked, interrupting his inner turmoil. "You wanna bite that Bunny as much as I do?"

Spinner laughed nervously and met his pal's eyes in the reflection of the mirror. "Like we'd be able to get close enough to do that. You saw that Miami dude. He's pretty determined to protect her. And Nally and Peter? They're just as whipped as he is." Spinner rubbed his middle and nodded to Geoffrey's reflected gaze. "But I'd like to. Oh, how that would make my day."

"It'd make my whole year," Geoffrey added wistfully and shrugged his shirt back on not bothering to button it up.

"It'd make my whole millennium," Spinner laughed and stood to cross to the sink.

"Huh. Me too." Geoffrey moved aside to allow him access and he paced the room behind him slowly, wondering how difficult it would be to get what he desired. He went over a few scenarios in his mind and then stopped pacing.

"Do you think you could take that Miami dude?" Geoffrey watched the younger Rakum as he doused his upper body with the icy cold water. The kid looked strong enough, but Geoffrey knew that true Rakum strength came from within and Geoffrey didn't think he had any special aptitude for battle.

"Uh," Spinner splashed water on his face one more time and then shook his head violently, sending water droplets in all directions. "I dunno. I don't think so. I've haven't really fought anyone since First Ritual." He shrugged his faded blue T-shirt back on and smoothed his spiky hair. "I'm a lover, not a fighter," he said with a wink.

"Lotta good that does us now." Geoffrey hid his disappointment and kept his voice even. Deep down, he hadn't given up on taking the

Rabbit from Miami by force, if he could. "I had my first Rabbit about twelve years ago. It was the only time, but I'll never forget it."

Spinner nodded appreciatively and leaned against the wall near the sink. "Oh, yeah. Back in '92, I ran across an Elder who had just marked a Rabbit. I was making my rounds when Elder Brandon showed up in the same building I was in."

"You're shittin' me!" Geoffrey said incredulous at his pal's fortune.

"Master Brandon stepped out of the elevator as it opened and told me where he'd left the Rabbit. Of course, I could smell him, and ohhh." Spinner rolled his eyes with the memory. "Ohhh, what a delicious week that was."

"A week? Incredible!" Geoffrey was truly jealous and he pounded the bench. "All by yourself? For seven whole days?"

Spinner nodded, shrugging his shoulders. "I took him to my apartment. I locked the door," Spinner laughed and his black eyes glittered. "I had this buddy named Joiner who finally convinced me to share. Man. That was a good time."

"You got that right." Geoffrey was still reeling with the knowledge that this short, lean and muscular youth before him had been host to a fresh Rabbit *alone* for an entire week. "You are one lucky dude."

"Yeah," Spinner agreed still smiling. "I sure used to be. But this..." He gestured with his hand to the room around them, "I never should've read that book."

"Me neither." Geoffrey leaned against the wall and watched the door. When the Miami dude returned with the Cows, he was going to test him. Push him a little. And perhaps see if he could take the Rabbit by force. It would be so worth it.

42

Don't be a Baby

The ride on the jet had been interesting. Simon sat beside Meryl in the back row with every other seat occupied by Rakum. They noticed him, but none overtly acknowledged his presence. Meryl also did not speak to him and he dozed most of the way. When Simon awoke, his neck and shoulder throbbed from the wound the Rakum had inflicted.

Presently, Simon was tailing Meryl down a long hall where black walls ran with thin rivulets of water, the air damp and musty. They were at least three floors below ground as he counted the elevator dings, and the doors they passed sported a three-digit number. Simon winced as he gingerly touched his neck. Meryl had bandaged it, but it burned as if still fresh. Simon understood that not all Rakum were healers, but why did Meryl have to draw from his throat? Javier never did and the Dracula bit was much more alarming.

The Rakum stopped walking and turned to meet his eye. "Is it so bad, little Simon?"

Simon shook his head.

"Good. Complaining doesn't become you and it pisses me off." Meryl pushed open the next door they reached and stepped inside. He flipped a light-switch and a gauzy pink light filled the room.

Simon took in the room's appointments. It was large, twenty-four feet long, and five twin beds lined the far wall. Through a wide, door-less opening to his right, he spied a bathroom, counting three toilets and three shower stalls with fiberglass doors.

"This is my room." Meryl pulled off his black T-shirt and stepped toward the bathroom. "Make yourself at home."

Simon watched him leave. He was hungry, but he doubted the room was stocked with tuna sandwiches. His eye fell on a small refrigerator tucked in between two '60s-style couches. He dropped to his knees to look inside only to find it stocked with booze and beer.

Meryl called from the bathroom, "My brother's bringing you a sandwich. I want you to be *really* nice to him." Then the shower came on and Simon's stomach grumbled louder. He settled into the stiff couch and his toe disrupted a stack of skin mags piled on the floor. As he stooped to straighten them, the apartment door opened.

"Oh, my," the stranger breathed, looking him over in a ravenous glance. "Are you for me?" he added his head to the side.

Simon came to his feet and his jaw dropped; Meryl had a clone. The Rakum who entered was identical to Meryl in every way.

The twin smiled with approval as he approached, a brown paper bag in his hand. "Meryl was right. I mean, *shit*..." he chuckled, shaking his head. "How ever did D'Millier let you go?"

Alarmed without knowing why, Simon looked to the bathroom door for Meryl.

"I'm Beryl. We serve Elder Jack Dawn. Do you know this name?" Beryl reached out to touch Simon's cheek, but Simon inhaled and fell into the couch. "Why are you so skittish? You're a Cow, right?"

"I—" Simon began, but Beryl shushed him and handed over the sack.

"You've been spoiled. Meryl and I can correct that. Here's a sandwich..." Beryl maneuvered around Simon to sit against him. "Go ahead. You'll need your strength," he snickered.

Simon opened the bag and removed the sandwich without taking his eyes from Beryl, still completely unnerved at looking into the face of Meryl's exact copy. Plus, Beryl was *creepy*.

"How can I be creepier than Meryl if we're exactly the same?" the Rakum asked, his winning smile to one side.

Simon peeled back the commercially-sealed sandwich wrapper and apologized. "I've had a weird day, I'm sorry."

Beryl laughed. "I guess you have. Dumped by a moron and picked up by a prince. You're one lucky dude. Hey, you know what? Maybe Jack will let us keep you. I guess you know he brought you here to die."

Simon lowered the sandwich as his chest tightened. That was not at all what he had signed on for. He was going to be Meryl's favorite. Simon shook his head. "No, Meryl said..."

"Don't be a baby. We'll put in a good word for you. Our master favors us, so who knows?" Beryl winked and bit his lower lip. "Are you going to eat that sandwich?" The Rakum made a grab for the wrapper and took it out of Simon's limp hand. "Show me your neck."

Simon's eyes grew wider wishing Meryl would return. As the thought crossed his mind, Beryl laughed and called toward the shower.

"Get in here, brother. Your new boyfriend's afraid of me."

"Stop scaring him. He's sensitive." Meryl exited the bathroom, bare-chested and still wet from a fast shower, wearing possibly the same black slacks. He grabbed his T-shirt off the floor and shrugged it on. "Simon, my pet, is wicked old Beryl scaring you?"

Simon hesitated recognizing Meryl's patronizing tone. He'd been played. The scene at Stone's house, a farce to get him to voluntarily follow Meryl. Simon shuddered and regretted it, because both Rakum smirked when he did.

"You're much too beautiful to waste, little Simon." Beryl wrapped his palm around Simon's near thigh and massaged the muscle. "Master Dawn might let you stay if you please him. Can you? Please all of us?"

Simon's face drained and panic struck his heart.

"I want to know—three at once? Hmm?" Beryl pressed and moved his hand to Simon's shoulder. He pulled him close and sniffed dramatically, stuffing his nose in Simon's blond hair.

"He can do it," Meryl said. "Look at him, I mean, *shit*. He's perfect." Meryl met Simon's eye and gave him an adoring gaze. "Don't fret," Meryl added. "Jack wouldn't want you to go to waste any more than we would."

Simon struggled to his feet, wishing more than anything to be home again, under the covers. "I-I don't understand. What are you saying? I thought… What do you want?" he sputtered, his mind racing with other uses the Rakum might have in mind.

"We want to be *pleased*," Beryl said also standing up. "We'll be careful not to hurt you too much. Anyway, Kite's a healer—he'll fix you if we go too far." Both Rakum stepped forward and each took one of his arms in their hands. "Now, show me your neck."

Simon pulled away, struggling in vain. He then closed his eyes and shouted Javier's name. Roman's face popped into mind and he belted his name out, as well.

One of the twins covered his mouth and the other stripped off his shirt. Simon twisted in their iron grip and when the gauze bandage ripped away, he shouted for Roman in his mind. The arrogant Elder was an asshole, but Javier swore he was just.

Attached to his fiery wound, Beryl bore down on him forcing Simon to his knees. He clenched his jaw under the heavy hand that covered his mouth and continued to call out to Roman in his heart. Then, before he passed out, he remembered the God of Israel; the God of his people. And he remembered the Messiah who healed so many people in His day.

Simon opened his eyes and looked at the ceiling in the strange rosy light and he asked the Messiah to help him. Even though he was losing consciousness, he knew he'd been heard.

43

A Protective Elder

When the other Rakum disembarked, Roman stood by the cockpit door and gestured for Javier to hang back.

"Better than any Elder, Kilmeade hears the chatter of the brethren. Brace yourself; Simon is here."

Roman's words pierced Javier's heart. "Where? What're they doing to him?"

"He's with Jack's men and they *will* abuse him."

Javier's chest constricted with worry over his friend. "What can we do? We have to do something!"

"We proceed as planned." Roman laid his hand on Javier's shoulder. "You're still a Rakum; control your thoughts." Then Roman added with a kind nod, "God will watch over Simon. Agreed?"

Javier took a deep breath, compartmentalized as he'd been trained, and nodded. In an even tone, he asked, "So, Elder Kilmeade... he's with us?"

An almost imperceptible smile touched Roman's lips before it disappeared to be replaced with the serious grimace of the hour. "Kilmeade is my blood brother. That is all you need to know."

Javier's eyes widened; Roman had a twin. The men only vaguely favored so he'd never considered such a thing. Roman refused to divulge more so Javier counted the stranger a friend and let it drop.

"Good boy. Now, come." Roman gestured for the open door. "Stay close. No one will lay a hand on you. I will protect you."

Javier accepted Roman at his word and headed down the steps. As soon as his foot touched the hangar floor, four burly Rakum stopped what they were doing a short distance away and headed toward them. Javier stood in place and Roman was by his side when the foursome arrived. After that, everything happened quickly.

Without a word, two of the brutes reached for Javier. One guy's fingertips actually brushed the material of his shirt, but neither got any closer than that. Faster than his eye could follow, Roman shoved both men away with enough force to leave them sprawled on the ground. Javier had seen similar moves as part of his education, but never in practical use.

The other two Rakum considered the punishment their brethren received and eyed the Elder dishing it out. Javier expected Roman to speak, but when he saw the guy on the left flinch and twitch his eye, he knew Roman was communicating telepathically. Whatever he said was giving the bullies pause.

Javier watched Roman's heroic deflections and did not notice one of the defeated Rakum crawl to his feet and come up behind him. A second too late, he looked back, only to be clocked over the head with a ball-peen hammer from a nearby toolbox. Javier stumbled forward and then to the side, but Roman caught him and eased him down. With his vision blurry, but his hearing acute, he heard Roman speak for the first time since they exited the jet.

"That is the last thing you will do tonight."

Roman grasped the man by the head, one hand on his chin and one at the base of his skull. He pulled the Rakum's face to his and thrust his hands in opposite directions. If he'd applied even one more ounce of strength, the Rakum would have lost his head altogether. But Roman was the picture of self-control as he dropped the limp body onto the hangar floor. He held his hand out to Javier, a dangerous glint in his eye. Javier took the offered hand and came to his feet. He rubbed his eyes until he could see clearly and inclined his head to Roman that he was ready. It was an impressive sight, seeing his Elder so inflamed.

The two aggressive Rakum stepped back, their faces a mixture of hate and fear. Several other Rakum had approached by now and they all studied the scene without a word. Javier thought it strange for no one to speak; Rakum weren't known to hold their tongues when angry. But then again, maybe the brethren that surrounded them were afraid of Roman's mood. Javier knew he would be in their shoes.

Across the room, Elder Kilmeade awaited standing in the opening of a set of double doors. He nodded to Roman who tugged Javier along, experiencing no additional provocations from their brethren. At the doors, Kilmeade gave Roman a private word and allowed them to pass. It was dark and since he no longer possessed the ability to see in such low light Javier reached for Roman's coat.

His Elder slowed his pace and then took his arm. After another twenty blind steps, a door opened and a dim bulb hung on an exposed wire in the small foyer.

"Kazak," [7] Kilmeade said quietly and disappeared the way they came. Javier smiled. So far, so good. Was Rider's God helping them? If He wasn't, it was an incredible coincidence that they had gotten so far without a hitch.

Roman pressed the down button on the elevator and turned to Javier. "Are you ready?"

Javier raised his eyebrows. "For what?"

"To meet God."

Before he could reply, the elevator door opened revealing a Rakum waiting inside. It was Beryl, who Javier recognized from past Assemblies.

"Going down?" he asked, stepping to the rear of the car.

Roman put his hand to the threshold holding the elevator door ajar and gestured for the kid to get out.

"I'll ride with you, Master. I've been ordered to escort you."

Roman remained where he was. "Exit the elevator, pup."

Javier looked between the two men. Was he about to see another Rakum nearly lose his head?

Beryl smiled and his little-boy dimples belied his evil heart. "I don't answer to traitors, Elder Roman."

Javier shook his head a fraction as Beryl met his eye, but the kid's arrogance was well advanced. He stepped toward Roman and reached for the lapel of his long coat. Javier stepped back as Roman reached past him, grasped the youth by his throat, and yanked him from the lift. Beryl was tossed through the air and he slammed against the far wall. The cinderblock didn't give way, but Beryl's bones *did*. Javier knew quite a bit about anatomy, but with such a multitude of fractures to identify and with his growing loss of Rakum abilities, he lost count at fifteen. The last to break was Beryl's coccyx as he slid down the wall to land hard on his rear.

Javier empathetically winced and boarded the elevator wondering if Roman had overdone it. Did his Elder have a previous beef with the young Rakum? Either way, the brutal sight replayed in Javier's mind.

"I suspect word will go out that you're not taking any guff," Javier joked as the doors closed on the sight of the broken Rakum.

---

[7] (Hebrew) literally, "Be strong", the common hello / good-bye for the Rakum race.

"Trust me." Roman gave Javier a small grin. "He had it coming."

"And you still got it," Javier mused truly thankful.

"I'm going to need it. Now we face the Population."

"And the other traitors?" Javier asked as the elevator stopped on their floor.

Roman didn't answer right away, but stepped out as the doors opened. The fourteen-by-fourteen hall led to another set of double doors. Javier remembered the location of the Population and he took a step, but Roman held him fast by one arm.

"There is an altercation in progress." Roman touched his temple to indicate how he knew. He then touched Javier's breast to encourage him to use his intuitive powers to stay one step ahead.

Javier nodded and concentrated on the group inside. When he gathered all the empathetic information he could, Roman pushed open the doors. Javier steeled his nerves and followed closely, as ready as possible for another fight, and hopefully, wherever Simon was, he was okay.[8]

---

[8] The titillating history between Kilmeade and Roman can be found at the back of this book, in BONUS: *Loose Rabbits*, #2, p.247

Jack & the Ten Fathers

Jack Dawn stopped at the Chamber of Fathers, rapped on the door, and waited to be admitted. He had Kite with him, but he motioned with his hand for his subordinate to stay behind. Only moments passed before he heard a reply in his mind and he pushed the heavy door.

The door opened into a large meeting room, devoid of chairs except for those in the forward section, where the ten Fathers sat in a wide semi-circle, their faces a mixture of expressions ranging from anger to amusement. Jack crossed the room, glancing down briefly at the glassy black marble floor that reflected the dim light in the room. The entire room was black, from the cold stone walls to the throne-like chairs that the Fathers occupied. The lighting was minimal since any Rakum could see in the practical dark anyway.

After he had crossed the wide room, Jack approached the center chair and the High Father reached out his right hand, palm down.

"Father Abroghia," Jack mumbled, and lightly brushed the old hand with his lips as his deep voice rumbled around the room.

Abroghia hated him—always had—and Jack reminded himself to control his temper. He threw his weight around among his inferiors nonstop, but before the Fathers, he would tread softly. Especially since he was the reason they had called an Assembly and they most likely blamed him for the entire affair.

Abroghia regarded Jack, his head tipped to the right, his eye hard. Though he was at least two thousand years old, he stood straight as a line, as balanced as a youth in his soft-soled shoes. His gray hair hung down to his mid-back like faded corn silk and his beard reached the top of his chipped leather belt. Like the other Fathers, he wore the floor-length gold and black open robe over a simple white belted smock. In his right hand, he carried a thick staff carved of Cedar as old as he was. Jack took a bowing stance and the High Father brought his free hand to rest at chest level, sighing with irritation.

"Explain yourself." Father Abroghia's voice spiked with fits and starts peculiar to him alone and Jack spoke the words he had rehearsed.

"There is a virus loose among the brethren and I believe its beginning and end is in a mortal woman named Beth Rider—" Jack was prepared to spill the entire story at once, but he was interrupted by a Father on the far end.

"Elder, come here."

Father Umbarto. Jack squared his shoulders and stepped to the end of the row of thrones. Of the Ten, Umbarto was the youngest and if there were such a thing as seniority among them, he would be at the bottom. Although any Rakum could instinctively discern a hierarchy among the Fathers, the official governmental position was that the Fathers stood before the Assembly of Rakum equally. Once he was before Umbarto, the old Rakum came to his feet and stepped forward to address him.

"*What is it, Father?*" Jack whispered, now only a few feet away.

"I am unhappy with the thrashing you gave Stone. We all are." Umbarto took a deep breath that rattled through his aged lungs, his black skin reflecting shining beads of sweat in the dim light. "For your sake, I am glad he survived."

"He's alive, then?" Jack asked with cautious interest.

"Indeed. You will face him again soon enough. And I will see you apologize and make restitution."

Jack nodded slowly and looked away, disgusted at the thought of humbling himself before the traitor he used to call a son.

"Look at me when I speak to you, pup."

Interrupting his inner worry, Umbarto's vibrato voice snapped Jack around again. He was not as tall yet he reached up for Jack's muscled shoulder and effortlessly forced him to kneel to one knee.

"Your carelessness should not be taken out on your inferiors. We are disappointed in you."

Jack remained as he was placed, one knee on the hard marble, and the hand of his Father pressed against his shoulder. He had no defense and he did not meet Umbarto's accusing glare. Instead he remained silent and waited. They were right 100% of the time and Jack knew better than to argue.

A few silent moments passed until Abroghia stood and crossed to Jack's side. He kicked the bottom of his staff and gouged Jack's calf.

"You have endangered many of our people. Explain this virus you speak of, and then explain what you think can be done to right the situation."

"But do not stand," Umbarto added hastily after his cohort. "I have always hated craning my head to see your ugly face."

Jack smiled sardonically and nodded in agreement. "Yes, Father. This is what has happened. A mortal woman named Beth Rider has written a few books and those books are casting a spell on our people. Already hundreds of the brethren are affected, and many are past rehabilitating."

"This does not sound possible, Elder. How can a book...words on a page, have power over your brethren? You're not making sense." This one was Theophilus, a Father with fiery red hair and bright green eyes. The other Fathers joined him in noisy agreement, but Abroghia raised his staff a few inches and the room fell silent. Jack shook his head and answered as best he could.

"Father, I cannot say exactly *how* it's done, just that it's happening. We have already gathered six Rakum in the dungeon who are ready to give up their lives for the words in this woman's book."

"Michael Stone was one of these?" Father Johann entered a query of his own. "Stone was infected?"

Jack swallowed and looked to his right to meet Johann's eye. "No, Father. No. Michael was guilty of betraying *me*. He was harboring the woman and trying to prevent me from acquiring her. I suppose I lost my temper with him."

"Lost your temper. Mmm-Hmm. Go on," Father Abroghia pressed, still standing beside Jack as he knelt on the hard marble floor.

Jack wrinkled his nose at the sulfurous odor emanating from the ancient Father. It was commonly known that if Abroghia smells of fire, then he is truly incensed. Jack spoke his next sentence as respectfully as possible.

"Yes, Father. I recommend you destroy her and every Rakum who is willing to die for her religion nonsense."

"Have you spoken to her about this religion? Did you try to contain this problem when you first were made aware of it?"

It was Johann again and he spoke with obvious disdain. Jack realized that so far, none of the Fathers appreciated the gravity of what he tried to explain.

"Father Johann, believe me, she is beyond reasoning with. I recommend you speak to one of the traitors that are with her in the dungeon. If you would only talk with one of them, you will see the problem right away." Jack looked to Umbarto and hoped the man would have even a small amount of affection left for him, at least for all of the years they lived and hunted together. "Father Umbarto, speak to David Walker from Miami. He's in the Pop with the Rabbit. You know that I have always worked for the preservation of our people."

Umbarto held Jack's gaze for several long moments, working up his response. Finally, he nodded his head and returned to his chair. "Yes, send him in."

Jack offered thanks and slowly rose to his feet, ignoring the creaking of his bruised knees.

"And Stone. I want Michael Stone in here right away."

Abroghia this time, and his glare gave Jack pause. He'd stepped over the line by crushing the lieutenant the way he did. Now Jack was afraid to admit he didn't know where Stone was and he drew his lips together and frowned.

"He is your lieutenant, Dawn. Call him in." Abroghia's eye glinted with ice then he gestured with his bony hand. "If you are not completely impotent, call him in. Right here. Now."

Jack swallowed and closed his eyes. He had hoped to never face the man again and now he was calling him in the most intimate way possible. Jack cleared his mind and begrudgingly sought Stone's thread. The search took longer than it should and the Fathers grumbled in disgust. With the man's mind all over the Rabbit business, Jack had a hard time reeling him in. After supreme effort, Jack yanked his thread and made an effort to be civil.

"Stone, the Fathers want to see you right away. Come now." Jack exhaled loudly and peeked at Abroghia who was paying close attention to his every word. Jack added a few placations for his sake alone. *"Michael, I apologize for trying to kill you. Now you need to tell the Fathers what you know."*

Seconds passed and then he heard Stone's clear reply.

"I will speak to High Father Abroghia alone."

Jack opened his eyes and met the Father's gaze. In another few seconds, he discerned that Stone was speaking privately now to Abroghia. The Fathers were being seduced by the traitors and Jack was nauseous at the realization.

Without a word, Abroghia turned and headed for a side exit, his heavy staff thudding every other step. Then the High Father disappeared into the private meeting rooms and sleeping quarters; places the everyday Rakum would never see in his lifetime. Jack watched him leave and when the door closed behind him, Johann pointed toward the large entryway.

"Bring David Walker. Now."

Without another word, Jack left the room and found Kite waiting for him outside in the huge foyer. He was delighted to be out from under the judgmental gazes of all ten Fathers. None understood the urgency of the problem at hand.

Jack popped Kite on the head and barked a command. "Bring me that kid from Miami. And don't speak to him. I want him scared."

Kite nodded his head and took off.

Jack paced the room, preparing to wait, and hopefully, contain his worry. It wasn't easy.

45

Beth peered around David's protective stance to see Geoffrey and Spinner facing off with him, grinning with evil intent. Whatever transpired in the restroom had now spilled over into her world. They made their demands a few minutes ago causing David guard her with his body. Peter and Nally stood on either side of David, further blocking her from the two hungry Rakum.

"I don't mind messing up that pretty face to get me some Rabbit. I won't tell you again." It was Spinner, his voice edgy. "Move over, or I'll move you over."

"You can try," David replied, his voice low.

A movement near the doors caught Beth's eye and she watched as two men walked in without escorts. Both of them scanned the room and looked her way. Beth recognized them at once.

"Roman!" she called and he approached with purpose.

The men around her stopped threatening each other long enough to see who was being added to the mix. When the Elder got close, Geoffrey and Spinner stepped back and Beth sighed with relief.

"Are these two giving you trouble?" Getting right down to business, Roman gestured to Geoffrey and Spinner. Beth nodded and Roman's mouth went to the side in a curious grin. He turned toward the two Rakum and grasped them by their shirtfronts, a fist on each kid. He then proceeded to walk them roughly to the bathroom. Beth and her group watched as he reached the door and all three disappeared inside.

"We won't see them again tonight," Javier said, drawing everyone's attention.

With a pang of concern for the lost, Beth touched Javier's arm.

He looked curiously at her hand. "Yes, ma'am?" His voice was softer than before and his eyes had a light in them she didn't notice before.

"What is he going to do? They're deceived. They've had it hard."

"He'll neutralize them. Make sure they can't interrupt us again." Javier spoke gently as if hoping to give her comfort. She nodded and exhaled with relief.

"Good to see you," David said to Javier and put out his hand in the human fashion. Javier shook it without missing a beat. Beth had only been around the Rakum a short while, but she recognized a difference in them already. Javier and David spoke words of encouragement to Peter and Nally. Had they already changed? Would she be able to tell if they had? And what of Michael? If Roman and Javier were outside all this time, perhaps they had news on her hero. Beth cleared her throat and Javier turned to look at her.

"What about Michael? Have you heard anything? Is he okay?"

"Let's see."

It was Roman and he was standing directly behind her. Beth gasped and whirled around. He had approached so quietly that Beth blushed, embarrassed that she'd jumped with fright.

"I will try to contact Michael Stone." Roman closed his eyes and the Rakum around her fell silent. The Cows had stopped moving, too, and the big room fell as quiet as a tomb. Had Roman done that? Could he control those crazy humans without even looking their way? Beth had too many questions and not nearly enough time to ask them.

After what seemed an eternity, Roman smiled and looked down on Beth, his eyes kind. "Stone is here and he has completely recovered."

"Thank God!" Beth gushed and grabbed David into a tight embrace. "Tell him I'm praying for him," Beth blurted and Roman shook his head.

"Michael's telepathy is practically nonexistent. He has Jesse Cherrie with him; he's the one I am reading. But don't worry. Young Michael knows you're as worried about him as he is about you."

Beth nodded, satisfied that he was okay. She remembered the man from the airport and was happy Michael's friend had come along to help.

"Is he headed down here?" Javier asked, but Roman shook his head.

"No, he has a private audience with Father Abroghia." Roman cleared his throat and clarified for Beth. "Abroghia is our High

184

Father, our oldest."

"Will he be all right?"

"The Fathers guard their thoughts, but Jesse has heard some curious things from Michael that may sway Abroghia's opinion in our favor."

All of the Rakum nodded, but none asked for an elaboration. Beth's lips parted to ask him herself, but Roman turned to Javier and pulled him one step aside.

"Jesse is only four doors down from where they stashed Simon. I will ask him to help the boy."

Beth watched Javier's face twist with concern and he took hold of Roman's right forearm. She remembered the blond college kid Javier brought to her house the night before. Beth was ashamed she hadn't asked about him before now. She thought to apologize, but with his eyes closed and brow furrowed, the tall Elder grunted for her to remain still. When finished, Roman turned to her, bowed a few degrees and then held out his hand.

"Miss Rider," Roman smiled as Beth took his hand. "Jesse will assist Simon and Michael will handle himself. Let me tell you what *we're* up against. Jack Dawn has been called before the Fathers and dismissed. I cannot read Dawn or his people..."

"They are coming for David." It was Peter and he spoke up as if he just received a new transmission. All eyes turned to him and he blushed bright pink. "Pardon me, I'm in contact with Meryl—he let slip that they're coming for David right now."

"Understood." Roman nodded and turned back to Beth, his expression tired, but sincere. "Miss Rider, what we need is for you to pray for us right now. All of us who want to follow your God need to pray for us to be transformed."

"Transformed?" Beth asked not sure what he meant.

"Miss Rider, you will pray for us to become human. This is what we desire."

Nally and Peter nodded their heads in agreement with David and Javier consenting verbally. David reached for her hand and she smiled.

"It will be my pleasure." Beth asked the Rakum to join hands and circle up. When all the words were said that she could think of, Beth led them in an old hymn that they didn't know, but joined in at the chorus as best they could. Beth sang two verses before the swinging double doors were pushed open by two Rakum she now recognized as Kite and Gage.

The two escorts reached the small circle and grabbed David's arm. Beth protested, but he smiled at her and shook his head.

"I'm not afraid anymore. It's okay."

Beth nodded and watched him being taken away. Before he reached the double doors, she heard him sing out, his voice echoing around the huge room full of emotion. Then he was gone.

Beth grabbed up the hands of the men around her and led them in a prayer for David. And they all said amen.

46

Guard Your Tongue

Michael left Jesse in Bunker F and headed for the Chamber of Fathers. They had successfully slipped into the Cave through a little-used tunnel that was older than the facility itself. In fact, Jack Dawn had shown him the tunnel at the first Assembly held there in 1951. During the year, Rakum would sneak in or out of the plant via the tunnel during working hours for various unofficial and clandestine excursions. Of course, successfully sneaking into Assembly was unprecedented and Michael was quite proud of the accomplishment.

Jesse agreed to lay low a little longer in the bunker while Michael confronted Abroghia. Now that he was only a short distance from the Chamber Annex—Abroghia's meeting rooms—Michael slowed his pace and took a deep breath.

The Annex door was always sealed and he expected the High Father to give him access when he arrived. Michael squared his shoulders, remembered who and what he was fighting for, as if he knew, and stepped bravely forward. When he was two strides from the smooth, flush black door, it opened unaided and Michael walked in without pause. Once inside, the door closed quietly, throwing the room in total darkness.

Michael stopped his forward motion and steadied his breathing. He had a private audience only once before, and that was during First Ritual. He was brought before Abroghia for wayward and illegal telepathy as a youth, and the severe punishment practically ruined his chances of ever being a gifted telepath. But he recalled what they had hoped to erase. Now Michael was going to use that information as leverage against the oldest creature on the planet.

"Light," he said, and thought his voice sounded normal enough. A candle came alive on his right and he walked toward it. When he was three feet from the source, another candle flickered to life to his left. Directly before him now, Father Abroghia held the bare candlestick in his left hand, ignoring the hot wax that slipped onto his leathery skin. His right hand curled around the cedar staff that never left his side. He did not need the staff to lean on, but rather to intimidate. Many Rakum had been publicly chastised by the long weapon, and many thought it contained mystical powers. Michael was one of those. He eyed the staff, unnerved at the thought of being brained with it.

Michael nodded to the Father who responded in kind. Reading his gaze was impossible so Michael watched closely every expression on the Father's face. After an awkward wait, Abroghia spoke.

"What have you to say to me, Stone?"

"Yes, Father Abroghia, I want the Rabbit, Beth Rider, to be set loose. She never intended to hurt anyone and she definitely never intended to enrage Jack as she did. I think—"

Abroghia lifted his staff a few inches, his eyes black and lifeless in the flickering candlelight. "What does she mean to you? She is beneath you. A mortal. Worthless. Easily replaced. Why do you care about this one over the others?"

Michael parted his lips to answer, but Abroghia was not finished.

"What do you know of *love*, Stone?"

Michael raised his eyebrows. He hadn't thought about love consciously since he and Jesse left poor Jeremy's loft. He opened his mouth and this time was allowed to respond.

"Yes, Father, I have tossed that word about since I met this woman. Honestly, I don't know exactly what it is, but…"

"Would you die for this woman? I believe that is the question you asked yourself. Stone, would you?"

Still Abroghia's face remained completely lax, revealing none of his true feelings on the matter. Michael shook his head a small degree, but his mouth mumbled the opposite of the gesture.

"Yes, I believe I would. I can't imagine standing idly by and allowing her to perish. What is that? Is that love?" Asking the oldest of their race, Michael was truly hoping for an answer.

Abroghia regarded him coldly and then expelled a weary breath. "Did you read this document Jack Dawn is complaining about?"

"Yes," Michael nodded speaking softly now.

"Did the document lead you to the human's God?"

Michael shook his head no.

"But you have a human compassion that you did not possess

previously? You have developed the ability to *love* since you read it?"

Michael thought back to the first moment he saw Beth at the airport, vulnerable, beautiful and innocent. Didn't he react oddly even then? He shook his head no and lowered his eyes. "I can't explain it Father, but when I first laid eyes on her, I began to feel differently."

"Do you believe she is a witch and has cast a spell on the Rakum?"

Michael scowled. "No, Father, that's ridiculous—if you knew her," he added the last apologetically. "Have you spoken to her? She's definitely not doing this to hurt anyone."

"I have heard enough." Abroghia blew out his candle and turned away. Michael took one step toward him, breaking protocol.

"Father—she could still be released. I know about the first Lost Rabbit."

Abroghia turned, but because of the single candle flame, his face was lost in shadows. Even with his special vision, all Michael could see were hollows of gray and black in the old Rakum's face.

"Watch it, Stone. You are on a precipitous point. Guard your tongue." Abroghia artfully stayed out of the light and Michael shivered at the tone of the voice in his mind.

"I will protect her, Father. With everything I have. I will use every weapon in my arsenal." Michael spoke softly, not certain that he could focus the thought clearly enough in his present state of excitement. He was threatening the oldest and strongest of their race and for the first time in his life, the exhilaration was akin to fright.

"You are mistaken. You were young, your meager talents muddied by exhaustion." Abroghia stepped up to him and into the light, his eyes now glowing red as if lit from within. *"And your memory was expunged."*

Michael heard the last in his mind only and he blinked instead of flinching. He steadied his nerves and sent a few words as carefully as he could and watched those red eyes flicker with an unknown emotion. *"No, it was not."*

Abroghia stared at him a few more moments and then turned out of the light and was gone, the thudding of his giant walking stick the last sound to dissipate down the stone hallway.

Michael looked at the brass candleholder in his hand and watched the flame dance. Abroghia couldn't face the truth any more than Michael could ignore it. And by leaving the way he did, Abroghia confirmed what Michael believed since First Ritual when Father

Johann let the secret out.

Abroghia was the first Rabbit.

And if he wasn't, he was willing to let Michael think so rather than tell him the truth. What could be worse than your entire race descended from a lowly and despicable Rabbit? Did Abroghia have a secret so terrible that he'd rather Michael believe the lie?

Michael shrugged. No matter how their race began or whether or not the High Father was the Lost Rabbit, he had bigger fish to fry. He would go find Beth and testify on her behalf. And he would no longer keep Abroghia's dirty little secret.

Michael walked to the exit and extinguished the candle. Love was *his* dirty little secret. Michael smiled and rubbed his face. He hoped she was worth it.

Shirtless, Blond, and Perfect

Jesse waltzed into his assigned dorm smiling. If he pretended everything was normal, maybe it would be. Perhaps his brethren would ignore him as they usually did. As Michael left to have a heart-to-heart with the High Father, Jesse showered off the day's grime. He was forced to redress in the same clothes he'd worn to work that day, but he felt cleaner nonetheless. And he shaved.

Jesse rubbed his smooth cheeks appreciatively. Now he looked like a stockbroker again even though the barbaric Rakum in his family would never notice. Jack Dawn's taste in proselytes had changed drastically over the years. A century ago, he discipled refined and sophisticated sorts like Michael and Jesse. But the last few decades, he collected raucous and predatory types that more reflected their Elder's personality. As a result, aside from Michael Stone, Jesse had few friends among his immediate brethren.

Now to business.

Minutes ago, an Elder named Roman asked him to locate and rescue a Cow that had wandered from his pen. Since when did he become the savior of the world? Jesse humphed and shrugged on his suit coat. Roman was a stranger, but he was also an Elder and he stood in the presence of Michael's Rabbit. What did they expect to accomplish? By the end of the night, every one of them would be dead. There was a good chance that Jesse would come under judgment for helping them. But there was that one glimpse Roman sent. That one peek into Brother Javier's psyche.

Javier loved Simon as Jesse loved Dae Lee.

That is how they got him; by evoking the memory the one human who stole Jesse's heart. So, yeah, he'd go help the kid. Why not? He was already in hot water as it was.

Jesse pulled open his door and stood in the hall. The dorm was practically deserted and he closed his eyes to listen out for the boy. Roman informed him that he was only a few rooms away so all Jesse wanted to do was pinpoint his location and avoid opening every door to find him. Jesse listened with his ears and his mind and waited. After a few seconds, various telepathic signals trickled in and he sorted them, but none of them sounded like a sad little Cow wasting away in a dark place. When a door opened fifteen yards ahead, Jesse opened his eyes.

It was a boy—shirtless, blond, and perfect, cast with an alarming pallor. He stumbled into the hallway and crashed heavily into the wall before collapsing on the stone floor. Jesse leapt into action and went to his side instantly sensing it was the kid Roman sought.

"Simon?" he asked and the boy looked at him, his blue eyes filled with tears.

"Javier. Where's Javier?" he whispered.

Jesse grasped him under his armpits and lifted him to his feet. After determining he couldn't walk, he heaved him over his shoulder and took the boy back the way he'd come. If he could get him alone, he might be able to heal him.

"Javier…I'm sorry," the boy whimpered and Jesse shushed him.

When they were back in his room, Jesse dropped him on one of the small beds and checked his pulse. His heartbeat was strong, but his breathing labored. By the look of the festering puncture wound in his neck he had been bled much too long

"Simon, I'm a friend. Be still." Jesse knelt beside the boy and placed his left hand over the hole in his neck. It was so easy, and it took no effort. Why didn't the Rakum who bled him get someone to sew him back up? It was wasteful and basically, stupid. Jesse scoffed and lifted his hand; the wound had disappeared.

"I'm sorry…" Simon was speaking to Jesse now.

"Shhh. Hey, let's try something else." Jesse lightened his tone and put his palms on either side of the boy's face. "Now, think of something nice. You have a girlfriend?"

"Uh-huh," he mumbled and looked intently into Jesse's gaze.

"What does she look like?"

"Like Halle Berry…with strawberry blonde hair…" Simon smiled and Jesse grinned back.

"Okay. Think of her face. I'm going to send you a little jolt, okay? Ready?" Jesse pressed his face firmly and held the boy's eye. "Ready?"

Simon nodded, completely trusting.

Jesse shook his head at the boy's faith in him and concentrated on sending a small amount of his own energy into the kid. He'd done it countless times with Rakum injured in one way or another, most recently on one Michael Stone, but never on a human. He measured his output carefully and within moments, the boy's breathing improved and his facial expression morphed into one of gratitude instead of misery.

"Wow. Oh, wow," Simon whispered. He took a deep breath and exhaled slowly. "Wow. Wow."

Jesse smiled and nodded his head. "Okay, sit up. You're an excellent patient."

Simon wowed a few more times, rotating his neck and then rubbing his face hard. "You're something...wow."

Jesse arose and rummaged in a nearby chest of drawers. The laundry was musty, but at least the boy wouldn't be naked in the damp atmosphere of the Cave. He selected a striped yellow and black Polo from decades past and tossed it to the kid.

"Put this on."

"Thanks." Simon pulled the shirt over his head without commenting on its distracting odor. "Do you know Javier?"

"No, but I know Michael Stone. I've adopted you until I can turn you over to Elder Roman."

"Oh! He heard me. I called him, I sure did. Man, he's one good telepath," Simon marveled.

"Come, I'll take you to him." Jesse stood and waited for Simon to find his feet. He looked strong and fully capable of walking down to the Population.

"Hey, will you contact Javier and ask him if he's okay? He was wigging out on me back in Montgomery."

Simon had stepped forward and taken a hold of Jesse's sleeve. Jesse regarded his touch and fancied the kid had a fairly familiar relationship with Javier to be so bold. But *whatever*. He kept his own Cows at arms' length, yet there was no rule against befriending them. He nodded his head and the boy released his arm.

Jesse sought out the Elder in his mind and found him in an instant. He sent his initial message first. *"I have the boy. I'm bringing him to you."*

"How is he?"

"I have revived him. He asked me to find out how his master is doing."

Jesse looked at Simon as he silently spoke to the Elder. The boy looked pensive, his hands clasped tightly together at his chest. The kid's demeanor caused him to spout another question to Roman before he answered the first. *"Is there something wrong with this kid? He doesn't look all there."*

"Tell Simon Javier is fine. And no, I don't think the boy is all there."

Elder Roman's mental voice carried no humor and Jesse smiled wryly. Many of the Rakum's Cows became pathologically attached to their masters. It was unfortunate that this handsome young man had fallen into such a trap so early.

Jesse made for the door and gestured for Simon to follow.

"Come, Javier is fine and waiting for you. I'll take you to him." Jesse pulled open the door, nodding at a random Rakum passing by. The guy didn't look in and ambled on oblivious. With a satisfied sneer, Jesse stepped out into the hall and waited for the kid to fall in beside him.

"Where're we going, Jesse?"

"Don't you call Javier 'master'?" Jesse looked back at Simon who wore a dumb expression, as if he'd never heard such nonsense. *Whatever.* Jesse shook his head and proceeded down the hall. Simon kept up with him and after they'd paced about halfway he tugged on his sleeve.

"Where're we going?"

"I prefer you didn't touch me. Are we clear?" Jesse regarded the boy with an icy glare and he pouted in response.

"Sorry."

"Elder Roman and your *master*—" Jesse stressed the word for the kid, "are in the Pop, a place where we keep all of our Cows when at Assembly." Jesse resumed walking and another brother opened his apartment door as they passed.

"Hey, Jesse, right?"

It was an older Rakum that he knew from years back. Jesse nodded casually.

"You going to Pop?"

"Yeah. Taking this Cow back." Jesse inclined his head to Simon, but didn't meet his eye.

"Pull Selene. I had her last night and believe me, you won't be sorry." With that, the old Rakum closed his door and walked away in the other direction. Simon made a noise of amusement and Jesse glanced over.

"He *had her* last night? Is she a Cow or something else?"

Jesse didn't see the humor and he didn't care for the pushy and clingy mortal. He ignored Simon's question and headed for the elevator at the end of the hall. Mentally he timed the distance to the Pop and how much longer he would be obliged to endure Roman's ward. But the Cow Selene...that information was intriguing.

Jesse put his hand to his middle and considered how long it had been since his last meal. Michael and his freaky friends were getting religion and some were going hungry for it, but Jesse had made no such oath. He picked up the pace and got the kid onto the elevator.

Maybe Old Man Mathers was still down there. Jesse attempted to reach him telepathically. Some Cows could receive him and Mathers had been with them over fifteen years.

Jesse ignored a few more intrusive questions from Javier's little friend and sent one message to Mathers repeatedly as the elevator went down. *"Get Selene ready. Get Selene ready. Have Selene ready. I'm coming for her."*

Jesse hoped the old man heard him because he was plenty hungry. Even her name sounded delicious.

Ask Him About God

David stood outside the huge black doors and his knees trembled. In his heart, he repeated the mantra Miss Rider taught him, the one about how God protects His own. Jack Dawn's angry goons led him roughly and neither would look him in the eye. The brother on his right struck his knuckles on the door three hard raps and stood still again. When the door opened, David found himself face-to-face with the Elder who so easily and cruelly incapacitated him hours before. He made a small sound in his throat as rough hands shoved him forward. He crashed into Dawn's broad chest.

"Here's the traitor, Fathers. David Walker, from Miami." Jack caught David's slight form in his strong hands and stepped aside to toss him to the ground. David hit the stone floor hard, but quickly righted himself and rose to his knees, unsure of whether to stand.

"Elder Dawn!" Father Johann called, his voice low and menacing.

David witnessed the tension in Jack's face as he steeled his jaw and stepped over to his superior.

"I do not care for the way you handle your brothers. Umbarto, is this behavior common for your man?" Johann instructed Jack to stop before him, but turned to Umbarto for his reply. "Is his barbarism your doing?"

Umbarto rose to his feet and shook his head. "No, Johann. When we were together, he was respectful. I do not approve his behavior."

David read the responding look in Jack's glare. It was widely known that Umbarto was the most vicious Rakum of them all, but Jack was in no position to rebut.

"And neither do I." Abroghia entered the room from the private side door and pointed his staff. "Jack Dawn, I will mete out punishment for you later. For now, I will humble you. Lie down on the floor here, face down. Right here." The High Father pointed to

196

the ground right before where David knelt.

David watched as the giant that he feared the most grumbled and went to all fours before him. It took him a couple of seconds to be fully lying down, but when he was, he turned his face away from the Fathers and looked directly at David. Avoiding his murderous gaze was difficult.

"David Walker?" Father Abroghia was now waiting for David to acknowledge him, his voice uncharacteristically gentle. "That marble hurts your knees. I want you to sit on Elder Dawn for the duration of this visit."

David raised his eyebrows and glanced at a couple of the other Fathers and they all waited expectantly. They may not have known their contemporary was going to proceed with this course of action, but they didn't contradict him.

Without thinking too hard about it any longer, David carefully crawled upon Elder Dawn's wide muscular back and sat, his feet on the floor in front of him. Dawn didn't make a peep, but he broke out in a sweat that David interpreted as immeasurable fury.

"David Walker, there is something different about you, isn't there? You don't seem...quite right to me." Father Theophilus spoke in a harsh whisper, took one step from his throne and then halted abruptly. He then put his hand to his nose and glanced questioningly to the Fathers on his right and left.

Out of the corner of his eye, David saw Abroghia motion with his staff and all of the Fathers fell silent, giving him the floor. Did they discern that he was being transformed? How would he know and what would it feel like? He trained his shaky gaze upon the High Father, still afraid to face his fate.

"David Walker..." Dispensing with the friendly act, Abroghia's voice changed into a low growl. "You have been excommunicated. Why?"

David swallowed and hoped for the best. He didn't know what to say or what was going to happen to him, but he had to speak. His lips parted and as Miss Beth taught him, he offered up a prayer in his heart. "I was weak. Tomás thought I was a weakling."

"Bring me Elder Tomás," Abroghia announced to no one in particular then continued. "Are you weak, David?"

"M-maybe, Father. But I'm not a danger to our people, and I'm not a burden. I'm just different."

"I can see that." Abroghia lowered his chin, but held David's eye.

"You smell like a *human*." He spat the word and a quiet filled the air for several long moments.

David concentrated on his breathing and tried to mentally convince his heartrate to slow.

Abroghia sighed angrily and rolled his eyes. "Tell me about the Rabbit named Beth Rider. Jack Dawn has told us that you are willing to die for her. Is that so?"

David looked at the faces around him and paused. Would he die for her? He had not been prepared for that question. "Father?"

"If I brought her in here to kill her, would you offer your life in her place?"

"I don't know. Maybe. I'm not sure. I've always been more empathetic than my brothers…" David stammered wondering if the Fathers were about to test their theory. He hoped they didn't, because he was afraid to die, even for Miss Beth. Then in a flash he knew the answer.

Of course he would.

Impatient for a response Abroghia cleared his throat. "Would you have given your life to save the Cow, Terrence?"

David grimaced at the mention of his friend's name. He had loved Terrence more than anyone he'd ever known. Would he have sacrificed his life for him, too? David concentrated on the possibility, his eyes darting from Father to Father. Before he could work up an answer, the heavy doors behind him opened with a swoosh of air and he looked back. It was Elder Tomás, and he didn't look happy.

"Tomás, join us."

Father Theophilus spoke up and motioned for him to enter and he did, taking in the scene before him. Tomás' eyes scanned the huge form of his compatriot spread-eagled on the floor, and then to the youngster planted on his back.

"Fathers. Elder Dawn." Tomás nodded in greeting to them and then turned his gaze to David. "Brother Snake."

"Master," David mumbled, not sure what the protocol was for a Rakum in his position.

"You excommunicated this David Walker. We have heard your reasons. They are a matter of record. But I want to hear it again. In your own words. Why?" Umbarto spoke now, as the remainder of the Father's listened in one accord.

"Father, I sent him out into the world to toughen him up. He was impotent and a disgrace to my clan. I despise his weakness." Tomás turned his gaze to the High Father. "He disdained my instruction. He fell in love with every Cow. He didn't fit in."

David watched Tomás' profile. His Elder's words stung and he must have flinched, because Father Abroghia stepped closer to him. He reeked of brimstone and David held his breath.

"Does it pain you to hear, David Walker?"

David swallowed. "Yes, it does. I know I'm weak, but I love my brothers. And I love my Elder. I didn't want to leave."

"Isn't that wonderful. Love, love, love." Abroghia slapped the back of David's head, his voice louder than before. "David Walker is too caring. Jack Dawn is too cruel."

David watched the High Father with round eyes and his fear escalated. Abroghia looked over to Umbarto and flicked his staff David's way.

"It is in Dawn's nature to be hateful and barbaric as it is in Walker's nature to be kind and gentle. Are we dealing with simple personality clashes here, brethren? What about Michael Stone? Jack, you punished him because he cared about the fate of the Rabbit. Maybe Stone is too kind and gentle for you." Abroghia scanned the faces of the other Fathers, pausing dramatically.

"Ask him about God," Jack mumbled from the floor, his face still away from the Fathers.

David looked to the front again realizing that the moment of truth had arrived. Rakum had no religion except self-preservation, and he could see that the challenge came as a surprise to his superiors.

"God? I am your god, Elder Dawn." Abroghia looked down at Jack and then over to David. He stepped a little closer and laid his hand on David's shoulder. "David?"

David swallowed. "I believe in the God of the mortals now, Father Abroghia."

"And you discovered this God by reading the Rabbit's document?"

David nodded once and could see the quizzical look in Abroghia's eyes turning darker by the second.

"Father Abroghia, are they going to destroy me now that I believe in God?"

Abroghia looked to Umbarto and then back to David. "Why not? You are no longer Rakum. How do you feel?"

David blinked, not understanding the question. Abroghia drew back his hand and hit him across the chin with a balled fist. David recoiled and tumbled off Jack's back and onto the cold marble.

"How do you feel?" Abroghia pressed, menacingly standing over him.

David sputtered and pushed himself up onto his hands. Blood dripped from his lip. He dabbed it with his thumb and looked at it closely. Nothing was right. His head spun from the violence of Father Abroghia's attack, his hip ached from landing on it so heavily, and his blood was bright red.

Bright red—the blood of a human.

David counted the seconds and the room fell completely still. He rocked his weight back and sat on his heels, still dizzy. His lip stung and continued to leak blood. David looked up at the High Father and whimpered. It had happened. He was fully mortal.

Abroghia snorted and slapped him hard enough to knock him back to the floor. "Bring me Beth Rider."

Tomás turned on his heel and exited the room.

David remained where he was and watched the doors from his prone position. Beth would know what to do. Mostly convinced, David prayed for her in his heart and did his best to ignore the pain that wracked his body. It was a new pain that did not dissipate. But it made him feel truly alive. Maybe for the first time.

49

A Nigerian Princess

Jesse pushed through the double doors happy to be free of Simon. Paying the boy no mind, he made a beeline for Mathers who stood a short distance away beside the most beautiful Black woman Jesse had ever seen. She was lithe and willowy, built like a dancer with an unmatched and ethereal countenance.

"Jesse, they're over there."

Simon had followed him and now pulled his coat sleeve. Thankfully, he dropped it when Jesse tossed him an agitated glare.

"Then go join them. Bye," Jesse hissed, and the boy scooted off.

He took a second to rearrange his attitude and then approached Mathers. The grizzled old Cow recognized him at once and stood off the wall to greet him. Selene cast her gaze to the floor and only fluttered up once to see who she was being handed off to. Her immodest string tank top revealed much of her natural gifts, but Jesse saw something else in his mind's eye; he saw an innocent, a child taken from the real world and thrust into a universe of monsters. He reached out and carefully took the woman by the forearm. As Mathers slithered away without a word, Jesse squeezed her arm gently to encourage her to look at him. He wanted to see her eyes and he hoped to see her smile. Most women smiled when they got a look at his face.

"Selene? My name is Jesse. How are you tonight?" Jesse used his softest voice and patiently waited for her to reply.

"I'm tired, Master." Her eyes remained trained to the floor and Jesse sighed.

"Haven't you slept?"

"It's difficult to find time to sleep. I've been popular."

Jesse looked aside and frowned. The woman was extremely

desirable and as he spoke with her, he sensed his hunger being aroused in more ways than one. But he didn't force submission; it wasn't his style. Jesse sighed again and squeezed her arm once more.

"Look at me." She paused only a second and then turned up her face to meet his. Jesse looked into the clearest brown eyes he'd ever seen. He couldn't imagine *not* taking her upstairs with him and making her his forever. "Why are you alone? Why haven't you a sponsor?"

"I was with Elder Yosef."

Selene glanced to her right and Jesse followed her gaze. She meant one of the traitors that huddled beside the bleachers. Jesse recognized none of them, aside from the boy, Simon, but as he eyed them, a tall and slender chap with glasses nodded to him politely. It was Roman, at the center of a group of some twenty-five Rakum. Michael's Rabbit was nowhere in sight.

"Yosef got religion, eh?" he asked still watching the close group.

"Two weeks ago. He tried to hide me, but they found me and brought me here."

"I understand." Jesse caught her eye and held her attention. "Selene, I want you to come with me. I'll keep you to myself."

Selene did not look relieved. On the contrary, her eyes welled with tears even as she tried to suppress them.

"I promise I won't hurt you." Jesse tried to read her expression, but he'd never been any good at discerning feminine emotions.

She looked back at the crowd of traitors and sniffed.

"What is it? Is it Yosef?"

Selene nodded and clenched her jaw. "He chose that book over me. He chose that silly religion nonsense over me." Selene opened her arms and stood square, posing. "Me. Who would give this up?"

Jesse smiled wryly and shook his head. "Honestly, Selene, no one in their right mind would give you up."

"You got that right, Master," Selene huffed, leaking a glimpse of her true personality.

"Which one is Yosef?" Jesse asked out of curiosity.

"There he is, with the pale yellow shirt. How could he dump me like that?"

Jesse wondered the same thing. Right now, Elder Yosef was deep in prayer with some of the other Rakum. Two of them were on their knees. Jesse opened his hand and caressed the silky underside of Selene's arm.

"Come with me. I want to take you out of here, away from this

Assembly. Will you come?" Jesse knew where the tunnels were located. He was 100% confident that he could spirit the two of them out successfully. It didn't matter where he went, so long as he kept his brethren away from Selene.

"What do you think about that Rider novel?" Selene looked at his hand and then met his eyes. "Are you going to get religion and dump me, too?"

"I'm not interested in religion. I like things the way they are." Jesse took a step back and dropped his hand, severing the contact. He wanted her to choose, no matter how risky it was. She had seen many sleepless nights in bed with more Rakum than he wanted to count, but she was still blameless in the ways that mattered. She was still helpless. She was too much like Dae Lee, and Jesse's throat constricted when the girl's name came to mind. He swallowed forcibly and lowered his head, nearly begging now.

"What do you say?"

Selene looked the praying crowd over once more and nodded her head. "Yes, I will go with you."

"Good," Jesse smiled. Her returning smile caused his stomach to flip uncomfortably in a way it hadn't since Dae Lee's death; something was happening. He walked the stunning goddess toward the exit and nodded to Roman as he pushed through the doors. So what if he was falling for one of them again? He survived the first time, and this time he'd get her away from those who would use her up.

Jesse led Selene to the elevators, planning their escape route. As soon as he could, he'd contact Michael and let him in on the plan, but for now, Jesse kept his eye on Selene and gave his heart away one more time.

†

Roman watched Stone's friend leave with the Cow and returned his attention to the Rakum around him. Not only did he have Javier, Peter, and Nally leading prayers for all involved, but two Elders and twenty more Rakum had joined the circle of traitors. Four of them had fully transformed and Roman marveled. When would it happen for him? For Javier? What were the magic words to make it so?

Roman listened to a few more prayers and his eyes fell on Simon. The kid was no better than he had been before they left him at Stone's house. He'd had a few frightening experiences since then, but he was no closer to God. He clung to Javier's right arm like a desperate lover and Roman shook his head. At least Javier was still focused on the Right. His beloved son was praying for the Rakum who stood beside him and Simon stood there, eyes wide open, watching the show. Was there no hope for the boy?

Roman closed his eyes and tried to concentrate on Beth Rider and what she must be going through in the Chamber of Fathers. She would be terrified, but Roman had to admit that he would be to. Every single time he entered their presence, he was unnerved. Roman prayed and hoped for the best, but even with his budding new faith, he expected the worst.

50

The Angel and the Demon

Beth followed Tomás closely. He was closing in on six feet, with shoulder-length black hair that shimmered when they passed under the low-hanging industrial lights. He had the sharp ethnic features of a champion Matador. If he wasn't a devil, she would have thought him attractive, but his eyes were dead. Beth was lost in her thoughts by the time they reached their destination and the Rakum Elder stepped aside, pointing to a fourteen-foot double door before them.

"The Chamber of Fathers. Enter, Rabbit."

Beth paused to gather her courage, but realized she wasn't truly afraid. She'd been calm since David was taken away and now she was almost startled by her lack of concern. She chalked it up to faith stepping up when it was all she had left and she pushed on the old door. At her touch, both doors opened wide and she stepped onto the threshold and looked around.

"STOP!"

A thunderous voice echoed from inside the chamber, reverberating off the walls.

"Do not come any closer!" the same voice commanded her with an edge of panic.

As her eyes adjusted to the low light in the room and still standing on the actual threshold, Beth focused and saw what looked like Jack Dawn sprawled out on the black floor, his face toward her. David was also on the floor, but sitting on his rear, legs out in front of him. Even from thirty feet away she could see he was injured.

"You cannot enter here!"

The voice again. Beth considered her options. She had been delivered to this room and now prevented from entering? She tried to see who was speaking, but the speaker was lost in shadows beyond the

Rakum on the floor. Beth took two steps forward and garnered another bellow from the dark.

"STAY BACK!"

Beth could see the entire room now, albeit not perfectly. The most curious thing about the room was the semi-circle of tall-backed thrones that sat on the far end. Old men stood before those thrones, their eyes all trained on her. Her gaze landed on the one in the middle, tall and willowy with a beard made of silk holding a red staff taller than he was. This one's hand was upraised, palm out, his face a mask of indignant horror.

Beth started to reply, but all at once the wizened old men to either side of the middle one turned and filed out of the room, one by one, in a line, out a side exit. A split second later, Jack Dawn pushed himself to his hands and knees and came to his feet.

"Now you'll get what you deserve, Rabbit," Jack whispered and glared at her victoriously as he lumbered out the door she entered.

David was the last to move.

He brought his feet together and rolled over onto his hands only to methodically push himself to a squatting position. Beth wanted to help him and she made as if to step forward, but the old man who was left shouted for her to be still and he helped David up himself.

"David, are you okay?" she asked him as he approached her. Although he was bleeding at the mouth and a welt had formed on his cheek, he was smiling.

"I'm better than okay, Miss Beth. I'm a new man." He winked and passed her slowly, limping on his right leg. As he stepped out, he blessed her, and the doors closed heavily behind him.

Beth looked at the old Father and put her hands on her hips. Was he afraid of her?

"You cannot come in here! It is not time. It is too soon!"

Beth realized then that the Father was not looking at her, but off her right shoulder. She turned her head and saw only the closed door.

"YOU LIE!" the old Father hissed and stepped backward until he was behind his chin-high throne.

Beth shook her head wryly realizing that the old Rakum was having a spiritual discussion with an entity that entered with her. Beth took another step forward and smiled.

"I will kill her," the old Father growled, but even Beth could see there was no power behind his words. She opened her mouth to ask his name when a stream of unexpected words filled her mouth.

"Your time is up, Ta'avah, Demon of Old. Relinquish your throne." And that was all. Beth's lips remained partly open, but no other ethereal sentences poured forth.

The old Father lowered is head, still hiding behind his chair, and he held up his hand in a sign of surrender.

"Just please, go."

His voice weak, Beth watched his eyes trained above and just to the right of her shoulder. Several seconds passed slowly and finally he sighed and came around his chair to slump into it heavily.

"What was that all about? Didn't you call me in here?" Amazed at the stern quality of her voice, Beth stepped closer to the old Father and stopped fifteen feet away.

He didn't meet her eyes as he responded. "You will address the Assembly. Tell them everything I show you tonight."

Beth blinked. "What?"

"You chose this path, Beth Rider, and this is where it has led you." The old Rakum tilted up his gaze, his eyes sunk deep into his brow. "Give me your hand."

Beth backed away and he repeated his command.

"Why? What're you going to do?"

The old Rakum rose to his feet and reached her in the blink of an eye. He grasped her wrist even as she was still gasping with surprise. "Show you. You must tell the Assembly."

Beth resisted, then submitted as she realized she was as powerless as when in the clutches of Jack Dawn.

"Okay, show me," she mumbled, sensing fear in the Rakum and growing stronger because of it.

"Close your eyes and see…"

Beth begrudgingly shut her eyes. Behind her closed lids, the blackness filled with light, pulsating white and red and then blue and green, until a picture formed of a man and woman sitting at a stone table inside a close earthen space. The room was dark, lit by a single oil lamp that flickered between them and out a small circular opening in the wall, she could see the full moon and a clear night sky. As she watched, the woman turned to face her and she saw herself—dressed in a rough off-white tunic sashed with a cloth tie, her head covered with a linen shawl.

With a whoosh of air Beth realized she was now the woman, sitting across from the man, seeing through her eyes as clearly as day. Beth turned her head both ways and could not discern what was vision and what was reality. As far as she knew, she'd been transported. "Where am I? What is this?" she whispered, but the thickly-robed man put his finger to his lips and shushed her.

"I will speak. You listen."

Beth started to protest and stopped herself. Something about the man's voice was familiar and as she looked into his eyes, she realized it was the old Rakum from the Chamber. Abroghia, Roman had called him, their High Father. But here, he was young, maybe eighteen, with bronzed skin and the aristocratic nose of a Bedouin Sheik.

"I am Ta'avah, the first of my kind, of a dynasty of mighty messengers, producing men of renown and terror with the daughters of men. Empowered by the Most High, I commanded my world, designed it to fit my needs, and carved out a niche unique to me alone. My brothers, Zahdone, Rah-keel, Zara, all of us assigned to plunder, kill, destroy and dismay the sons of men until the Time of the End. Together we are the *Nephilim*, Legion of Infamy, and my portion has been fulfilled."

"Nephilim—the sons of God," Beth whispered. The old Rakum from the Chamber of Fathers was not a man at all, but a spirit manifest in the flesh. And somehow, using the powers of darkness, he orchestrated events in such a manner that thousands of years later, he multiplied his offspring to a steady one hundred thousand. How was this accomplished? And even more bewildering, why did God allow it? Abroghia-Ta'avah scoffed as if he read her thoughts.

"You will tell the Assembly to disband. Each man will go his own way. I, Ta'avah, no longer cover this people." Ta'avah lifted his hand and dangled his pointer finger in the air in front of Beth's face teasingly. "But you warn them to choose wisely. The Most High wants them for Himself. Each will make a choice..."

Was he truly cutting them loose? This devil of old, this demon masquerading in the body of a man—could he turn it off so easily? And what did it mean for Michael, Roman, Peter, and Nally? The faces of each Rakum she had come to know over the last week flashed before her memory. Would they all be set free?

"You try operating outside the will of the Most High and see how far you get, Rabbit." A little of the old arrogance shone through and Beth pursed her lips. He continued. "Go now. That is all I will say."

Beth sighed and made as if to ask him another question when his eyes widened and he stared over her right shoulder.

"You again!" Ta'avah hissed and stood up from the stone bench.

"What now?"

Beth instinctively turned to look, but as before in the Chamber, there was no one there. But of course she knew that there *was*. An angel of the Most High God—likely the same angel who had frightened the old demon back at his throne room, and as before, Beth watched Ta'avah have a conversation by himself.

"I DID. YOU HAVE NOTHING ON ME!" Ta'avah shouted like a child with a tantrum and then he rattled off a few sentences in what sounded like Aramaic to Beth's unlearned ears. When the old Rakum realized he was getting nowhere, he sulled up and turned away, pouting like a toddler. It was then that Beth felt a hand on her shoulder from behind.

She didn't startle, as if she expected to relive her experience with the angel in her dream of years past. She imagined her angelic visitor to be nine feet tall with shining garments and fierce eyes. She only had to wait a few seconds before the angel spoke, words she heard with her ears.

"At the dawn of mankind, the Four fell and were sent to earth…"

Beth gasped as the room dissolved into a new vision, but this one was more like a television show, a recording of a past event. So much so that around the edges she could still see the room where she sat with Abroghia-Ta'avah. She remembered to breathe as she studied the scene laid out before her. It was a desert, flat and lifeless, stretching as far as the eye could see. Four dark shapes descended from the air until they touched the sand, solidifying into human-shape, yet retaining their shadowy silhouette.

"Zahdone, prince of pride and arrogance. Rah-keel, prince of false witness and gossip. Zara, prince of every sickness, affliction and trouble. And Ta'avah, prince of covetousness, lust and murder…"

Beth watched the four figures approach at a walk, casually kicking through the sand with no eyes in their featureless faces.

"The Four spread to the four corners of the earth…"

As the words left the angel's mouth, the apparition on the right, Zahdone, fell into a million pieces, fanning out 360 degrees in every direction, disappearing beyond the distant dunes, completely disappearing until there were three.

Beth thought to speak, but the gentle hand on her shoulder squeezed slightly and she remained silent. The wispy specter on the right, Rah-keel, was the next to go. Like his predecessor, he split off into countless shards and vanished in every direction. The third followed closely after, this one departing with an ear-piercing screech that caused Beth to cringe and cover her ears. And when only Ta'avah remained, he dissolved into millions, like his brothers, but when the minions scattered to the four corners of the earth, one man-sized apparition remained.

It continued stepping forward until it was only a few feet away, and as it came to a halt before her, it solidified into a man. It was Abroghia—young and strong—the Rakum who brought her out of the Chamber and into the ancient stone hut.

"These things the Lord hates," the angel continued in his rich baritone, "pride, a lying tongue, hands that shed innocent blood, hearts that devise wicked plans, feet that are swift to run into evil, false witness, and the one who sows discord among the brethren. These are an abomination to the King of the universe."[b]

Beth nodded with understanding and sensed the angel behind her smiling in agreement. The Four Brothers went out with their particular talents and afflicted the men of earth who refused to follow the ways of God. And this last one, Ta'avah, the prince of lust and murder, fashioned an entire race of men with his evil intentions.

"And the world was wicked, corrupted by the Four, effortlessly deceiving the sons of man. So God sent a flood to cleanse the earth."

And the Nephilim were on the earth in those days as well as after...[c] Beth remembered the Scripture and nodded; the answer to an old Sunday school question finally answered. If everyone died in the flood except Noah and his family, how were there Nephilim on the earth afterwards? Now she had her answer. The Nephilim were spirits; they didn't drown because they couldn't.

But what about the timing? Abroghia ran his kingdom for over two thousand years, why now? Beth asked without turning.

"Ta'avah knew his time was short," was the angel's cryptic reply.

"What about the others?" Beth looked at Ta'avah as she spoke; he was still sulking across from her.

"Their time is here, but not yet."

"What about this one?" Beth gestured toward the Rakum's back. "What happens to him?"

Ta'avah turned half-way and looked at her, his chin lowered. "I'll be around."

His eyes darted behind her and his smile faltered. Then without another word, he faded away even as she watched, his enormous staff clattering to the dirt floor as he left.

Beth stared at the massive cedar staff and shook her head. Thousands of years reigning on earth, over like that. She looked around and waited for instructions. Something else was coming. Why did God think she was capable of such a big job?

Beth laughed softly. It boggled the mind that He figured insignificant Elizabeth Louise Rider to be such a valiant and capable soldier.[9]

---

[9] Read how Abroghia-Ta'avah called the first Father in the time of Jesus Christ. BONUS: Loose Rabbits, #'s 4 & 5. p.258

51

Jesse Decides to Run

Michael stepped out the door of his Barracks F dorm room and looked up and down the hall both ways. He expected to find Jesse waiting for him as instructed, but the man was nowhere to be seen. As he stood on the threshold, frustration building on his face, a door opened across the hall and a familiar face poked out.

"I thought I heard you come back, Stone. There's no mistaking that walk of yours." It was Gage, one of Jack's newer proselytes. He was a thick Rakum of medium height, mottled pink skin and unassuming features. The low light shimmered off his bald head making him look even shorter than he was. Not to mention he was disgusting. This one was there when Jack came to collect the Rabbit. He had manhandled Beth Rider and by the odor slipping through his pores, he'd taken her blood.

Michael bristled involuntarily and Gage laughed.

"I can't believe you survived. You were a goner, man. I wish you could've seen the wrestling move Jack put on you." He laughed harder and hit the wall with his palm.

Michael held his tongue and planned his next move. He wanted to find Beth, but first he had to know where she was. Thankfully, Gage was no telepath and only sensed his train of thought.

"She was delicious, Stone, and skin like satin. If only you weren't such a Nancy you could've had the same pleasure as the four of us."

Michael stood up off the wall to work the guy over, but the elevator opened down the hall at the same time. He looked up reflexively and watched as Jesse exited and headed toward them with a gorgeous woman trailing respectfully behind.

"Selene, good choice," Gage said lasciviously as he watched the duo approach.

Fed up, Michael snarled and crossed the hall to reach the man. He shoved Gage's chest repeatedly until he stumbled backward into his room. "Stay out of my sight. This is private."

Michael had not been to Jack's wrestling parties in years, but he remembered everything he'd been taught. He was prepared to smash the jerk to bits if he didn't comply. Thankfully his reputation outweighed his questionable behavior and the guy didn't strike back.

"Don't touch me, you traitor. Hands off." Gage was now several feet inside his own room, but he didn't return to the hall. Michael cursed him and closed the door in his face.

"Everything okay?" Jesse had reached them now, the Cow standing behind him watching everything with gigantic brown eyes that missed nothing. Michael nodded his head in the affirmative and met Jesse at the door to their room.

"Where've you been?" Michael tried not to pay the woman any notice, but she was undeniably alluring. She had been serving Rakum for a long time, and he sensed that although she'd been handed around quite a lot recently, her original Master was an Elder. For the life of him, Michael couldn't imagine why Jesse had her.

Jesse noted his obvious interest and stepped aside to maneuver his companion to stand before him, his hands on her shoulders.

"This is Selene. She's coming with me." Jesse lowered his voice and looked to the side suspiciously. "I'm leaving Assembly. Right now."

"What do you mean?"

"Just what I said. You can come with me if you want to. Something's happening, Michael. Something terrible. Your Rabbit has done something unimaginable; something has happened to the High Father."

"What do you mean? What could Beth do?" Michael pointed to the room to get his pal to enter, but Jesse shook his head.

"No, we're on the move. In a few minutes, you're going to get the announcement that Father Abroghia is gone."

"What? Gone where? What're you talking about?" Michael worked at understanding Jesse's words, but he couldn't imagine a world without Abroghia. All he could think of was that he must have misheard. "Nothing can hurt him. He must be 2500 years old. Jesse, I think he's the first Rakum. Remember what I was trying to tell you earlier? Abroghia is likely the original Lost Rabbit."

Jesse paused and as he did he dropped one hand from Selene's shoulders and pulled her to him in a half embrace. Michael wondered what the movement meant; Jesse was not one to touch or handle the Cows.

"No. Not a Rabbit, but something more."

"Something more? More than a Rabbit? How are you getting this? Telepathically? Are you divining it? What?" Some Rakum could predict the future, but Michael couldn't remember a single instance where Jesse exhibited such a talent. But his friend was shaking his head as he pulled the woman tighter to his side.

"I just know. As I was coming up the elevator, I knew that he was gone. And when the word gets out, everything is going to break loose from the top down."

"What about Beth? Where is she? Can you at least tell me that?" Michael caught the woman's eye briefly and she looked away. "I need to know where she is."

"She's in the Chamber of Fathers."

"Then that's where I'm headed." Michael started moving toward the elevator even as he spoke and Jesse was right behind him.

"I'm taking Selene out."

Michael looked at his watch. "You know it's only two hours to daybreak out there, right?"

Jesse nodded. "I'll take my chances."

"We're in the middle of the desert. Hide in the tunnels until dark. Don't be stupid."

They reached the elevator and hit different floors.

"No, we're leaving." Jesse waited to catch Michael's eye then finished his thought telepathically. *"They killed Dae Lee. I'm going to save Selene. Help me or stay out of the way."*

Michael shook his head and the elevator lurched to a stop on his floor. "I'll do anything for you Jesse. Just name it. But first, I must get to Beth."

Jesse nodded and put his hand to Michael's neck. "I will miss you," he said and touched his forehead to Michael's.

"That's sort of squishy," Michael half-joked, projecting the condition of his own softening heart. He stepped off the elevator and left the two of them aboard.

Jesse offered a small grin. "Look me up when this is over. If we're alive, that is." He sighed without apparent grief. "This is the end of the Rakum Race. By sundown tomorrow, we will be scattered to the wind. Be careful, and be safe."

Michael still didn't understand his brother's far-fetched prophecy, but he watched the doors close before he turned for the Chamber of Fathers. If Beth was having an effect on Abroghia, why wouldn't he feel it? The High Father was his *actual* father.

Michael attempted to locate the ancient Rakum telepathically, but received nothing in return. He wasn't too surprised. Of all the nights to be without that helpful gift; Michael wished he could call Beth. Comfort her. Encourage her. Perhaps even receive some comfort and assurance in return. She was small and fragile, but there was a power behind her that he didn't comprehend. A power he could see when he looked into her lovely face.

Was that power the One from her novel? And should he be seeking to know more about it instead of worrying about the fate of a Rabbit and the end of his race?

Michael picked up his step and ignored every Rakum he passed. Beth was before the Fathers and no human had ever stood in that position before tonight. That fact alone put a new urgency in his heart and Michael fell into a jog.

52

Who Is, Who Was, & Who Is to Come

When the invisible messenger spoke again, he placed his other hand upon her opposite shoulder.

"Take the Staff of Ta'avah to the Assembly of One Hundred Thousand. They will listen to the one who carries this symbol of their people."

Beth picked up the staff with effort and looked it over closely. Carved of cedar, it was over six feet long. The surface was smooth from years of elements and atmosphere, and although the top was six inches in diameter, it tapered to a fine tip of less than one inch. The craftsmanship was astonishing and it weighed at least forty pounds. Beth lowered the head and studied a set of characters carved into the top. Her basic knowledge of Hebrew allowed her to discern the letters *resh* and a crude *kof*—which she surmised made up the word 'Raka', and underneath were four more characters, of which she could only read the first, a *tav*.

"Raka Ta'avah?" She asked, hoping the angel would answer. He didn't. Instead, he squeezed her shoulder and the room shimmered like sound waves on a pond. With a slight breeze of cool air, she blinked and was back in the Chamber of Fathers. The room was empty, as she left it, and the angel's hands were removed from her shoulder. Beth spun around.

"Wait, please. Can I see you?"

"You have seen me."

Beth thought a moment. The tall, bronzed, strong and shining angel in her imagination was very likely what he actually looked like. It was easy to forget that because she belonged to the Most High she had spiritual eyes. Beth smiled and asked, "What is your name?"

"*Emunah*, who stands in the presence of the One Who Is, Who Was, and Who Is to Come."

Beth suppressed a 'wow' and smiled.

"Emunah," she repeated softly, then, "will I die tonight?"

"No, your time has not come. Call the Assembly. Your God will put the words in your mouth. Go, Elizabeth Louise Rider, daughter of the Most High God."

Beth nodded and headed for the gigantic double doors, dragging the staff and bursting with purpose. Just as she reached out for the brushed brass handle, a door to her far right opened on squeaky hinges and a ruddy and wrinkled face peeked at her from behind the door. Beth had an idea.

"What's your name?" she asked and the elderly man looked behind him before meeting her eyes from across the room.

"Theophilus, Madam."

"Theophilus, we need to call the Assembly together. Can you do that?" Beth watched him deliberate, look back the way he'd come, and then sigh as he stepped in hesitantly.

"Abroghia is gone?" His voice cracked.

He wasn't asking Beth, but addressing someone behind her who, by the angle of his gaze, must have been Emunah. Beth lifted the staff off the ground with effort and allowed it to land back on the stone floor with an impressive sound.

"Yes, and we need the Rakum assembled immediately. Please, get to it."

Her action with the staff had a visible effect on the old Father as he startled and then shuffled into the room, followed by one, then two, then three, until all nine Fathers who remained were in the Chamber with her. They filed toward the thrones, each one stopping in their place. When all had reached their assigned seat, they sat in one accord, eyes stuck on Beth in the center of the room holding the Staff of their master like a shield.

At first nothing happened. Beth watched the Rakum Fathers become still, so much so that she thought they were being obstinate. But momentarily, she noticed that they were indeed busily at work, albeit telepathically, each making slight and differing gestures of concentration. The one named Theophilus shook his head ever so slightly, and the dark muscular one on the end held a pointer finger to his temple. When a minute had passed, a Father with snow white hair and fair skin looked up and gestured in Beth's general direction.

"The Rakum are assembling." He looked at her warily from his seated position and his eyes darted from her face to the staff, to the space above her right shoulder. Having her giant comrade so close at all times caused her courage to increase exponentially.

"I want every Cow and every Rakum in the Population also brought to Assembly." She spoke confidently and couldn't suppress a tight smile when the old red-headed Theophilus nodded and sent a command telepathically, humming an eerie monotone at the same time.

"It is done."

The pale one again. Beth asked him his name and he identified himself as Father Johann.

"Johann, the nine of you need to assemble there, too. Anyone who doesn't come will be destroyed." Beth hadn't known she would say such a thing, but she believed her words.

Johann and two others inclined their heads that they would comply and Beth saw that they kept their eyes on the staff in her hand or over her shoulder and rarely met her gaze. The pride, arrogance and false superiority that the Rakum exhibited ever since she fell into their world had departed. The same was replaced with hollow eyes and shaky hands.

The reign of the Rakum was over and she was the one God chose to bring it to an end.

53

Going Human

"Abroghia is gone."

Standing in the Grand Hall that led to the Chamber, the phrase reverberated painfully through Michael's skull and he stopped his forward motion to lean against the damp wall. It was the voices of the Fathers, speaking at once and in perfect unison. The power behind the telepathic utterance nearly brought him to his knees. After a moment, the knife that pierced his brain receded and he opened his eyes.

Two Rakum fifty feet down the hall were lowering their hands and also standing off the walls where they had been thrust. Michael blinked several times and looked at the portal that led to the actual Chamber. Beth was in there and in a few seconds he would be, too. He took one step toward his goal when another telepathic bomb dropped behind his eyes.

"ABROGHIA IS GONE!"

This time, the voices of nearly a hundred Elders thundered through his mind and he was on the ground writhing under the weight of their words before he realized what happened. Michael clutched his head with both hands and squeezed closed his eyes. As he waited for the excruciating pain to fade, he peeked down the hall only to see his brethren sprawled out on the hard floor, as miserable as he was.

Something had happened to the High Father.

Just as Jesse predicted.

†

In the Population, Roman and Yosef gripped their heads, hoping to alleviate the pressure that threatened to break open their minds. When the first announcement came through, Roman was happy that aside from the one Elder, Javier and every other Rakum that stood with him hadn't heard a thing. They had all been transfigured into the form they desired most and were therefore immune to the telepathic warning issued down from the top of their kind. But when the second broadcast rang through, Roman was incapacitated and brought to the hard floor, along with Elder Yosef. The High Father was gone and Roman was shocked by the turn of events.

Slower than he wished, the pain receded and he got to his feet, helping Yosef up along the way. He opened his mouth to speak, but noticed a strange sensation behind his eyes. He focused on Yosef and wondered if the man's shocked expression matched the one on his face. Within seconds he realized why his brain buzzed so…he was lighter. As if Abroghia's invisible hand that held him down his whole life was miraculously lifted. Roman was free.

"Roman!" Javier came to his side and grasped his arm tightly. "What happened? What's going on?"

Roman blinked and looked down on his son. Javier had been fully human only ten minutes, but he was as comfortable already as if he'd been born that way. And he was jubilant. Roman smiled and saw Yosef step away to simultaneously speak to his own pups.

"Abroghia is gone."

"Gone? Dead?"

Roman paused thoughtfully and then shook his head. "No. Gone. He has deserted us. Beth Rider's God has chased him off."

"What happens now?"

"We go to Assembly." Roman approached the close crowd of newly-turned humans and pulled Javier along with him. "Everyone, head for the elevators. We're going to the Main Hall."

Instantly, comments, questions, and alternate suggestions went up all around, but Yosef intuited the same call and began rounding up everyone on his side. Roman hung back, ushering the crowd with his free arm. He looked at Javier and wiggled his elbow.

"You're safe, Javie. You can let go of my arm."

Javier looked at his hands on Roman's coat and smiled sheepishly. "What will we do in Assembly? What will they do without Abroghia? Where's Beth Rider?"

"In time. Help me herd this company of brothers and we'll watch history unfold."

Roman worked side-by-side with Javier and Yosef to move the people toward the exit. Before long, the Cows would be ordered to

Assembly too, but he wanted to get his own to the top first. Someone would be along to help the lunatics who voluntarily populated the underground dungeon.

When the cluster of twenty-five former Rakum and a handful of believing former-Cows stood in the foyer to the elevators, Javier once again pulled on Roman's arm.

"Simon's not here."

Roman looked around and sighed. A young bearded man stepped forward then and cleared his throat.

Roman inclined his head. "Yes?"

"Your blond friend went under the bleachers," he said with a sympathetic frown and then wandered off.

Roman nodded. He'd seen that one praying with the others moments ago, and he trusted his sincerity. With little effort, he mentally located the stubborn youth, but didn't attempt to make contact. He laid his hand on Javier's shoulder and shook his head.

"You did all you could," Roman said frowning. "He's not afraid. He's hiding from us. He wants to stay behind and see if there is a future for him with our kind."

"But without Abroghia, do we still have a kind?" Javier asked as the elevator headed up with the first load.

Roman shook his head. There would be no more Rakum. When the dust settled in a few hours, there would be a small collection of blood-sucking, long-lived miscreants, but no organized and protected Rakum Race. By sunrise, there would be no more Brotherhood, period.

Javier read everything in his face and grinned. "I'm not worried about Simon. He's going to be okay. I believe."

Roman smiled and nodded his head. The kid was hearing from God now. It was going to be okay.

†

Jack shrugged Meryl off violently when the kid attempted to help him stand. He participated in sending the second transmission and even he was knocked to the ground by the force employed by all viable Elders at once. Now they had two choices; head for the exits and run, which would be a direct disobedience since all of their Fathers commanded them to assemble, or go to the Main Hall and face the Rabbit and her fearsome God.

It was clear from the miniscule telepathic images that

accompanied the Father's announcement, that not only had the High Father abandoned them, but it was Beth Rider who initiated his defeat. Jack shook his head in wonder that such a tiny inconsequential waif could bring down an entire race. And wasn't there something else?

Jack glanced at the faces that surrounded him. Beryl was recuperating in their Barracks from an attack by Elder Roman, but Meryl, Kite, and Gage stood before him. Each man looked terrified and Jack hoped his feelings didn't show on his face as theirs did. What was different?

He looked at the ceiling absently and then behind him toward the Chamber of Fathers still a hundred feet down the hall. Something was amiss.

Meryl stepped forward as silently as a cat and cautiously placed his hand upon Jack's arm. *"Unprotected, master. We're unprotected."*

Jack growled and yanked his arm away. But the kid was right. Whatever powerful forces kept them vital and potent as Rakum had lifted and was gone. He was vulnerable now as he never had been before. Infuriated by his helplessness, Jack whirled around and hurried toward the Chamber. A familiar Rakum stood just outside the door. Maybe he'd break him over his knee again for fun. With Abroghia gone, he might be able to get away with it.

†

Jesse stood fifteen feet from the tunnel opening, but couldn't decide if he should leave. The edicts sent down from the Fathers and then the Elders were dire. After the two announcements of Abroghia's desertion, and the command to assemble, Jesse heard a fourth transmission that now gave him pause. Any Rakum who refused to attend the Assembly would be destroyed, and Jesse didn't scoff. A Father had the ability to stop a Rakum's heart by thought, or burst the blood vessels in his brain if so inclined.

"What's wrong? Is it daybreak?"

Selene was standing to his right, closer to the small, boarded-up opening that would empty into the desert outside. Jesse looked at her absently, his mind still racing with the possibility of being exploded from within.

"Are we going or what?" Her voice was plaintive and Jesse was able to give her an answer finally.

"No." He touched his temple. "I must go to Assembly. The

Rabbit has destroyed the High Father and she commands us to assemble. If I don't go, I will die."

Selene looked to the exit and then back. She could go. She had no telepathic connection with them. They would allow her to leave. Jesse released her hand.

"You go, Selene. You don't need to come with me. You can go outside."

Selene must have thought about it, but when he made his suggestion, she took his arm and shook her head.

"No, if the Rabbit is in charge, then we'll be safe. Her religion is peaceful. I could tell that when Yosef fell for it."

Jesse studied her face a moment, remembered everything he and Michael had shared regarding the Rabbit, God, and life in general. The light in the tunnel was nearly nonexistent and Selene's feminine silhouette made her appear even more regal than he imagined earlier. She was a prize to be cherished and Beth Rider's God *was* the good kind. They had a decent chance of making it out alive and together.

"You're right. Come." Jesse slipped his arm through her hand until their palms clasped and he led her back toward the main floor.

"Can you send someone a message that we're coming? Just to be safe?"

Jesse put a finger to his temple and stopped moving. Michael was right outside the Chamber door and he sent him a short message in keeping with his ability. He then turned to Selene.

"It is done. Let's hurry."

They made their way to the crumbling hand-dug steps in the dirt floor and climbed up. The Rabbit's God would let them be. Convinced, Jesse walked faster toward the light, pulling a willing Selene behind him.

Jack Dawn Meets Emunah

Ready to exit the Chamber of Fathers, Beth once again reached for the brass handle on the old door, but it opened on its own, swinging in toward her at a stately pace. She took one step over the threshold and was ecstatic to find Michael there, his expression one of pure joy.

"Michael!" Beth rushed forward dragging the heavy staff along with her and wrapped her free arm around him tightly. Instead of returning her embrace he cupped her face in his hands.

"You're okay!" Michael then pulled her close and impulsively pressed his lips against hers. After a few heart-stopping seconds, Beth wriggled loose and gestured to the staff in her hand, hoping to avoid any discussion regarding their impromptu display of affection and how hugely it affected her.

"Will you carry this for me?" she whispered, the few syllables sounding raspy to her blushing ears.

Michael's eyes grew wide at the sight of the six-foot symbol of Abroghia standing like a banner of victory at her side. He shook his head no, but reached for it anyway.

"Don't you *DARE*, traitor!"

Michael and Beth both startled and looked down the hall to the entrance of the primary foyer where Jack Dawn and three of his thugs filled the doorway.

"Drop it, Rabbit! No human and no traitor shall ever hold the Staff of Abroghia!" Jack advanced at a brisk walk, his bear-like stance meant to intimidate, his minions following a few steps behind.

Beth repositioned herself to face the Elder and steadied the staff in her left hand, as she'd seen Abroghia do earlier. Jack's reaction was to slow his pace and then stop twenty feet away.

"What are you going to do, Rabbit? Who do you th—"

Jack stopped midsentence, his eyes darting up over Beth's

224

shoulder. Familiar now with this reaction, Beth smiled and motioned for Michael to get behind her.

"Elder Jack Dawn, turn around and lead us to the assembly hall," Beth said firmly and ignored the glance Michael threw her. He did maneuver to her side and allow her to stand inches in front of him, but he kept his eye on his nemesis. It was apparent that her Rakum guardian didn't see her invisible defender and this encouraged her all the more. So far, only the doomed could see him. Michael belonged to God, whether he knew it yet or not.

Jack didn't move, but stood in place, mouth ajar, chest heaving. Like his Fathers before him, his eyes flitted around from Beth to the invisible giant over her shoulder to the staff in her hand. In the moments of indecision, Kite backed two steps and turned away. The clatter of his heels as he tore off down the stone hall didn't distract anyone left standing in the foyer.

"I will not ask you again." Beth lowered her voice and her chin, and lifted the staff with two hands to allow it to drop and sound on the rock beneath her.

Jack jumped visibly at the noise and stepped back. Beth took one step forward and Jack matched her effort the opposite direction, his eye now planted on the angel behind her.

"Lead us to Assembly, Jack. You can still choose. You can choose life."

Jack snarled and dramatically expressed himself with the middle fingers of both hands. "I'd rather die than serve your God, Rabbit. I'll never bow down. Never. My allegiance is to my true king, my true father."

"Jack, you will die if you try anything stu—"

Beth didn't get to finish her sentence. Jack lunged for her, taking two long strides and then leaping into the air in an attempt to hit her head-on. Beth straightened her back to prepare for the blow, but she needn't have worried. Milliseconds before they made contact, the Elder hit an unseen barrier and crumpled to the floor with a ground-shaking thud.

Beth and Michael looked down on him, stunned and unsure if he was dead or unconscious. Michael moved forward with his boot to check and Beth eyed the two Rakum standing nearby. With morbid curiosity they also examined their Elder from a few feet away.

"You two will lead us to Assembly. Let's go. March." Beth made a slight motion forward, handed the staff to Michael and then took another step to encourage the boys to start moving.

"He's dead," Michael whispered, a strange mixture of emotions in his voice.

Beth frowned. "I know. I'm sorry. I really am." She started walking behind the frightened Rakum and Michael kept step easily managing the gigantic staff with his magnificent strength. "I hope they listen, or a lot more of them will die like Jack. Their time is up. The day of the Rakum is over."

"I know," Michael replied as Meryl glanced back, fear in his eye. Michael placed his hand on Beth's shoulder as they gained on the Main Hall. "Beth, what're they looking at? They're not looking at us."

Beth met his eye briefly. "You don't see him, do you?"

"See who?"

"Thank God." Tossing Michael an assuring smile, Beth hurried to the giant archway she knew would open in to the Main Hall. She had a big job ahead of her and she wanted to get to it.

55

Hiding from God

Simon hugged his knees to his chest and watched the exodus through the slats in the steel gray bleachers. All of the praying Rakum filed out the double doors, and more than a few humans tagged along with them. Simon eyeballed the heads as they passed his position looking for one in particular, some throw-back hippie that he'd been dodging since Jesse brought him in. This guy was praying with the Rakum before the call to Assembly went out so he probably wanted to save Simon's soul or something like that. He leaned more forward, but didn't see the guy anywhere.

Roman and Javier were there though, in the rear, herding their fellows to the exit.

"It's wonderful, Simon. Please, give it a try. Please." Javier's last words before he abandoned him once again.

Simon sneered and relaxed against the cool mason block wall. Javier was being sincere, he could tell. He knew the guy well. But...

Simon looked at his hands layered in alternating shadows. Javier wanted him to let go of the past and move into the future. With him, maybe. If he could imagine life without Rakum. Simon didn't know if he could.

"Hey, whatcha doin' under here?"

Simon looked to his left and the hippie was walking toward him, stooped down to fit under the bleachers. He reached him and stuck out his hand.

"I'm Larry. Whatcha doin'? Are you hiding?"

Simon huffed and shook his head. What did the guy want? He was a few years older, with an adolescent beard and kind eyes, but Simon had enough friends, and he definitely didn't want to be pals with a weirdo Christian Cow.

"It's okay. I'm not gonna tell anyone. I'll hide with ya if you want." Larry settled on the dusty floor beside Simon about two feet away and leaned against the wall, mimicking his posture. "So you were with Master Jesse?"

Simon shook his head.

"Oh. I saw him bring you in. Master Jesse's all right. He's called me a few times. He's a gentleman."

Simon looked at Larry sideways. "He was cool."

"So, who's your Sponsor?"

Simon smirked sideways and studied his fingernails. "Nobody."

"Huh, I doubt that," Larry laughed.

Something about his tone caught Simon's attention. "What do you mean?"

Larry held up his thumbs and forefingers in a three-sided box and peeked through it to Simon's face, then scanned down to his feet.

Simon shook his head. "What?"

"A guy like you is never passed around."

"What do you mean? Like me?"

"Don't play dumb." Larry opened his hands, palms out and framed his own face. "This mug will get you passed around. That one will make you someone's pet."

"Oh. Huh." Simon understood. "It's not all wine and roses, I can tell you that."

Larry caught his drift. "They're not all so nice as Master Jesse."

"No," Simon agreed quietly.

"I know hundreds of Rakum. Wanna hear about my first time?" Larry was looking at Simon's profile, but he shrugged without returning his gaze. "I was sixteen, playing bass in my friend Tommy's garage band. We were awful." Larry laughed. "But we had a gig at a tiny club off the Strip. I saw my first Rakum there in the john."

Simon looked up briefly. "In the john?"

Larry laughed again. "Yeah, I had to whiz and I busted into the bathroom and slammed into a guy coming out. I knew there was something different about him right away. I don't know exactly what it was, but I have a sort of sixth-sense about things. Anyway, after our set I walked up to the guy and introduced myself."

"What did he say?"

"He invited me to his place for a party."

"And you went? With a strange man? Are you nuts?"

"I told you, he wasn't a man. I knew he was something else."

Simon considered his assertion and then nodded his head. He was the same way with Javier. Love at first sight. No questions asked.

"And he was the first one to show me the ropes. He worked here, at the Cave, so I started coming here off and on, and that was eight years ago."

Simon looked back to Larry's face, glanced at his smallish but strong frame. This wanna-be rock star let blood for hundreds of Rakum for eight years. It was hard to imagine. And a little chilling.

"You want to know why most Cows are men?"

Simon's eyebrows went up. The question had occurred to him in the past, but Javier never had an answer for him.

"Because women are too emotional. They get hysterical. And men are easier to seduce. Weird, huh?"

Simon had no response. He couldn't deny either claim so he remained mum and hoped he wasn't blushing.

"They prefer female blood because of spiritual reasons, but it's not worth the trouble to get it from those who resist. If they don't submit, it's not any good."

"Spiritual reasons? Like what?"

"God made women more spiritual. They have a direct phone line to the Big Guy." Larry read disbelief in Simon's eyes and shrugged. "Honest!"

"That's bull."

"I know lots more about these guys, too. Did you know they can't swim?"

"What? Yes they can," Simon argued. He'd been camping with Javier. They'd been out on the boat at night. Javier hadn't worn a life vest bragging he couldn't drown.

"No, they can't swim. Something about their body density. They sink to the bottom. It's true." Larry held up his hands. "Honest!" Simon scoffed. "So, who's your sponsor?" Larry continued.

"His name was Javier."

"Was? Oh, he left with the believers?"

Simon nodded, eyes on his shoes.

"Is he human now?"

Simon nodded again and sifted some dirt through his fingers. "It's stupid. Why can't he stay the way he is *and* believe in God? It's just stupid."

"Oil and water, Frank. Oil and water."

"Frank?" Simon met his eyes with a tiny spark of humor.

"You haven't told me your name, so I'm calling you Frank. Ol' blue eyes." Larry threw him a goofy grin.

Simon chuckled, feeling a little lighter for it. "Sorry, man. It's Simon. Simon Miller."

"Okay, Simon. God and Rakum are like oil and water. They don't mix."

"But why not?"

"Haven't you ever read the Bible, Simon?"

"Yeah. Some of it."

"Rakum are the opposite of God." Larry shrugged, his tone as matter-of-fact as if they discussed the weather.

"I don't believe that. Javier was always good to me. He loved me. Still does..."

"And as soon as he became a believer, he turned into a human. There's your proof. Hey, I've been seeing it all week. Back where I come from, three Elders changed at the same time. It was pretty cool."

"It still doesn't make sense."

"A good Jew should know that drinking blood is bad."

"How'd you know I'm Jewish?" Simon wasn't offended, but he was surprised. He had absolutely zero ethnic markers that he was aware of. Larry winked and put a grimy fingernail to his eye.

"I see things, Simon. I knew you were a Jew when you came in with Master Jesse."

"Weird."

"One of the Fathers is Jewish."

"Huh? You're kidding." Simon didn't think much about the difference between Jew and Gentile.

"No. His name is Theophilus."

"Duh—that's a Greek name. Greek. Gentile. Dig?"

Larry laughed. "There are Jews in Greece, Simon. Anyway, I heard that Father Theophilus once met Jesus, in the flesh."

Simon flashed a glare at the mention of the Name, more out of habit than authentic emotion.

"No, it's true. He actually heard Him preach. He taught all day and when the evening fell, Father Theophilus followed after Him for a few days before he met Father Abroghia."

"Abroghia—he's the boss, right?"

"Yeah, he was the boss. I think he's gone now. He was the oldest. Anyway, Theophilus, according to the story, was given a choice and he chose Abroghia over God."

"I can dig it."

"But it was a stupid choice. See, Jesus *loved* Theophilus and Abroghia only wanted to use him."

Simon scoffed and held up his hands as imaginary scales. "The guy had to choose between power and immortality *or* submission and love? Not much of a choice."

"I chose God. Now I have immortality and love. And nobody is using me and I am nobody's slave." Larry hugged his knees now, his voice growing softer.

"Humans are not immortal and they're weak," Simon argued, but Larry only smiled.

"Shows what you know. Because I joined up with God, I will live forever. And who do you think caused all this ruckus? Who do you think is changing the Rakum into mortals? Who won the war if the Rakum are being destroyed? It's God."

Simon was silent, the guy was right. Larry was on the winning team. Javier was on it with him. Why couldn't Simon get on board? What was keeping him from turning to his Creator and asking for a little help? A little guidance? A little shove toward the good side?

The amazingly intuitive Larry nudged him then and offered to pray for him. Simon hemmed, but finally consented. He repeated a few phrases and he thought of a few prayers of his own. When all was said and done, the room had been emptied and Simon was smiling.

He knew some secrets now. Had some answers. Asking God to take over his life had cleared the cobwebs from every corner of his mind. Things made sense.

Oil and water.

Blood and life.

Rakum and Human.

Good and evil.

He'd become foolish and God lifted him up and gave him some wisdom.

And the Name didn't bother him anymore.

56

The Truth

Beth stepped into what the Rakum referred to as their Main Hall and gawked at its sheer immensity. The Population had been large, but this place took her breath away. Lighted electrically, but with minimum glare, the huge space diminished all who entered. As far as the eye could see, Rakum sat or stood in layers, some as small as ants in the sky-high bleachers. The floor space was also entirely peopled with bodies moving one way or the other, vying for a place to stand when the Rabbit was to speak.

Michael cleared his throat to get her moving and Beth smiled sheepishly.

"It's just so *big*," she remarked and continued into the room doing her best to appear casual. She had absolutely no fear and her confidence had emboldened her Rakum guardian. Michael walked tall and gestured with the staff to those they neared along the way. As a result, a generous path opened up for them as they made their way to the center of the floor.

Beth spied the raised platform ahead and the nine Fathers already assembled there, standing stooped and defeated in a queue reminiscent of their position in the Chamber. When she reached the steps to climb onto the stage she heard her name behind her.

"Miss Beth! Miss Beth!"

It was David. Beth grabbed the youth into her embrace.

"Look! I'm a man! A regular human man!" He pointed to his black eye, misjudged the distance and made contact. Even as he winced from the discomfort, he laughed with glee. Then he spun around and shook hands with Michael whose face lit up in response.

Another figure came close and pulled Beth into a hug before she could refuse. It was Javier, and Beth squeezed him back as he spoke in her ear.

"It's happened." Javier's mouth was right up against her cheek and his excitement barely bottled. "Roman, too. It's a miracle. Everyone who was with us in the Pop, we've all been brought near to God!"

Beth held him close and tip-toed up to ask him about Simon. Javier stepped out of her arms and pointed behind him.

"Simon, too..."

Beth's heart seemed about to burst with joy. She grinned at the college kid and then nodded her head to Roman. He smiled back with a subdued but sincere grin.

"Come up on the stage with us, all of you," Beth called over the noise of the crowd and headed up the steps.

Michael followed David, Javier, Roman and Simon as they positioned themselves five abreast in the center of the nine remaining Fathers.

As soon as she took the stage, the crowd grew quiet. The thousands of faces in the room turned toward their fallen leaders and the Rabbit's Rakum partner that held the symbol of their power in his strong left hand.

Beth inhaled and then released the air slowly, waiting for some words to come to her from on high. After another two seconds, she heard a familiar baritone over her right shoulder respond.

"It is time, Beth Rider, daughter of the Most High God, for the destruction of those not present."

Beth looked to the distant black ceiling and spoke to the air. "But Father! Please wait! Ten more minutes. What if there are more Peters out there? More Nallys? More Davids? Let's give them one more chance to come in!"

When she heard no reply, Beth turned to the Rakum Father on her right and touched his sleeve. Theophilus shied away, but awaited her command.

"Contact those who are on the run. Tell them they only have ten minutes to get to the Main Hall or they will be destroyed." She waited for a nod and an obvious action before turning to the Father on her left.

"Johann, how many Rakum could not make it to Assembly this time? David said sometimes they are incapacitated."

"One hundred and fifty," Johann answered without a pause. But in her other ear, Emunah corrected him.

"One hundred and fifty-three."

"Okay. Johann, contact every single one of these Rakum right now and repeat my words exactly. Understand?"

The shaky old man's eyes widened, but he consented with a slight nod of his regal head.

Beth gave a brief overview of what their brethren were facing at the Cave and then asked them if they would consider giving their allegiance to the God of Israel from this day forward. It was all she could do long distance and she hoped that any Rakum God called would soften his heart and receive His salvation. The rebellious were about to be destroyed and she knew it was God's will that none should perish.

Next Beth turned her attention to the hush-quiet crowd that surrounded the stage. Taking the staff from Michael, she stepped forward and caused it to strike the platform with a tremendous noise that reverberated off the distant walls. Sending up a prayer in her heart and then garnishing a quick look of encouragement from Michael at her side, Beth opened her mouth to speak.

"In the beginning God created the heavens and the earth..."

She told them about their Creator.

She told them about His love.

And she shared the most wonderful Truth of all: Redemption was nigh. For whosoever sought it.

Epilogue

Seven Years Later

Beth leaned on her desktop and watched as her husband finished reading the first draft. She'd finally completed the manuscript of the account of her incredible experience with the Rakum a mere six years ago. Here, in her comfortable suburban home, with the Saturday afternoon sun streaming in through her office window bathing her in warmth, the events of that dark week seemed more fiction than not. But the proof sat across from her, reclining in a new La-Z-Boy, the spiral bound book draft in his massive but gentle hands.

The sunlight framed Michael's face and did not burn his skin as in days of old. His broad shoulders and muscular build still intimidated his co-workers at the airport, but now he was their Chief, working full time, Monday through Friday, eight-to-five. Life was good and had never been sweeter.

Michael looked at her then over his wire-framed reading glasses, a look of love and awe on his handsome face.

"What? Where are you?" She leaned forward over her knees, eyebrows raised. This was the first look she'd given him of the writing project that took her three years to commit to paper.

"I had no idea. I'm...I'm blown away." Michael shook his head and pulled the spectacles from his face. "Abroghia—he was one of those devils that fell from heaven in the beginning? I just never..."

Beth nodded slowly in tune with his wonder. "I wasn't permitted to divulge everything at the Assembly, you know. But yeah, that is what the old demon said. And that is what the vision looked like when Emunah told me about Abroghia's origins."

Michael shook his head again and laid the book on his lap. "It's unbelievable. I was half-demon. Abroghia was my natural father and he was a devil? It blows my mind."

"We're all half-demon, Michael. We're all born into sin. You just

235

had a little extra boost, is all." Beth stood and crossed the room and removed the book from his lap. "God let me have you, that's my favorite part of the story. That's my reward."

Beth fell into Michael's lap and he held her gently and ran his hand through her hair. It was only shoulder-length now, but he still rarely took his eyes off it.

"You didn't mention the staff."

Beth shook her head. "No, I left that out." She shrugged and looked at him out of the corner of her eye. "Since I'm not certain where it is, I didn't want to mention it. I mean, what if someone starts a quest to find it? Maybe I'm being paranoid, but it needs to stay missing."

Michael nodded in agreement and kissed her forehead. "How many do you suppose made it out, Hon? How many are still out there in the dark?"

Beth didn't answer. She only knew what she saw that night in the Cave. Half of the Rakum present believed her words and committed to at least learn more about God. Ten thousand of them walked out of the facility into the daylight and were not burned. No matter what the numbers were, a miracle took place that night. And Beth promised herself to never think on the rebellious and evil Rakum who disappeared into the fabric of the night to regroup and survive any way they could.

Without Abroghia, the Cave shut down entirely. The NCJ transportation system, too. All across the globe, Rakum businesses and associations fell like dominoes until all were destitute. Any Rakum who slithered into the dark, did so penniless and alone. Beth caught Michael's eye and knew he was thinking on the same things, only he was recalling specific brothers he cared about, brothers he'd discipled and known. Beth wrapped her arms about his neck and hugged him tight.

"I love you, Michael Stone."

"I love you, too—"

"Daddy! Daddy!"

Just then, a precious voice piped in from the doorway and a tiny figure rushed into the room, all pink lace and ruffles. Michael received the child's flight into his lap and balanced her on Beth's so he was holding both of the women that had stolen his heart.

"Daddy! Daily's here! Daily's here!" Excited about the arrival of their guests, Grace Louise grasped her father's face in her miniature hands and squeezed his mouth into a pucker. "Hurry! I saw her pull up! Come on!"

Beth laughed and shimmied out from under the bouncing five-year-old and left her to her father's care. Jesse and Selene were married the same month as she and Michael, and their daughters were born only three days apart. Michael stood to his feet, Grace dangling around his neck like a priceless necklace.

"Dae Lee, sweetie. It's Dae Lee." Michael supported his daughter with his arms and sent his wife a wink. Beth shooed him with her hands.

"Go let them in. And will you send Selene up here? I want to show her the book before we leave for dinner."

"Sure," Michael said and turned for the door.

Beth smiled and shut down her computer as Michael clomped down the stairs. The sounds of greetings and kisses wafted up the stairwell and an immeasurable sense of joy filled her heart to capacity until she wept grateful tears. It was a wonderful thing to be used by the Most High God, and an even more wonderful thing to survive to do it again. ...But only if necessary.

Beth wiped her tears from her cheeks and sent up a prayer of thanks to her God. It was good to be a daughter of the King.

END BOOK ONE

The Rabbit Trilogy

The Rabbit Saga *includes 6 novels. The first 3 involve the Rakum becoming aware of a Creator, and the last 3 bring every last one to choose sides.* Books 1-3 Now Available.

The Rabbit Saga Book Four

Expected Fall 2018

BONUS

....Delightful "Easter egg" chapters delving into the characters of The Rabbit Trilogy.*

Loose Rabbits of the Rabbit Trilogy

These are only a few of the available Loose Rabbits. Visit www.ellencmaze.com and click LOOSE RABBITS for more!

A Few Loose Rabbits of the Rabbit Trilogy:

1: Javier's First Time

1897

Javier caught Roman's eye, aware that his goofy grin irritated his Elder immensely. Elder Roman detested his emotive tendencies, but how could he not be excited? Since he moved in with Roman twelve years ago, he'd only been in the company of mortals a handful of times, and all of those had been aware of his supernatural propensities. Now they were on a steam locomotive traveling to New York City to reside in a *hospital*. One literally filled with humans, most of them unaware that he was a Rakum, and all of them as helpless as babes. Javier couldn't even begin to imagine the adventures in store.

So, he grinned like a lunatic.

Of course, Roman frowned.

"Why don't you go for a walk," Roman ordered.

"Where to? We're on a train," Javier replied smiling, but Roman was not amused. "Okay." Javier dropped the silly grin and stepped to the door of their private room. "I've been feeling strange. Maybe it's too stuffy in here."

"Wait." Roman stood and touched Javier's sleeve. "Explain."

Javier turned. "What?"

"Explain this feeling."

Javier was thoughtful as Roman was not one to mince words or waste time with worthless conversation.

"Yes. Right here." Javier made a circle around his midsection. "I feel a lightness, and then," he made a popping noise with his mouth, "it changes to a feeling of heaviness."

"And you first discerned this when?"

Javier grinned, enjoying Roman's undivided attention. "When the train got underway. I assumed it was the motion."

"No." Roman shook his head. "There's a Cow on this train. I sensed him myself. You've inherited the radar. *Finally, a step forward.*"

Roman said the last under his breath with disdain, but Javier's jaw dropped. It was the first time he'd experienced a draw for the mortals who willingly gave blood to his people.

"Cow-dar?" Javier chuckled, but as before Roman didn't crack a smile. He resumed a poker face and fell quiet.

"Yes. So, go for your walk. Track him."

"It's definitely a man?"

"Yes." Roman managed a very tiny smile. "See if you can find him."

"And if I do?" Javier's heart rate increased and he swallowed with anticipation of the hunt.

"Bring him here. Do not take his blood outside of our quarters." Roman released his sleeve and gestured with his hand. "Go, now."

Javier nodded and left the room, walking purposefully down the narrow aisle that ran the length of the private sleeping car. He had no instructions to follow except to go and do, so he proceeded as far as the exit and paused.

Nothing.

His stomach still ached, longed, but...nothing. Curious but not frustrated, Javier opened the door and entered the dining car.

Dinner was over and half of the tables sat empty. Those who remained drank brandy and smoked, creating a veritable cloud. No one took notice of him as he walked slowly down the center of the car, peeking at the other passengers out of the corner of his eye. Of course, he wouldn't be able to *see* the Cow so much as sense him—he knew that much from his lessons. Still, using his vision was easier, and he scoped the car's occupants. When he reached the end of the car, he sighed and yanked open the door. The next box was for livestock so he stood between and listened to the rails.

It was not nearly as noisy as he expected and he could see the track passing at a good clip through a narrow opening in the floor. He watched the ties zip past one after the other, shining in his special vision, for several minutes. Just before he became mesmerized by the repetitive movement his stomach lurched. At the same time, the door from the dining car came open behind him. Javier turned, leaned against the wall of the next car and met the eyes of his visitor.

The man was 60, if a day, with white hair sprouting from his head as well as his chin. His eyes were translucent blue and a life of hard labor was etched in the wrinkles of his face.

"Evenin'," he said, nodding to Javier in a style reminiscent of the brethren. The man positioned himself against the door of the dining car, the placement of his thick frame preventing accidental interruption.

Javier opened his mouth to speak, but was at a loss for words. His midsection flopped again and he subconsciously put a hand to his belly. The stranger eyed him up and down and smiled, revealing only a few good teeth.

"Name's Chester. Harold Chester."

He spoke in a curious American accent and stood motionless, allowing Javier a moment to process. Finding his voice, Javier spoke his name.

"Javier d'Millier."

Old Chester inclined his head to Javier and gave him a knowing wink. "I recognized you, master."

Javier exhaled and nodded his head. This guy was familiar with his people. That was good. Some of the pressure relieved immediately.

"I recognize you, too," Javier joked weakly. Chester nodded and a partial smile could be seen beneath his copious beard.

"You look like a kid," he said with humor.

"I am a kid," Javier answered, matching the grandfather's attitude.

"Do you mean you're not a cuppla hundred years old, masquerading as a teenager?" Chester chided and scratched his chin.

Javier shook his head, liking the stranger more and more. "I'm twenty."

Chester chuckled and swore jovially. "You have a long life ahead of you son. My master was pert near 2000 years old when I met him. He looked fifty, at the most. And that was, well…" Chester removed his weathered newsboy cap and rubbed his head thoughtfully. "Thirty years ago."

"Where is he now?" Curious, Javier asked the next obvious question.

"When I came back from the War, he was gone. I fought for the South." Chester winked, replaced his hat, and grinned wistfully. "Damien was his name."

"Damien is a Father," Javier blurted, but the old man only shrugged.

The Rakum were governed by the Ten Fathers, ancient and powerful creatures whose lives were shrouded in mystery. Perhaps Damien did visit this Cow as a youth. Why would the guy lie?

Javier chuckled again at the irony.

Father Damien was *his* true father.

"So, you hungry?" Chester asked, and unbuttoned the top of his canvas duck coat. Javier stepped forward, covering the man's gnarled hand with his palm.

"Wait. Follow me."

Chester moved away from the door and fell in behind him as they re-entered the dining car. Javier paced his breathing and grew more excited as they neared their destination. By the time he reached the door to his quarters, he could no longer hide his excitement nor quell his longing. He pushed open the door and shoved Chester inside. Roman was waiting, obviously telepathically aware of all that had transpired outside. He gestured to Javier, palm up and greeted the Cow with a nod.

"Chester, remove your coat."

Javier's hands clenched into fists as he stood behind the old man, watching him slowly remove his overcoat and then push up his sleeves. The bloodlust was nearing a level that frightened him. He met Roman's eyes, but his Elder's hand was still upraised and Javier made a small sound in his throat.

"Chester, you're Javier's first catch, but far from his first mortal. He will be careful." Roman glanced at Javier then, his eye hard. Then he looked down on the old man and took his coat. "Don't be afraid."

"No, Master, sir," the old soldier answered stoically and faced Javier.

"Javier, hand me your knife."

Roman held out his hand now and Javier dug around in his trouser pockets, his eyes red. Once he grasped it he tossed it to his Elder not at all concerned about what he was going to do with it. All he could see was the blood. The sound of his own heart beating nearly drowned out that of the stranger that shared their small room. Again, a small noise escaped his throat and he watched the knife in Roman's hand.

"Javier, step over here."

Roman only had to wait a millisecond and Javier was by his side his hands open and ready to grab Chester's bared arm. As he watched, Roman sliced the man's flesh quick and deep and Javier dropped to his knees to take his portion. At one point during his meal, Roman spoke to the Cow, and then a minute later, spoke to him. But Javier drank on, oblivious.

His first Cow.

His brain buzzed with delight, and he did not let up until he was forcefully pulled off the man's arm by his Elder.

244

"Now sew him up, Javier," Roman said sternly, his fingers tugging Javier's hair.

Javier's eyesight blurred and his brain was stuffed with cotton, but as if from far away, he recognized Roman's terse tone. His Elder was instructing him. Javier focused as well as he could and covered Chester's still-leaking laceration with his palm. Taking only about fifteen seconds, Javier was able to convince the man's blood to clot and for the skin to knit together. Finished, Javier dropped his arm and sat on the floor.

"Where're you headed, Chester?"

Roman was speaking to the Cow, both of them ignoring the smiling Rakum on the floor. Javier looked between them, amused at nothing and everything.

"Boston, master." Chester looked at Javier and shook his head. "Unless you think you might need me again."

Roman glanced at Javier on the floor. "No, thank you, Chester. You go on to Boston. Do you miss your Rakum master?"

"Sometimes I do. I'm right lonely now, Master."

Roman nodded and handed the man his overcoat. "If you go to a lounge called the Red Herring and ask for Beatle..."

Chester smiled at the name.

Javier laughed out loud, saying, "Beatle!"

Roman glared at his proselyte on the hard floor. "Yes. Beatle's master will use you. Mention my name, Elder Roman."

Chester's eyes widened. "Elder..."

"That name will open doors for you, Chester."

"Thank you, master." Chester turned his cap around in his hands and bowed low. He then turned to Javier and bowed to him, as well. "Thank you. It's been a pleasure. Thank you..."

"Chester!" Javier called as the old gentleman put his hand to the door handle. "The pleasure was all mine."

Flattered, Chester nodded and exited the room. Javier looked dumbly at the door, his buzz finally passing. Roman cleared his throat and he made an effort to stand.

"My first catch," Javier whispered as he pulled himself up using the bench that doubled as a bed. "Who'd have thought I'd meet my first catch on the midnight train to New York?"

"Amazing," Roman dead-panned and rolled his hands at his disciple. "Shake it off. You barely held it together. That was pitiful."

"There'll be Cows in New York, won't there?" Javier watched as Roman nodded. "And I'll get to practice over and over, right?" Roman nodded again, this time allowing a twinkle in his gray eyes. "Good."

"Yes, good." Roman gestured to the opposite bench. "Now sit. We have two hours until our stop. I would appreciate some peace."

"Yes, Master," Javier agreed. He settled across from his Elder and crossed one leg over the other. "Do the Fathers keep Cows?"

Roman caught his eye, apparently annoyed at Javier's impertinence.

"I thought it was ironic Chester knew Father Damien. So…they use Cows then?"

"Drop it, Javie."

"We're not permitted to know?"

Roman sighed and lowered the newspaper he was reading. "When you meet Father Damien, why don't you ask him?"

"I'm meeting Father Damien in New York?" Javier sat up, his mind crystal clear. He'd never met any of the Fathers, but he knew that he was supposed to before he graduated First Ritual. His Elder nodded his head and returned to his reading. The subject was closed.

Javier smiled as his mind raced. Soon he would meet his blood father and his Rakum Father for the first time. What adventures he was in for, and at the moment, he was as serene as he'd ever been. His stomach was full and his eyes heavy, yet a satisfaction filled his soul that he'd never known. Things were looking up.

He had Cow-dar now and he laughed aloud at his new word. He'd never go hungry again. On top of his thoughts as usual, Roman scoffed and fell silent.

Javier looked out the window, feeling better than he had in his whole life. It was good. *All good.*

2: The History between Roman and Kilmeade

Roman left Javier alone with the junior Rakum and pulled open the side door leading into the attached dwelling. His superb sense of smell picked up Kilmeade's scent right away and he had no trouble locating him in the sprawling residence. He and Kilmeade were born of the same mother on the same evening, three minutes apart. Among Rakum, no familial ties were acknowledged, and the boys were kept apart until their teens. But when reunited at the close of First Ritual, the two 17-year-olds became inseparable.

Being fraternal twins and first-rate telepaths, they were able to keep their blood connection secret, and for decades they traveled the world as Rakum comrades. Life was good. But politics among the brethren being as they were, when they were both promoted to Elder months apart, they were separated by the Fathers to settle different areas of the North American Continent. In 1838, at 200 years old, Kilmeade was sent to establish a Rakum presence in New York City, and Roman to the villages and forests of Canada. Now it was 1897 and Roman hadn't seen his brother since their split nearly sixty years earlier.

"Enter, brother."

Roman recognized the voice on the other side of the closed door. He wondered what he'd see in his brother. The Fathers warned him that Kilmeade had been taking the dying buzz and had been horribly disfigured by the effects. A heinous crime among their people, Kilmeade's punishment would be meted out in private in the wilderness of Montreal. Kilmeade was slated to move into Roman's forest cabin as he and Javier assumed his situation at the hospital. Now as he opened the door and approached his brother, Roman readied for anything.

"Roman, having you here gives me great pleasure." Kilmeade spoke facing away from his guest, and Roman stepped up, waiting for him to turn. "I hope you're as strong as ever, big brother. I've been up to no good here at the hospital." Kilmeade turned slowly and met Roman's eye, a glint of humor shining deep down, and a smile playing on his lips.

Roman's eyes widened, but he returned the smile and tilted his

247

head to the side. "You've looked better, my brother."

Kilmeade laughed aloud and leaned against the wall behind him. Roman marveled at his countenance. Kilmeade was naturally tall, like Roman, but where Roman was slender, Kilmeade had always been broad shouldered and thick-necked. Now, he appeared more muscular and hunched over by inches. Since his youth, he'd worn his auburn hair at shoulder-length, but now it drizzled down his chest on either side as long as a woman's. His formerly smoke-gray eyes were an unnaturally bright robin-egg blue, and his lips ruby red. Roman snickered and gestured toward his brother.

"Please don't show this face to my pup, Javier. He'll have nightmares for years." Kilmeade returned his grin and nodded.

"You read my mind. Let's go see him right away—" Kilmeade stopped abruptly, lost his grin, and looked off to the right, no doubt telepathically spying on Canaan and Javier. Roman chuckled, knowing what Kilmeade was about to remark.

"Ohhhh," his brother dragged out the word and looked back to him, smiling. "You are devious. You'll make a fast friend with Canaan that way. That boy will drink anything."

"Canaan is not my concern," Roman scoffed. "Javier, on the other hand, has a lot to learn."

"I want to meet him. That pup of yours is special, isn't he?" Kilmeade's eyebrows went up with interest, but Roman artfully changed the subject.

"This is because of the dying buzz?" He gestured to Kilmeade's face.

"Nice, eh?" Kilmeade smiled wider and revealed his eye-teeth, now extended several centimeters and sharpened to a point. "Check these out."

Roman walked up to him and putting one hand behind his brother's head, he put the other in his mouth. The tip was serrated and Roman's flesh was nicked as he made contact.

"Those must come in handy. Wrong or not, I could use teeth like that."

Kilmeade laughed and ran his tongue over and around his teeth. "I'll miss them. If they go away, that is."

"They will. The Fathers will put you in isolation. You will drink only Rakum blood for a year. You'll be restored completely, trust me." Roman spoke confidently, rehashing the same story the Fathers told him when he was ordered to report to New York.

"That Canaan is gung-ho to save me," Kilmeade giggled and covered his mouth. "Pardon me," he snickered, "another effect is joviality. Feels good, Roman."

"Too good." Roman assumed a serious expression and waited for his brother to do the same. When Kilmeade finally quieted, he sighed and continued. "When you reach the cabin, there are a few small things you'll need to tend to. I regularly pay the village brothel keeper fifty dollars a month in silver. He doesn't know about our people." Roman lowered his voice. "He thinks Javier and I are vampires." Resisting the urge to smile, Roman pulled up a chair. "But he is agreeable. The woman at the brothel who knows our people is Agatha, and I have told her to watch for you. I didn't know about Canaan, so please inform him."

"They won't allow me human blood for at least twelve months, and as for sex—do you think Agatha would mind this face?" Kilmeade was joking and Roman didn't answer.

"Tell Canaan. I shouldn't have to."

"So serious," Kilmeade laughed and reached for an old fashioned bell-pull. In the basement of the house, Roman heard a tinkle of brass as his brother yanked it twice. "Let me introduce you to my Cows. They're quite disgusted with me, so forgive them their insolence."

"Because you haven't used them?" Roman waited for him to nod, the idiotic smile still in place. "I hope you haven't coddled them, Kilmeade. I do not suffer humans."

His brother stepped up, slapped his chest, and headed for the door. "Relax. You can retrain them. I have no doubt you will."

Roman steeled his jaw at the sound of heavy footfalls in the hallway. Kilmeade pulled open the door and two men ambled in, barely looking in their master's direction. Instead, they fixed their eyes on Roman and stopped ten feet away. Kilmeade shadowed the men dramatically and then stood behind them, a hand on each man's outside shoulder. The theatrics wore thin and Roman cleared his throat.

His brother began the introductions. "Poppy Jaster."

The man on Kilmeade's right removed his cap with one quick nod. He seemed tame enough and was a sturdy man, built for labor.

"He's in charge of the grounds. Poppy, this is Elder Roman, your new master."

"I'm your servant, Master Roman," Poppy mumbled sincerely and lowered his eyes. Roman indicated his approval and looked to the other man.

"And this is Kelly O'Brien, Hospital Administrator."

The second man was older by twenty years with the same height and thick build. His main oddity was a bulbous deformity of the nose and the diagnosis hit Roman with no effort at all.

"Your tumor is cancerous, O'Brien. If you don't have it removed soon, the disease will spread to your facial tissue and you'll die within months."

Kilmeade's eyebrows went up and he touched the man's nose from behind with one elongated finger. "Oh, how about that."

Dodging Kilmeade's poke, O'Brien took the news in stride. "Thank you, master. I'll have the doctors look at it this week."

"Good. Now let me set the ground rules so that our time together will be as pleasant as possible." Roman had their full attention. "Do not touch me or my pup, Javier. And if I touch you, keep your hands to yourself. I prefer Cows to untrained mortals, so I will use you often. But Javier will use the human patients here. Help him in choosing who to tap and who to avoid."

"I vow to do this for you, master," O'Brien said and dared a peek over his shoulder where Kilmeade stood. "And I'm glad you're here."

Kilmeade ruffled the man's oily white hair jovially and then made a fist against his scalp, pulling his head backward. "Been lonely, have you? I could tap you now, you old goat. I long to do it. Just grab on and not let up until you—"

"Elder Kilmeade," Roman said sternly, addressing his brother formerly before the Cows. Because of his condition, Kilmeade's behavior was unpredictable and he decided to finish up. "You men may go. Report to me tomorrow night at sundown."

Both men nodded and waited for Kilmeade to dismiss them. Roman's brother opened his hand on O'Brien's hair and patted it down as if stroking a kitten.

"Bye now, old Cow," he cooed and bowed low, snickering as they scooted around him and left the room. Roman frowned.

"You've really lost it, brother."

"I know, but oh, I feel good."

Roman commiserated with a small grin, but then flinched. The Fathers were sending him instructions and he held up his hand and closed his eyes. Recognizing the moment, Kilmeade was silent and waited several seconds before Roman sighed and nodded to himself.

"When was your last human blood meal, brother?"

Kilmeade's eyes grew round. "Fourteen days. I haven't relapsed since the Fathers called me on it."

Roman sucked his teeth and shook his head, pondering the capricious nature of their leaders. They wanted him to buzz his brother. Why? It didn't matter; probably for their own entertainment. Roman unbuttoned his cuff and rolled up his sleeve.

Kilmeade didn't need a formal invitation. He closed the distance between them, grasped Roman's forearm and jerked it to his mouth. Roman looked away and counted the seconds. Sixty should do it. As he neared the time, he faced his brother and placed a hand on his frizzy hair.

"Come see me when you are well, brother. I've missed you."

Still pulling blood as hard as he could, Kilmeade responded in Hungarian telepathically. *"A bátyám. Barátom."*

My brother. My friend. How appropriate.

Roman smoothed his hair and gave him an extra minute. Why not? What were brothers for?

3: How Michael Met Jeremy

At Dannelly Field Regional Airport, Michael unbuckled his firearm and tucked it away in its custom case. The new janitor had followed him into the locker room and once again, Michael ignored him. There was an art to cultivating such a relationship and Michael had years of practice. The guy was a good candidate—healthy, young, male, and in a hopeless state of awe.

Michael arranged and rearranged his belongings as slowly as possible to give the little guy a chance to get closer. Three days ago, the airport's newest employee caught wind of Michael strolling down the concourse checking doors between arrivals. Michael barely gave him a glance that first night. The second and third nights, the kid watched him with an expression Michael had seen countless times before, a hopeless and unidentified longing.

No doubt the janitor was confused and embarrassed that he experienced such a draw for another man, but Michael was glad for it. It was the way he chose all of his Cows.

Or more correctly, how they chose him.

Most Rakum sought out the oddball humans who lived to let their blood, but a few, like Michael, attracted the donors with no effort on their part whatsoever. And this, the fourth desperate night, Michael decided to toss him a bone. Tonight, as he stood looking into his chest-high locker, the janitor came up alongside him and inched forward, until he was an arms' length away. The kid was short, maybe five feet, with spiked black hair that belied his Hispanic heritage. He was cute in a puppy-dog way and Michael had no trouble seeing him as a future pet. He slammed the locker door to watch him jump and tilted his head, meeting the kid's eye.

"What?" Michael asked, playing coy.

"Officer Stone? My name's Jeremy," the kid said without an accent. He paused after stating his name and licked his lips.

Michael knew that he had no idea what to say. He regarded Jeremy with a long look and then gave him the smallest smile.

"Jeremy, what's up?"

"I…well, I…" Jeremy stumbled over a reply and then reached into his pocket, his eyes glazing over.

As Michael watched, he pulled out a retractable box cutter,

pushed out the blade, and put it to the soft rise of his palm below his thumb. The guy was hooked and Michael hadn't even lifted a finger. With a grunt, Michael reached forward and snatched the blade from his hand.

"Not here, Jeremy."

"Oh, I…I'm sorry. I…" Jeremy stuttered and blinked his eyes several times in succession. Michael gave him a reassuring smile and leaned toward the kid to tuck his blade back into his coveralls.

"Meet me in the employee parking lot at 10:45."

Jeremy nodded, his huge brown eyes watery and dazed.

Michael smiled and chuckled, amazed at his good fortune. All over the planet, his brothers were bending over backward to find two or three crazy humans to donate blood for free, where for Michael it was easier than taking candy from a baby. What was it about him that attracted the freaks? He had no idea, but the saying among his brethren was "easier is always better." So, he accepted his lot. He had seven Cows already, and this young man would make a nice even eight. What else could a Rakum lieutenant ask for?

At 10:45 p.m., Michael approached his Saab and noted a familiar figure standing by the right quarter panel.

"Hey, Jeremy." Michael nodded to the kid and gestured to the car. "Get in."

The kid pulled open the passenger side door without hesitation and slipped into the seat. Michael was seated behind the wheel and as they left the airport, Jeremy sighed. Michael looked over at him briefly and tipped his head.

"What?"

"Where're we headed, Officer Stone?"

"Call me Michael for now, Jeremy."

Jeremy nodded his head and then unbuttoned his collar. He was no longer wearing his gray work coveralls, but a green-striped dress shirt and black jeans.

"I feel weird," he mumbled, watching Michael's profile as he drove.

Michael smiled. "I'll bet."

"I gotta get outta this shirt." Jeremy pulled at the second button and then the third as Michael chuckled. Underneath, he wore a white T-shirt stained with sweat.

"Hang in there, buddy." He laughed again, and shook his head. "Where do you live?"

"Martha Street."

"You live alone?" Michael had no desire for an audience when he took the young man's blood. The kid lowered his eyes.

"I'm crashing with my cousin. I'm sorta between places right now."

"Is your cousin likely to disturb us?" Michael glanced over for a brief second and Jeremy looked at him, unblinking.

"He'll be asleep. He has to work at four. He sleeps pretty hard."

"Good." Michael nodded his head and turned onto Madison. Once he was a few streets over from Martha, he caught the kid's eye again. "You feeling better?"

Jeremy shrugged fully out of his over-shirt and shook his head. "I don't feel bad...just weird."

"I can only imagine," Michael smirked and pulled up in front of Jeremy's house. What else would it feel like? An otherwise normal man suddenly has an urge to let his blood as soon as he can to a guy he just met? It must be the strangest sensation in the world.

Michael followed the kid to the door and listened out for signs of movement inside. By the time the front door was open, he heard snoring in an adjacent room and was satisfied that the kid's cousin was indeed fast asleep. Standing in a cluttered foyer, he put his hand on Jeremy's shoulder.

"Where do you sleep?" Michael asked in a whisper, and Jeremy gestured to a door at the end of the hall. Michael nodded and followed him in. Once inside the bedroom, he closed the door and turned to the kid, his hands on his hips. "Where's that knife?"

Jeremy fumbled through his pocket and this time retrieved a small folding knife that he pulled open with care. He put the sharp edge to his palm as he did in the locker room, but once again Michael stepped forward and removed it from his hand.

"No, Jeremy, never cut your hand. I'm not a healer, so whatever you cut will have to heal naturally." Michael reached for the boy's wrist and pulled his forearm out toward him.

"What does that mean, 'not a healer'?" His voice was faraway, but Michael answered him nonetheless.

"Some of my people can heal with their touch, but I have other talents." Michael positioned the tip of the small blade in the crook of the kid's arm and met his eye.

"Other talents…I'll bet," Jeremy cooed and fell into Michael's gaze.

"Focus on my eyes and this won't hurt—ready?" Michael pressed the point in a few centimeters and waited for the go-ahead from the kid. When Jeremy mouthed "okay," Michael held his gaze and pressed the knife nearly an inch through the skin, creating a generous puncture wound that he immediately brought to his lips so not a drop was wasted.

Jeremy gasped, but never looked away. Even when Michael closed his eyes to concentrate on his meal, Jeremy continued to watch him with wonder in his child-like gaze.

After four deep pulls on the young man's arm, Michael realized what a treasure he had discovered. Jeremy's blood was pure, untainted. Of all his Cows, none carried such ambrosia in their veins. When he sensed his balance being affected by the pleasure of the moment, he moved the two of them to the untidy daybed against the wall. His people referred to the experience as a *buzz*, and Michael was buzzing like crazy. He sat heavily and Jeremy plopped down against him. Just before the kid lost consciousness, Michael let up and pressed his handkerchief against the wound.

"Oh, Jeremy," Michael moaned quietly as he leaned over his knees, his head spinning. The boy's blood centered in his belly, warming him head to toe. It had been decades since he'd enjoyed the like. It was several minutes before his head cleared and he opened his eyes with effort to look at the kid beside him. Jeremy leaned against him, eyes closed, his breathing steady.

"Jeremy." Michael jostled his shoulder to rouse him. "Hey, kid."

"Michael…" Jeremy whispered without looking up.

"You okay?"

"Yeahhhh…" Jeremy dragged out the word.

"Good." Michael was nearly back to normal and he turned at the waist to tie his handkerchief securely around Jeremy's elbow. "What do you eat, Jeremy? Your blood—it's perfect."

"Hah," Jeremy laughed and looked languidly into Michael's face, only inches apart on the small bed. "I'm a vegan, Michael. How 'bout that?"

"Me likey," Michael replied, and the boy smiled.

"Me likey too, Michael. I can see things so clearly now…"

"Like what, Jay-Jay?" Michael put his right arm behind the kid supporting him.

255

"Paintings, Michael. I'm going to make a million dollars with these new ones. And I owe it all to you, Michael...all to you, my new friend."

"An artist, eh?" Michael looked around the dank, dimly-lit room. He was keeping this one, and he would take no chances on losing him to economic shortcomings. "An artist needs a studio, Jeremy. I want to put you up in a loft downtown. How would you like that?"

"Put me up?" Jeremy opened his eyes and focused with effort.

"Exactly. You'll stay there rent-free until you sell enough paintings to pay. Sound good?"

"Yes. Yes." Jeremy sat up, more awake now. "Yes. Yes."

"But there's one condition."

"Anything, Michael, anything. What can I do for you? I'll do anything for you. You are my *muse*, Michael. I've been waiting for you for so long..."

"I'll keep you to myself, Jeremy. You'll meet more of my brethren, but you belong to me, got it?" Michael waited until he nodded, not fully understanding, but willing to obey. "I'll move you into the loft on Friday night. Be ready." Michael reached for his wallet and pulled out three crisp hundreds. "Quit your job at the airport by phone. Don't go there during the night, got it? Take this money to carry you through."

Jeremy nodded again.

"One more thing." Michael stood up from the bed and Jeremy remained where he was, looking at Michael in reverent awe. "When we're alone, call me Michael. But anytime my brothers are present, refer to me as 'master'. Got it?"

Jeremy nodded, a shy smile playing across his face.

Michael stepped toward the door and tossed Jeremy a parting grin. "You're a good kid, Jeremy. I'm glad we're friends."

"Best friends, Michael. Best friends."

"Indeed," Michael winked, put his hand to the knob and had one last thought before he exited. There was something else about the kid that purified his blood. Something that wasn't outwardly noticeable. Michael inclined his head to the kid and whispered his next question.

"Jeremy, do you have a girlfriend?"

"No time for girls, Michael. Gotta paint." Jeremy grinned and flashed pearly white teeth that contrasted his coffee-colored skin. "I'm a good Catholic, Michael. I don't fool around."

"Good," Michael nodded, his gaze serious. "For me, for the

blood, keep it that way, okay? Can you do that, Jay-jay? Will you stay pure for me?"

"Yeah," Jeremy nodded, blushing.

"So, I'll see you Friday. We'll move you into the loft."

Jeremy nodded and waved, a silly grin on his face.

Michael chuckled and left the house silently. What a fortuitous find, a kid who was dying to give blood, who didn't pollute his body with processed food or meats, and who hadn't given his body over to lust. He was a true virgin. Michael was surprised, Jeremy had to be at least twenty-one. *But easier is always better...*

Michael headed home, smiling the whole way.

4: Abroghia Calls Theophilus

"A Man Named Salvation"

32 AD Galilee

The time had come to share his rule and he had the first man picked out. Abroghia nodded to the inferior Rakum to his left and sent him off on the night's mission. Ionious was already in place, now it was only a matter of timing.

Abroghia shifted his weight to his other foot and peered at the crowd gathered on the hills, sitting around small fires, some laughing, some crying, and others tossing lots for baubles and Caesar's coins. Few of the mortals that peppered the Galilean landscape knew what Abroghia knew: that arriving any minute was a walking God. Thankfully, the majority of the men and women that mewled and tittered on every side were blissfully unaware of the change coming upon their world. Abroghia aimed to do his best to keep them uninformed.

One hundred yards away on the next rise, silhouetted by a Gibbous moon, Markus gestured with a slight movement of his head and sent his message telepathically. *"One hundred paces north, master. The Man from Nazareth approaches."*

Abroghia straightened his spine and stepped from behind the acacia. He had no intention of being seen by the traveling Rabbi, he knew enough about Him to stay out of His way. Abroghia had his eye out for a certain red-headed and fascinating man called Theophilus, expected to approach the Man when he arrived.

Hailing from an orthodox Jewish family and squatting in a small village near Athens, Theophilus had traveled with a large group to reach the City of David in time for Sukkot. Abroghia was aware of all of the Pilgrim Festivals and made the best of them by picking off stragglers as they came through his Samaritan valley. A dozen nights ago, Theophilus' convoy wound its way past Abroghia's home, carved as it was into the hillside. They pitched camp only a stone's throw away and as the men folk reclined about the fire telling tall tales and swapping lies, Abroghia listened intently from the shadows.

When the conversation turned to the Son of Joseph canvassing the countryside, teaching repentance and calling people to return to the Torah of Elohim,[10] Abroghia's ears pricked. Many believed the Man fulfilled enough prophecies to warrant closer scrutiny—Abroghia was one of these. He wasn't one to take chances with the Creator. He was given a measure supremacy and he knew his parameters. As long as he played by the rules, Elohim would hold up His end of the deal.

The red-headed Hebrew recounted a story he'd heard about the Nazarene, calling Him the Messiah they'd all been waiting for. He shared several second-hand accounts of miraculous healings and deliverance from demonic beings. Then he swore to every man in the clearing that if he could only speak to Jesus, he would follow Him to the ends of the earth.

"I have thrown a fleece out for Elohim. If this Man is our Messiah, then He will speak to me when we meet. If I am instead lost in the crowd, I will know He is a fraud."

The young firebrand said those words to his brethren and Abroghia smiled. Now, the night had come and the twain would finally be in the same place at the same time. If Elohim showed Theophilus that this Man was the Messiah, Abroghia was going to do his best to steal him away. It was his main mission—to foil the works of the Creator for as long as he was able.

Across the way, Markus pulled his cloak over his head and turned away as a gaggle of men hurried past his position.

"Stay out of sight or you'll be sorry." He sent the eager youth the message and proceeded to walk through the sand toward the crowd. His leather sandals kicked up the loose earth and his rough linen robes swished and scratched at his thighs. It was doubtful the Man would harm Markus if He saw Him, but this was no night for maybes. Abroghia had one shot and this was it. After tonight, the caravan of devotees would head for Jerusalem and he had no desire to enter that spiritual hornet's nest.

"Twenty-five paces and you'll see them crest the far hill," Markus sent over without looking Abroghia's way. The crowd had already gotten wind of the Rabbi's arrival and began to shift and shove, stand and move toward the far rise. Abroghia pressed between a hefty couple and fell into a slow jog to parallel the Man when He reached the zenith. He'd already pinpointed Theophilus' position and now wished only to observe their interaction, if any. Would the Man called *Salvation* stop long enough to speak to a man whose name translated

---

[10] (Hebrew) Law of God

259

to *Loved by God?* Abroghia hoped so.

For two thousand years, Abroghia had painstakingly experimented with the human flesh that populated the planet; molding, killing, pillaging—whatever was necessary to create a Kind unto himself. He had the power and authority to do almost anything he set his mind to, so long as the mortals he toyed with were unclaimed by their Creator. And there were plenty who spent their entire lives outside of the protection of Elohim.

At present, he had collected nearly five hundred underlings, almost all of which were born to women. One hundred were temporary Wraiths he animated himself to serve his purposes. The spirits he compelled to do his bidding were happy to have a body to inhabit, even if it was temporary and false. The shells started out as corpses, so Abroghia had only a few months' use out of them before they fell completely apart. He was extremely powerful, but maintaining cohesion on one hundred separate entities stretched his abilities to the max. Several nights ago when he looked into Theophilus' eyes, he knew the time had come to distribute his reign among nine others. The Rakum Race was ready for official leadership.

Theophilus would be the first called to Father the new race of beings that Abroghia fondly named Rakum, after his true name, Ta'avah Rakha, or *Vain Lust*. A joke perhaps to the Creator, but the name meant power to Abroghia. The name represented his reputation and his renown and finally the time to build his empire had arrived.

"Blessed are you poor, for yours is the kingdom of Elohim…"

The Rabbi's words floated on the wind and carried much further than a normal man's would. Abroghia reached his watching post and crossed his arms, training his gaze on the Man fifty paces downwind.

"Blessed are you who hunger now for you shall be filled…"

A ruddy cheek, a flash of a bright orange beard, and stepping between the low fires and toward the Man, Theophilus moved to test his fleece. Rabbi Yeshua,[11] as the locals called Him, faced east, arms wide as He spoke words that soothed some and abraded others. Theophilus was ten paces behind and closing in. Several primary disciples surrounded the Rabbi, watching for trouble as much as listening to His words. The Greek-speaking Jew pressed on.

"But I say to you, love your enemies. Do good to those who hate you, bless those who curse you, and pray for those who spitefully use

---

[11] Yeshua is Jesus' Hebrew name, it means literally, "Salvation"

you…"

Abroghia arched his eyebrows and looked at the faces on all sides. For the most part, they were entranced. Mouths agape, hands either hanging limply at their sides or upraised to the heavens above. It would make more sense if the crowd laughed, but not a single soul found the Rabbi's words amusing.

Theophilus was one man away from the Rabbi from Nazareth. Abroghia watched as he stretched out his hand and touched the disciple directly before him.

"Love your enemies. Do good and lend, hoping for nothing in return…"

The Man turned then and as He spoke He reached around the wild-eyed black-haired man guarding Him, and bid Theophilus near. The stunned Pilgrim stumbled forward and stopped an arm's length away only to be pulled into a one-armed embrace. Jesus looked into Theophilus' eyes and smiled before continuing.

"If you do this, your reward will be great, and you will be sons of El Elyon, for He is kind to the unthankful and evil…"

"But Rabbi," one in the crowd called out, "the Torah allows one to collect from those who owe us. Are we to go poor so our enemies may eat?"

The Rabbi's smile went to the side and he squeezed Theophilus' shoulder. "Just as you want men to do to you, you also go and do likewise to them."

With that He released Theophilus who stepped back as if freed from a spell. His face shone with revelation and even as a brutish disciple called Kefa caught him and pulled him out of the way, the red-headed Jew was smiling.

Abroghia nodded to Markus who in turn motioned to Ionious with one finger. With triangulated precision, they closed in on Theophilus lying peacefully on the scrub that covered the arid hills. Jesus and His people moved off as Abroghia and his men moved in. By the time they reached the red-head's side, the crowd had shifted fifty paces away and Theophilus was alone.

"Now to make him mine," Abroghia mumbled and knelt to his side. The time had arrived and he was ready.

Oh, was he ready.

5: Abroghia Calls Theophilus, Part II

"The Promise of Power"

"Theophilus, come. I need you," Abroghia whispered, kneeling over his target, his two men flanking his position. The man recognized him from their previous meeting, when Abroghia had introduced himself in private outside the travelers' camp. It was then that Abroghia knew he had found the first Father of the Rakum race. "I need you to rule beside me. Teach these younglings what you know. Help me to grow a great nation of men who live to serve their leaders."

"Why me, Abroghia?" he asked, still lying flat on his back. "I'm a tailor, not a leader. I've never married nor owned land. I have seen the Son of God and I want to follow Him." Theophilus met Abroghia's gaze and didn't give Ionious or Markus any notice. His face still glowed from meeting the Rabbi and Abroghia turned up the heat.

"You have no choice, Theophilus. You have been chosen to help me raise the Rakum race from the dust. You are the first of nine that I will call. You will help me choose the others. You will father thousands of sons directly from your loins. Through your seed you will do a great service to the world."

Abroghia had hit a nerve; Theophilus had secret dreams of grandeur. Fantasies of bringing the nation of Israel out of bondage all by himself.

"Come," Abroghia said, "say not a word until I show you what I am capable of. Rise up, and come."

Markus lifted Theophilus off the ground and when he found his feet, the Rakum steered him to follow Abroghia across the now-empty field. Within minutes, they reached the trees and Abroghia pulled a full-sized sword from a sheath at Ionious' side.

"You will serve a master who can never die. Thrust this blade through-and-through, Theophilus," Abroghia said. He held out the sword, but didn't expect the man to take it. When Theophilus began voicing his doubts, Abroghia handed the blade to Markus who shoved it into his middle without a thought.

Theophilus exclaimed and rushed to his aid. "Stop! Abroghia!"

Turning side-to-side twice, Abroghia demonstrated how the sword penetrated, making certain Theophilus saw the blood oozing from both sides of his body before he put his hand to the hilt and drew it slowly out. As Theophilus watched, Abroghia ripped the already torn tunic wide so he could witness the closing of the wound in the bright moonlight.

"Impossible!" the red-head gasped.

"With man, perhaps, but not with me," Abroghia chuckled. "I cannot die, Theophilus. I am a powerful god and I need you to help me with these young ones." He gestured to Markus, who stood obediently by awaiting command. "We will populate the earth with men who are stronger, smarter, and longer-lived than the world has ever seen."

"Who do you follow, Abroghia?"

"I have inhabited this earth in different forms for four thousand years. I have power beyond your imagination and if you join me, I will lend that power to you. You could never imagine what you will be capable of once you devote your life to my purposes."

Theophilus considered his words, looked at the two young men on his either side, and then back to Abroghia.

"And the Elohim of Yisrael?"

"Who do you think gave me this power?" Abroghia replied. "Will you come? I will prove myself to you a million times over, but you must consent. You must submit to my authority. I will reward you. You will never be without fine food, luxury, and all the pleasures of life." Abroghia paused. He allowed the silence to fill the world around them before whispering, "And, Theophilus ben Ya'acov, you will *rule.*"

The red-head pondered Abroghia's promises several seconds before sighing from deep within. He nodded his head a fraction and lowered his eyes, saying, "If you can do all you say, then yes, I will follow you."

The light that emanated from Theophilus' visage as he left Jesus' side began to ebb and Abroghia smiled, grasping him by both shoulders.

"Good. You will never regret it, my son." Abroghia held onto Theophilus tightly as Markus and Ionious stepped closer. "Answer me this. The life is in the blood, correct?"

"Er, yes. So says Elohim."[12]

"Then it stands to reason that if I pour my life into you, you will

---

[12] Leviticus 17:11, 14; Deuteronomy 12:33

263

take on my attributes. Yes?"

Theophilus furrowed his brow, nodding slowly.

"Tonight we begin the process of making you over into a god, Theophilus." Abroghia produced a small bone knife from his sash and sliced deep his wrist. He thrust it toward the man's face and his eyes widened. "Take my life into you, Theophilus. Then you will know power like you've never imagined. Do it now."

Markus stabilized the man with a palm to his neck and Ionious stood by with a hand on his chest. Theophilus didn't pull back when the blood rushed into his mouth, spilling over his lips and down his beard. Abroghia was aware that it would pain the man greatly, and within moments, the two youngsters were supporting a thrashing new leader in their strong hands. For five minutes, the Greek Jew seized in their grasp, gagging and coughing spittle tinged red with mingled blood. When the effects passed, Theophilus hung in Markus' arms, gasping for air. Abroghia waited until his eyes were clear once more and took his chin in two fingers.

"From this moment on, you are Father Theophilus, a powerful force to be reckoned with. And these men are your servants," he said, gesturing toward the Rakum behind him. "Greet your Father, pups."

"*Kazak, Abba,*"[13] Markus said in Hebrew. Ionious repeated the phrase in Greek and Abroghia smiled. *Be strong*, indeed. Be strong.

And given a few months of conditioning and alchemy, the mortal born outside Athens would shed his humanity and claim his deity alongside his master. He'd be stronger than man was meant to be and he'd owe it all to a spirit manifest in the flesh named Ta'avah Rakha Abroghia; his god and king.

It was good.

---

[13] (Hebrew) Be Strong, Father.

Rabbit Legacy Book Two of the Rabbit Trilogy

Seven years have passed since novelist Beth Rider escaped the clutches of Jack Dawn and his ilk. Yet the war rages on as a Rakum remnant rebuilds under the thumb of a tyrannical and unbalanced Elder. Determined to destroy everything Beth stands for, Elder Rufus initiates a deadly plan to draw her and her allies into his trap. With the aid of a disaffected Elder named Canaan and a mysterious, legendary Rakum youth known as *The Last*, the 'Rabbit Army' will confront the demonic forces behind those who threaten their freedom and their very lives.

Rabbit Redemption Book Three of the Rabbit Trilogy, *Early 2018 from LRP*

Whittled down to a few thousand, the decimated Rakum race has been scattered to the wind. Isaac Akaron purposes to rebuild under his own power. Ruthless, ambitious, and hungry, young Isaac's plan requires the blood of the surviving Elders. As he seeks them out, a powerful Elder previously thought dead reappears with mighty plans of his own. Serving under duress, Elder Canaan and Beryl seek assistance from those who helped them before. Utilizing his courage with unimaginable faith, Javier D'Millier charges headlong into the fray with a bloodthirsty secret that can be the end or the beginning of the New Rakum Race. **In a violent and climactic battle that spans dimensions, Javier and Isaac will fight to the death as the redemption of thousands of souls hangs in the balance.**

Read the Book that Started it All...
The Judging The Corescu Chronicles Book One

Hungary, 1640. With the sharp stab of the demon's fangs, village priest Markus Corescu finds his world turned upside-down, coming to the realization that he has been transformed into an abomination—a vampire. Immediately, the newly-undead clergyman assigns a divine calling to his bloodthirsty nature and satisfies his despicable hunger on the humans around him without remorse. Fast forward to the present, and the priest has suppressed and forgotten his past. With the aid of two mortals, and despite the violent protests of his immortal contemporaries, the old vampire is finally able to see the Truth. As he wrestles with his very soul, he discovers that the thousands of people he has judged were not killed within the will of God, but rather they were exsanguinated to satisfy his lust for blood. Now he must make amends with God, but even if his eyes are opened, his ways are not easily changed.

For more information on other works by
Ellen C. Maze
visit **www.ellencmaze.com**

End Notes

a Beth Rider wrote a vampire series entitled The Corescu Chronicles, with The Judging being the first installment. This is the book referred to by the Rakum who read or hear of it. YOU can read this stand-alone series, too, written by Ellen C. Maze. Find it online and at many fine bookstores.
b. Proverbs 6: 16-19, p. 210
c. Genesis 6:4, p. 210

Made in the USA
Columbia, SC
14 July 2018